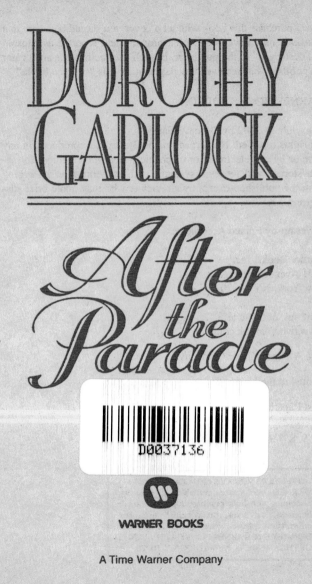

# DOROTHY GARLOCK

## After the Parade

WARNER BOOKS

A Time Warner Company

WARNER BOOKS EDITION

Copyright © 2000 by Dorothy Garlock
All rights reserved. No part of this book may be reproduced in any
form or by any electronic or mechanical means, including information storage and retrieval systems, without permission in writing
from the publisher, except by a reviewer who may quote brief pas-
sages in a review.

Cover art by Franco Accornero

Warner Books, Inc.
1271 Avenue of the Americas
New York, NY 10020

Visit our Web site at
www.twbookmark.com

A Time Warner Company

Printed in the United States of America

First Paperback Printing: April 2000

10 9 8 7 6 5 4 3 2 1

DEDICATED TO

82ND U.S. NAVAL CONSTRUCTION
BATTALION
—THE FIGHTING SEABEES—

AND IN MEMORY OF

MY HUSBAND
HERBERT L. GARLOCK, SR.

WHO SERVED WITH THE 82ND IN THE
SOUTH PACIFIC
1943–1945

## TO A HOMECOMING HERO

After the victory and the parade,
After the hometown band has played,
After the cheers and four long years,
Can we, at last, break free of our fears?

After the bombs and cannonade,
After the bravery you displayed,
After the pain and wounds that bled,
Can you face with me what lies ahead?

I stand and I wait and I long for a sign.
The love you once gave, will it still be mine?
Can we recapture the passion mislaid?
Will you come back to me, after the parade?

—F.S.I.

# Chapter One

OCTOBER 15, 1945
RAWLINGS, OKLAHOMA

> *"Hurrah for the flag of the free.*
> *May it wave as our standard forever.*
> *The gem of the land and the sea,*
> *The banner of the right—"*

*T*he Rawlings high-school band, decked out in full uniform and lined up beside the platform at the depot, played with gusto John Philip Sousa's "Stars and Stripes Forever." A crowd of a hundred or more had gathered to greet a group of the men who had fought to keep them free. When the huge WELCOME HOME banner that stretched across the front of the depot was loosened by the wind, willing hands hurried to hold it in place.

The gigantic engine, belching smoke, whistle blasting, wheels screaming against the rails, slowly passed the station and came to a jerking halt. There was a sudden expectant quiet. The conductor stepped down from the coach and stood with his hands clasped in front of him.

When the first of the weary war veterans, a surprised Marine, came through the door, the music from the band mingled with the cheers of the crowd and the horns of the cars parked along the street. The Marine stood hesitantly before he bounded down the steps, swung the heavy duffel bag from his shoulder to the platform, and was soon surrounded by laughing and crying relatives.

At the back of the crowd, Kathleen Dolan Henry watched six more veterans alight from the train. All were greeted by loved ones. She waited anxiously for her first glimpse of Johnny Henry in more than four years. When someone waved a flag in front of her face, she hurriedly brushed it away just as a tall sailor, his white hat perched low on his forehead, a duffel bag on his shoulder, stepped down and stood hesitantly on the platform. His eyes searched the crowd. There was a sudden hush, then the band began to play the Civil War song they had practiced for a month.

> *"When Johnny comes marching home again,*
> *hurrah, hurrah.*
> *We'll give him a hearty welcome then, hurrah,*
> *hurrah,*
> *The men will cheer, the boys will shout,*
> *The ladies, they will all turn out,*
> *And we'll all be gay, when Johnny comes marching*
> *home."*

The band stopped playing and the crowd took up the chant: "Johnny, Johnny, Johnny—"

*The hero of the small Oklahoma town had come home from the war.*

Johnny Henry was stunned. At one time the people of this town had blamed him for bringing disgrace and death to one of their own. Now they were cheering him.

Everyone had heard how Johnny Henry, on an island in the Pacific, had lifted the blade of the bulldozer he was operating and, amid a shower of gunfire from the Japanese entrenched on the beach, had driven it straight toward an enemy machine-gun nest that was preventing his platoon from building a landing site. The powerful dozer had buried the men and their guns inside the concrete structure, permitting the large-scale landing that had secured the island.

Johnny grinned at the young girl who dashed up to take his picture, waved to acknowledge the crowd, then walked slowly toward a small group at the end of the platform. His father, Barker Fleming, his black hair streaked with gray, stood with his arms folded across his chest, his Cherokee pride preventing him from showing emotion. The lone tear that rolled from the corner of his eye was seen only by his daughter, who stood by his side.

Kathleen watched as Johnny shook hands with Barker and his young half brother, Lucas. He said something that drew a laugh from his older half sister, and he patted the younger one on the head. As proud as she was of him and thankful that he had survived the war, Kathleen couldn't force her feet to carry her to the platform and greet him with all the town looking on. Feeling vulnerable, knowing that some in the crowd were watching her, she hurried off down the street to watch the parade from the window of the *Gazette* office.

*Beneath the brim of a brown felt hat a pair of ice-blue eyes watched Kathleen with keen interest as she watched her husband step off the train. Noting with satisfaction that she didn't go to meet him, the man, his face darkened by a week's growth of whiskers, casually moved away from the cluster of people at the depot and slowly followed her down the street.*

At the war's end, two months earlier, Kathleen had been working at the Douglas Aircraft plant in Oklahoma City.

The front page of the August 15, 1945, *Daily Oklahoman* had screamed the news.

## JAPS QUIT, WAR IS OVER

### TRUMAN TELLS OF COMPLETE SURRENDER.

WASHINGTON, August 14. The Second World War, history's greatest flood of death and destruction, ended Tuesday night with Japan's unconditional surrender. From the moment President Truman announced at 6 A.M., Oklahoma time, that the enemy of the Pacific had agreed to Allied terms, the world put aside for a time woeful thoughts of cost in dead and dollars and celebrated in wild frenzy. Formalities meant nothing to people freed at last of war.

Tears had filled Kathleen's eyes, overflowed, and rolled down her cheeks. Brushing them away, she hurriedly scanned headlines.

### DISCHARGE DUE FOR 5 MILLION IN 18 MONTHS.

Another headline made her smile.

### OKLAHOMA CITY CALMLY GOING NUTS!

Johnny would be among the first to come home because of the time he had spent in the combat zone. Kathleen thought of the ranch outside of Rawlings where, for a while, she had been happier than she had ever imagined she would be and where, later, she had sunk into the depths of despair. She had thought that she could never go back there, but she knew that she must . . . one last time.

Kathleen folded the newspaper carefully. This edition she would keep to show to her children someday . . . if she ever had any more. The ache that dwelled in her heart intensified at the thought of the tiny daughter she had held in her arms that night five years ago, while the cold north wind rattled the windows in the clinic and she waited for death to take her child.

*The war was over.*

Soon she would be free to leave her defense job, go back to Rawlings, tie up some loose ends, and decide what to do with the rest of her life. She was still part-owner of the *Gazette*. Adelaide and Paul had kept it going during the war, but they'd had to cut it from an eight-page paper down to six pages once a week.

On that wondrous day when the war's end was proclaimed, Kathleen had volunteered to work an extra shift in the payroll department of Douglas Aircraft. The pay was double overtime for the day. The money would come in handy when the plant closed.

Tired after the twelve-hour shift and the long bus ride into town, she had stepped down onto the Oklahoma City street thronged with shouting and cheering people. Cowbells, horns, and sirens cut the air. Hundreds of uniformed airmen from Tinker Airforce Base and sailors from the Norman Naval Base mingled with the crowd. Total strangers hugged and kissed one another.

"How 'bout a hug, Red?" A young sailor threw his arm across her shoulders and embraced her briefly. "You got a man comin' home, honey?"

"Thousands of them."

"Bet one of 'em can hardly wait to see ya."

The sailor went on to put his arm around another girl, and Kathleen stood back against a building and watched the jubilant crowd. Her eyes filled with tears, and her heart flooded with thankfulness. This celebration was something she would remember for the rest of her life.

Vaugh Monroe's voice came from the loudspeaker on the corner.

*"When the lights come on again, all over the*
*world,*
*And the boys come home again, all over the*
*world—"*

Kathleen stood for a short while and listened to the music. When the next song was "Does Your Heart Beat For Me," she felt a pain so severe that a lump formed in her throat. The last time she had been with Johnny before he went overseas, they had sat in a strained silence in a restaurant. Someone had put a coin in the jukebox, and she had been forced to listen to that song.

Kathleen walked hurriedly on down the street to get away from the music. As she waited on the corner to catch the bus that would take her to the rooming house where she had lived since coming to the city to do her bit for the war effort, she looked around cautiously.

Several times during the past weeks she had seen a man standing in the shadows near the bus stop, and she had been sure he was a man from the plant, the one who had seized every opportunity to talk to her. He had not been persistent with his attentions but had offered several times to take her home.

Not many people were leaving the downtown area, and the bus when it arrived was almost empty. After she was seated, Kathleen caught her reflection in the window and wondered if she had changed much during the war years. Her hair was still the same bright red. She had tried to tame the tight curls into the popular shoulder-length pageboy style but had given up and let it hang or wrapped it in a net snood.

Johnny had teased her about the color of her hair, saying that since he could always spot her in a crowd, so could a bull, so she'd better carry a head scarf when she went to the pasture.

Walking up the dark street to her rooming house, Kathleen felt . . . old. In a few months she would be thirty-three. It didn't seem possible that seven years had passed since Johnny had saved her from the hijackers on that lonely Oklahoma road outside Rawlings. For a few years she had been extremely happy, then her world had fallen apart. Their baby was born with no chance to live, and Johnny's stupid feeling that his "bad blood" was responsible had dug a chasm between them. After this length of time, she doubted it ever could be bridged.

Kathleen had not filed for a divorce even though Johnny had asked her to during that last meeting. As his wife she had received family allotment money sent by the government. Every penny of the money had gone to Johnny's bank in Rawlings. He would have a small nest egg to help him get started again.

When he came home, Johnny would be free to make a new life for himself and with whomever he chose to share it. As for herself, she was sure that she would never be completely happy again, but she could, if she tried hard enough, find a measure of contentment in her work. She had stayed in contact with her editor at the pulp magazine where her stories were published. Now that he had moved on to work for a book publisher, he had suggested that she write a book. It was something she planned to do when her emotions were not so raw.

Johnny had not expected the welcoming party and was embarrassed by it. He wished, in hindsight, that he had stayed on the train until it reached Red Rock to have avoided all this. In the back of his mind had been the hope that Kathleen would be at the station. It was stupid of him. She had probably met and fallen in love with a 4-F'er or a draft dodger while working in that defense plant in Oklahoma City.

*He wondered if divorce papers were waiting for him.*

During the ceremony at the depot, the mayor welcomed the veterans home, gave each an envelope containing gift certificates to be used at various businesses in town, then escorted them to the hayrack that had been decorated with flags and welcome-home signs. Johnny sat with the other returning veterans and waited patiently for the ordeal of being paraded through town to be over. He searched the crowd that lined the street for a head of bright red hair and chided himself for hoping that she cared enough to be here when he came home.

Two months ago Johnny, with the rest of his battalion, had watched the Japanese plane with the huge green cross painted on its bottom fly over Okinawa on the way to meet with General MacArthur and surrender on the battleship *Missouri*; he realized then that a phase of his life had ended. The siren that in the past signaled an air raid blew triumphantly that day, announcing that the war was over.

*The racket was enough to raise the dead!* The celebration had begun.

Lying on his cot, trying to read, Johnny grimaced at the thought because there were plenty of dead on the island to raise.

"Damn fools are going to shoot themselves," he muttered. The other man in the tent couldn't hear his words over the racket going on in the camp.

"The war's over, Geronimo! We're goin' home!" His exuberant shout reached Johnny above the sound of the gunfire.

As the only Native American in the construction battalion of Seabees attached to the 3rd Marine division, Johnny had been dubbed Geronimo.

"Yeah, we're going home."

Four years was a long time to have been away from home, yet he could clearly visualize the clear blue sky and the broad sweep of rolling prairies of southwestern Oklahoma. He longed to get on his horse and ride to a place where there was not another human being within miles and miles.

He had discovered firsthand that war was hell. Would he ever forget the bombings on Guadalcanal while they were trying to build an airstrip for Allied planes to land? Would he forget the steaming Solomon Islands with their coconut plantations and hut villages of ebony-skinned natives, bearded, short, stocky, and superstitious? He knew that he would never forget the stench of burning flesh as flamethrowers drove the enemy out of the caves of Okinawa.

"Ya know what I'm goin' to do when I get home, Geronimo?" The excited voice of Johnny's completely bald tentmate interrupted his thoughts. "I'm going to take my woman and my kid in the house, lock the door, and not come out till spring. Do you think my kid will remember me? Hell, she was only two years old when I left. It's hard to believe that she'll be startin' school."

"Sure, she'll remember you, Curly," Johnny assured him. Then, "Goddammit!" he exclaimed, as a bullet tore through the top of the tent. The celebration was out of control.

What a relief it was when finally a voice came over the loudspeaker. "Cease fire! Cease fire!"

"It's about time," Johnny growled. "Damn officers sitting up there with their heads up their butts while the idiots shoot up the place!"

He had come through the war with five battle stars for major engagements and had only a few minor shrapnel wounds to show for it. He was grateful for that. *But, hell, he had no wife to go home to.* If Kathleen hadn't divorced him yet, she would as soon as he reached the States.

His sister, Henry Ann, had written every week and would be glad to see him, but even she didn't need him anymore. Her life was with Tom and their kids. Barker, working hard at playing the father, had sent him a package once a month. One package had contained a camera and film. He'd used it. Adelaide had sent him the *Gazette* each week. Sometimes the issues were a month old, but he had read every line, looking for news of Kathleen.

Johnny clasped his hands under his head, stared absently at the bullet hole in the tent, and thought of what he'd do when he got home. He still had the land that he'd bought before he and Kathleen were married. As his needs had been few, every month his pay, except for five dollars, had gone back to pay on the mortgage. Keith McCabe had paid to run some cattle on his land. That money, too, had gone toward the mortgage. Considering that he had given almost five years of his life to Uncle Sam, he wasn't in too bad shape financially.

After the first six months he had stopped looking for mail other than V-mails from Henry Ann and occasional letters from Adelaide and his half sister, Maria.

The first Christmas he was in the Pacific Theater, he had hoped for a card from the only woman he had ever loved. He had made her a bracelet out of aluminum from a downed Japanese aircraft. Many hours of painstaking work had gone into engraving it with her name. From a Guadalcanal native he had stupidly bought her a comb made out of trochus shells, from which pearl buttons are made.

Weeks dragged into months and he began to dread mail call, fully expecting one of the *Dear John* letters that a few of his fellow Seabees had received from wives who had found new lovers.

He had packed away the bracelet and comb and concentrated strictly on trying to stay alive while he raced out of a flatboat onto an enemy-held island and while he drove the big bulldozer to clear the land or the packer that rolled the coral to make the landing strips.

But, dammit to hell! No matter how hard he'd tried to forget, there was still a vacant place in his heart.

Preoccupied with his thoughts and waving automatically to the crowd that lined the street, Johnny was suddenly jolted back to reality when he saw Paul and Adelaide frantically returning his wave. Behind them he could discern a slender figure standing in the window of the *Gazette* office. Was it Kathleen? Hell, no. If she'd been in town, she'd have been at the depot to take a few pictures and get a story for the paper. Now he wished he'd asked Barker if he had heard from her. His father and Kathleen had always been thick as thieves, and at one time he had feared that she was in love with the guy.

When the truck pulling the hayrack stopped in front of the courthouse, Johnny jumped down and hoisted his duffel bag to his shoulder. Barker was waiting there.

"Your sisters and I would like you to come out to the ranch for dinner. Lucas thinks that you won the war all by yourself."

"Thanks, but I think I'll go on out to the Circle H. It's been a long time since I've seen it."

"It's up to you. You know that you're always welcome. The car is just down the street. The kids are down at Claude's."

"That old coot still fryin' hamburgers?"

"He's still at it."

Barker slid under the wheel of his '41 Dodge, one of the last cars made before the automobile plants shut down and converted to making war materials.

"When Elena graduated from college she got a teaching job in Boston." Barker reported the news of Johnny's half sisters casually as they drove out of town. "Carla and her husband are in New York."

Johnny grunted a reply, looked out the window, and watched the fence posts fly by. Barker had always driven like a bunch of wild Apaches were after him. He did that now, dust trailing behind them like a bushy red tail. Johnny considered asking about Kathleen, then thought better of it. Instead he brought up the town's main industry, a tannery that Barker owned.

"How's the business doing?"

"Good. We're getting summer and fall hides and keeping more of the good stuff for our own factory. The government cut down their orders when the European War ended and then almost stopped completely a few months ago. We're looking for another market."

"I'm sure you'll find one."

Johnny's hungry eyes roamed the flat Oklahoma plains and then lifted to the eagle that soared effortlessly in the clear blue sky. It was good to be home. He noticed along the road things that he had once taken for granted, like the occasional oak or hawthorn tree that was heavy with mistletoe. The white berry parasite was the state flower of Oklahoma. The first Christmas after he and Kathleen married, he had put a clump of mistletoe in each doorway of the house as an excuse to kiss her.

Thank goodness Barker knew when to be quiet. Johnny glanced at his father's stoic profile and the hair that was broadly streaked with gray. That had been a surprise. He'd had only a little gray at the temples four years earlier.

Johnny's mind stumbled back to the present. In a few days he'd buy some kind of car and go over to Red Rock and see Henry Ann and Tom. He wondered if his cousins Pete and Jude Perry had come through the war. The last he'd heard Pete was in the navy. Jude had gone to medical school, then had been thrust into the army. Grant Gifford had written that he was in the 45th Infantry out of Fort Sill. The Thunderbirds had seen heavy action at Anzio and had taken heavy casualties. God, he hoped Jude had come through. He was the best of the Perrys.

Barker stopped the car in front of the small unpainted frame house but kept the motor running. After Johnny got out of the car he lifted his duffel bag from the backseat, bent over, and peered through the window.

"Thanks."

"Don't mention it."

Johnny straightened, and the car moved away. The first thing he noticed after distance had eaten up the sound of the motor, was the quiet it left in its wake. During the years he had been away, there had always been a racket in the background, even on the boat going and coming across the Pacific. He stood still, not wanting to break the silence even with his footsteps.

The small four-room house looked lonely and unloved. Grass stood a foot high in the places where Kathleen had long ago planted flowers. The old washtub he had nailed to a stump to serve as a planter was still there, but dried weeds had replaced the colorful moss rose that once filled it. He eased his duffel bag down onto the porch and walked slowly around the house.

The stock pen was empty. The windmill towered like a still, silent skeleton against the blue sky.

Johnny sat down on the back steps, rested his forearms on his thighs, and clasped his hands tightly together. Coming back was not as he had imagined it would be. In the jungles of Guadalcanal, New Guinea, and Bougainville he had dreamed of this place. After that first Christmas when he had not heard from Kathleen and realized that he had lost her, the desire to get back to his ranch was the force that had kept him sane during the long months of bombings and shelling.

*Now that he was here, what was it but one small lonely speck in all the vast universe?*

Johnny watched the sun sink slowly beneath the horizon before he made a move to go into the house. The craving for a drink of cold well water stirred him to his feet. He removed the key from a small pouch in his bag, unlocked and pushed open the door.

*Oh, Lord! It was so dearly familiar that it brought moisture to his eyes.*

The green overstuffed chair and couch he and Kathleen had bought a week after they married were just as he had left them. The table where the battery-powered radio had sat now held a kerosene lamp with a shiny chimney. Electricity still hadn't made its way to the Circle H. A large framed picture of a covered wagon on the trail west hung on the wall over the couch. On the opposite wall was a picture of an Indian on a tired horse. Kathleen said it was called *Trail's End* and, because she liked it so much, had named one of the stories she wrote for the *Western Story Magazine* after the painting.

Johnny eased his duffel bag down to the floor and took off his sailor hat. From the peg on the wall he lifted the battered Stetson and rolled it around in his hands for a long moment before he set it on his head. It felt strange and . . . big. He returned it to the peg.

In the doorway leading into the kitchen, he stood for a long while, letting his eyes take in every familiar detail. The room was spotlessly clean. The windows shiny. The blue-and-white checkered curtains were freshly ironed. On the table was a square cloth with flowers embroidered in the corners. A mason jar with a ribbon tied around the neck was filled with yellow tiger lilies and brown-eyed daisies. A note was propped against it. Johnny's fingers trembled when he picked it up.

*Welcome home, Johnny.*

*I am truly thankful that you came home safe and sound. We will need to meet soon and tie up the loose ends of our lives so we can get on with whatever is ahead. I have an apartment above the Stuart Drugstore.*

*Your dinner is on the stove. Adelaide made your favorite chocolate cake.*

*Kathleen*

Johnny replaced the note carefully against the jar as if he hadn't touched it. She was in Rawlings and hadn't come to the depot to meet him, nor had she showed her face in the crowd that lined the street.

*You are a stupid fool, John Henry. Get her out of your mind. It is over.*

He went through the kitchen to stand in the doorway of the tiny room she had fixed up as a place where she could write her stories. It, too, was spotlessly clean. What caught his eye first was the table he had given her for her typewriter when she first came to Rawlings. The typewriter was gone, as was every other trace of her.

He went back through the kitchen to the bedroom. The fluffy white curtains Kathleen had bought were freshly washed. The white chenille spread with a spray of blue and pink flowers in the middle covered the bed without a wrinkle. The multicolor rag rug was still at his side of the bed. Kathleen had put it there after he had complained about putting his bare feet on the cold floor.

Nothing of Kathleen's remained in the room, not even their wedding picture, which had stood on the bureau. But she had been here, cleaned the house, and taken her things. Had she taken the picture? He went to the bureau and opened the top drawer. There it was, facedown, on the folded flannel shirts. *She hadn't wanted it.*

He gazed at the smiling faces for a long while. He was wearing a dark suit, the first one he had ever owned. Kathleen's dress was blue with short puffed sleeves and a V-neckline. His wedding present, a locket in the form of a book, hung from a chain around her neck. Inside the locket, he remembered, were their faces. Kathleen had cut them out of a photo taken at a rodeo. Her hair, fluffed on top, hung to her shoulders in soft curls. Her eyes were laughing, her lips parted and smiling. He remembered how proud he was that day on a street in Vernon when they met a cowpuncher he knew who worked the rodeos, and he introduced her as his wife. The man couldn't take his eyes off her.

Johnny looked at himself in the photo that had been taken the day after they married; the second happiest day of his life. He had lived two lifetimes since that day.

*Had he ever been that young and happy and so crazy in love that he foolishly believed he, with his trashy background, would be a fit mate for a woman like Kathleen?*

He looked up at his image in the mirror above the bureau. Crinkly lines fanned out from the corners of his eyes. The skin on his face stretched over his high cheekbones. He had never looked more like his ancestors who roamed the plains hundreds of years ago than he did now. His hair was still thick but shorter than when he left for the service. Some of the men in his battalion had lost their hair in the hot, humid jungle.

Suddenly feeling the pressure of his lonely homecoming bearing down on him, he set the photo on the bureau and took one more glance around. His eyes were drawn to the bed where he and Kathleen had spent endless, wonderful nights making love.

Did she miss the cuddling, the whispers, the slow loving kisses, and the passion they had shared? Did she have it now with someone else? The thought sent shards of pain knifing through him. Shaking his head to rid his mind of the thought, he went quickly to the back door and out of the house.

# Chapter Two

$K$athleen watched the parade pass, unaware of the tears that wet her cheeks. Her eyes fastened on Johnny until he was out of sight. He looked as if he wanted to be anywhere but sitting on that hayrack being paraded through the town. He appeared older, thinner. Was it the tight, sailor uniform that made him look so thin? He had seen and done unimaginable things in the jungles of the Pacific; they were bound to have taken a toll on him.

She had tried to make his homecoming more pleasant by cleaning his house. When she went to collect her personal things, she had found the house littered with mouse droppings and covered with layer upon layer of red Oklahoma dust.

After packing her car with what she intended to take with her, she had begun scrubbing and cleaning the house, handling with loving care the things she and Johnny had bought the first few weeks after they were married: a tin measuring cup, a mixing bowl, and a set of glasses. She washed the multicolor Fiesta dishes given to them by the McCabes for a wedding present and returned them to the shelves.

The second day she had brought out the washtubs and, while crying what she was sure was a bucket of tears, washed the clothes he had left behind. She laundered bed linens, towels, and curtains. As soon as she took the dried clothes from the line she sprinkled and ironed them, put them away and rehung the curtains at the windows and on the strings that stretched across the kitchen shelves. The chore brought to mind how Johnny hated her having to use the scrub board and had insisted that they buy a washing machine with a gasoline motor. It was in the barn. She didn't have any gasoline, and, anyhow, she didn't know how to start the motor.

This morning, she had hurried out to the ranch with a block of ice melting in the trunk, a kettle of beef stew with potatoes and carrots on the floor of the sedan, and a chocolate cake that Adelaide had insisted on sending.

She had written the note three times before she finally arrived at what she wanted to say. Now she wished that she had added that living with an uncertain future was driving her insane.

*Oh, Lord. As soon as we come to some arrangement about the divorce, I'll leave here. I'll not be able to live here and see him with someone else.*

Adelaide and Paul were interested in buying back her share in the *Gazette* if she planned to sell. The paper had been in Adelaide's family for generations. She had sold an interest to Kathleen only because during the lean years she had been about to lose it. The banker had refused to lend her money for the day-to-day operation of the small-town newspaper.

Times were much better now than they had been seven

years ago when Kathleen had used the inheritance from her grandparents to buy into the *Gazette*. During the war she had received a little income from the paper after Adelaide and Paul had taken out their salary, and she had saved money. Her stories were bringing in more money now that the pen name K.K. Doyle was gradually becoming known to Western fiction readers.

"Did you see him?" Adelaide and Paul came back into the office. "I can't believe that he's home. He looks so thin and . . . dark. He was always tan, but that sun over there has baked him as brown as a berry. Oh, honey—" Adelaide exclaimed, when she saw the stricken look on Kathleen's face. She hurried to her and put her arm around her. "He was looking for you. I know he was. Wasn't he, Paul?"

"I can't be sure, honey. He was scanning the crowd, that's sure."

"No. He doesn't even know I'm here. He doesn't know anything about what I've been doing unless you or Barker told him."

"You asked me not to tell him, and I didn't. Barker may have. Anyway, he'll know when he gets out to the ranch. No one else would have gone in there and cleaned like you did." Adelaide and Paul were Kathleen's dearest friends and were sensitive to her emotional hurt and confusion.

"I left him a note."

"He would have known if you *hadn't* left a note. Barker said that he was going to meet him and take him home."

"He'll not have a way to get back to town." Kathleen worried her bottom lip with her teeth.

"That old Nash of yours has about seen its last days, even if it was up on blocks during the war. I'm surprised

Eddie could find tires to go on it." Paul stood behind his petite wife, rubbing her back. "Feel good?" he whispered.

"I could stand here all day."

"You're a glutton," he said softly in her ear.

"Eddie told me he could have sold the Nash a dozen times," Kathleen said. "He wouldn't take a dime for storing it all this time. He did it for Johnny not me."

"I got two rolls of pictures." The dark-haired girl announced as she burst through the door. She was a bundle of energy, small, quick, and pretty. "I got several of Johnny when he got off the train and again while he was on the float. Lord-dee mercy, he's good-looking. I don't think he knew who I was."

"When he left, you were just a kid. You've grown up while he was gone."

"I'd forgotten he was so handsome." Judy rolled her eyes. "Maybe I was too young to notice."

"Want me to develop these? We should decide on the pictures we want for this week's paper." Paul opened the camera and took out the film. Judy was like a daughter to Paul and Adelaide, although she had lived with her father, Sheriff Carroll, since her mother's death three years ago.

"I'll do it." She picked up the film and headed for the darkroom, her skirt swirling around her bare legs.

"I can hardly remember when I was that young. She gets prettier all the time," Kathleen said wistfully. "It's hard to believe she's twenty-three. When she came here looking for her real parents, she was just sixteen."

"And already mighty gutsy," Paul added.

"She was worried that she'd be out of a job when you came back," Adelaide said to Kathleen.

"I hope you told her that I'd rather not come back full-time. I want to take a stab at writing a book."

"She knows that now."

"I'm thinking about moving to Elk City or maybe back to Liberal. Barker said he'd help me find a place in Elk City. He invited me to come stay at the ranch. They have plenty of room. Wouldn't that set the tongues to wagging?"

"You're not moving out there . . . are you?" Adelaide had a worried look in her eyes.

"No. It would only make a deeper rift between Johnny and his father. Just before Johnny left he brought up his old suspicion that I was attracted to Barker because I was spending so much time out at the ranch. He just couldn't understand that I just liked his father."

"I think it was a little more than that. Johnny was jealous and afraid you'd like Barker more than you loved him. To his way of thinking Barker was everything he wasn't: well-off and educated." Adelaide seldom criticized Johnny. She was terribly fond of him. She did so now because Kathleen was so miserable. "Barker was a shoulder for you to lean on when Johnny let you down."

"I've got to see him and tell him that I'll do whatever he wants to do about the divorce. If I divorced Johnny Henry, a hero who spent four years fighting for our country, I'd be the most hated woman in Oklahoma. I'll do it if that's what he wants, but I'd rather he'd do it."

"He might think that you've already filed."

"I haven't, even though the last thing he said to me was: 'Get a lawyer to make out the papers. Tell him that half of the ranch is yours and, if you want your money now, to put it up for sale. Send the papers. I'll sign them and send them back.' He turned and got on the train and didn't even look at me again."

"He loves you, Kathleen. I never knew a man who loved a woman as much."

"Ah . . . hum!" Paul cleared his throat loudly.

Adelaide gazed lovingly at her husband. "Don't get in a snit, love. I was not including you."

"If he loved me, he wouldn't have left me to grieve by myself. I lost my baby and then my husband," Kathleen said with a sudden spurt of spirit.

"It's a well-known fact that women can handle grief much better than men."

"It was his damn feeling of inferiority that caused the trouble. He firmly believes that our baby was born deformed and without a chance to live because of him. He thinks that the Perrys, his mother's family, are an incestuous clan and that any children he has will be like our little Mary Rose."

"That's nonsense."

"I told him so. The doctor in Frederick told him. Another thing that bothers him is that he feels inferior because he can only read on a very low level. I didn't know that and asked him to read one of my stories. He went through the motions, but when I asked him about it, he threw the magazine down and walked out. I gradually became aware that he could read only the simple words."

"That must be why he'd never take the test to become a Federal Marshal."

"I would have taught him if he had given me the slightest hint that he wanted me to."

"Johnny is a proud man."

"I have pride and feelings, too. Did he ever ask you about me when he wrote to you?"

"He never wrote anything except his name on the V-mail he sent. It was usually a cartoon or a copy of their

Thanksgiving or Christmas dinner menu they gave to the men to send home. Barker said all he ever heard from him was '*thanks for pkg*' on a V-mail after he had sent him a package."

"He hated to write even a grocery list."

"Most men would have made an effort to keep in touch with their loved ones even if they couldn't write very well."

"He never asked me to write when he left. He didn't want to hear from me. I think he thought it was a good time to cut me loose and forget me."

"If he doesn't make an effort to make up with you, he's a fool."

"I'd better go," Kathleen said, eager to leave because talking about her pain seemed to make it worse.

"Would you like to stay and have supper with me and Paul?"

"Thank you, but I'd not be very good company. I've got some reading to do about the Shoshone Indians. The book I'm going to write will take place up north on the Shoshone Reservation."

"Why don't you write about the Cherokee? You could get the information straight from the horse's mouth and not have to do all that reading."

"Barker would love to know that you called him a horse." Kathleen smiled, but only slightly.

"I'm thinking that he's been called worse."

With her head bowed, she walked down the alley toward the stairs leading to the rooms above the drugstore and slowly trudged up the steps and into the darkened hallway. While fitting her key into the lock, she heard a door farther down the hall close softly. For only a minute she wondered about the occupants of the other two apartments in the building.

The window in Kathleen's one-room efficiency apartment looked down onto the alley. She went there now and stood gazing at the bleak landscape. Her head was pounding. She wanted desperately to cry but refused herself the luxury.

She had come to Rawlings as soon as her job at the plant had been eliminated. It had been a couple of miserable weeks, made more so by living in this dark, dreary place. She could not write here. Her imagination refused to function. She longed for the bright and cheery room she had at the ranch, where she could look out onto the wide stretches of grassland and envision the scene she was writing about.

Where would she go when she left here? Rawlings had become home. Her friends were here. But they were Johnny's friends, too. She hated the thought of leaving, and she hated the thought of staying and seeing him with someone else. Could they meet on the street and give each other a civilized greeting just as if they had not at one time meant the world to each other?

While she was considering her options, there was a light tap on the door. She opened it to see Barker with his hand lifted to rap again.

"Adelaide said that you were here."

"Hello, Barker. Come in."

"I thought you might want to get out of this rathole for a while," he said after he entered and closed the door.

"You're speaking of my home." Kathleen allowed humor to surface briefly.

"Home, my hind leg. I'd not stable a horse in here."

"Of course, you wouldn't. You'd not be able to get him up the stairs."

"I took Johnny out to the ranch. I didn't stay."

"How did he . . . seem?"

"Quiet. But then he's always been quiet around me. He never mentioned . . . anyone."

"Did you expect him to?"

"I thought he might." Barker noticed the tired lines in her face and the circles beneath her eyes.

"He'll not have a way to get back to town or down to the McCabes' to get his horses."

"In the morning I'll drive out in my truck and leave it for him to use until he gets something. Marie will follow and bring me back."

"That's good of you, Barker. I'd offer the Nash, but more than likely he'd not take it."

"He may not accept the truck from me. Do you want to go out with me?"

"No. I'll wait for him to come to me. He will when he is ready."

"Are you sure he wants out of the marriage?"

"I'm sure. Before he left he told me to file for divorce, and I never heard one word from him all the time he was gone. He couldn't have made it plainer than that."

"He's a fool to let you go."

"You're a dear man, Barker. I wish things were different between you and Johnny."

"He thinks that I deserted him even though I didn't know he existed until he was twenty years old. It took me years to find him." Barker folded his arms across his chest as he sometimes did when he was in a serious mood. "He didn't have a pleasant childhood living with that . . . woman."

"You can say it outright, Barker. She was a whore. Johnny said she was one because that was what she wanted to be. I've thought about it a lot. You've done your part to make it right. It's up to Johnny now."

"He tolerates me. It's more than he did at first."

"He wants to like you. His darn pride gets in the way."

"Are you going to stay here in Rawlings, Kathleen?"

"I don't know what I'm going to do."

"I want to show you a house. You can't stay in this place. I won't allow it."

"And I'll not allow you buy me a house, Barker. You know that."

"The tannery owns the house. One of the men left, and we don't plan to replace him. The house will stand empty or be rented out. I'd rather you rent it."

"How much is the rent?"

"Ten dollars a month. You'll have to pay your gas and electric. That's another five a month. Telephone, and there is one already installed, will be another couple of dollars. But what the hell, you'll be rich as soon as you finish your book."

"Not unless friends like you buy a trainload."

"I just might do that and give one to everyone in the state. Not every man has a daughter-in-law who is an author."

"I may not be your daughter-in-law much longer. Johnny will want this thing settled."

"You'll always be my daughter, little redbird." Barker's hand reached out and stroked her shining hair. He seldom touched her. It was at times like this when he most revealed his Indian heritage. His handsome coppery features looked as if they were chiseled in stone.

"Thank you." Kathleen turned away so that he'd not see the tears that came suddenly to her eyes.

"Get your coat. It's cold when the sun goes down. I want to show you the house."

"We won't be gone that long, will we?"

"We will, if you come home with me for supper."

"All right. I don't think I could face an evening alone tonight."

The watcher in the upstairs window had opened the door a crack after Kathleen and Barker passed it. He saw them walk down the front stairs, then hurried to the window to watch them cross the street to where the Indian had parked his car. He knew that the Indian was her father-in-law and that he owned the tannery. The watcher took the stairs two at a time; and by the time Barker had backed out of his parking space, he was in his own car.

*I'll write down in my observation diary that she wore a blue dress today and that for a while I stood close behind her at the depot. I was so close that I could smell the lemon rinse on her hair. I managed to touch her back. She didn't know that it was me, didn't even look my way. All her attention was on that son of a bitch that got off the train.*

The small, square, three-room house sat on the edge of town. Kathleen was surprised that it was in such good condition and that it had a large, freshly painted bathroom. The tub, lavatory, and toilet were like new. The hot-water heater was in a closet on the back porch and had a thermostat so that she would have hot water all the time.

"The furnishings were for sale," Barker said. "I bought the lot for twenty-five dollars. You can have them for that. I don't intend to make a profit off my daughter."

"You're kidding!"

"About making a profit?" His dark eyes twinkled at her.

"No. That you paid twenty-five dollars for all this."

"He was in a hurry to leave and couldn't take them with him."

Kathleen's eyes swept over the upright stove, the small icebox, and the kitchen table and chairs. In the bedroom was a brass bed and a dresser with a hinged mirror. The front room had a brown-leather couch, a chair, and a library table. The carpet on the floor was maroon and of good quality.

Barker wasn't looking at her. Kathleen knew immediately that he had paid more than twenty-five dollars for the furnishings. She thought about the fact for a moment and decided to accept the gift graciously and not to question him about it.

"Who do I pay the rent to?"

"The tannery."

"I'll take it, and I thank you for thinking of me. I wish that I could move in tonight, but tomorrow will have to do."

"After we take the truck out to Johnny, Marie and I will come by and help you move."

"You'd better be careful, Barker. I might start thinking that you're about the nicest man I ever met."

"Ah . . . Chief Wonderful. I like the sound of it." He smiled, and his dark eyes shone with pleasure.

Kathleen had been at the Fleming ranch many times, but only once since her return from Oklahoma City. The ranch house and outbuildings were a reflection of the owner, richly furnished without seeming to be so. Orderly and well tended, the one-story house appeared to have no inside walls because one room flowed into another.

The Flemings were proud of their heritage. Indian art covered the walls and Indian-designed rugs, the floors. It was a lived-in house with comfortable leather couches and chairs and a large fieldstone fireplace.

Barker's father had amassed a fortune in oil, cattle, packing plants, and tanneries, making his family one of the richest in the state. The ranch and the tannery were Barker's special responsibility. He ran both with an easy hand, having learned the value of delegating authority to responsible people.

His home was managed by Thelma Fisher, a distant relative who had lived with them for years, and Marie, who had graduated from high school, but had not the desire, as had her two older sisters, to go on to college. Janna, 15, and Lucas, 12, went to school in Rawlings.

Kathleen was greeted warmly by Marie.

"Daddy told us he'd try to get you to come for supper."

"He didn't have to try very hard."

Kathleen was fond of the small girl with the dark hair and coppery skin. Marie was a born homemaker, eager to have a home and children of her own. While waiting for the right man to come along, she was content to live in her father's house and help tend to her siblings.

"Hello, Mrs. Fisher." Kathleen spoke to the woman who came to the dining room with another place setting.

"How ye been doin', Kathleen?"

"All right. You?"

"I be all right." Mrs. Fisher, who came from the Scottish side of the family, adopted the dress of the Cherokee while she was at the ranch. Today her loose brown dress hung from her shoulders to just inches above her beaded moccasins; but when she went to church in town, she dressed as stylishly as any woman there. "Get washed up, Lucas," she called. "Your daddy will be here in a minute."

"Hello, Kathleen." The boy who stuck his head out of the kitchen door to speak could have been Johnny at that age. He was handsome, and his straight black hair framed a serious face.

Barker came to stand behind his chair at the head of the table. He had put on a fresh shirt, and his newly combed hair hung to his collar.

"Where's Janna?"

"She's coming," Marie said.

"I'm coming! I'm coming! I'm . . . here!" Janna dashed into the room, smoothing her hair back with wet palms. She was as tall as Marie, but much thinner. She was an outdoor girl and was happiest when she was astride her horse, riding for pleasure or helping the hands with the cattle. "Hi, Kathleen. I didn't know you were here."

Kathleen loved every member of this family. She had felt at home with them as soon as she met them, which was before she and Johnny were married. Johnny had felt nothing but anger when he learned seven years ago that Barker was his father. Having endured taunts since childhood that his father had been a drunken Indian, Johnny could not accept Barker's explanation of why he had been left all those years with a mother who was a whore. The pain was too deep.

While he and Kathleen were together, he had warmed to the family a little; but when the strain in his marriage occurred, he had begun avoiding being with them.

*Johnny, Johnny, you're missing so much. You could be a part of this family, if only you'd forget how you were conceived and let them love you.*

# Chapter Three

"The truck is at Johnny's. Marie and I left it before he could come out and make a fuss." Barker took a heavy box from Kathleen. "Where do you want this?"

"In the backseat."

"What do you have left to bring down?"

"The only heavy thing is my typewriter."

"I'll get it."

Kathleen had carried suitcases and boxes down to the Nash, swearing that never again would she live in a place where she had to carry anything up or down a steep, rickety stairway.

"This is everything," she said later, as Barker placed her typewriter on the front seat of the car. "I'll be glad to see the last of this place. I'll go tell Adelaide I'm moving."

The three of them walked down the alley and went into the back of the *Gazette* building. In the pressroom, Paul and Judy were looking at the pictures she had taken at the depot and during the parade. Kathleen's eyes feasted on the two pictures of Johnny: one as he stepped off the train and the other a close-up of him smiling down at Judy.

"These are good, Judy. You've turned out to be quite a good photographer."

"What did you expect?" Paul said with a smirk. "She had a darn good teacher."

"There's nothing modest about this guy." Judy winked at Kathleen. "I'll make copies of the pictures of Johnny for you. Would you like copies, Mr. Fleming?"

"I sure would. Could you make them about . . . so big?" He held his hands about eight inches apart.

"They should blow up to eight-by-tens and still be clear. If they are grainy, I'll make five by sevens."

"Listen up, you-all. I've got news." Adelaide came from the front office. Her Oklahoma drawl was always pronounced when she was excited. "I just heard that a new doctor is coming to take over the clinic."

"It's about time. Rawlings has been without a doctor for almost three years." Paul continued to trim the photos. "The old man who replaced Dr. Herman died on us."

"This one is a veteran who was injured in Italy. He's fully recovered and is ready to practice. Claude came by and told me."

"Did Claude say why he chose Rawlings?" Barker asked. "Every town around is begging for a doctor."

"All I know is that Claude was contacted by Mr. Gifford, the attorney general. He asked Claude what he planned, as mayor, to do about the clinic and told him about a crackerjack of a young doctor who wanted to start a practice. Claude said that we were eager for the clinic to be reopened and that if Mr. Gifford recommended him, the doctor was bound to be all right."

"Gifford isn't one to make a recommendation lightly."

Barker's remark went unheard by Kathleen as her mind wandered back to when she first arrived to work at the

*Gazette.* She remembered Dr. Herman, who had been mayor, a cold-hearted monster with such a hold on the town that no one dared to do anything without his permission.

"Has anyone heard anything about Louise Munday?" Kathleen wondered what had happened to the big blond woman who had been Dr. Herman's nurse.

"She must still be serving her ten-year sentence for helping Dr. Herman with his little scheme. Want me to ask Daddy about her?"

"Don't bother. I really don't care as long as she stays away from me. Adelaide, I came by to tell you I'm moving to one of the houses owned by the tannery. It's the last house on the road going west."

"A small white house with the porch on two sides?"

"That's the one. I've got the Nash loaded. Barker said he'd stop here and get my trunk in a day or two."

"I'm glad you found a better place, although it was nice having you so close. Do you have everything you need?"

"Before I leave, I'll go to the five-and-dime and get a couple of plates, a cup or two, a pan and a skillet. That's about all I need."

"You'll not go to the five-and-dime. Paul and I will be down this evening. I have plenty of extras."

Tears sprang to Kathleen's eyes. Her heart had been pounded to a pulp and her emotions so mangled that tears were always near the surface these days. Her only escape was to force her numb mind to come up with a sassy retort.

"Feed Paul before you bring him. My cupboards are bare."

"I'll pick up a block of ice and follow you down to the house."

"I don't have anything to put in the icebox, Barker."

"It'll be cold when you do."

"But, Barker, you don't have to—"

"You might as well give up and let him have his way." Marie laughed and grasped Kathleen's arm. "Once Daddy gets the bit in his teeth there's no stopping him."

"I'm beginning to find that out."

Barker headed for the door. "Marie and I will help you unload, then I've got to get out to the tannery. See you later, folks."

Before she got into her car, Kathleen said, "I don't want to like that little house too much. I may be moving on."

"Oh, I hope you stay, even if you and Johnny . . . don't work things out." Marie's expressive face creased in a worried frown.

"I've no hope of that, Marie. No hope at all."

Above the drugstore the man watched both cars leave the alley.

*She's moving into the house the Indian took her to last night. Having her down the hall has been wonderful for me, but she's too bright and lovely to have to spend time in that dingy place.*

*I knew the minute I saw her that she was the one. Since that time she's been all that has made my life worth living. I live only to be near her. Someday she will really look at me, see that I love and cherish her, and will love me back . . . I know it.*

By noon, Kathleen had put her things away and made her bed. Her mind returned constantly to Johnny. She was unable to get used to the thought that he was so near, yet so far away. He looked like the same flesh-and-blood Johnny she had married, but older, somehow different.

She herself was not the same, she thought, as she drove

to the store. She hadn't realized how much until she looked at the wedding picture. She had wanted to take it from the ranch house, wanted badly to take it, but remembered that Johnny had paid the photographer with silver dollars he had won at the rodeo. After the divorce she would ask him to let her have it.

Her mind was so busy that she sat in her car in front of the grocery for a long moment. They had been so in love. At least she had been. Her mind had been his, her heart his, her body his, just as his had been hers. She had been sure that they would be together always. How could the feelings they'd had for each other vanish because the child they had together had been less than perfect? The love he professed to have for her had not been lasting. She just must face that fact and go on. People didn't die of broken hearts . . . or did they?

Suddenly the thought that Johnny could be in town today occurred to her. Anxiety cut through her. She scanned the street for Barker's truck, then dashed into the store. She needed to be calm when she came face-to-face with him, and she certainly didn't want to be wearing this grubby old dress and dirty white sandals.

Fifteen minutes later she carried two sacks of groceries to the car and hurried back to the sanctuary of the little house. Kicking off her shoes, she put the milk, eggs, and butter in the icebox and the rest of her supplies in the cupboard above the sink.

A sudden rap on the door startled her. *Barker was back*. He had promised to come turn on the gas and light the water heater. Kathleen raked her fingers through her hair, looked around for her shoes and didn't see them. Oh, well, he had seen her barefoot before.

She didn't see the tall figure in the cowboy hat until she

reached the door. He was standing on the edge of the porch with his back to the house. She gaped, unable to utter a sound, incapable of accepting that Johnny was just a few feet away. Panic struck fresh and sharp. Her heart began to pump like a piston. Her first thought was to turn and run out the back door. She feared it would take more courage than she possessed to face him and hear him say that he wanted to be rid of her. Shaken to the core, she was unaware that a small sound had come from her throat.

Hearing it, he turned. His face seemed frozen. His dark, intense eyes beneath the brim of his old hat were fixed on her face. From somewhere the realization came to her that he was wearing a shirt that she had ironed two days before.

*Oh, God! Oh, God!* A strange sensation began seeping rapidly through Kathleen's mind, a fuzziness, a distant humming noise sounded in her ears. She sucked in her breath.

"Hello, Kathleen." The pounding in her ears made the words seem to come from far away.

"Hello." Her throat was tight, and she just barely managed the word.

They stared at each other through the screen door. It seemed an eternity before he said, "May I come in?"

Unable to speak for the chaos raging in her brain, she pushed on the door. He pulled it open and stepped into the small room and took off his hat. Kathleen backed up and turned away. Suddenly it was too much for her. She felt the tears and couldn't bear for him to see them.

"Excuse me for a moment."

She stepped into the bedroom then darted into the bathroom, closed the door, and leaned against it. She had mentally rehearsed the meeting with him a thousand times during the past four years, and never had she imagined it would be as devastating as this. She wet her face with her hands and dried it. Not wanting to see how terrible she looked, she avoided the mirror, picked up a brush, and smoothed her hair.

Going back through the bedroom, she paused in the doorway. He was sitting on the edge of the couch. Her eyes clung to him as he flicked a match and put it to the cigarette he held between his lips. The light shone for an instant on his dark face. He drew deeply on the cigarette, and the end flared briefly. Before he blew out the match he raised his lids, and she had a glimpse of steady dark eyes.

"Looking for your shoes?" he asked quietly.

She nodded, came into the room, and sat down on the edge of the chair across from him. She had regained control. Her mouth was taut, and there was an air of unconscious dignity about her poised head. She clasped her hands in her lap and pulled her bare feet back close to the chair as if to hide them.

"You always liked to go barefoot."

"I was raised on a farm. Remember?"

"I remember a lot of things." His eyes held hers while he drew deeply on the cigarette.

"I'm sorry. It was rude to run out. I didn't mean to behave like that. It was the strain of . . . moving . . . the uncertainty of . . . things and seeing you so suddenly."

"How did you plan to behave?"

She lifted her shoulders, trying to encompass a world of explanation with the silent gesture.

"How did you know I was here?"

"I went by the *Gazette*. Adelaide told me."

"I couldn't stand that room above the drugstore.

Barker told me about this house being for rent and I grabbed it. I bought the furniture . . . for a song."

"Does Barker own the house?"

"The tannery does."

"Same thing."

"I pay my way. I don't expect you, Barker, or anyone else to feel obligated to help me." Her eyes were wide and dry. She was startled by her own tone of voice and her bluntness.

"You haven't changed. You still don't need anyone."

"I needed you . . . once." The words burst from her. She hadn't meant to say them and tried to soften them, by saying, "You look good. Maybe a little thinner."

"You should have seen me after Guadalcanal. I sweated off so many pounds that I looked like a walking bag of bones."

"I watched the paper for news of your battalion. The only time I saw it mentioned was when you covered the Japs with the bulldozer. I have the clipping if you'd like to see it."

"Hell. That was overblown. The newsboys needed something to stir up the folks back home so they'd buy War Bonds." He looked around for a place to put the ashes from his cigarette. Kathleen hurried to the kitchen and returned with a cracked saucer she had found beneath the sink.

"I don't have an ashtray or dishes yet. Adelaide is going to lend me some."

"Still don't smoke?"

"I never acquired the taste for it."

"Why didn't you take the dishes out at the ranch? They're just as much yours as mine."

"Your friends gave them to us. You should have them."

A long, silent minute went by before he spoke. "How did you like working at Douglas Aircraft?"

"How did you know that?"

"Was it a secret?"

"No. I just didn't think you knew where I was. Adelaide said you didn't ask her, and she didn't tell you."

"She didn't. Were you Rosie the Riveter?"

"I worked in the payroll department. We paid twenty thousand people every Friday. I could work as much overtime as I wanted, so I usually worked ten or twelve hours a day."

"I heard that the defense workers made a pile of money."

"I wanted to do my part to help end the war."

"Commendable of you," he said dryly.

He seemed to be studying her, seldom took his eyes from her face. It made her nervous.

"Did you see your name on the sign on the courthouse lawn? Over four hundred went to the service from this area."

"Some of them didn't come back."

"Thank God, you did. I said a prayer for you every night and hung a banner with a star on it in the window."

"Thanks," he said, and looked away from her.

"I wanted to write."

"No stamps?"

"I didn't know where to send it."

"Henry Ann would have given you my address."

"Would you have read it?"

"A man away from home gets pretty desperate for mail."

*I wrote you a thousand letters in my mind. I would have mailed them, but couldn't bear the thought that you might return them unopened.*

"I just came from the bank." Johnny's voice broke into

her thoughts. "From the size of the account, you didn't use any of the family allotment money the government sent you."

"I didn't need it."

"Didn't want *even* that from me, huh?"

"That wasn't it at all. I was getting along on what I was making and saving a little. I knew you'd need money to get started again."

"Why didn't you send me the divorce papers?"

"I didn't think it was right to divorce you while you were over there fighting for our country."

"Several of the men in my battalion got *Dear John* letters from wives who wanted a divorce."

"I'm sorry if you were disappointed that you didn't get one."

Her words penetrated his cool armor. He was getting angry. Lines around his mouth became deeply etched, and his nostrils flared. She knew the signs.

"Did you find someone else?" The words seemed to be snatched out of him.

She saw that he was waiting for an answer to his question. Her mind was too confused to tell him anything but the truth.

"No. I didn't have time for anything but work."

"You wouldn't have had to do much looking. There must have been plenty of 4F's and draft dodgers working at the plant."

"They did their jobs, too. They built the planes that helped end the war."

There was a silence while he lit another cigarette. *He was still wearing his wedding ring!* She could feel her heart beating through her fingertips and spoke before she thought.

"You're wearing your wedding ring."

"I'm still married. Where's yours?" He looked pointedly at her hand.

"I . . . didn't think you'd want me to wear it."

"Horse hockey!" he snorted. "Do you have a lawyer?"

"I'm not filing. You'll have to file to get rid of me."

"Kathleen," he said her name menacingly. "You're trying my patience."

"That's too bad. I don't mean to be contrary. How would it look if I divorced a hero as soon as he came home from the war?"

"You're concerned about what folks in this town will think?" When she didn't answer, he said, "Then you plan to stay here?"

"I haven't decided. I've been selling more and more of my Western stories. My editor is urging me to write a book. One thing about being a writer, you can do it anywhere. I should take that back. I couldn't write a line in that dark apartment above the drugstore."

"I read some of your stories while I was overseas."

Kathleen's mouth dropped open in surprise. "You . . . did? I didn't think that you liked to read."

"We had little breaks between campaigns. When you have nothing else to do, you can learn to like most anything. The Salvation Army brought in boxes of magazines and books. I picked out the ones with stories written by K.K. Doyle."

*Was there pride in his voice?* Kathleen smiled for the first time since he had come into the house. Their eyes caught and held. It was so wonderful to look at him. It was hard for her to believe that it was Johnny sitting across from her.

"You . . . read my stories over there?" she managed to ask, her heart thumping painfully.

"Yeah. They were pretty good." His lips quirked a little at the corners.

He had felt a surge of pride when some of the men remarked, *"That fellow Doyle writes a damn good story."* After his tentmate had taught him how to sound out words, he had read everything he could get his hands on. Practice makes perfect, Curly had said, and he had been right. During the first year, his reading had been painfully slow, but because he felt closer to her while reading her stories, he'd stuck with it. By the end of his tour of duty, he could get so immersed in a story that he didn't want to go to his foxhole when the air-raid sirens sounded.

Johnny had intended to wait a few days before coming to see her; but when Adelaide told him where she was, he was on his way before he had given it much thought. He wanted to find out if what they once shared was still there. Now he knew that it was for him, and stronger than ever.

"I'm surprised that you got books and magazines over there." Her voice broke into his thoughts.

"Some of the magazines were so old they were held together with tape. You had a story in an old *Western Story* magazine that was about to fall apart. It was called 'Hot Lead . . .' and something."

"'Hot Lead and Petticoats.' It was the first story I sold. I think now that it was not very good."

Johnny put his cigarette out in the saucer and set it on the floor. Kathleen's eyes followed the movement and for the first time noticed that he wore black shoes.

"I've never seen you in anything but cowboy boots. You even wore them to our wedding."

"You saw me at the depot when I left to go back after my leave."

"That's right I did."

"I put on my boots, but they were so stiff and dried-out, I couldn't wear them." Dead silence followed the remark, then he said, "Thanks for washing my clothes."

She lifted her shoulders in a noncommittal shrug and tried to think of something to say so that he wouldn't leave. Her love for him was as intense as it had been seven years ago when they met and fell in love. At times, during the past four years, an almost unbearable longing for him had swept over her. It was more than a physical need, as it was now. Only pride kept her from throwing herself in his arms and begging him to stay with her forever.

"Eddie didn't charge me for keeping the Nash." The comment came from some small corner of her mind.

"He said that three of the four tires he put on for you are pretty good. The fourth one will bear watching."

"When did you see him?"

"A little while ago. I bought a car from him. I wanted a truck, but there isn't one to be had around here. He's putting a hitch on behind the car so I can pull a flat rack." He looked at the watch on his wrist. "He should be about done by now."

"You could have had the Nash."

He ignored the remark, stood, and reached for his hat. "The car I got isn't much, but it'll do for a while."

"What do you plan to do?" Kathleen got to her feet. "Besides ranching, I mean."

"I've had a couple of offers. I was discharged at the naval base at Norman. During the week I was there I called Grant Gifford. Remember him? He's still the attorney general. He came out to the base to see me and said that he was sure that there was a place for me with the Oklahoma Highway Patrol or the Marshal's Office, if I wanted it."

"Do you?"

"I've not decided. A representative from a construction company came to the base trying to hire bulldozer operators. The pay is good, but the work is in Central America."

Kathleen's heart gave a sickening leap. She tried to control her sudden shivering and failed.

"Are you going?"

"I'm too glad to be home to leave right away. I'll not have any trouble finding a job driving a bulldozer around here if I decide to do that. It stands to reason that there'll be a building boom now that the war is over."

"You loved the ranch."

"It's hard to make a living on the number of acres I have." He stepped out onto the porch, and she followed. "I'm glad you're doing all right. If you need anything, let me know."

"Thanks." Her voice was shaky.

"Half that bank account is yours and half the ranch when you're ready to take it."

She felt as if he had kicked her in the stomach. The strength seemed to drain out of her, and her usually straight shoulders slumped. Her mouth suddenly went dry, and she felt sick.

"I'll *never* be ready to take it." Her voice was firm and convincing. She looked down to hide the hurt he was sure to read in her eyes.

"Sure you will," he said confidently. "You'll take it because you're entitled to it."

"You'll see." She clamped her lips tightly together to keep from telling him to take the bank account and the ranch and shove it. Not for anything would she let him know that his words had cut her to the quick. "Are you going to see a lawyer here?"

"Why? Do you have someone on the string you're anxious to marry?"

"I told you that I didn't have. But this isn't fair to you. You'll meet someone . . . want a family—"

"I've been through that, Kathleen. Don't be trying to arrange my life." He stepped off the porch and headed for the truck he had parked in the road in front of the house.

"I wouldn't even think of trying to arrange your life," she sputtered, her head tilted proudly, but color draining from her face, a sure sign of her anger.

"No, I guess not." He lifted his shoulders. Kathleen saw for an instant a forlorn expression on his face. It prompted her to say:

"I put a marker on Mary Rose's grave," she called.

He stopped and turned. "I saw it this morning. I'll pay you for half of it."

She was so jolted by the remark that the walls holding her emotions in check suddenly crumbled. Anger at all she had endured came boiling up out of the pit of her stomach. Words when they came, were unguarded and loud. Her voice, shrill and breathless didn't even sound like her voice.

"You don't owe me a blessed thing, you . . . horse's ass," she yelled not caring who heard. "You didn't even like her! You wouldn't even hold her. I'll not take a penny from you for her marker. She was *my* baby. Mine! I was the only one who loved her, grieved for her. The great Johnny Henry, Best All-Around Cowboy, was ashamed of having a deformed daughter. Get the hell away from

here and don't come back or ... I'll get my gun out and
... shoot you!"

Her eyes were fiery now. Her head felt tight, and her
eyes smarted; and for the first time in her life she wanted
to really lash out at someone, to do something violent.
She turned and ran back into the house.

Johnny went taut as he listened to her outburst. A muscle twitched in the corner of his mouth as he stood for a
minute and looked at the empty porch. Her words had
shocked him. He had only offered to help pay for the
marker. Why did that make her so angry?

In the house, Kathleen threw herself down on the bed
and cried with deep disappointment. She had always held
out a tiny hope that when Johnny came home he would
tell her how sorry he was for his rejection after their
daughter was born and that he had been as hurt when they
lost her as she had been. Now, she knew that it wouldn't
happen. It was over. The finality of it was crushing.

*Why didn't you take the job in Central America? I had
reconciled myself to the fact that I had lost you forever
and was going to go on with my life. Now ... I don't
know what to do—*

# Chapter Four

*D*uring the week that followed, Kathleen doggedly tried to keep her thoughts from dwelling on Johnny, although twice she woke up in the middle of the night with tears on her cheeks.

She worked on her book and became immersed in the story. She concentrated on the scene she was writing, then the next scene and the next, until she had written the first chapter. She had followed the advice her editor had given her. *You have only a minute or two to catch the interest of the readers. Open with a hook that will keep them reading to see what happens.* Scanning the typed pages, she was pleased with what she had written.

Kathleen had not left the house since Johnny's visit, but Adelaide and Paul had been to see her, as had Barker and Marie. This morning she needed to go to the grocery store and then to the ice dock to pick up a card to put in her window so the iceman would stop. It was still warm in southern Oklahoma and would be for another month.

Her intention had been to walk to town, but noticing that one of the tires on her car was low, she decided to drive it to the station to get air before it became completely flat. She drove slowly down Main Street past the Rialto Theatre where *Sergeant York* was playing. She and Johnny had seen the film while she was pregnant with Mary Rose. So many memories were here. The town of Rawlings had become home to her. She would hate to leave it.

At Eddie's station she pulled up to the air hose. A man came slouching out of the building, a cigarette dangling from his mouth. He stopped in front of the car, placed his hand on the hood, and looked at her through the windshield. She looked steadily back at him. He wore a battered felt hat and his clothes were so greasy he must have been wearing them for a month. He also needed a shave. Finally he took a last puff of the cigarette, dropped it on the paving, and stepped on it.

"My front left tire is low. Will you check it, please?"

"Sure. You wantin' gas too?"

"A couple of gallons."

She heard the hiss as the air went into the tire, then the gas cap being removed. She reached for her purse when he came to the side of the car.

"How much?"

"Four bits. You're Kathleen Henry, ain't ya? Ya married Johnny Henry, then run off when he went to war. Heard ya was up in the city a raking in the dough at the airplane plant. Back for good?"

She recognized him then as a man who had been around town when she came here seven years ago. He had been one of the toughs who hung around doing as little as possible.

Kathleen ignored his question, handed him a dollar, and waited for her change.

"I ain't blamin' ya for leavin' Johnny. He was a high-handed, know-it-all sonofagun. Still is, if ya ask me. Folks are fallin' all over him 'cause he killed a few Japs."

"What did you do during the war?" Kathleen looked straight at him, her temper overriding her desire to get away from him.

"I didn't have to go." He grinned, showing tobacco-stained teeth. "Draft board gave me a 4F card 'cause I got four toes shot off while I was hunting squirrels back in '40."

"How could you be so lucky?" she said with heavy sarcasm.

"Better'n gettin' my legs blowed off. Cletus Birdsall came home with stumps."

"I'd like my change, if you don't mind."

He pulled a handful of change from his pocket and picked around in it with greasy fingers.

"Need any help out there let me know."

"Why would I need any help from you?"

"You're out there in Chief Big Shot's house, ain't ya? It's right on the end of town, ain't it?"

"I rent the house from the tannery."

"If you say so." He let his eyelid droop in a wink and raised the corner of his mouth. "Ain't much goes on in this town that folks don't know."

The gesture disgusted her. "My change?"

He dropped the change in her palm with one hand and with the other he deftly lifted the windshield wiper, unhooked it and took it off before she could start the motor.

"What are you doing?"

"Washing your windshield." He lifted a mop on the end of a stick out of a bucket of water and slopped it on the windshield. "I danced with ya at the shindig they put on for the Claxtons when their house burned. Guess ya don't remember?"

"No, I don't."

"Gabe Thomas. Does that ring a bell?" He used the squeegee to take the excess water off the windshield.

"Yes. I remember. Your name was on the police log at the city office for bootlegging and stealing gasoline. I'm surprised Eddie lets you work here."

"I'm the best mechanic in Tillison County, that's why." He grinned. He seemed to be terribly pleased that she remembered him. "Ya hadn't been knocked up when we danced."

Kathleen's face reflected shock on hearing his crude words. She sat tight-lipped, staring straight ahead. The instant he snapped her wiper blade back in place, she moved the car ahead so fast that he had to jump out of the way.

"Be seein' ya," he called.

She was so angry that she didn't care if she ran over him when she drove out of the station. *That's what you think, you ignorant horse's patoot.*

Gabe stood in the drive and watched her until the Nash turned the corner. *Yeah, babe, ya'll be seein' me all right. Always did want to get in yore pants. I'm thinkin' it won't be too hard to do. Ole Johnny broke ground, but now he's outta the picture.*

From a car parked next to the vacant lot down the street, the encounter was watched through powerful binoculars by her *Guardian* as the man liked to call himself. This was the first time that she'd left the house in a week. He could tell that she was agitated about something when she drove out of the filling station. He started his car and followed slowly.

Two nights ago he had given himself a treat. He had left his car on a side street, walked across a vacant field, and approached her house from the back. The kitchen window shade was halfway up and he could see her sitting in her nightdress at the table working on her manuscript. The radio was on and Eddie Arnold was singing, "I'm Alone Because I Love You." He had become so excited he could hardly breathe when she lifted her arms, arched her back, and stretched. *The gesture was so familiar it made him doubly sure that she was the one.*

He watched her and daydreamed that someday he would walk into the house and she would greet him as if he belonged there. He would tell her what he had done with his inheritance, and she would be proud that he had invested it in a company selling arms to the British at the time when the world was at war and that he had made a vast amount of money. *My very own dear, he would say, we can afford for you to have whatever you want.*

A dog began to bark, breaking into his dream. She looked toward the window. He hurriedly backed away and went back across a field to where he'd left his car.

Months ago, when he'd discovered that she wrote stories for a Western magazine, he'd had a searcher find every magazine that had a K.K. Doyle story in it. He had read them all, over and over. He kept the magazines locked in a suitcase. They were his treasures.

*The nerve of that trashy, whopper-jawed, nasty, dirty polecat,* Kathleen fumed as she shifted into second gear and tramped on the gas pedal. She was so angry that the Nash went over the curb and swerved to the wrong side of the street before she realized it. *Johnny would tear him apart if he knew what he had said to me.* A block away, she slowed the car. *Or . . . would he care?*

The Greyhound bus had come into town and was parked in front of the drugstore. Kathleen passed it on her way to the icehouse, where she picked up a card to put in her window on delivery day. Coming back she stopped at Miller's grocery store and was about to get out of the car when she saw Johnny come out of the store with a sack of groceries. He went to a dark sedan, said something to a woman in the front seat, then put the grocery sack in the back.

With two cars angle-parked between them, Kathleen could see only the back of the woman's head, but she knew that she was young. Old ladies didn't wear bleached, shoulder-length hair. Kathleen felt as if the air had been sucked from her lungs. She turned her head, hoping and praying that he wouldn't see her, and, if he did, he'd not know that she'd seen him and . . . the woman.

Johnny backed the car out and drove down the street. On a sudden impulse Kathleen followed. *He may be taking someone home*, she reasoned, remembering how concerned he had been for her when she first came to town. At the library corner the sedan turned south. Kathleen turned, then stopped. She could see all the way down the street to the flatlands outside of town. The sedan continued on out of town, and it was clear to Kathleen that Johnny was taking the woman out to the ranch.

She put her hands to her head, and her fingers massaged her aching temples. She was grateful that he hadn't seen her and wouldn't know that she had followed him.

*She had thought that she would be prepared for the in-*

*evitable when it happened, but it had happened far sooner than she had expected.*

Kathleen began to shake all over, and it was such a peculiar sensation that it frightened her. Fear ate into her very being. Would she never be free of this power he had to hurt her? Would she ever be able to empty her mind of Johnny and the love they had shared?

Of course not, she chided herself. Heavens! He had been a part of her life for seven years. They had made a child together. There was no way she could ever get him out of her mind. But she hoped someday to get him out of her heart.

Suddenly she was ashamed.

Where and when had she lost her pride? Johnny had made it plain that he didn't want her, and here she was, following after him like a puppy. She stiffened her resolve to do her utmost to hide her love for him. She would never, she vowed silently, allow him to use it as a weapon against her.

The man following Kathleen stopped his car a block behind hers. He waited to see if she was going to get out and go into the library. When she didn't, he picked up from the seat beside him what he called his observation diary and read the entry he'd made earlier.

*10:30 A.M. Kathleen, Kathleen, Kathleen. I love to write her name. It is as beautiful as she is. She wore a skirt today that came to just below her knees. Thank goodness, she no longer wears that awful leg makeup she wore during the war. I hated to see her wear it, and I hated it when she wore her beautiful hair in that ugly net snood.*

*At the 66 station, she bought gas, got air in a tire, and talked for a while to a greasy, uncouth individual who made her angry. When I find out what it was he said to upset her, he'll be sorry.*

When he finished reading, he took an expensive Sheaffer fountain pen from his pocket and added another entry.

*11:00 A.M. My beautiful Kathleen is hurting because the son of a bitch she's married to has another woman. From the looks of the blonde in his car, he scraped the bottom of the barrel. My beautiful girl was faithful to him all during the war, and as soon as he gets home he takes up with a bleached-blonde floozy. He isn't fit for her to wipe her feet on. She's leaving now—going home. I wish I knew what it was that she needed from the store. I'd buy it and leave it on her porch tonight.*

In the middle of the week Adelaide came out to tell Kathleen about the reception to be held for the new doctor.

"Please come, Kathleen," she said after they sat down at the kitchen table. "I'm heading the welcoming committee. We'll serve cake and coffee and iced tea. Claude is seeing to the cake."

"He's taking his duties as mayor seriously."

"We've discovered he has talents other than making hamburgers."

"Was this reception your idea or his?"

"Mine. I'm taking care of the decorations. I'm going to use my lace tablecloth, and Paul is polishing my mother's silver service."

"Silver service? This is going to be a fancy affair."

"The service hasn't been used since Mother died fifteen years ago. I'm not sure how it's going to shine up; but Paul says it will, and he's usually right."

"When is this shindig you're so excited about?" Kathleen smiled at the woman she loved like a sister and handed her a glass of iced tea.

"Tomorrow afternoon, two o'clock. We've put posters in all the store windows. Dr. Perry arrived yesterday, and Claude took him out to Doc Herman's house. The arrangement is that if he stays, he can buy the house for what the bank has in it. They took it and the clinic after Doc died."

"I hope he stays after you've gone to all this trouble, but maybe his wife will not like a small town and they'll go back to the city."

"He isn't married."

"Well, unless he's got an eye in the middle of his forehead and all his teeth are missing, every single woman in town will be after him."

"We may be able to use him to make Johnny jealous." Adelaide lifted her brows in question. "That boy needs someone to give him a swift kick. I'd ask Paul to do it, but he likes him too much."

"Don't even think about trying to get us back together, Addie. Johnny wouldn't care if I paraded through downtown Rawlings as naked as a jaybird."

"I think you're wrong."

"We won't argue that now or ever. Tell me about the new doctor," Kathleen said quickly, hoping to change the subject. She didn't want to hear about the woman Johnny was keeping company with.

"Claude said that this is his first civilian practice. He went into the army after medical school."

"He should be pretty good at patching up gunshot

wounds. The trouble is that there may not be many of those now that there isn't a draft to dodge."

"What brought that on?"

"I ran into Gabe Thomas today at the filling station, and he was bragging about not being drafted because he'd had four toes shot off squirrel hunting. He got under my skin. I don't know why Eddie hired him."

"It irked a lot of people, including me, that he was here during the war, bragging that he had been too smart to get caught in the draft." Adelaide took the last drink from her glass and set it on the table. "I've got to get back to the paper. I'll come by for you tomorrow."

"You talked me into it. I'll have on my best bib and tucker to meet the new doc, and I promise that I won't pick my nose or tell him dirty jokes."

"Oh . . . you— I'm glad to know that you still have your sense of humor."

Kathleen watched her dearest friend drive away. Adelaide was fifty years old but didn't look or act a year older than thirty-five. Love for her husband, Paul, was keeping her young. They adored each other as much today as they had when she first met them seven years ago.

Lucky, lucky Adelaide.

John J. Wrenn, president of Oklahoma State Bank of Rawlings tried to conceal his amazement as a cashier's check was placed on his desk by the man who sat across from him.

"Deposit the check in the name of Hidendall, Incorporated. We wish to pay for the property outright. The balance is to be kept in a checking account."

"Of course. The house has historic value. It was built by a cattle baron in 1912."

"I'm not interested in the historic value, Mr. Wrenn. It suits my purpose. I insist on privacy."

"The Clifton place is one of the largest holdings here. Only the BF Ranch is larger. We have been leasing the land to local ranchers for grazing."

"Continue to do so. I'll have a man down here in a few days to look over your books."

"Folks will wonder—"

"You are to tell the curious that I'm a weather observer, which I am part of the time. My main occupation is that of writer. My books are published under a very well known pen name. I don't want to be bothered by people knocking on my door seeking autographs. I hope you understand that my name is not to be mentioned to anyone at any time nor under any circumstance. Is that clear?"

"It is," the banker hastened to say.

"How long before I can move in?"

"In just a few days. I'll send a crew out tomorrow to clean the house. It's been vacant since old Mrs. Clifton died last year. She left the house and the property to a nephew in New Jersey. He told us to sell it. The furnishings, as you could tell, are old, but good quality. We decided to sell them with the house rather than hold an auction."

The man who stood looked more like a movie star than a writer. A few months short of his thirty-ninth birthday, he was average height, with ice-blue eyes and blond hair turning gray at the temples. He wore a dark shirt, a string tie, and a mohair jacket with dark brown oval patches on the elbows. There was an air of purpose to his movements that was particularly evident when he strode to the door of the bank president's office and turned for a final word.

"I'll be doing other business with this bank if my wishes for complete confidentiality are respected. I'll return day after tomorrow and sign the final papers."

"They'll be ready." The banker stood, but before he could get to his feet, the man calling himself Robert Brooks was out the door, so he sat back down.

*Will wonders never cease to happen?* He had unloaded that old Clifton estate, and he couldn't even brag about it to anyone.

He had been surprised when the man phoned and inquired about the Clifton place. It had been on the market for a year and had been shown only one time. The man who called wanted to see the inside of it, as he had already inspected the grounds and the surrounding property. Wrenn had sent a junior clerk out with a key, and not two hours later he was looking at a cashier's check for *fifty thousand dollars.*

John Wrenn pulled the telephone toward him and told the operator to get him the First National Bank in Oklahoma City. While he waited, he wondered how much longer it would be before Rawlings Telephone Company would install dial telephones.

"Hidendall, Inc., is as solid as the Rock of Gibraltar," the officer of the bank in Oklahoma City assured him. "Theodore Nuding is the sole owner of the corporation. His check is good."

"Mr. Nuding bought a property after seeing it only one time. Does he usually leave a balance of five thousand in a checking account?"

"Nuding is an unusual fellow. However, his needs seem to be few. He does not live high on the hog, even if he is able to."

"He's . . . well-off?"

"To put it mildly. If you want his business, I advise you to follow his instructions to the letter. He's got an uncanny business sense, and he's a man who demands anonymity."

"Thanks for telling me. If that's what he wants, I can assure you that's what he will get."

"Ah . . . I thought you'd agree. He's not hard to get along with unless you try to put something over on him. Then watch out. He can be vicious."

John Wrenn hung up the telephone and leaned back in his chair. Damn. Theodore Nuding, alias Robert Brooks, was well-off. Did that mean he was comfortably rich or a millionaire? The banker regretted that he hadn't added another five thousand to the estate and made himself a nice little profit.

The man who walked into the hotel down the street wore a well-worn suit coat and an old brown felt hat on a head of dark brown hair. He shuffled as he crossed the lobby to the desk. He removed his glasses and massaged the bridge of his nose.

"Any mail?" he asked the desk clerk in a meek voice.

"A couple of letters, Mr. Brooks."

"Thanks." He put his glasses back on and glanced at the letters. Both were from business places back East. He put them in the pocket of his jacket and headed for the stairs.

In his room, Theodore Nuding took a bulky notebook from his inside coat pocket before he hung the coat on a hanger. He adapted easily to any environment. He liked the smallness of Rawlings, although he realized that it would be harder to blend in than it had been in the city.

But he could do it. He knew how to make himself into a forgettable fellow or into a man long remembered.

He sat down at a table near the window, looked across at the courthouse, and then down on the street. He recognized the man who was getting out of a car in front of the bank, and reached for his ever-handy binoculars. He studied Johnny Henry as he stood beside the car talking to his father, Barker Fleming. He had made it his business to find out all he could about Kathleen's husband and rather admired him for his attitude toward a father who had abandoned him. Johnny's mother had been a whore and his sister was a slut who worked in a honky-tonk in Oklahoma City.

Nuding was a man with an extraordinary memory for detail and a knack for picking up information, especially anything pertaining to Kathleen Dolan Henry. His obsession with her was a fact that he readily admitted and reveled in.

Theodore Nuding's own father had died when he was nine years old. It had been God's gift to him and his mother. Thank God he'd had no brothers or sisters. He'd had his darling mother all to himself for almost thirty years.

He took out his fountain pen and began to write.

> 4:00 P.M. *I'm so glad that I found her, Mother. Her hair is gloriously red like yours, but then you know that because you urged me to take the job in the aircraft plant so that I would meet her. I bought a house for her today. It's a big old house, somewhat like the one you and I lived in when I was taking care of you. It will take a while to get it ready for her. Then I'll look after her and keep her safe just as I did you.*

*And after a while, like you, she will come to depend on me and will love me for my gentle care. So much to be done. I wish I didn't have to waste time sleeping.*

# Chapter Five

*K*athleen dreaded going to the reception for Dr. Perry. She didn't fear that she would run into Johnny because she couldn't think of a reason why he would be there. Her fear was that someone would mention him and the blond woman.

Night after sleepless night, she had pictured Johnny and another woman in the house that had been hers for almost three years and in the bed she had shared with him. Had he been writing to someone here in Rawlings while he was away? Was she from here or from out of town?

*Get out of my mind, Johnny Henry, or I'm going to lose it.*

Kathleen was ready when Adelaide came by. Forcing herself to show some enthusiasm for her friend's sake, she hurried out to the car with a perky smile on her face.

"You look so pretty I'm surprised Paul will let you out the door without him."

"He knows that no one but he would have me." Adelaide moved her purse to make room on the seat for her friend. "Judy will be at the reception taking pictures. Paul thought that he'd better stick around the office in case the bank was robbed or the schoolhouse caught on fire."

"Every newspaperman's dream."

"We'll be a little early. I want to get things set up before the crowd arrives. It's open house, thank goodness. Everyone won't come at the same time."

"Don't count on it. Mrs. Smothers, our number one complainer about paper delivery, will come early and stay late."

"And try to get free medical advice from the doctor," Adelaide added.

"I'm not much in the mood for small talk. I'll help you get set up, stay a polite length of time, and walk home. I need the exercise."

"I can't afford to stay the entire afternoon either. I've got plenty to do back at the paper," Adelaide said as she parked behind a row of cars in front of the clinic. "We can carry in everything in one load if you help me."

"I wasn't planning on it," Kathleen teased, "but I will."

Claude had set up a table in the reception area of the clinic. It was covered with a lace tablecloth. In the center of the table was a large decorated sheet cake. WELCOME TO RAWLINGS, DR. PERRY was written in green icing. Around the edge of the cake were large red roses with green leaves.

"The cake is beautiful. Did Claude bake it?"

"One of the restaurants made it." Adelaide unwrapped the silver service and set it up at the end of the table. "I'm glad for the chance to use Mother's silver. Oh, hello, Dale. Are the coffee and tea ready?"

The woman who came down the hall and into the reception room was, as Adelaide would describe her, pleasingly plump. From the starched cap perched proudly on top of dark brown hair to her gleaming white oxfords, Dale Cole was the classic nurse and so efficient that most people didn't realize that she was not an RN.

"The coffee is perking. We even chipped the ice for the tea."

"Dale, meet Kathleen Henry."

Dale's smile was beautiful. "Hello. I've heard a lot about the young reporter who came to this town and broke the hold Doc Herman had on it."

"For heaven's sake! I didn't do it all by myself."

"She gave us the push that we needed to get rid of that tyrant." Adelaide fanned the napkins out on the table.

"Have you met Dr. Perry?" Dale asked. "If I weren't already married to the most wonderful man in the world, I'd be after him like a shot."

"That good, huh?" Adelaide winked at Kathleen.

"He's just as sweet as he can be, a crackerjack, and a caring doctor to boot. Every single woman in town and some of the married ones are going to suddenly get a bellyache, a sore throat or palpitations." Dale picked up a clipboard. "Nice to have met you, Kathleen." She tilted her head toward the inner office, where the murmur of masculine voices could be heard. "You're in for a treat," she said brightly, and scurried down the hall.

"She's nice. How long has she—" Kathleen cut the words off in mid-sentence when the office door opened, and her eyes collided with Johnny's. He came into the room followed by a man with a thin, pleasant face and curly blond hair. Kathleen's eyes went from Johnny to the man, and down to the cake.

"Hello, Johnny, we didn't know you were here."

*Thank goodness for Adelaide.* Kathleen wouldn't have been able to say fire if her clothes were ablaze.

"I came to see if my old friend had time to go squirrel hunting." Johnny's eyes were still on Kathleen. "Have you met Mrs. Leahy, Jude?"

"The publisher of the newspaper? We've not met, but Claude White spoke of you. He warned me not to get on your wrong side." The doctor held out his hand.

"Did he tell you that I charge him too much for his ads and that he wants to pay me in hamburgers?"

"Now that you mention it, he did say that he'd trade me burgers for house calls." The doctor's voice was warm and friendly.

Kathleen was slightly breathless by the time his eyes left Adelaide and turned to her.

"Jude, this is my wife, Kathleen," Johnny said without taking his eyes off her. "Kathleen, do you remember me telling you about my cousins, Jude Perry and his brother Pete?"

Kathleen's eyes flicked to Johnny, then back to the smiling man who was holding out his hand. She put hers in it.

"You mean . . . from down on—"

"—Mud Creek," the doctor said. "A lot of water has gone under the bridge since we were down on Mud Creek, huh, Johnny?" Smile lines fanned out from the corner of large brown eyes. "I knew that you were Kathleen as soon as I opened the door. Karen and Grant Gifford told me about Johnny's pretty redheaded wife." Jude Perry was still holding her hand. He turned and spoke to Johnny. "How did an ugly old cowboy like you manage to talk her into marrying you?"

Kathleen's face flushed at the compliment. Her eyes shot to Johnny. He stood on spread legs, his arms were folded across his chest, his eyes daring her to explain their separation.

"It wasn't easy," he said with a raised brow and a quirk at the corner of his mouth.

*You . . . you horse's patoot! Why haven't you told him that we're separated? How will you explain the blonde you took to the ranch?*

"How are the Giffords?" She had to say something.

"Fine. They are coming down in a few weeks. I was just telling Johnny that we'd have to get together and catch up on all that's happened since we were last in Red Rock." He released her hand and moved away. When he turned she noticed that he limped. "As much as I'd like to stay and visit, I've got two patients to see to before this shindig gets under way. See you in a day or two, Johnny?"

"I'll give it a try, Jude. Thanks."

"See you in a while, ladies," Dr. Perry said, and limped down the hall.

Johnny waited until the sound of a door closing reached them before he spoke, his direct gaze on Kathleen.

"About ready to leave? I'll give you a ride home."

Kathleen almost choked, and her heart pounded in response to her anger. A hectic flush stained her cheeks, and her eyes, when she glared at Johnny, shone like those of a wildcat he'd once treed.

"When I'm ready to leave, I'll walk."

"When will that be?" He gave her back stare for stare.

"I've not decided yet."

"You came to meet the doctor, didn't you? You met him. Do you need her help, Adelaide?"

"Hey, I'm out of this." Adelaide picked up the silver coffee server and headed for the kitchen.

"I hope you're satisfied." Kathleen's blue eyes sparkled angrily. "You've made Adelaide uncomfortable."

"Adelaide's skin is thicker than that. If she's embarrassed, it's because you've got your back up."

"All I said was that I'd walk."

"I saw you in front of the store the other day." He dropped the news in a calm, sure voice that unnerved her even more.

"I usually buy my groceries at the store."

"Why didn't you go in?"

"I changed my mind. Is there a law against that?"

"You followed me out of town."

"I went to the library!" Her face was fiery now, her eyes like blue stars. Her head felt tight, and her eyes smarted. She wanted to hit him. It was a ridiculous notion. *He knew that she had seen him with the blonde. But why was he trying to humiliate her?*

"I want to talk to you."

"Well, talk. Dammit!"

"Not here. These walls have ears." A muscle twitched in the corner of his mouth.

"I'm home most nights," she said in a voice wooden with control, but some of the desperation she was feeling made itself known by the quivering of her lips.

"Don't be difficult, Kathleen. I know that you can hardly stand the sight of me, but unbend a little. I need to talk to you."

"Is it safe to come back in?" Adelaide asked from the doorway.

"Of course. I'm sorry you were uncomfortable. I'll be going now if there isn't anything else you want me to do."

"I wasn't bothered in the slightest. Go on. In a few minutes I'll have more help than I'll know how to manage. You're excused." Adelaide made a little shooing motion with her hand.

Kathleen picked up her purse and walked out the door, conscious that Johnny followed close behind her. At the end of the walk, he took her elbow and turned her toward his car. After she was settled in the seat, he went around to the driver's side, opened the door, and got in. It was then she noticed the extra space between the seat and the dash. He had evidently unbolted the front seat and moved it to make room for his long legs.

"It isn't like riding in a Buick, but it's a shade better than my old truck." He glanced at her set profile before he started the car. "Do you want to go someplace and get something cold to drink?"

"No. I've got iced tea at home."

"Will I be invited in, or do you want to talk in the car?"

"You can come in. That is if you can spare the time." She turned to look out the window and failed to see the frown that puckered his brows.

Nothing more was said until they reached her house and he had parked the car behind her Nash. Kathleen got out and led the way into the house.

"I'll fix the tea," she said on her way to the kitchen. Her nerves were a tangled mess, and her hands shook as she threw back the top lid on the small icebox and chipped enough ice from the block to fill the glasses.

*He's made arrangements for the divorce. She should be prepared for it, but she wasn't. Oh, Lord, help me not to blubber like a baby when he tells me.*

Johnny was sitting on the couch in much the same place he had sat when he was there before. In his hand was a page of her manuscript he had taken from the stack on the end table. Smiling dark eyes met hers. He was grinning as if he were terribly pleased. Kathleen drew in a deep breath and tried to remain calm.

"Pretty good," he said, and replaced the page before reaching for the glass she held out to him.

"That's one of the exciting scenes. There are several pages of dull narrative leading to that. Writing a book is different from writing a short story. It requires much more detail."

"I kind of got hooked on Western stories." When she didn't speak, he said, "What are these things on the glasses?"

"Socks. My landlady in Oklahoma City knitted them. They help to keep the glass from sweating and the ice from melting so fast."

"Socks for tea glasses—what'll they think of next?" He turned the glass around and around in his large hands. Kathleen's eyes were drawn to them. *He was still wearing his wedding ring.*

An uneasy silence hung between them. Johnny clasped his hands 'round his glass and looked at it intently. Kathleen was confused. She had prepared herself for what she was sure he was going to say. What thoughts were going through that handsome head?

"What did you want to talk about? Have you seen a lawyer?" She decided to jump in and get the agony of suspense over with.

"Are you in a hurry to break with me?"

"You left me. Remember?" she said quietly. "I'm sure you want your freedom to—"

"—To what?" His body was still except for the slight flicker of his eyelids.

"Marry someone else." The words almost choked her.

"What gave you that idea?"

"Let's don't beat around the bush. Come right out with what you want to say."

"I don't know if I should even bother to ask you now. You seem in such an all-fired hurry to get me out of your life."

"Under the circumstances, what choice do I have?"

"Have you got someone else?" Looking intently at the glass in his hand, he spoke softly.

"No." Then she added, "Not yet," in order to keep a little of her dignity intact.

"Does that mean that you have someone in mind?"

Kathleen's anger flared. "How dare you sit there and question me about my private life when you ... when you—"

"All right. Let's forget it." He set his glass on the end table and stood.

Kathleen remained seated. Her voice shook with anger when she spoke. "I can't forget it. Maybe you can, but I can't. You came to say something, so say it."

Johnny sat back down, leaned over, and rested his forearms on his thighs. His hands were clasped together tightly. He seemed to be studying his new boots.

"Tell me this, Kathleen. If you don't have another man, why are you in such a hurry to divorce me?"

Kathleen looked at him. His face was leaner, harder. His hair had grown during the past few weeks, and he looked more like the old Johnny. She thought of herself. Too much time had been wasted. She should have confronted him years ago, instead of taking his repeated rejections in silence. She didn't want to wait any longer for fate to make its play.

"How can you ask . . . under the circumstances? What did I do to you to make you want to humiliate me?"

"I never wanted that." His head came up. "I know how bad you want . . . a family. I can't give you children . . . not the kind that will make you happy."

"So you cut and run. You don't want to risk another Mary Rose, is that it?"

He was silent for a long while, then he said, "You don't understand me at all, do you?"

"I tried to. Are you afraid that I'll demand part of your ranch if we get a divorce? If that's what's holding you back, you can get that thought out of your head."

"Goddammit!" Suddenly his shoulders slumped. "I was going to ask if you would be willing to sign papers at the bank so I could get a loan to rebuild my herd. The government will guarantee a loan to a veteran for a home or business; but since you're my wife and co-owner of the ranch, I needed your signature. But forget it." He went to the door.

"I'll sign the papers." Kathleen followed, but stood back so she could look up at him. "Isn't there enough money in your account to help you get started?"

"I won't use that." It was his tone of voice more than the words that wounded her.

"You don't want even that from me," she said, throwing back at him words that he'd said to her previously. Her control broke like a dam being pushed by flood waters. She balled her fist and pounded him on the chest to emphasize her words. "You make me so damn mad!" Tears of frustration filled her eyes when she realized what she had done.

"Still the fiery redhead. You can't hold your temper any better today than you could seven years ago."

"You, more than anyone else, can cause me to lose it. Why won't you use the money?"

"Pride, I guess. I can't explain it. I don't have a way with words like you do. I only know that I can't take the money you saved when you don't want anything from me."

"It was the allotment money the government sent me as your wife."

"Not all of it. I can add. Think about it; and if it's something you're willing to do, stop by the bank and ask Mr. Wrenn for the papers." He slapped his hat down on his head and stepped out onto the porch. "I'll understand if you don't want to be obligated, because if I can't make the payments, they'll come after you."

"I'll go in tomorrow."

"Thanks." He looked at her for a long while, then headed for the car. Before he got in, he turned. " 'Bye."

" 'Bye, Johnny."

He lingered by the car, Kathleen on the edge of the porch. She was thinking that he might come back to the house when he finally spoke.

"Isabel is out at the ranch. She's sick and didn't have any place to go."

"Your sister?" Kathleen's breath caught in her throat, and she felt the heat come up her neck to her cheeks.

"My half sister. I told you about her."

"I remember. What's the matter with her?"

"I'm not sure. I'm going to try to get her into the clinic to see Jude."

"Does the doctor know her?"

Johnny snorted. "Oh, yes."

"Was she the woman with you . . . the other day?" The words came even as she thought them.

"Yeah. She came in on the bus. She'd called Sheriff Carroll before she left the city. He sent word out to me."

"I'm sorry. If there's anything I can do, let me know."

He snorted again. "You'd not be able to stand her."

"Why didn't she go to Henry Ann?"

"She hates Henry Ann. She hates me, too, but hates Henry Ann more."

"Poor miserable thing."

"She's hard. I'm sorry to say, I've never known a woman as hard and as selfish. Whatever is wrong with her, she's brought on herself." He got in the car and started the motor. He continued to look at Kathleen standing on the porch as he backed out. On the road he lifted a hand and drove away.

Kathleen could do nothing but smile. A weight had been lifted from her heart. He hadn't been taking a woman out to *her* house. The one in his car had been his sister.

"Where have you been? I've been here all day by myself. You knew I wanted to go to town and you slipped off without me. You're a son of a bitch, Johnny."

Isabel began raving at Johnny the minute he stepped upon the porch carrying a chunk of ice. While Isabel continued to berate him, he slid the block into the icebox and shut the door.

"Did you bring me any cigarettes? This place is so damn quiet I heard a bird fart when it flew over. I don't see how you stand it out here without electricity or an indoor toilet. Talk about backwoods! I thought Mud Creek was back in the sticks, but here there ain't even any sticks, for Godsake."

"You didn't ask for cigarettes."

"I told you last night I only had two packs left. Jesus Christ!"

An ashtray with a dozen butts in it was on the table, the dishes hadn't been washed and the dish towel was on the floor. He picked it up.

"This place is drivin' me crazy." Isabel's breathing was uneven. "I've been stuck here for over a week. I want to go to town. I've not seen a soul but you and that old coot that works for you. I can't understand a word he says. He's not got a tooth in his head."

"Don't take your spite out on Sherm. It isn't his fault that you're here. I told you to listen to the radio all you want. I'll keep the battery charged up."

"All you can get is that old station down at Vernon." She grasped the back of a chair to steady herself.

Johnny was embarrassed to look at her. She wore only a single sleeveless garment, the armholes so big that her flat breasts were visible. Her trembling legs were so thin they looked like sticks.

She was thirty years old and looked fifty.

"You're sick, Isabel. You should see a doctor."

"Hell, I know I'm sick. I've seen a doctor. He told me to rest. Why do you think I came here? There's nothin' to do here, but rest. I've had about all the *rest* I can take."

"You're not in any condition to go anywhere. You couldn't walk fifty feet."

"Ha! Just give me the chance."

Her voice was weak, and she was breathing hard; but there was defiance in her eyes. The skin on her bony face had a yellowish tinge, and dark circles surrounded her deep-set eyes. Her dry, straw-colored hair had come out in patches, revealing her scalp.

"Remember Jude Perry?" Johnny hurried on before

she could interrupt. "He's a doctor now. A good one. He just took over the clinic in town. You should go see him."

Isabel hooted. "Jude, Hardy Perry's smart-mouthed, sissy-britches kid? How'd he ever get to be a doctor? Well, never mind. I'd not let that flitter-headed ninny treat my sick cat, if I had one."

"He left medical school at the head of his class and went into the army with a commission. He was wounded at Anzio. He's a long way from being a flitter-headed ninny."

"Anzio? Where's that?"

"Italy. He was shot in the thigh while tending a wounded man."

"If it'd been his head, it wouldn't hurt him. All he wanted to do was read his damn books. He wouldn't even help with the still unless Hardy threatened to beat the tar outta him. God, it was funny seeing him dancing with Hardy."

"When you're young you do things you don't want to do to keep a roof over your head and food in your belly," Johnny said tightly.

"Yeah, well, he'll never be the man Pete was. That man knew how to dance."

"I remember that you lied about your age to be in the dance marathon with Pete and got both of you thrown out of the competition."

"He was madder than a pissed-on snake." Isabel laughed. "It was probably a good thing that the sheriff got me out of there. Pete wanted to kill me."

Johnny went through the living room and paused in the doorway leading to the bedroom. Letters, pictures, and mementos from his rodeo days that Kathleen had saved lay scattered over the unmade bed. A bureau drawer hung open.

"Goddammit," he swore. "I told you to stay out of my things. You were to use the bed and that was all."

"Hell, what'er you riled up about? I was just looking at your old pictures. There's nothin' else to do." Isabel watched as Johnny put the pictures, rodeo clippings, and souvenirs back in the drawer.

"You could do some cleaning around here." Even as he said it, he knew that she hadn't the strength even to keep herself clean. She made him so angry he had to say something.

"Did you go to see your wife while you were in town? Is she a whore? Bet that red hair in the picture came out of a bottle at the five-and-dime."

"You would try the patience of a saint."

"Saint? I ain't no saint. Is the redhead givin' you a little tail now and then?" She laughed nastily. "You didn't go without it while you were gone. I'd bet my life on that! Ain't no man I ever heard of can go without it that long."

"Shut up, Isabel."

"God, I don't blame her for leavin' you. This place is deader than a graveyard."

Johnny picked up the drawer and walked out of the house. Isabel followed him to the porch.

"What'er you goin' to do? You afraid I'll tear up the pictures of your darlin' Kathleen? I want to go to town, Johnny."

On his way to the barn, Johnny turned. "Not until you agree to go to the clinic and see Jude."

"You . . . horsecock!" Isabel yelled, before she went back into the house and slammed the door.

Inside the barn, Johnny looked at his and Kathleen's

wedding picture for a long while before he turned it face-down in the drawer, then slipped the drawer into a gunnysack and tied the end securely. He climbed a ladder and carefully placed his burden on the support beams, where it would be safe from Isabel's prying eyes.

# Chapter Six

$D$r. Jude Perry sank down in the chair behind his desk and rubbed his aching thigh. The open house had been a success. According to the mayor's count, more than a hundred people had showed up to give him a warm welcome. He was tired, but elated too.

He had Grant Gifford to thank for arranging the purchase of the clinic. This is what he'd always wanted. He'd had no desire for a big-city practice. Being in the same area as Johnny was an extra bonus. It had been good to see him. Grant had told him about Johnny's war record and that he suspected that Johnny's marriage was breaking up. According to Grant and Karen, Johnny and Kathleen had been terribly in love when they wed. Jude wondered what had happened to drive them apart.

Kathleen was a pretty woman. Jude could understand why Johnny was still in love with her. Now how did he know that? he asked himself. Was it the way Johnny's attention had been drawn to voices in the reception room while they had been in the office, and the fact he'd not mentioned a separation? Grant had said they'd lost a child before Johnny went to the service. He wondered if that had anything to do with the rift between them.

Jude hadn't thought of Isabel Perry in years. When she first came to Mud Creek, a fourteen-year-old who didn't have the brains of a flea, he sensed she would come to a bad end, just as her mother had. Johnny had said that she was sick and had come to stay with him because she didn't have anyplace else to go.

Johnny suspected, because of her lifestyle, that she might have a venereal disease. If that were the case, there wouldn't be much he could do if the disease was in the advanced stage. What an ironic turn of events. Isabel had hated him when they were young. He hadn't had much use for her either.

"Doctor?" The nurse had entered the office quietly and broke into his thoughts. "Someone to see you."

"A patient?"

"No. He could be a salesman."

"How are you doing, Theresa? You've been here since six this morning."

"This has been a special day. I'll be leaving soon. I wanted to make sure the night nurse had a handle on things."

"Is Mrs. Cole still here?"

"Her husband came for her a few minutes ago. He apologized for taking her away early. He said something had come up, but didn't say what it was."

"Do you like her?"

"Yes, I do. She's very pleasant, very capable."

"I want you to tell me if you think there should be any changes in the staff. You're in charge."

"It will be a while before I know if there should be

changes. So far everyone seems efficient and enthusiastic."

Jude studied the woman. She was an excellent nurse. Saint Anthony Hospital in the city was sorry to lose her. She was not much over five feet and had a round, full figure. Although she weighed more than she should for her height, she was neat as a pin. Her uniform looked as if she had just put it on. The starched cap with the black stripe sat atop short, dark brown hair that was pulled back and pinned. Soft brown eyes in a pretty face with a flawless complexion looked back at him.

Theresa's husband had been killed on the Normandy beach, leaving her with a son he had never seen.

"Has Ryan settled in?"

"He's glad to be out of that apartment in the city. He's crazy about Mrs. Ramsey and her daughter Emily." Theresa's eyes lit up when talking about her son. She was glad, too, to be away from her in-laws, who were trying to take over the raising of their grandchild.

"Then you're happy here?"

"If my son is happy, I'm happy. I was lucky to find a place to rent just a block from the Ramseys."

"I'm glad you're with me."

Theresa blushed at the compliment and lowered her head to study a chart she was holding.

"I'm glad to be here, Doctor."

"I'm not sure sometimes how to proceed in a private practice," Jude continued. "All I've done lately is work in a veteran's hospital. You've worked with general practitioners. You'll have to help me stay on the right track."

"You took your brush-up courses and have all the right qualities to make a fine small-town doctor."

"I appreciate your confidence."

"I'd better show in your visitor before he seduces our receptionist. He's already got her in a twitter."

"He's probably going to try and sell us some new equipment. I'll lay out our bank statement. That'll discourage him."

Theresa went out and closed the door, but not before Jude heard a male voice and a woman's nervous titter.

He was lucky to have Theresa. She'd met her husband during her last year of nursing school. They had been married two months when he was drafted into the service. She had given birth to their son without ever seeing him again and had worked for four years in Oklahoma City. Jude wondered what had caused her to accept a job in a small clinic at a third less pay.

When the door opened, all thoughts of Theresa, the clinic, and his aching thigh rushed from Jude's mind. Fourteen years had passed since he had seen the big blond man who filled the doorway. Pete Perry had joined the navy back in 1932 as soon as he was cleared of the murder of Emmajean Dolan. His ship had been sunk in the Battle of the Coral Sea, and Jude had not heard whether his brother had survived. Now here he was!

"Pete? God Almighty! Pete!" Jude got up from behind his desk on numb legs and without taking his eyes off the man, managed to meet him in front of his desk.

"Hello, little brother." Pete's voice was husky with emotion. He grabbed Jude's hand.

The two men stood looking at each other. Pete's eyes were unnaturally bright, and Jude's were misty.

"Lord, Pete, I never was able to find out if you made it after the *Lexington* was sunk."

"Broke my leg is all. While I was in the hospital on

New Caledonia, I got word the old man had died; and I didn't know how to get in touch with you."

"It's good to see you. Lord, it's good to see you." Jude gripped his brother's shoulders in his two hands.

"It's good to see you, too. My little brother is a doctor. I was over at Red Rock looking for a trace of you. Henry Ann told me where you were. I hightailed it right over."

"You always had a crush on Henry Ann," Jude said with a nervous laugh.

"Yeah. Reaching for the moon, wasn't I? I realize now that we'd not have suited each other and that I wanted something I knew I couldn't have. I'd have made her miserable with my wild ways." Pete grinned the devilish grin that women loved. "She said that Johnny came through the war and that he lives near here. She's talked to him several times on the phone."

"He was here today. Isabel has come to stay with him."

"I thought sure that someone would have killed that little split-tail by now."

"She's sick. Johnny said that she's very sick and didn't have anywhere else to go. She turned out just like her mother, Dorene."

"A whore, huh? I figured she would."

"Are you going to stay awhile?"

"I didn't re-enlist. I got a hankering to see familiar sights. I gave the navy sixteen years and saved a little money. I'd like to raise horses and dogs."

"Stay with me until you decide what you want to do. I've got plenty of room."

"I'd planned to stay at the hotel for a day or two."

"No need for that. The doctor who built this clinic owned a house just a short distance away. I bought it along with the clinic."

"Lord, but I'm proud of you, Jude." Pete grasped Jude's shoulder. "Never thought I'd see a Perry become a doctor. And you did it all by yourself."

"You helped me once in a while. I know you slipped old Mrs. Hunting a little money now and then to help me with my studies."

"I should have done more. I should have gotten you away from Mud Creek. All that was on Hardy's mind was women, dancin', and bootleggin'. He was no fit father to you."

"I don't think about it anymore. Our pa lived the way his pa lived. What's important now is what we do with our lives."

"Looks like you're doing pretty good."

"That's yet to be proven. Let me show you around. This is a clinic, but we have bed patients. It's a clinic/hospital because we do minor surgery. It is well equipped thanks to army surplus. Our X-ray rooms and the lab are the first ones on your right. I'm hoping to get a couple of good technicians soon. I've contacted old army buddies who may be interested. The surgery is at the end of the hall."

Jude led Pete through a door and into a long hallway. They met Theresa, who had removed her starched cap and changed her white shoes for black ones with heels that made her appear taller.

"I'm leaving, Doctor. See you in the morning."

"Theresa, I'd like for you to meet my brother, Pete Perry. Pete, this is Mrs. Frank. I was lucky enough to lure her away from a big-city hospital to work with me here."

"Your brother?" Theresa looked up at the tall man. A slow smile started in her eyes and spread to her lips. Pete responded to the smile with one of his own. "We were sure that you were going to try and sell us bandages or bedpans," Theresa said. She was really pretty when she smiled, Jude noticed.

"Now what would give you that idea?" Pete held on to her hand and looked down at her as if she were the only woman in the world. It was his natural response to a pretty woman. "Brother," he said to Jude, "you do have all the luck."

"You'll have to excuse him, Theresa. He's fresh from the navy."

"That accounts for it. Welcome home, sailor." She pulled her hand from Pete's and turned to Jude. "I checked Mr. Case's temperature. It's steady at one degree above normal."

"Good. Did you tell Miss Pauley to call me if it goes up as much as two degrees?"

"I told her, and she will. I'd better get going. It's time to pick up Ryan. Nice to have met you, Mr. Perry."

"Nice to have met you, ma'am."

Jude continued with the tour of the clinic, introduced Pete to the night nurse, Miss Wanda Pauley, a no-nonsense spinster, and to Mr. and Mrs. Tuttle who were employed to do the cleaning and the laundry.

"Is Rawlings big enough to support all this?" Pete asked when they were outside, standing beside his car.

"I hope so. It's the only clinic in the county with a full-time doctor. The next town of any size is Frederick. Anything we can't handle here we'll send over there. We'll be ready for most things. Of course, there's always the unexpected. We're getting an iron lung from the government. I'm hoping we don't need one before it gets here."

"Polio isn't particular who it hits. A couple of young fellows on board ship came down with it. They took them off at Pearl and put them into iron lungs. I don't know if they're still alive."

"So far, there have been only four cases identified in Tillison County. I don't know if the records are correct. Sounds low to me, considering the number of cases in Oklahoma during the past ten years."

"Do I get free doctoring?" Pete asked with a twinkle in his eyes.

"You'd trust me?"

"Well, now, I'll have to think about it. How long is your memory?"

"Long enough to remember you knocking me on my butt a few times and cussing me out a lot of times."

"That's what I was afraid of. How far did you say it was to Frederick?" Pete laughed and slapped Jude on the back so hard he staggered. "Let's go get those hamburgers. My belly button is rubbing against my backbone."

When Dale Cole was told by the receptionist that her husband was waiting for her in the reception room, she blanched. She turned quickly back to the cabinet and returned the package she had removed. This was the second time Harry had been to the clinic during the four months she had worked here. She trembled at the memory of what had happened that day when they got home.

"Dale, did you hear me? Mr. Cole said something important had come up and wanted to know if you could leave early. Mrs. Frank was there and said for me to come find you."

"Thanks, Millie. Tell him I'll be there in a minute."

Dale needed that minute to compose herself. Her mind raced back, trying to think of something she had done to set him off. She had seen him briefly when he had made an appearance with other members of the Chamber of Commerce. He had been in conversation with John Wrenn, the banker, and appeared to be in a good mood. She had been busy cutting and serving cake and unable to leave the table to speak to him. Had that been her mistake?

Dale picked up her purse and walked down the hall to the reception area on legs that trembled. Before she rounded the corner she took a deep breath and squared her shoulders. Her eyes went directly to her husband. He would notice if she looked frightened of him in public. He got to his feet when he saw her. He was a man of medium height with a head of thick brown hair and heavy brows. He worked as a supervisor for Oklahoma Gas and Electric Company.

"Harry, what has happened? Is Danny all right?" Dale asked with a worried frown.

"He's all right. I had a call from your sister." He said the last loudly enough for it to be heard by Millie Criswell, the receptionist. Then he grasped Dale's elbow and steered her out the door.

"Which one?" Dale hurried to keep pace with him. His grip on her elbow was getting tighter and tighter, and her heart began to thump. *What have I done? Oh, Lord, what have I done now?*

"Get in the car," he said when they reached it. He opened the door. He didn't shove her; he was always careful in public.

Dale's fearful eyes followed him as he rounded the front of the car. He was terribly angry. When he started the motor, he eased the car slowly away from the curb. He said nothing, which was not a good sign.

"Who called, Harry?" Dale asked when they were almost home.

"No one called," he answered calmly.

"Then why did you want me to leave early?"

"I wanted to talk to you before Danny got home. I saw you rubbing up against that son of a bitch from the furniture store. You really think you're something, don't you, Dale? It was disgusting, is what it was. You must outweigh him by fifty pounds, and you were acting so coy, so *cute*. You were in his face, practically licking it, like a lapdog."

"I wasn't. I was serving cake—"

"—You fat bitch! Are you calling me a liar? You were slobbering all over him. You've been getting out of hand since we moved here. That job has gone to your head. The only reason I let you work was because of the labor shortage. Well, that's almost over. Defense workers are being let go by the thousands. There'll soon be more nurses looking for jobs than you can shake a stick at." He stopped the car in front of the house. He turned and looked at her with pure hatred in his eyes. "Get in there unless you want the neighbors to see me kick your fat ass all the way up the walk."

"Harry, it was my job to cut and serve the cake."

"Your job is to see to the one who feeds you and keeps a roof over your head. All you do is embarrass me, Dale, and talk behind my back. I can hardly look people in the eye anymore."

"I've never, ever said a word about . . . anything." *I've kept the secret, hidden my bruises.*

"I'm tired of your lies. Lie, lie, lie. You're lucky I put up with you. I should have sent you packing years ago.

Jesus! You're about as sexy as a fat cow. I'd be better off sticking my pecker in a bucket of lard."

Dale had heard the same demeaning remarks over and over. Last week it was because she had put too much salt in the corn bread. His insults had become so foul she had asked him if Danny could leave the table.

She thought about not getting out of the car. But in the mood he was in she didn't know what he would do. Why was he like this? Dale answered her own question. He wanted wild, hard sex and accusing her of something helped him get aroused. It was always the same and had been since they married.

Harry had shown a little jealousy while he courted her, and she had been dumb enough to think it was because he loved her. Now she knew that he was incapable of loving even his own child. He wanted to possess her, humiliate her. It was the only way that he could feel superior to her. She felt the same hopelessness that she'd felt a hundred times before

*Lord, how can I endure it?*

It was best to get it over so that she could get herself composed before Danny came home. She was sure that their five-year-old son would know that something had happened between his parents, but he wouldn't say anything. He was unusually quiet at times like this as though accepting that this was the way life was supposed to be. Someday Dale hoped to make him understand that not all men hit their wives and that she was enduring this so that she could be with him.

When she got out of the car, she looked to see if any of the neighbors were in their yards or on their porches. Harry's fear that one of them would come over was the only thing that might stall for a while what she knew was coming, and even that would only prolong the inevitable.

For the past four months her work at the clinic had given her a new sense of self-worth. For the first time in years Harry was not supervising every move she made. She had enjoyed a freedom that had begun slipping away from her from the day she married him. Now he was going to take it away again.

Inside the house, Dale set her purse down and turned. She was unprepared for the open-handed blow that caught her on the side of the face, and she stumbled. Harry was on her in an instant, pushing her against the wall and holding her with his forearm against her neck.

"Get in there and get your clothes off, you fat slut. You been wantin' a hard pecker, and you're goin' to get one." Harry always talked nasty when he was in a rage. He emphasized his words by pushing his arousal against her.

"All right." Dale had learned that to defy him enraged him more.

He released her and shoved her toward the bedroom. She stumbled into the room as she heard him going toward the bathroom for the razor strop. She knew what was coming. He would whip her bare buttocks until he was about to climax, then he would plunge roughly into her.

*I'm afraid, she thought, that someday I will kill him.*

# Chapter Seven

Kathleen put on her coat, flipped a scarf over her head, and tied the ends beneath her chin before she left the house to walk to town. The sun was still warm this first part of November, but a brisk wind shook dried leaves from the trees that lined the street, and they crunched beneath her feet.

She'd had a restless night. Once, she had even left her bed to look out a window when a dog barked furiously. Was that a man leaning against her car? She hurried to another window, mistakenly thinking that she would have a better view. When she returned, no one was there. Kathleen stood at the window for a long while, finally deciding that she had seen a shadow, that the man had been a figment of her imagination.

This morning the incident had left her mind as she crossed a street and stepped up on the sidewalk. Coming toward her was a woman wearing white shoes and white stockings. She wore a hip-length coat and a scarf on her head. Kathleen recognized her as Mrs. Cole, whom she had met at the clinic the day before.

"A nice cool morning, isn't it?" Kathleen said.

"Yes, it is," Dale answered. "But the wind isn't doing my hair any favors." Her jaw hurt when she spoke, and this morning she'd not been able to eat. There was a bruise on her cheekbone that she managed to cover with rouge. She had smeared salve on the welts on her buttocks before she pulled on her underpants, but she could not bear to put on the girdle Harry always insisted she wear. He would be angry when he found out.

"We haven't had a frost yet, but when we do, the leaves will fall like rain."

"My chrysanthemums are still blooming." Kathleen Henry was a person Dale would like to have for a friend, but she knew that Harry would never allow it. "I'd just as soon the cold weather hold off for a while."

"Was the reception as much of a success as expected? I had to leave early."

"Oh, yes. We used all of the first cake that served fifty and most of the second cake. Many people had only coffee or tea. Theresa estimated that over a hundred came during the afternoon. A photographer was there taking pictures for the paper." Dale glanced back to see a car coming slowly down the street toward them.

"I'd better scoot or I'll be late at the clinic. Nice seeing you again." She hurried away.

Kathleen wondered if the woman was not feeling well. She certainly wasn't the friendly person she had met at the clinic. Her eyes had a haunted, or was it a frightened look, especially when she noticed the approaching car. When Kathleen glanced over her shoulder, she saw the car stop and Dale walk over to it. Later when she looked back again, Dale was still walking and the car had gone on.

As Kathleen entered the *Gazette* office, Adelaide looked up from her desk with a broad smile.

"Good morning. Can I interest you in a full-page ad?"

"Do I get a discount?"

"Of course. How's the book coming?"

"Good. I'm really getting into it. I'm on chapter ten."

"How many chapters?"

"I don't know. I've set up the conflict and introduced the characters. That took care of the first third of the book. The last third will be tying up the loose ends and seeing that the villain gets what's coming to him. The hard part is the middle third."

"Interesting." Paul came in from the back room. "What are we talking about?"

"Kathleen's book," Adelaide said. "Have you decided on a title?"

"I may call it *Gone With the Wind*." Kathleen pulled off her scarf and fluffed her hair.

"Hummm. Seems to me I've heard that before."

"A publisher would never allow me to use it even though a title can't be copyrighted. I had thought of calling it *The Heart Rustler*, but my male readers might think it was a love story. So I'm naming it *The Hanging Tree*."

"That should clear up any notion about its being a love story. When do I get to read it?" Paul asked.

"Not for a while. Did Judy get some good pictures at the reception for the doctor?"

"She sure did. I've been trying to get her to set her cap for the doctor, but she's got a cowboy on the string. I don't know what it is about cowboys that dazzles the girls."

"Here, love." Adelaide pulled a sheet of paper from her typewriter and handed it to Paul. "We met the doctor's brother last night. They were having hamburgers at Claude's."

"Johnny told me the doctor had a brother named Pete who had been in the navy for a long time. Did you know that they are Johnny's cousins?"

"Not until Johnny mentioned it yesterday. The brothers are both blond, but don't look much alike otherwise. The doctor isn't as heavily built as his brother. I wonder if Pete's going to be around here for a while. He is a good-looking man in a rough sort of way."

"I heard that, Addie." Paul paused in the doorway leading to the back room.

"He isn't as good-looking as you are, love." Adelaide's eyes shone when she looked at her husband.

"I'm relieved to know that." Paul pretended to wipe sweat from his brow. "I was about to go mess up that guy's pretty face. I've got a couple of pages ready for a proofer if anyone is interested."

"I'll do them for you, Adelaide." Kathleen took off her coat and hung it on the hall tree. "I can't get into the bank until nine o'clock."

A man in an old felt hat and a shabby coat followed Kathleen into the bank. He was standing behind her when she told the teller that she was there to sign papers regarding Johnny Henry's loan. The man known in Rawlings as Robert Brooks could have reached out and touched her; but it would not have been wise, and he resisted the temptation.

That she didn't recognize him as a coworker whose desk had been less than fifty feet from hers in the office at Douglas Aircraft for two years was a source of satisfaction to him. He was good at changing his appearance.

His mother had told him many times that he should have been a movie star or an actor on the stage.

After Kathleen was directed inside the partition that separated the lobby from the office area, Mr. Brooks produced a bill and asked the teller for change. He put the bills in his pocket and went out to his car to wait for Kathleen to leave the bank. While waiting, he opened his *observation diary* and began to write in a small neat script.

*9:30 A.M. Johnny Henry is taking out a GI loan. Kathleen went to the bank to sign the papers. She must have agreed to do that when he took her home from the clinic yesterday, but that does not necessarily mean they are getting back together. If they do, it will make it harder for me to do what I plan.*

*Last night that lowlife from the filling station went by her house a couple of times. Had he stopped, I would have been forced to take action. Using the night glasses I ordered from the Army Surplus store, I saw her standing in her bedroom window in her nightdress. Kathleen, Kathleen, it won't be long until you will be safe. I will take care of you forever.*

It was the middle of the morning.

"We're getting there." Johnny and Sherm, an old man he had known since he first came to the ranch, had been working since dawn on the corral. "In a day or two we'll go down to McCabe's and get my horses. You'll have to go along to drive the car and trailer back. I've already made arrangements to buy a load of hay."

"I ain't never drived no car pullin' a trailer, but reckon

I can." Sherm scratched his grizzled head and looked toward the house when the sound of singing reached them.

> *"Way down yonder in the Indian Nation*
> *I rode my pony on the reservation,*
> *In the Oklahoma hills where I belonged—"*

"I don't know why she has to play the radio so damn loud," Johnny grumbled. He was not in a good mood. He wanted his house back. He wanted his wife back and in his bed. He was tired of sleeping on an army cot in the barn.

"Is she goin' to stay long?"

Sherm glanced shyly at Johnny. It wasn't his nature to ask questions, but he was thinking of moving on if Johnny's sister was going to be here from now on. Before she came, he and Johnny had fixed decent meals, talked a while, or listened to the radio for an hour or two before he went back to the shack he lived in behind the barn. Now he dreaded going in to eat.

"I don't know, Sherm. She's sick, awful sick. I'm trying to get her to see a doctor. I'd consider it a favor if you'd overlook some of the things she says."

"I ain't ort to be sayin' it, but she goes outta her way to be mean. It don't seem like you and her could rightly be kin a'tall."

"We had the same mother. That, I'm sure of." Johnny hung the hammer on a strand of wire and squinted at a car that turned up the lane, came alongside the house, and stopped. "Now who can that be?" When a tall man in a light-colored Stetson hat got out of the car, Johnny let out a whoop and hurried forward. "Holy hell! Pete? Pete Perry, where in the world did you come from?"

"Howdy, Johnny. It's been a long time." The two men met and clasped hands.

"Doggone, Pete!" Johnny's broad smile lit his face. "Doggone, I can't believe it's you. Golly-damn, Pete. It's been many a year. It's damn good to see you."

"Same here, Johnny-boy. How ya doin'?" The two tall men continued to clasp hands and smile at each other.

"Good. You?"

"Good. What's it been? Sixteen years? When I left to go to the navy, you and Jude were kids. Now you're men. Hellfire, where did the time go?"

"It didn't go very fast in the Solomons. I heard you were on the *Lexington*. When it went down, I figured you were a goner."

"Only the good die young, Johnny-boy. I was the meanest son of a bitch on Mud Creek. Remember?" Pete laughed. He was the same, just older. His blue eyes twinkled in the old devilish way. His blond hair was still thick and wavy.

"I don't know about being the meanest, but you were working pretty hard to get there."

"Yeah, I was. But I was taken down a notch or two when Grant Gifford beat the tar outta me that Sunday afternoon I crashed Henry Ann's ice cream party."

"I remember that. And I remember accusing you of rustling our beef."

"That I *didn't* do. Not because of you, but because of Henry Ann." Pete clapped Johnny on the shoulder and grinned. "I wonder what ever happened to Chris Austin and Opal after he finally got the guts to leave home and take her to California?"

"Henry Ann said they came back when Mrs. Austin took sick. They have three boys and Rosemary, Opal's daughter. Henry Ann said that she heard Rosemary had turned out real pretty."

"She wasn't mine," Pete said quickly. "I know folks thought she was, and I let them think it. At the time I didn't want to think that it was my pa who forced himself on the girl. I was afraid that if I knew for sure, I'd kill him."

"That's probably why Opal never told who raped her."

"I look back now and wonder how Jude turned out the way he did, considering what we come from."

"You didn't do too bad either, Pete. Considering—"

"Considering what?"

"Well, considering you did everything you could to make folks think you were wild as a hare and horny as a billy goat."

"Yeah, I did, didn't I?" Pete grinned sheepishly.

"Remember Marty Conroy?"

"Tom Dolan's brother-in-law? I remember that I was itching to knock his teeth out. I still think he was the one who set Tom's house on fire."

"He's over at McCalister serving life for murdering a girl right here in Rawlings."

"Well, hallelujah! He was a son of a bitch if there ever was one. Not that I wasn't one, too."

"I'll not argue that." Johnny laughed, and slapped Pete on the shoulder. "Come meet Sherm. He lives here on the place and helps me out. I've got maybe thirty head of horses on a ranch down near Vernon. We're trying to get this corral in shape so that I can go get them."

"Let me give you a hand for a day or two. Your line of work is more up my alley than Jude's. Isn't it something 'bout Jude being a doctor? Little shit knew what he wanted and went after it."

"From what I hear, he's a damn good doctor. The three

of us were damn lucky that we came through the war. Eighty-two men from right here in Tillison County didn't come back. A lot of them were in the 45th Infantry out of Fort Sill."

"That was Jude's outfit. We talked last night until we were hoarse. I've decided to settle down around here someplace. Jude's all the family I've got. I've saved a little money these last fifteen years and want to put it into a little place to call home."

"What was your job in the navy?"

"Chief machinist's mate. But that's behind me. I'd like to have a horse ranch, but it takes a wad of money to get started."

"That's what I've got here, but on such a small scale it's darn hard to make a living. I've applied for a GI loan."

"I've been thinking about doing that."

"I'd be glad for your help for a few days, Pete, but I can't offer you bed and board. Isabel is here. She's in bad shape. You'll understand when you see her."

"Jude told me."

"She's about as pleasant as a boil on the butt. I've been trying to talk her into going in to Jude's clinic, but she won't hear of it. She can't walk across a room without stopping to rest, but she'll nag you to take her to a honky-tonk."

"What's wrong with her?"

"Damned if I know. But considering her line of work for the past ten years, it could be most anything. She looks fifty years old."

"Turned out like her ma, huh? I figured she would."

"I get angry with her, but I pity her, too."

"How is your wife making out with her here?"

"My wife lives in town." Johnny turned, picked up the tools, and spoke to the old man. "I'll fix us some grub, Sherm. You come on up to the house for noon. Hear?"

Sherm grunted a reply and shuffled off toward the shed.

"Come on in, Pete. Isabel has probably been looking out the window and wondering who is here. She can smell a man a mile away."

As soon as Johnny opened the door and saw his sister sitting in a kitchen chair, he knew that she had tried to fix herself up in case the visitor came to the house. She was a pitiful sight. She had dampened her hair, brushed it behind her ears, and rouged her hollow cheeks. Her mouth was a slash of bright red. She wore a low-necked dress that showed her bony neck and a large sore on her collarbone.

"We have company." Johnny walked in, then stood aside for Pete to enter.

"Hello, Isabel."

Isabel attempted to put out her cigarette. With her eyes on Pete, she missed the ashtray completely and jabbed it repeatedly onto the oilcloth that covered the table.

"Pete . . . Perry? S'that you, Pete?" She attempted to stand and then sank back down on the chair. The pain in her lower back caused her lips to tremble and brought tears to her eyes.

"Yeah, it's me. It's been a long time, Isabel."

"I . . . never thought . . . I'd see you again." Her voice was weak and hoarse. "You look just the same."

"I doubt that, Isabel."

"You're heavier, is all."

Johnny went to the living room and turned off the radio, then went to the sink to wash. He felt pity for the half sister who had taunted him all his life about his Indian blood. Yet when she needed help she'd come to him. She had wasted her life, and she had just turned thirty. He was probably the only person in the world who cared if she lived or died . . . and he wondered why he cared. She'd not throw a bucket of water on him if he was on fire.

"Have a chair, Pete. I'll rustle up something to eat."

"I'm so glad to see you." Isabel had eyes only for Pete. "This place is deader than a doornail. Nobody comes here. The only thing that happens around here is that the wind blows. The damn wind blows all the time. It's enough to give a body a duck fit!" Isabel's voice turned into a whine. "Johnny won't take me to town, Pete. He slips off and leaves me with that harelipped old billy goat that hangs around here. I'd give a man anything he wants for a night at a honky-tonk with good music and dancin'."

Embarrassed, Johnny kept his head bent and his shoulders hunched over the frying pan he'd placed on the stove. Pete, however, didn't seem to be uncomfortable with Isabel's proposition.

"You don't look like you're up to a night on the town, Isabel, much less a night in a man's bed. Johnny said you've been sick. What does the doctor say?"

"That crackpot said rest was all I needed. Hell's bells, Pete. People rest when they're old and can't do nothin' else. I'm sick of restin'."

"What doctor told you that rest was all you needed?"

"One I saw in the city."

"I'd not take his word for it. You need something more than rest. Why not go in and see Jude?"

"Jude! You're kiddin'. That smart-mouthed shithead wouldn't know a snotty nose from a dose of clap."

"You're wrong. Jude went in the army after medical

school. They had the best equipment, and he learned a hell of a lot from the best doctors. He may be able to help you."

"I ain't turning my ass up . . . to that pussyfooter unless he's payin' *me*. He did ever'thin' he could to turn Hardy against me. He'd do his damnedest . . . to see that I croaked." Isabel had to stop and take a breath.

Pete shrugged. "It's none of my business if you'd rather sit here, dry up, and blow away."

"We could go to town and have . . . some fun," Isabel said hopefully.

"I'm not taking you to town and have you keel over on me. No, sir. I'll take you to see Jude. If he says you're up to it, we'll go honky-tonkin'.'"

"Shit!" The cigarette between Isabel's fingers shook, dropping ashes on the table. "Jude always thought that he . . . was something on a stick. Bet now he thinks he's Jesus Christ."

"You're wrong about that. Dead wrong. Jude isn't like that at all. He went out onto the battlefield and dragged a wounded man to his foxhole. That's how he got shot. Even with a bone sticking out of one of his legs he managed to get that man to safety." There was pride in Pete's voice. Anger too.

"Well, when I knew him . . . he was a smart-mouthed little bastard."

"No, he wasn't. Hardy married his ma. He didn't marry mine. I'm the bastard in the family." Pete got up from the table and went to the washbasin. A couple strokes from the water pump filled it.

"You . . . didn't act like a bastard."

"How is a bastard supposed to act? I'm not going to argue with you about Jude, Isabel. It's up to you whether or not you want to help yourself." He splashed water on his face. After he dried it on a towel, he turned his back on Isabel and spoke to Johnny. "Fried potatoes and onions. Lord, I haven't had that in a long time."

"It's about all we have around here. I don't know why we can't have something decent to eat," Isabel grumbled. "I'm hungry for spaghetti and tomatoes, but Johnny don't care what I'm hungry for." Both men ignored her.

"Are you planning on raising horses for the rodeo, Johnny?" Pete asked.

"Yeah. Quarter horses mostly. I had a Tennessee Walker once and got kind of interested in show horses. But, I don't know enough about training and couldn't afford to hire a trainer."

"I remember that little pinto you had. You practically slept with that horse."

"Ed Henry gave him to me when I was fourteen. I brought him over here when I bought the place. He was getting pretty old, so I put him out to pasture. He was struck by lightning the summer before I went into the service. It was like losing a member of the family."

"Pete," Isabel said, breaking into the conversation.

Pete ignored her for a minute, then looked her way. "If you're going to continue to run down Jude, I don't want to hear it."

"I'm not going to say anything . . . about the wonderful *doctor*." Isabel paused. "What I'm saying is, I'll go."

"You'll go? Where?" Pete acted disinterested. He passed behind Johnny and nudged him in the back with his elbow.

"I'll go to the damn clinic if . . . you'll take me honky-tonkin'." Isabel's face was white and her eyes feverish.

"Let's get this straight. We'll go to the clinic, and if Jude says you're able, we'll go honky-tonkin'."

"He'll not want me to go just for . . . spite." Isabel's voice was shrill.

"If that's going to be your attitude, it may be best if you don't go see him. You'll not do what he tells you." Pete turned to Johnny. "When are we going to get your horses?"

"How does day after tomorrow suit you?"

"I said I'd go see the damn doctor and I'll . . . and I'll do what he says," Isabel added irritably.

"All right. I'll take you this afternoon. Want me to slice the bread, Johnny?"

# Chapter Eight

*"You'll never know just how much I love you.*
*You'll never know just how much I care—"*

Kathleen switched off the radio. That song always left her weepy, and she was trying desperately to keep her emotions under control. It was stupid, she told herself, to pine for a man who didn't want you.

After leaving the bank, she had stopped at the grocery store and bought a jar of peanut butter and two packages of strawberry Jell-O. Jell-O, one of her favorite foods, had rarely been seen in the stores during the war. After making up one of the packages and leaving it to cool before putting the bowl in her icebox, she treated herself to two slices of bread and peanut butter before she settled down to work on her book.

Her fingers worked the typewriter keys rapidly, but her thoughts raced ahead of them. By the middle of the afternoon she had written six pages. She rolled her seventh sheet into the machine.

*Beulah heard the clink of shod hooves on pebbly ground and, almost immediately, the thud of booted*

*feet. A shadow fell in front of her, a shadow with
wide shoulders and large cowboy hat.*

*"Having trouble?" asked a deep voice she recog-
nized as belonging to a man she knew and feared.*

Kathleen paused, read what she had written, and realized it wasn't heading in the direction she wanted her
story to go. She pulled the sheet of paper from the typewriter, turned it over, and rolled it back in. For five long
minutes she sat staring at the blank page, trying to bring
forth a mental vision of the scene.

After a while, she came to the conclusion that her cre-
ative juices had dried up for the moment. She would
wash her hair and think about the scene while she was
doing it. Fifteen minutes later she squeezed the excess
water from her hair and wrapped a towel around her
head. Carrying in her hand the bottle of vinegar she'd
used as a rinse, she left the bathroom and headed for the
kitchen.

"Ohhhh—" The word was scared out of her. A man
holding a tire pump was standing in the middle of her living room. "What . . . are you doing in my house?"

"I knocked." Gabe Thomas, the mechanic from Eddie's
service station, grinned at her.

"Get out!"

"I knew you were here." He was wearing the same old
greasy clothes he'd worn the day she went to the station
and the same battered felt hat.

"Get out of my house."

"Ah . . . don't be that way, Kathy. I've had my eye on
ya for a long time. Since we danced 'fore the war. Ya ain't
got no man now 'n yo're the kind a woman who needs
one. Ya and me'd match up pretty good." He lifted his

eyebrows and touched his crotch. "If ya know what I mean."

"I know what you mean, you uncouth piece of horse hockey! I'd rather match up with a warthog. Now . . . leave."

"Ya don't mean that. Ya need a man, Kath—"

"What I need or don't need is no concern of yours. Get out of my house!"

"I told ya I was willin' to give ya a hand. Yore tire's goin' down again. I'll pump it up . . . or pump you, if ya ask me right nice." He took a step toward her.

"Leave now, or I'll call the sheriff." She gripped the neck of the vinegar bottle, determined to hit him with it if he came a step closer.

"Ya ain't gonna call no sheriff. Yo're just actin' hard to get." He stepped sideways, blocking her path to the phone, and she drew her arm back.

"Get out or I'll scream my head off after I bash you over the head with this bottle."

"Sh . . . it! You'll not hit me with that, and ya ain't gonna to yell neither. Who'd hear ya? Ya'd like to have somethin' big—"

A loud knock sounded on the door, then another. Kathleen darted past him and threw open the door before the slow-thinking man could prevent her. A stranger in a brown felt hat and an old worn coat stood there.

"Ma'am, do ya know if some folks named Woodbury live 'round here?" His Southern accent was heavy.

"I believe so. I'll have to think a minute. This man was just leaving." She opened the door wider and jerked her head toward the man still standing in the middle of her living room. "You are leaving!"

"I ain't through here yet."

"Yes, you are. Good-bye."

"Ain't nobody by that name in Rawlings," Gabe said irritably.

"Leave," Kathleen said through clenched teeth, and opened the screen door. When he hestitated, she said angrily, "Leave now!" With a deep scowl on his face, he went through the door, shouldering the other man out of the way.

"I'll be back . . . to fix your tire."

"No! Don't come back here. Ever!"

"Was he givin' ya trouble, ma'am?" the man asked, after Gabe got into his car.

"Nothing I couldn't handle. I don't know of anyone around here by the name of Woodbury. I was just stalling so that awful man would leave. He came here with the excuse of pumping air in my tire."

"I have a tire pump in my car. I'd be glad to pump up your tire. I noticed it was goin' flat."

"That's nice of you, Mr.—"

"Brooks. Robert Brooks."

"You look vaguely familiar, Mr. Brooks. Have I met you before?" She wrapped the towel more snugly around her wet head.

"I doubt that, ma'am. I've not been in town long. But maybe you saw me at the bank or in one of the eating establishments. I'm staying at the hotel for a while."

"At the bank. I saw you this morning at the bank. I hope you find the people you're looking for."

"It was a long shot, thinkin' they were here."

"Well . . . good-bye." Katheen stepped back to close the door, his voice stopped her.

"Ma'am, you should keep your door locked. I don't like the looks of that fellow."

"You're right, and I will. Thank you."

After Kathleen closed the door, a niggling memory caused her to go to the window to get another look at the man. Something about him struck a chord. She watched him go to a mud-splattered car and take out a tire pump. Then for a while he was out of sight behind her car as he pumped air into her tire. She was still at the window when he returned to his car and drove away.

Surprised that she still had the vinegar bottle in her hand, she walked into the kitchen. Just as she was about to set it down, another knock sounded on the door.

"Lord, have mercy!" Thinking Gabe Thomas had returned, she angrily flung the door open. "What now?"

"Does that mean you're glad to see me or not glad to see me?"

"Johnny!" Joy and relief made her gasp his name. "I'm glad to see you. Come in."

"For a minute I thought you were going to hit me with that bottle," he said after he'd stepped inside.

"I would have if you'd been that, that . . . disgusting horse's patoot that was here earlier."

"Who's that?" Johnny's brows beetled in a frown.

"Gabe Thomas. He works for Eddie."

"I know who he is. What was he doing here?"

"He said he came to fix my tire. I don't know why a nice guy like Eddie hires scum like him."

"What'd he do?" Johnny asked quietly. If Kathleen hadn't been so giddy at the sight of him, she would have recognized the sign of smoldering anger.

"I was washing my hair and didn't hear him knock. I came out of the bathroom, and he was standing here in the living room. I asked him to leave. He wouldn't until a man came to the door asking directions."

"Are you saying that he came in uninvited and refused to leave?"

"He thought we'd match up, as he put it. He made a few off-color remarks. Nothing worse than some things I'd heard while working in the city."

"The son . . . of . . . a . . . bitch! Did he put his hands on you?"

"If he dared, he'd have had this bottle upside the head."

"I'll take care of it."

"Someone should tell Eddie what kind of man he has working there."

"He'll not bother you again." Johnny followed her to the kitchen. He reached over and took the vinegar bottle from her hand and set it on the table. "You've got water running down the back of your dress." He tossed his hat on a chair, gently pushed her down in another, then unwound the towel from around her head.

"He said he knocked. If he did, I didn't hear him because I was washing my hair." Kathleen's voice was strained, and she wondered why she had stated the obvious. She was breathless from the rapid beating of her heart.

"I just came over to thank you for signing for the loan." Johnny said as he rubbed her hair with the dry end of the towel. She closed her eyes and reveled in the wonderful feeling of his hands on her. When she opened them and glanced up, she was surprised to see his reflection in the small mirror that hung on the wall beside the door. His eyes were closed or very near it. Was he remembering the times he had dried her hair while she sat beside the wood cookstove in the ranch kitchen? *Sit here close to the oven door. I don't want you catching a cold.*

"Your hair isn't as long as it used to be," he said quietly.

"It's easier to take care of . . . this way."

"It's curlier."

"I'm getting too old to let my hair hang down my back."

"Too old? Where did you pick up a dumb idea like that? I like the short curls, but I liked it long, too."

"I'm seven years older than I was . . . back then," she said, hoping he hadn't noticed the squeak in her voice.

"But just as pretty. I'll never forget you standing in the road the day the hijackers stopped you. You looked like a beacon with the sun shining on this bright red hair." The dark eyes that fastened on the top of her head held a familiar hint of sadness.

"You rescued me."

"Yeah. You've got this hair to thank for me even seeing you."

"You're kidding!" Kathleen glanced up at him. "You'd not have ridden to my rescue if I'd a been a blonde?"

"I'd have gotten around to it after a while," he teased as he hung the towel on the back of the chair and forked his fingers through the short tight curls. "You'll be dry soon, but don't go outside. The wind is pretty cool."

"Yes, sir," she said, and saluted.

"You'd better get that bowl of Jell-O in the icebox if you want it to set up."

"Right away, sir!"

"Smart aleck." He grinned, and her heart thumped wildly. "How's the book coming?"

"Pretty good. I wrote six pages today, then suddenly the ideas stopped coming."

"Does that happen often?"

"It depends on how far I am into the book."

"I suppose I'll have to buy a copy when it comes out."

"If you do," she laughed nervously, "it might be one of the three copies sold in Tillison County: to you, Adelaide, and Barker."

"I suppose Barker comes by now and then," he said, making her wish she hadn't mentioned his father.

"Not a lot. I see more of Marie. Barker comes by and lights my water tank. The pilot goes out at the drop of a hat, and I haven't got the hang of how to light it."

"I'll take a look at it sometime. I tinkered around a bit with that sort of thing while I was in the service."

"Would you? It's handy having hot water when you want it. How about an egg sandwich? My landlady taught me how to make a good one. I'm not sure why, but she called it a Denver."

"I was going to invite you out to eat and meet a cousin of mine. Pete Perry is in town. He's Jude's brother."

"Adelaide told me about him this morning. She and Paul met him and Dr. Perry at Claude's." She sat down after Johnny straddled a chair and folded his arms on the back.

"Pete took Isabel over to the clinic. He had to promise to take her to a honky-tonk if Jude said she was able to go. There isn't much chance of that. She's in bad shape."

"Do you have any idea what's the matter with her?"

"I've got an idea. Every man in the service was lectured on venereal disease."

"Oh, no!"

"I'm boiling everything she's used in the big iron pot. "

"Johnny, I'm sorry." Kathleen placed her hand on top of his. He turned his hand over and gripped hers tightly.

"I feel guilty because I don't want her in my house. I

have no feeling for her. I'm sorry for her as if she were someone I didn't know, but that's all."

"That's understandable. You don't really know her."

"I knew her when she was very young, and then for a few months when she was fourteen. I didn't like her even then." Johnny looked down at Kathleen's hand clasped in his. "I don't know what will become of her. I can't keep her at the house much longer. She pays no attention to anything I tell her. Pete can handle her better than I can."

"He's her cousin, too, isn't he?"

Johnny snorted. "Yeah, but he's a man first, and that's all she's interested in."

"Do you think Dr. Perry can help her?"

"I don't know. They do great things now days with penicillin." Johnny looked at his watch. "I'm to meet Pete at the clinic in a little while. Would you like to come along?" His voice had a velvet huskiness to it.

"If you want me to." The normal rhythm of her breathing and heartbeat had flown, and she feared she would not be able to regain them before she made a complete fool of herself.

"I do. I'd like for you to meet Pete. He's very different from Jude." *What I really want is for Pete to see my beautiful wife.* The thought raced joyously through his mind.

"I'll change my dress." She raked her fingers through her hair next to her scalp. "I think my hair is dry enough."

Johnny reached over and ran his hand across the top of her head, fluffing her hair with his fingers.

"You can put a scarf over it until we get to the clinic."

With a fluttering in the pit of her stomach and every cell in her body surging to life, she hurried to the bedroom. *There was a chance that he loved her still.*

\* \* \*

Theodore Nuding kept his face expressionless, hiding the emotions that engulfed him until he had stepped off the porch. A messy mixture of feelings swirled through him: elation at being so close to her and talking to her, and cold hatred for the man who had invaded her privacy and caused her discomfort.

He lifted a hand and slapped himself on the cheek. Damn! He should have done something about the man days ago. He had been busy with the house and establishing the image of himself he meant the town to accept.

Thank goodness he had been watching when that disgusting son of a bitch stopped at Kathleen's house. If that mongrel had as much as put a hand on her, he would have killed him then and there. It would still have to happen, but now he had time to decide where and when.

Kathleen was watching when he returned with the tire pump. This was the first of many services he would perform for her. As he attached the rubber tube to the valve on the tire, he felt a warm glow of unqualified delight. He wished that he could stay all day and pump tires for her, but all too soon he was finished and feared he would blow the tire if he continued. He glanced to where she stood in the window and wanted to wave to her, but he didn't want her to know that he knew she was watching.

He drove out of town and parked the car on a rise where he could view Kathleen's house with his binoculars. His response was prepared should anyone be curious about what he was doing there for hours at a time.

The story had been tested two days ago when Sheriff Carroll came by and asked what he was doing. He had explained that he was studying cloud formations for the United States Weather Department because of the number of tornadoes in this part of the country. He had shown the sheriff the notes he'd written and the chart he was keeping. He threw out a few words like *vertical updraft* and *cumulonimbus*.

The lawman had bought the story. Robert Brooks was free to sit here on this rise all day if he wanted to.

When he swept the area with his binoculars, he was surprised to see that another car had stopped at Kathleen's house. The husband's car. He wasn't pleased that Johnny Henry was there, but he knew that he wouldn't hurt her. He hoped that she'd not go back to him, but if she did, it would be only a mild stumbling block in his plan for her. Nuding took his journal from under the seat. He'd filled one notebook and had started on another.

*3:30 P.M. Today I helped my Kathleen, maybe saved her from an unpleasant experience. She is so pretty, Mother. Even with a towel wrapped around her head she is the only woman I've ever seen that compares with you. I could believe that you have come back in her body, except she is independent, like the women of today, but not as bad as some. Mother, you would be shocked to know that some try to be like men, working at men's jobs and wearing trousers. I've not seen her in trousers but a time or two, and I didn't like it.*

*The man from Eddie's station went into her house today. He is the one that made her so angry that she pulled out of the 66 station and ran over the curb. I get extremely angry when I think about him going into her house uninvited and refusing to leave. He will not bother her again.*

*The room I'm fixing for her is coming along. I'm determined that she have every comfort, and I'm grateful that I'm handy with a saw and a hammer. I've had to take boards from other parts of the house and I work only at night, so it will be a while. But no hurry. I know where she is, and I know that she is mine. Even if she goes back to that cowboy, she is still mine.*

He closed his notebook and settled down to watch. He liked to think of himself as the *Guardian*. He was good at watching and guarding. Today, however, he had something else on his mind. He had to plot carefully his next move, one that in no way could be connected with him or with Kathleen. Nuding took great pride in the fact that he planned things very precisely. His cunning mind sorted through several scenarios and finally settled on one.

Now all he had to do was wait until the right time.

# Chapter Nine

$D$r. Perry came to the reception-room door and motioned to Pete to join him in his office.

"Is Johnny coming?" Jude asked after the door closed behind the two men. "As Isabel's next of kin, he's the one I should talk to. Lord, she's got a mean mouth. She was a brat when she was young, and she's worse now. Mrs. Cole and Theresa shouldn't have to put up with her. But they're doing what needs to be done despite her calling them and me every foul name in the book."

"She's got an advanced case of syphilis." Pete's diagnosis brought a nod from his brother. "I've seen it in the islands."

"I hope Johnny has been careful. The disease is most commonly transmitted by sexual contact, however transmission can occur through infected blood or an open wound. Isabel has a number of eruptions on her skin. Syphilis also damages the brain, bones, eyes . . . places not so obvious. It can be treated successfully with penicillin unless there has been extensive damage to the nervous system." The office door opened. Jude said, "Come in, Johnny."

"My wife is with me."

Jude stood. "Do you want to ask her to come in?"

"I did, but she said she'd wait. I want her to meet Pete. Has Isabel been causing trouble?"

"She has the honor of being the most unpleasant patient I've ever had." Jude sank back down in the chair, grateful to be off his aching leg. "I've been telling Pete that Isabel has an advanced case of syphilis for one thing."

"I suspected that. What else?"

"Several other things to be exact. I can't say absolutely, until I can X-ray, but I'm reasonably certain that she has breast cancer. It's lumpy, it's draining, and I believe it has spread to the lymph glands. I wanted to X-ray, but she put up such a fuss, I didn't press the matter further for now."

Johnny shook his head. "If that's the case, what can we do?"

"Keep her as comfortable as possible during the time she has left. She also has an erratic heartbeat, which is not unusual under the circumstances, and it's possible her kidneys are failing."

"Then . . . it's a matter of time. Is that what you're saying?"

"It's my opinion that it's too late for treatment."

"What do you suggest we do?"

"The logical place for her is here. Large doses of morphine will be needed soon."

"I'll pay for it somehow."

"Don't worry about that now. Hope that my nurses will put up with her and not quit on me."

"She's a hard one," Pete said. "She told Jude in front of the nurses that he didn't know his ass from a hole in the ground."

Johnny shook his head again. "She's gone downhill fast this past week."

"She has a number of open skin lesions. Syphilis can be transmitted through infected blood or open wounds."

"I knew about that. This morning I put the towels and the bedding she used in the boiling pot. Sherm is watching them for me. Her clothes are in a pile on the bedroom floor."

"Burn them."

"She's not going to want to stay here. You may have to tie her down."

Jude answered a knock on his inner door. When it opened, Dale Cole stood there with a worried look on her face.

"Doctor, Miss Henry is swearing a blue streak and calling for someone named Pete."

"Has she been given a sedative?"

"Not yet. We'll have to restrain her to do it."

"I'll go see if I can calm her down." Pete went to the door where Dale waited and followed her down the hall.

"She refuses to give us any information about herself," Dale said. "Perhaps you can help us fill in a few blanks."

"I doubt it. This morning is the first time I've seen her in sixteen years."

Dale stopped and looked up at him with a puzzled frown. "Sixteen years? The way she talks . . . well, never mind."

"Yeah. I've been in the navy sixteen years."

"Oh, then it was before . . . that."

"What'a you mean . . . before that? Before that, I knew

the little twit for about three or four months. She's a distant cousin . . . of sorts."

"Interesting." Dale started walking again.

"What has she been telling you?"

"Not much about herself. She says plenty about Dr. Perry and Johnny Henry and about you. I was sure you'd be wearing a halo."

Pete chuckled, and Dale smiled into his eyes. "Wait until I tell her she's got to stay here. She'll be singing another tune. Nurse," Pete put his hand on her arm to stop her before she went into Isabel's room. Dale tensed and looked up at him. "Don't let anything she says get to you. She can't help being what she is; and if the truth were known, she's scared spitless."

"Don't be concerned, Mr. Perry. I've been cussed at, called every unflattering name that can be thought of, even spat upon and knocked off my feet. This poor, sick, miserable woman cannot do more than that." Dale's voice quivered. She hoped that this rough, but kind man would never know the humiliation that she had described had been at the hands of her own husband.

Pete looked at Dale with a new respect. "You've got guts, ma'am. It's a shame that people you try to help are mean to you. I'd like to blame Isabel's meanness on damage to her brain, but she's always been meaner than all get out."

"We need to give her a sedative. Nurse Frank doesn't want to strap her down."

"Let's see if I can charm her into being nice. I used to be pretty good at it, but I'm a bit out of practice at the present time."

Pete's attempt to put a smile on Dale's face succeeded. She even laughed and rolled her eyes to the ceiling. His face was soft with charm; his eyes moved over her warmly. Dale felt suddenly young and almost . . . giddy. She felt free enough to say the first thing that came to her mind.

"Then come on, Romeo. Do your stuff." The hand that rested lightly on her back was comforting as he ushered her into Isabel's room.

Sitting on the side of the bed, Isabel squealed at the sight of Pete.

"Get me outta here, Pete. You promised we'd go . . . honky-tonkin'."

"I promised to take you if the doctor said you could go. He wants you to stay here a while for treatment."

"I'm not stayin' in this shithole, and that's that!" she yelled, and flung the hospital gown aside until it barely covered her crotch.

"Stay in the bed, Miss Henry," Dale said firmly, and hurried to the bed.

"Don't touch me, you snotty bitch. I don't have to . . . stay here if I don't want to. And I told you my name is Perry. Perry. Can't you get that through your dumb head? My name is Perry, just like Pete's, just . . . like that bastard who calls himself a doctor. Shit fire! I knew him when his pecker was the size of a peanut. Ain't much bigger now if ya was to—"

"That's enough!" Pete's voice was so loud it thundered in the small room. "Goddammit! Get back in that bed! Call yourself any damn thing you want to, but your legal name is Henry. Keep that foul mouth shut, too, Isabel. You straighten up and let these folks take care of you, or I'll see that you're put in the asylum where you belong."

"Asylum? You can't. I won't go," she shouted.

"You won't have anything to say about it. You've got

syphilis, did you know that?" When she didn't answer, he said, "That's what I thought. You knew you had syphilis. It drives people so crazy they end up in an asylum."

"That other doctor told me to rest. I don't have . . . be here to do that."

"You're lying, Isabel. If you went to a doctor, he would have put you in the hospital. Now listen to me. I won't put up with you mistreating the people who are trying to help you."

"You ain't my next of kin. Johnny is." She was lying down, but still defiant.

"Johnny has washed his hands of you. He turned you over to me. I'm a hard-ass, Isabel. While I was in the navy I whipped hundreds of whining kids into shape. Some of them worse than you, if that's possible."

"I thought . . . you liked me."

"I like the side of you that's nice and reasonable. I don't like a foul-mouthed, stubborn woman who hasn't got sense enough to take care of herself."

"I've been doin' it all my life."

"You've made a hell of a mess of it, too."

"I don't like . . . her!" Isabel's hate-filled eyes moved over to Dale. "She don't like me. She thinks she's better'n me. She thinks she's so goddamn smart prancin' around in that white dress with that shitty cap on her head. She's a fat—"

"—Shut up!" Pete shouted. "You're rotten, Isabel."

"Maybe, but I ain't never had no trouble gettin' a man. Ask her how many she's had."

Pete stood by the bed and looked down at the wasted body of the girl he'd known so long ago. The only feelings he had for her were revulsion and pity.

"I don't think Jude can help you here," he said quietly.

"Your brains are already scrambled." He headed for the door. "I'll tell him to call the asylum—"

"Pete! Nooooo— Please! I don't want to go there."

"It seems we have no choice, Isabel."

"I'll do what they want. I promise," she said in a rush, tears filling her eyes.

"Yeah? As soon as I turn my back you'll be talkin' nasty to the folks who are trying to help you."

"I won't. I swear I won't."

"All right. Prove it. They need to give you a shot."

"What for? Does Jude want to put me out so he can cut off my breast or a foot or screw me?"

"Dammit, Isabel! The shot is for pain."

"I don't hurt nowhere. I could dance all night, if that son of a bitch—"

"Dammit, you forgot already."

"Will you stay a while, Pete? I won't say a word if you'll stay. I don't like bein' here by myself. They won't even let me have a cigarette."

"I'll stay if you'll behave."

"I will. Sit down . . . please—"

"I need to go out for a minute, but I'll be back."

"When?" She raised up in the bed.

"I'll be back before you can count to a hundred."

"Are you goin' out with her?" Isabel's feverish eyes went to Dale.

Pete leaned down and murmured. "Not unless she's going with me to the head." He followed Dale out and closed the door. They moved a short way down the hall. "Damn! She's worse than I thought. I'll go in with you when you give her the shot."

"I'll not be doing it. Nurse Frank will. I'll tell her to get it ready."

"I'm sorry she's given you such a bad time. The last time I saw her she was a pretty young girl of fourteen. She had a mean mouth then, but nothing like now. Will the shot put her out?"

"For about six hours. I don't understand why she isn't in terrible pain."

"She may be, but too stubborn to admit it."

"You did a fine job in there. That's a kind of charm I've not seen used before." Dale's eyes smiled up at him.

"Oh, I've got other kinds of charm I drag out and use once in a while."

"Is her name Perry or Henry? I need it for the records."

"Her legal name is Henry. Her mother was married to Ed Henry when she was born. She took her mother's name later because Ed wasn't her natural father."

"Do you know the date of her birth?"

"No."

"Maybe I can get the information from her brother."

"Pee . . . te! Pee . . . te!"

Pete quirked a brow and glanced toward the room. "I guess she's counted to a hundred."

"Pete, dammit, you said you'd come back. Pee . . . te." Isabel's voice could be heard up and down the hall.

"Kind of nice being wanted, isn't it?" Dale was surprised at how easy it was to tease with him.

"Careful, nurse, I might not go back in there."

"Please, please, don't do that to me." Dale let out a grunt of laughter. Her jaw hurt so bad she could hardly open her mouth.

Pete was reluctant to end the conversation. He kept trying to see if Dale wore a wedding band, but her fingers were wrapped around the chart she held.

"I'll tell Nurse Frank to bring the sedative."

Pete ignored the calls from Isabel and lingered a minute to watch Dale walk down the hall. *If a man held her, he'd know he had a real woman in his arms and not a bag full of bones. She's nice, too, and got plenty of horse sense.* Dale passed out of sight, and there was nothing for him to do but go back into Isabel's room and try to quiet her.

Dale could feel Pete's eyes on her and wished that she were young again. When she married Harry, she had been slim and pretty and trying to finish her nurse's training. Her family had been dirt-poor and pleased that a man with a good job was interested in her. Over the years she had put on weight. Harry reminded her constantly of it and of her poor background. Now she felt . . . big and ugly. Pete Perry probably had known plenty of young, slim girls and was thinking that she looked like a fat cow waddling down the hallway. She didn't know why that mattered to her, but it did.

"Let's go sit in the car. Jude said he would send Pete out," Johnny said to Kathleen when he returned to the reception room. He took her elbow to help her stand up. "Better put that scarf back on. It's windy." He anchored his hat on his head.

Kathleen didn't speak until they were in the car and she had pulled the thin, flowered scarf from her head.

"You look tired."

"I am. I've been sleeping on a canvas cot in the barn and worrying that Isabel was going to burn my house down."

His dark eyes soberly searched her face. If she could believe what she saw in his eyes, it was loneliness. Without thinking about it, she reached for his hand.

"Did Dr. Perry tell you what was wrong with Isabel?"

"There's a lot wrong with her. She has syphilis and breast cancer."

"Can he help her?"

"She's too far gone. It's only a matter of time."

"I'm sorry. Is there anything I can do?"

"No. I don't want you in the same room with her. You've never heard a mouth as dirty as hers. Jude said that syphilis damages the brain. Hers must have been damaged long ago. She's always been mean.

"I remember one time Henry Ann and I were trying to chop weeds so we'd get a cotton crop. When we made Isabel help us, she deliberately chopped out a half a row of cotton plants. She laughed because she had outsmarted us. I wanted to slap her."

"Did you?"

"No. After that she went down to Mud Creek to stay with the Perrys."

"I heard the nurses talking. Isabel isn't a very good patient."

"That's an understatement. Jude said he'd never had one as bad. Pete thought he might be able to calm her down. She offered to go to bed with him if he would take her honky-tonking."

"But . . . she's got— You mean she would—?"

"You don't know Isabel. I wonder how many men she has infected."

"Oh, Johnny." Kathleen hugged his hand to her. "I'm not sorry that I never met her, but I still feel sympathy for her. She's all alone and dying."

"It's her own fault. I'll pay to keep her here. That's my only obligation to her."

"Will you call Henry Ann? She's her sister, too."

"I thought I would. She can decide whether she wants to come. Isabel won't thank her for it."

"Regardless, her kin should be with her. You all had the same mother—"

"You still don't get it do you?" Johnny pulled his hand from hers. "Isabel and I are the unwanted results of a horde of men who slept with Dorene. Her blood was so tainted from years of incest that whoring was the logical thing for her to do. She saw absolutely nothing wrong with it. And Isabel is just like Dorene, a whore because she wants to be."

"Henry Ann—"

"If I've got any decent blood in my body," he continued angrily and turned his head to look out the car window, "I have to thank that Indian who paid Dorene to let him screw her." After a minute or two he turned back and took Kathleen's hand, looked at it intently, and plucked at her fingers. "I never intended to get started on that subject. I'm sorry."

"Don't be." She wanted to say more and would have if this sudden closeness between them were not so fragile.

"Jude told me to burn her clothes," he said after a silence. "I'm going to use Lysol to—scrub down everything she's touched."

"I could help you."

"Pete'll help me. He's going to stay with me for a while. I'll put a bed in the little room off the kitchen."

Disappointment was a lump in Kathleen's throat. *He had no plans for her coming back to the ranch. He couldn't have made it plainer.*

"You'll like Pete. All women do." Johnny didn't notice that she had drawn her lips between her teeth to hold them still. "The navy changed him. Hell, the war changed

all of us. Pete used to be a hell-raiser. I've told you some
of the things he used to do. He was in love with Henry
Ann when they were young. He did dumb stunts trying to
impress her. He laughs about it now." Johnny tilted his
head so he could look into her face. "I'm rattling on. I
guess I've been hungry to talk to you."

"Who did you talk to while you were overseas?"

"I had a tentmate when we had tents. I daydreamed a
lot."

"Were you ever scared?"

"Lots and lots of times. I'm scared now."

"I can understand that. Your sister is dying."

"That isn't it. I'm scared every time I'm with you."

"With me? Now I *don't* understand that."

"I can't explain it. I'm not good with words, as you
well know."

"Are you afraid that I'm going to demand something
from you? I've already told you that I'm not going to. I'm
willing to go along with whatever you want to do."

"And what if I don't know what I want to do?"

"Then I guess I'll have to wait until you do."

"You, of all the people in the world, have the power to
make me so damn mad, so damn quick. I wanted us to
have a nice evening. I wanted to show you off to Pete.
We're not alone ten minutes until your temper shows up."

"I'm not in a temper. I stated a fact."

"That you're not going to demand anything from me.
You want nothing from me at all." Annoyed, he gripped
her hand so tightly it hurt. She knew he was unaware of
it.

"There are things I want from you, Johnny, but you're
not willing to give them."

"How do you know until you ask?" His dark eyes were boring into hers.

*Oh, Johnny. I want your love back. I want to go back to our house and sleep in your arms every night. I want us to make a baby again, and when it comes, I want you to love it. I want us to grow old together. I want to share everything with you . . . the good and the bad.*

Knowing that she could not voice any of those desires, she said instead, "I would like to have our wedding picture, if you don't want it."

His eyes scanned her face for a long while before he spoke.

"What makes you think I don't want it?"

"Well, you . . . seem anxious to get that part of your life behind you. I thought you might not want reminders—"

"—Why didn't you take the picture when you came out to collect your things?"

"I wouldn't do that. You paid for it with your rodeo winnings. Forget it. If the photographer down in Vernon is still in business, he may have kept the negatives."

"You can have it."

"No—"

Suddenly his hand was behind her head jerking her to him. He put his mouth against hers and muttered, "You make me so mad I've either got to kiss you or hit you."

Kathleen was incapable of moving. The lips that touched hers were warm, sweet, and demanding. The kiss became possessive and deepened. Her lips parted, his tongue touched hers, his fingers forked through her hair, and his hand slid over her breast. This was Johnny, her love. Her arm moved up and around his neck, holding him to her.

A rapping on the window brought them to their senses. Johnny lifted his head and frowned at the man grinning at them through the glass.

"Don't you know it ain't nice to neck right out here in public?"

Johnny reached over and jerked open the door.

"You wouldn't know *nice* if it jumped up and bit you. Pete, this is my wife, Kathleen."

# Chapter Ten

*K*athleen decided that she liked Pete Perry. He acted as a buffer between her and Johnny as they ate T-bone steaks at the Frontier Cafe. After a brief conversation about Isabel on the way to the restaurant, she was not mentioned again.

Pete flirted outrageously with Kathleen, and Johnny didn't seem to mind.

"How did a pretty girl like you settle for this ugly old cowboy?"

"He was the only Best All-Around Cowboy in town," she retorted. "I had to settle for him or nothing. It was an accident that we met." Kathleen glanced at Johnny's relaxed and smiling face. "I was being hijacked out on the highway when this cowboy came charging over the hill on his trusty steed, his six-guns blazing. The bad guys knew when they were outgunned and hightailed it before a shot was fired. I swooned," she said dramatically, "in the arms of *my hero*."

Johnny chuckled. "Horse hockey. You never swooned in your life."

"That explains how you met; but after you were around him for a while, couldn't you tell that he didn't have much between his ears?"

"Well, I did wonder what was holding them apart, but he was so . . . pretty and . . . he *was* the Best All-Around Cowboy at the Tillison County rodeo. What's a girl to do?"

"All right, you two. You've had enough fun at my expense. I've got some pretty good stories I can tell about Pete. You see there was this older, married woman who lived over in Ringling and Pete—"

"Whoa, there partner. You start telling that, and I'll have to tell Kathleen about the time you and Jude went to town and swiped a freezer full of ice cream off Mrs. Miller's back porch. Henry Ann was mad as a hornet when she found out about it."

"She was really afraid that someone had seen us and we'd get caught. Mrs. Miller, the old busybody, had been spreading gossip about Henry Ann and Tom, so Jude and I decided to get even." Johnny flashed a grin at Kathleen.

"Poor Henry Ann. I bet she had her hands full with you."

"When will I get to read some of the stories you've written?" Pete winked at the waitress and slipped the check she placed on the table into his shirt pocket.

"How . . . did you know about that?" Kathleen's eyes darted from Johnny to Pete.

"Jude told me. Then Johnny told me that you're writing a book. I've never known anyone who wrote a story, much less a whole book."

"I've not written the whole book yet. I'm just working on it."

"I've not known anyone who was even working on

one." Pete placed a generous tip on the table for the waitress and stood. "Where do I buy the magazines?"

"You don't have to buy them. I've got copies I can lend you . . . if you're serious about reading them."

"I've got on my serious face. Didn't you notice? Say, Johnny, what say we stop off at the town hot spot and have a beer so I can dance with the town celebrity."

"Only if you give me the check. This was my idea." Johnny helped Kathleen on with her coat, then reached to yank the check out of Pete's shirt pocket.

"Keep your cotton-pickin' hands to yourself. You can pay for the beers. Is he always so grabby, Kathleen?"

"Always." Kathleen felt light, airy, giddy, happier than she had been in a long time.

They crowded into the front seat of Johnny's car. Kathleen sat close to him, her shoulder tucked behind his. His hand brushed her knee as he shoved the car into gear and they took off. When he turned to look at her, their faces were only inches apart. Tremors of joy went through her. She wondered if he could feel the beat of her heart through the breast that was pressed tightly against him.

*You're happy tonight, my Johnny. Is it because you are with me or your cousin, Pete? Are you remembering how it was between us after we discovered our love and before Mary Rose was born?*

"I was discharged in San Diego." Pete's arm lay across the top of the seat behind her. "I could hardly wait to get into civilian clothes and go to a beer joint without keeping an eye out for the MPs. Know what? It wasn't as much fun as I thought it would be. I was lonesome for the red hills of Oklahoma."

"At the Norman Naval Base where I was discharged,

they loaded us on a bus and took us straight to the train station."

"He came home to a parade through town." Kathleen glanced at Johnny and saw his teeth clench and a muscle jump in his jaw.

"How do you know?" Johnny asked.

"I was there." Kathleen wished she'd not mentioned his homecoming.

"I didn't see you."

"You were too busy looking at the girls swooning over the returning hero." She turned toward Pete. "The band played, 'When Johnny Comes Marching Home.'"

"Golly-bill, I'm out honky-tonkin' with a real live hero and a celebrity."

"Dry it up," Johnny growled as he turned in and parked in front of the Twilight Gardens, "or I'll leave both of you here and you can walk back to the clinic."

"The place is jumpin' tonight," Pete said dryly, observing that only two other cars were parked at the joint.

"Just the way I like it," Johnny said in a faint faraway voice that only Kathleen could hear.

She wondered if he was remembering the night they sat in front of this place in his old truck? It was strangely the same, even though some of the neon had dimmed from around the windows and the building needed a coat of paint. The parking lot was as full of chuckholes as it had been seven years ago.

Kathleen struggled to keep her breathing even as memories swamped her, making her eyes misty. It was here that she and Johnny said the words that bound her to him forever. Not even their marriage ceremony was as binding to her as the declarations of love they made that night.

She had given him her love unconditionally. She was still his, even if he no longer wanted her.

"Let's go in and liven up this place." Pete got out of the car and held out his hand to Kathleen.

Inside, Kathleen paused to allow her eyes to adjust to the darkness. A row of booths lined three sides of the small dance floor. The bar was at the end. Neon beer signs provided the only light except for the dim glow from the jukebox selectors at each booth. None of the booths were occupied.

"This is our lucky night," Johnny said dryly, and Kathleen wondered if he was sorry that they had come here. "We have our choice of booths. Choose one, and I'll get the beers."

Kathleen slid into a booth at the back.

"Don't want anything to happen to my new hat," Pete said, and hung his light-colored Stetson on the peg above the selector before he sat down opposite her. "It cost me three dollars. Imagine paying three dollars for a hat."

"It's a nice one."

"You love him, don't you?" he asked abruptly.

There was no doubt in Kathleen's mind what he was talking about. She looked straight into serious blue eyes that seemed even bluer because of his tanned face and answered honestly.

"I'm crazy about him. Always have been and always will be."

"I thought so."

Johnny returned and set two bottles of beer and a cola on the table. He placed several coins in front of Kathleen and sat down beside her.

"It's a little early for much activity here. Crowd comes late," he explained after a drink from his bottle.

"Are you going to let me dance with Kathleen?"

Johnny took another long drink from his bottle before he answered. "It's up to her."

"How about it, Kathleen?"

"Sure."

"What do you like, fast or slow." Pete picked up one of the coins from the table and put it in the slot.

"Anything but the 'Beer Barrel Polka,'" she said with a nervous laugh.

"How about, 'I'm in the Mood for Love'?" He punched the correct number and looked over at the jukebox to see if the record had fallen in place.

Without comment, Johnny got up and waited for Kathleen to slide out of the booth. She didn't look at him as she took Pete's hand and let him lead her to the postage-stamp-sized dance floor.

They swayed to the music for a short while before they began to dance. Pete was an inch taller than Johnny. He held her firmly, lowered his head and pressed his cheek to hers.

"Johnny's crazy about you." The words were a soft whisper in her ear.

"Why do you say that?"

"The signs are there."

"I don't think so. Too much time has passed."

"What went wrong?"

"It's a long, long story, very complicated."

"What's complicated about two people who love each other? If I had a woman like you lovin' me, I'd move mountains, dry up rivers, and chop down forests to keep her."

"It's sweet of you—"

"Johnny's glaring at us. He thinks I'm whispering sweet nothings in your ear."

"He wouldn't care—"

"I bet with just a little effort, I could make him jealous as hell." Pete's lips were against the hair at her temple.

"Please don't. Don't jeopardize your friendship. He needs you now."

"Then you think he'd want to bust me up?"

Kathleen pulled back so that she could see his face. "I'm not sure."

"We won't rock the boat . . . yet. But that dumb Indian had better wake up and see what he's got before someone else takes it."

That *dumb Indian* knew what he'd had, and had convinced himself that he could never have it again. But that didn't mean that he'd stand by and see Kathleen hurt by a man like Pete Perry. Pete loved women, any woman that was available. It came as naturally to him as eating and sleeping. Kathleen might not understand that and fall for his line of flattery. To see her in another man's arms was like a knife in his guts.

When the music ended and Kathleen and Pete headed back to the booth, Johnny slipped a coin in the selector and stood.

"My turn," he said, and took Kathleen's hand.

On the dance floor, he put his arm around her and pulled her up close. She turned her head so that her forehead nestled against his cheek. The hand on his shoulder slipped up and up until her fingers could feel the hair at the nape of his neck. When he moved, it was impossible not to move with him. Had he selected this song on purpose, or had he just punched in a number?

*"You'll never know just how much I love you,*
*You'll never know just how much I care.*
*And if I tried, I still couldn't hide my love for you—"*

Kathleen's heart throbbed in her throat. She closed her eyes and for a while forgot that anyone else existed except for her and Johnny. She floated in a haze of happiness as they glided around the floor to the strains of the slow tune.

He moved his head, and she tilted hers to look at him.

"It's been a long time, hasn't it?" His dark eyes were fastened to her face.

"Do you remember the last time we danced together?"

"Of course." His arms tightened convulsively when her lashes fluttered down. "I had four and a half years to remember everything we ever did. I even remember the song we danced to." He pressed his cheek to her hair and sang softly, *"The moon stood still, on Blueberry Hill, on Blueberry Hill where I found you."*

"You remembered that!"

"And a lot more."

Kathleen let him mold her body to his. Her half-closed eyes were filled with a look of intense longing. For a while she wanted to forget that he no longer wanted to live with her as husband and wife. She nestled closer and moved her arm farther around his neck.

The music stopped. Johnny didn't. He continued to dance until the music came on again. The song made Kathleen's heart ache with longing. The Ink Spots were singing,

*"If I didn't care, would I feel this way?*
*If I didn't care, more than words can say—"*

Johnny became aware that they no longer had the dance floor to themselves when he led her nearly into a collision with another couple. He was also aware that his longing for her was causing his sex to harden. Hoping that she hadn't noticed, he pulled back until their bodies were no longer pressed tightly together from chest to thighs.

When the music ended, he steered her by the hand back to the booth, where two more cold bottles of beer waited. Pete was at the bar talking to the bartender. When he saw them sit down, he came back to the booth.

"The bartender is a navy man, Johnny. He served on the USS *Saratoga*. He asked me to join the VFW here. Have you joined?"

"No. I'm not much of a joiner."

"I think I'll join. We veterans should stick together so that what happened to the World War I vets won't happen to us."

"I'm not interested in pressuring for a handout from the government. I managed before I went to the navy."

Pete grinned. "Still stubborn and independent. How'd you get along in the Seabees? I heard that those guys were tough as boot leather and had a short fuse. Anyone knock you on your ass?"

"A couple tried to. One succeeded, but I got even." Johnny smiled, remembering.

Pete looked at Kathleen. "There's a story here, and if you ask him nicely, he'll tell it."

"Tell it, Johnny," Kathleen urged with her hand on his arm.

"If you insist." He covered her hand briefly, squeezed it, then wrapped both hands around his beer bottle.

"We had a guy in our outfit who had a huge chip on his

shoulder. One night we got into a squabble about something or other. He outweighed me by fifty pounds and got in a good punch that knocked me six ways from Sunday. I let it go, knowing that I'd get even.

"This sucker was scared spitless when the Japs came over. We all teased him about it. While we were on Sterling Island, he found himself a little hole in a rock shelf and hung a white cloth over it so that he could dive in when the sirens went off. One night I moved the cloth to the side. When he dived for his hole, he hit his head on the rock and knocked himself out."

"Did he know you did it?" Kathleen asked.

"He suspected. Another time one of the guys tied his shoelaces together while he slept and when the sirens went off, as they did every night, he got up and fell flat on his face. We all hooted and ran for the foxholes."

"We had one of those on our ship." Pete turned the beer bottle around and around with his big hands. "He was so scared he'd wet his pants. I felt sorry for him, but every man had his spot to fill and I had to see to it that he'd fill his. He was finally shipped out to stateside duty. It was a relief to all of us."

Silence stretched between the two men like a taut rubber band. Both were remembering other times.

"We had quite a few close calls," Pete finally began again. "I really never thought I'd make it back."

"I did my damnedest to do my job and stay alive. That's all any of us could do."

"Did you ever listen to Tokyo Rose?"

"Yeah, we heard her when we were secure enough to have a radio. It made us plenty sore when we found out that she was an American citizen who went to visit a relative then turned traitor for the Japs. She had a soft coaxing voice and fed us a bunch of bull about what was going on."

"She's been arrested and is being tried for treason."

"If they don't hang her, I hope that they put her away for life."

"Yeah. The war was an experience I'm glad I had a part in as long as there had to be a war, but I wouldn't want to do it again."

"Me too," Johnny said. "It already seems as if that was another life, or that it happened to someone else." He turned to Kathleen. "Are you ready to go? I doubt this conversation is interesting to you." He stood and held her coat.

"You're wrong about the conversation, but it is getting late."

They drove Pete to the clinic, where he had left his car. When he got out, he told Kathleen that he was going to hold her to her promise to lend him some of the magazines so he could read her stories. She laughingly told him to come by anytime and pick them up.

"I've got a few extra copies at the ranch, if he really wants to read your stories," Johnny said grumpily, while driving Kathleen home. He was quiet after that and didn't speak until he stopped at her house.

"Do you have locks on your doors?"

"I checked them today. I have the telephone, too."

"I'll be in tomorrow. I'll have a talk with Eddie at the garage; and if Thomas isn't there, I'll look him up. If he ever pulls such a stunt again, call the sheriff. If there's anything left of that mechanic after I get through with him, he'll go to jail."

"It's a shame when a person has to lock her doors in broad daylight. I've never had to do that before."

Johnny got out of the car, came around, and opened the car door. They walked to the porch.

"Did you lock the door when you left?"

"Oh, shoot. I didn't even think about it. It was daylight when we left."

Johnny turned the knob, pushed open the door and switched on the lights.

"I'll go through the house."

Kathleen waited in the living room while he made the circle through the kitchen, small back room, the bathroom, then through her bedroom. When he returned to the living room, Kathleen swallowed hard, knowing that he had seen the panties she had washed in the bathroom and left hanging on a line stretched across the bathtub.

"I locked your back door and hooked a chair under the doorknob. Do the same to this front door. These locks are flimsy."

"I'm not afraid, Johnny. I was by myself at the ranch when you were away."

"Times have changed, and you're in town now. I'll take care of Gabe Thomas. But there are others out there just as bad or even worse than he is."

"Don't get into any trouble on my account."

*He was concerned for her.* Kathleen tried her best not to be thankful that Gabe Thomas had come into her house.

"Your car running all right?" he asked, dismissing the subject.

"Good enough. The tire keeps leaking air. Didn't we used to have a tire pump?"

"It may be out at the ranch. I'll take a look."

"If there's anything I can do to help with Isabel, let me know."

"I'm going to call Henry Ann tomorrow and tell her about Isabel. If she decides to come, would it be all right if she stayed with you?"

"Of course. I'll be glad to have her."

"I'll tell her that when we talk." He pulled open the door. "I'd better get going, I'm going to stop by the clinic."

"Good night, Johnny."

He reached out and placed his hand on her shoulder, squeezed it gently, and nodded. Then he was out the door, his long legs taking him in swift strides across the porch and to his car, as if a mad dog were on his heels.

"Shitfire, shitfire," he cursed.

*She looked at me with those big, sad eyes, and I know she wanted me to stay. God, I wanted to stay and love her all night long; but if I did, it would have been the same thing over again. She should be with a man who can give her healthy babies. Tonight Pete watched her like a hawk stalking a chicken. I don't dare let him think she and I are through for good or he'd be after her like a shot, and his blood is as bad as mine.*

A light glowed in the three-sided shed behind Eddie's service station. Gabe Thomas lay under the wreck of an old car, removing parts. He was allowed the use of the shed as part compensation for helping out at the station when Eddie had to be away.

The wheels of the wreck had been removed and the frame set upon blocks. With light from a single bulb on the end of a long cord, Gabe was pulling out the bolts that held the engine in place and thinking about Kathleen Henry. Damn, but she was pretty, and with that red hair, she would be hotter than a pistol.

He'd'a had her today if that fool hadn't knocked on the door. But . . . there would be another day. A woman like her, who had had *it*, couldn't go without very long, and he hadn't heard of her being with anyone since she came back to Rawlings. She wasn't going back to Johnny or she wouldn't have moved into that house. He'd give her a little more time . . . let her sweat a little, it would make her all the more eager. Next time, he'd not be so stupid as to try for her in broad daylight.

The wide crack between the boards gave the watcher a full view of the shed. He had studied the wreck sitting on the blocks and now waited patiently for Gabe to position himself beneath it. The shed was a dark, quiet area. Nothing had moved up or down the adjoining street for half an hour. The man in the dark clothes calculated distance, angles and how much of a bump it would take to move the wreck before he turned away and walked quickly back to where he had left his car.

Minutes later, a car without lights came slowly down the alley, picked up speed when it neared the shed, turned sharply, and rammed the wreck, knocking it off the blocks and into the side of the shed. The light went out. Darkness and quiet prevailed.

Satisfied that he had accomplished what he had intended, the man calmly drove out of the alley and away.

# *Chapter Eleven*

"*T*ell that doctor you're quitting."

Harry dropped the words into the silence while his face was still behind the newspaper.

"What?" Dale was so startled that her hand shook as she returned her cup to the saucer.

"Have you lost your hearing, Dale?" He lowered the paper, frowned at Dale, then smiled pleasantly at his son. "Danny, if you've finished your breakfast, run get your coat, and I'll give you a ride to school."

"You wanted me to have this job, Harry." Dale waited until the child left the room before she spoke. She did her best to keep her voice from quivering.

"That was then. This is now. Your place is here at home taking care of Danny."

"He's in school all day, Harry. He spends an hour after school with Mrs. Ramsey. I'm home and dinner is ready by the time you get here."

"I'm not going to argue with you." Harry gave a deep sigh and shook his head as if talking to a stubborn child.

He moved his coffee cup aside, carefully folded the *Gazette,* and placed it on the table beside his plate.

Dale watched the action. During the six years of their marriage, she had cataloged in her mind every move he made leading up to one of his black moods. First his voice would soften, then he became overly neat and orderly; breaking a matchstick before he dropped it in the ashtray, dusting lint from his coat sleeve, smoothing the hair at his temples.

Next would come the questions. *Don't I provide for you? Don't you have everything you need? Didn't I take you off that dirt farm and put you in a house with a flush toilet?*

Dale began to quake inside, but as usual she stood up against him as long as she could.

"They are short-handed at the clinic, Harry. A terminally ill patient was admitted yesterday. I should give a month's notice so they can hire another nurse."

"Jesus Christ, Dale. We both know that you're not a nurse. Did you graduate from nursing school? Did you get your certificate? You empty bedpans and clean up vomit and shit. It doesn't take brains to do that. Tell him that you'll be gone in two weeks. That's my limit."

"No." Dale stood. "They need me, and I need the job."

"Why do you need the job? Don't I provide for you?" Harry got slowly to his feet, his eyes boring into hers. "What's got into you? You're getting more difficult all the time."

"I won't give the doctor notice, Harry." Dale hoped and prayed that Danny's being in the house would keep Harry's fists from lashing out.

"Then I guess I'll have to do it myself." He walked slowly around the table, then as fast as a striking snake, his hand was at her throat shoving her up against the wall. He knocked her head against it repeatedly until a plate on a plate holder bounced off the shelf and crashed to the floor.

"I'm tired of you defying me when I tell you to do something. Who pays for the roof over your head and food that goes into that fat belly? Huh? Who took you from that dirt farm and set you up in a decent house? Huh?"

Dale clawed at the hand squeezing her neck, closing off her windpipe. Over the ringing in her ears, she heard her son's pleading voice.

"Daddy, Daddy. Stop . . . please stop—"

Dale gasped for breath when the hand left her throat, only vaguely aware that Harry was talking calmly to their son.

"Your mother and I were just having a little fun. She fell against the wall and knocked your grandmother's plate off the shelf. You know how she is . . . not the most graceful mother in the world, huh? We'd better move, son, or both of us will be late." With his hand at the back of Danny's head, Harry urged him toward the door. The child resisted for just a moment, looking back at his mother.

Dale didn't move until she heard the car start and was sure he was leaving. When she did, her foot crunched the broken glass. She stroked her throat gently and swallowed to be sure that she could.

*Someday he will kill me.*

Johnny was up at dawn after a sleepless night. Last night Sherm had finished boiling the sheets and had hung them on the line to dry. After making up the bed, Johnny had stripped and fallen into it. But sleep had not come as he had expected. He continued to feel Kathleen in his arms, warm and moving, to smell the scent of her hair when he buried his nose in it, and to see the curve of her lips when she smiled.

She had not been outraged, as he had expected, when he kissed her. Lord, how many nights had he crouched down in his foxhole while the Japs strafed and bombed their building site, thinking of kissing her and more . . . burying himself in her soft body? He relived in detail the hours, during the dark of night, that they had spent making love, whispering, teasing, making plans. At other times, dark times, he had remembered her turning away from him after they had buried their baby, refusing to understand his determination never again to father a child.

Five years had dimmed the pain he had felt on seeing the small piece of deformed humanity he and Kathleen had brought into the world. It had not, however, dimmed his resolve never again to put her through the agony of giving birth to a child of his. But would he be able to endure seeing her stomach swell with another man's child. Good Lord! He should have taken that job in Central America when it was offered.

When morning came, Johnny put the coffeepot on, then began clearing the house of Isabel's belongings. He piled her clothes in the yard, poured gasoline on them, and set them ablaze. Thanks to his navy training he had already been careful with the cups, glasses, and eating utensils she had used, washing them separately and letting them sit in the boiling water.

He told Sherm when he came in for breakfast that Isabel wasn't coming back.

"I knowed she warn't well but didn't figure it was so bad."

"I've got to go back to town this morning. When I get back, I'll scrub this place down with lye soap. I don't think she ever went to the outhouse."

"I ain't never seen her go there."

"That's one less thing we have to worry about. I set the chamber pot on the porch. I'll build a fire under the wash pot and scald it good. I never use it, but I don't want it sitting around here with germs on it."

"I can do it while yo're gone. Is that feller comin' back to help drive up the horses?"

"I don't know. Pete seems to be the only one who can do anything with Isabel. She's so ornery, the doctor is afraid his nurses will quit."

"Hit's a pity, is what it is. Her bein' young and all."

Johnny drove slowly into town. After he tended to the business with Gabe, he would go to the telephone office and call Henry Ann to tell her about Isabel. He believed that she would come to Rawlings. She would think it the decent thing to do. He would have to watch Pete when she got here. Johnny wasn't sure whether Pete still had strong feelings for Henry Ann, and he didn't want his sister to have to deal with that on top of everything else.

When he rounded the corner to drive into Eddie's station, Johnny could tell that something out of the ordinary had happened. Several cars were parked in the alley and along the street, one of them a hearse. Jude, wearing his overcoat over his white jacket and holding his black bag, was talking to the undertaker. Johnny parked and crossed the street.

"Morning. Has something happened to Eddie?"

"No, to Gabe Thomas." Douglas Klein, the undertaker and owner of the furniture store, answered. He was a friendly man with a husky body, dark hair, and a small mustache.

"What happened?"

"The old wreck he had up on blocks fell and crushed him flat as a fritter."

"Not quite that flat," Jude said. "But he died instantly."

"Too bad. Where's Eddie?"

"He went to find a jack to lift the wreck so that we can get the body out. He said Gabe was usually pretty careful about blocking up those old wrecks."

"He must have slipped up this time. Are you through here, Jude?" Johnny asked.

"Just about. As coroner, I've got to sign the death certificate. The sheriff and I can't see it as anything but an accident. What are you doing in town so early?"

"I was going to speak to Eddie. Guess I have no reason to do that now." Johnny put a cigarette in his mouth, struck a match on the sole of his boot, and held the flame to the tip. "I plan to call Henry Ann this morning. She has a right to know about Isabel. How was she this morning?"

"About the same. She won't let us check her vitals. We have to do it when she's sedated. We're trying to keep her quiet. She wastes a lot of her strength yelling and thrashing around. Miss Pauley, the night nurse, said she made so much noise she woke everyone in the clinic."

Eddie returned with the jack and several men went with him into the shed to help the undertaker recover the body.

"Jude, I don't have much, but I'll pay for Isabel's keep somehow. Just give me a little time."

"You'll not owe me a thing for my services, Johnny. The clinic is another matter. The board of trustees will give you as much time as you need to pay them. So don't worry about it."

"I'll worry about it. There's just not much I can do about it right now."

"I'll keep her as comfortable as I can until the end. There will be an end, Johnny, and soon."

"Does she know?"

"I'm not sure. I think she has brain damage. That's not my line, so I can't be absolutely sure. A completely sane person would understand the seriousness of her condition."

The stretcher bearing Gabe Thomas's body was placed on the cart from the hearse, and Mr. Klein came to speak with Jude.

"If you've seen enough, Dr. Perry, I'd better get him on down to the parlor. He's going to take a lot of fixin' before his folks see him."

"I have. I'll finish up at the clinic and give the death certificate to the sheriff." Jude and Johnny crossed the street to their cars. "After you talk to Henry Ann, come by the clinic. We need to get some background information on Isabel."

"You know as much about her as I do. All I know is that she was born in Oklahoma City. Dorene listed the father as unknown. The only reason I know that is when Isabel tried to get part of Ed Henry's farm, the lawyer Henry Ann hired got a copy of the birth certificate."

"I don't suppose it matters all that much," Jude said, getting into his car. "I hope Henry Ann comes. It'll be good to see her."

\* \* \*

Jude parked his car at the clinic and went into the side door to his office. He removed his overcoat and sat down in the chair behind his desk to complete his paperwork.

*Would his damn leg ever stop aching?*

He was a little puzzled as to why a man who had worked on cars for most of his life would crawl under a wreck without making sure it was up on solid blocks. Judging by the congealed blood, he presumed the accident had happened around midnight. The body hadn't been found until early this morning. It wouldn't have mattered if it had been discovered minutes after the accident. The man had died instantly. Jude filled out the death certificate and left it on his desk for delivery to the sheriff.

"You were out early, Doctor." Theresa Frank came in as he was preparing to make his rounds.

"Yes. An accident."

"I heard about it."

"Sheriff Carroll will be by for the death certificate. I was about to make my rounds. Anything you need to tell me?"

"Mr. Case is better. You may want to consider dismissing him. He's worried about the cost of being here." Theresa consulted her chart. "Mrs. Warren has developed large welts on her body and her lips are swollen. We should check and see if she's allergic to some of the medication."

"Check to see if the medication she's been taking has codeine in it."

"I did that, and it does."

"That could be the cause. Take her off it."

"I told Dale to hold off giving it to her until I talked to you." Theresa continued with her report. "Mrs. Smothers is in the reception room, insisting on seeing you right away. She says that her legs are swelling. We have a patient with an infected toenail and a six-year-old girl with tonsillitis. Marie Fleming is here with her brother, who poked a nail in his hand. She thinks he needs a tetanus shot."

"He won't need me for that. You give better shots than I do."

"I don't know about that, but I'll give it."

Theresa was certain that Marie Fleming would be disappointed at not seeing the doctor. She had noticed how the girl had looked at him during the open house. She was young, pretty, and her daddy was rich—surely Jude had been aware.

"How about Miss Henry?"

"She refused to eat the oatmeal, but drank the coffee. She's fussing for a cigarette and calling for your brother to come get her out of here."

"Pete will be along soon. He sat up with her half the night."

"She's taking the oral sedatives, but soon she'll need something stronger. Her breast is swollen and draining. She did let me put a pad over it." Theresa folded her arms over the charts and held them against her. "If we have a few minutes, I'd like to talk to you about something."

Jude saw the concerned look on Theresa's face and backed up to sit down on the edge of the desk. He rubbed his aching thigh.

"What is it? You're not going to quit, are you?"

Theresa smiled. "No, I'm not going to quit."

"That's a relief. You scared me for a minute. How's Ryan? I've not seen him for a while."

"He's fine. He likes going to Mrs. Ramsey's and says

he's going to marry Emily when he grows up." Theresa's eyes brightened when she talked about her son.

Theresa Frank had had a hopeless crush on Dr. Jude Perry since the day she met him. He was the kindest, most thoughtful man she had ever known besides being so darn handsome it almost hurt her eyes to look at him. She was realistic enough to know that when he took a wife, it wouldn't be a dumpy nurse with a four-year-old child. But she daydreamed, and went on crash diets trying to look thin and desirable. In the meanwhile, she helped him in the only way she knew, by being the best nurse possible.

"Now, what is it that you wanted to talk about?"

Jude studied the woman who stood a short distance from him. He liked what he saw. She was pretty, quiet, and dependable. He wondered how many hours she spent washing and ironing her uniforms. They were always fresh. The starched cap was carefully perched on top of her soft brown hair, and she had a complexion some women would give five years of their lives for.

Most of all Jude liked who Theresa was: her attitude toward life, her compassion for the ill, her dedication to service, and her love for her child. She was just what he thought a woman should be—far from the sluts he had grown up with down on Mud Creek.

"It's about Dale Cole." Theresa's voice broke into Jude's thoughts. "I'm sure she had been crying when she came in this morning. I asked her what was wrong and she tried to assure me that nothing was wrong, that she just had a headache."

"Maybe that was true. Did she take some medication?"

"She took some because I was watching her. That's not all, Doctor—"

"Can't you call me Jude when we're alone? I call you Theresa."

"Yes, but you're . . . the doctor. I'm only the—"

"—Very important part of my practice. I want us to be friends as well as associates."

"I . . . want that too." Theresa's cheeks turned rosy red.

Jude laughed. "You're blushing, Theresa."

"I am not!" she insisted, but knew that she was. "Sometimes you get me so . . . flustered."

"I do?" He looked surprised. "I thought that you were . . . unfluster . . . able." They both laughed at his difficulty in pronouncing the word. "I'll not interrupt again. Tell me about Mrs. Cole."

"She has bruises on her neck. She tried to keep them covered just as in the past she has tried to keep me from seeing the bruises on her arms."

"We can't draw any conclusions from that," Jude said slowly.

"You may not be able to, but I can. I think that cold-eyed husband of hers is mean to her."

"Has she ever said anything?"

"No. She talks about him as if he was the most wonderful man in the world."

"Humm— What do you think we should do?"

"There probably isn't anything we can do as long as she keeps denying it. There's one more thing that has caused me to come to the conclusion that her husband abuses her."

"All right, Sherlock Holmes, what is it?" Jude enjoyed teasing her.

"Dale's son, Danny, stays with Mrs. Ramsey after school until Dale gets home. He was playing with Ryan and got pretty rough. He put his arm across his neck and held him against the wall. When Mrs. Ramsey got after him, he said he wasn't hurting Ryan, his daddy did it all the time."

"Did Mrs. Ramsey tell you this?"

"Yes, but she assumed Mr. Cole did this while playing with Danny. She didn't think it was the thing for a father to do even in play."

"I agree there. A little too much pressure could crush a windpipe."

"Dale is a natural-born nurse. She's dedicated, efficient, and soaks up knowledge like a sponge. I'm sure that with just a little study she could pass the nurses' exam. She was just a few months from graduation when she married Mr. Cole."

"Does she know that she's got such a good friend?"

"Now, there you go again." Theresa feigned annoyance.

"I like to tease you, Theresa. You're so pretty when you blush."

Theresa opened her mouth, then closed it. Her heart had jumped in her throat, making speech impossible. He was looking at her with warm, smiling eyes. He looked younger and less tired when he smiled. Determined to make light of the situation, she shoved the stack of patient charts in his hands.

"Go tell that to Mrs. Smothers. You may get her out of here in less than two hours."

# Chapter Twelve

Johnny stared at Kathleen when she answered his knock on her door. She was wearing the blue-silk negligee he had given her the Christmas before the baby was born. She appeared to be totally unaware of the effect it had on him.

"Johnny. Come in. Have you had breakfast?"

"Hours ago, but I'll take coffee if you have it made."

"It won't take a minute to make it. Meanwhile you can have some toast and Mrs. Ramsey's peach jam."

"I forgot that you drink tea." He followed her into the kitchen.

"Did you talk to Henry Ann?"

"She'll be here in the morning about ten-thirty. Would you mind picking her up?"

"Of course I don't mind. The bus stops at the *Gazette* office. I'll go early. I like Henry Ann and have from the minute I met her. I bet she misses Aunt Dozie."

"Aunty was like a mother to her and to me. I was on Bougainville in the Solomons when I got the letter that she had died. It shook me up. When I was a kid Aunty and

Henry Ann were the only two people in the world that gave a hoot about me."

"I wish I had known you then."

"Why? I had a chip on my shoulder the size of a boulder."

"And I would have tried to knock it off. How many pieces of toast?" Kathleen struck a match and lit the waist-high oven on the stove.

"How many do you have?" He grinned when she rolled her eyes to the ceiling.

"We'll start out with four, how's that?" She buttered the bread, arranged it in a flat pan, and slid it beneath the flame. "Coffee will be ready in a minute or two." She stood beside the stove, peeking at the toasting bread every few seconds.

Johnny was terribly conscious that all she had on beneath the negligee was her nightgown. Her feet were bare, and her hair was a mass of curls. He liked looking at her when her face was scrubbed and she wore not a trace of makeup. Lord, how he would like to tumble in bed with her and let her ease the ache as only she could. Thank God, he was sitting down and she couldn't see the lump that had suddenly appeared in his jeans.

"Whoops! I'd better get it out." Kathleen grabbed a potholder and pulled the pan from the stove. "A few seconds more and you'd have had burned toast."

"What are you going to have?"

"A piece of your toast with peanut butter, while more bread is toasting." When the toast was on a plate in front of him, she buttered more slices and slid them under the flame.

"It looks like I'm going to owe you a whole loaf of bread."

"You can pay me back . . . sometime."

When Kathleen sat down across from him, her knees came in contact with his beneath the small table. She moved them to the side and reached for the peanut butter. It seemed so natural to be sitting at the breakfast table with him.

*Johnny, Johnny, what happened to the love we once shared?*

He waited until they had finished eating before he told her about Gabe.

"You won't have to worry about Gabe Thomas anymore. He was killed last night."

"For goodness sake! What in the world happened?"

"He was taking parts off an old wreck of a car when it fell on him. Jude said it probably happened around midnight."

"I hate to hear it. He wasn't a very nice man, but he was someone's loved one."

"I was going to read the riot act to him this morning and threaten to break his neck if he came near you again. Fate stepped in and took care of it."

"I don't know what possessed the man to walk in here yesterday. It scared the life out of me to come out of the bathroom and find him in my living room."

"Lock your doors. Especially at night."

"We didn't even lock the doors out on the ranch."

"This is different. You're a good-looking woman living here by yourself."

"I don't feel good-looking. I feel like a clock that's running down. I'll soon be thirty-three years old."

"That's not old?"

"But . . . I feel old. Where has the time gone? Life is going by so fast." Tears came to her eyes. She blinked to hold them back, but they rolled down her cheeks. "Sorry—" Her eyes shone like stars.

"What's the matter? Why are you crying?"

"I'm . . . crying because . . . I'm just a silly woman."

Johnny was on his feet and reaching to lift her out of the chair. She wrapped her arms around his waist and hugged him to her. He stood for a minute holding her, then moved to the chair, sat down, and pulled her down on his lap. Her arms went up and around his neck. She burrowed her face into a broad shoulder that was soon wet with her tears. It felt so luxurious to be in his arms that she melted against him, loving the familiar feel of his hard body.

"Shhh . . . don't cry. Don't cry, honey—"

Sensitive fingers played lightly with the curls over her ears, then plunged into the soft masses to work gently at the nape of her neck. When her sobs ceased, he tilted her face to his and kissed her tear-wet eyes.

"Are you all right now?"

"No. I'm . . . getting old . . . and I—"

"Hush. You'll never get old. When you're sixty, you'll be as fiery as you are now." The words were murmured against her ear in such a tender voice that she cried again.

"But . . . I'll be alone . . . Johnny."

"No, honey—"

His mouth slid over hers. Kathleen closed her eyes and felt her lashes scrape his face before feathery kisses touched her lids, then moved across her cheek, searched for her mouth, found it and melted her lips to his. After the first deep pressure of his mouth he lifted it.

"Oh, God! Oh, God, honey—"

Then he made tender, adoring love to her mouth with warm lips and exploring tongue. He nibbled, licked, caressed until they both felt they were slipping into oblivion. He pulled on the bow at the neck of her nightdress, his hand burrowed inside to cup her naked breast, his thumb stroking the hard point. Kathleen's blood, suffused with fire, flooded riotously through her body. It suddenly wasn't enough and she wiggled to get closer.

"Be still, honey," he muttered urgently. "Be still or I'll not be able to stop. Dear God. It's been so long. I want to crawl inside you, feel every inch of you." He buried his face in the curve of her neck and took deep, gulping breaths. Their hearts beat together in thunderous pounding.

Kathleen wriggled again on the part of him that throbbed so aggressively beneath her hips.

"Don't stop. Please don't stop. I've dreamed every night of being with you like this. I love you. I'll always love you—"

"We . . . can't—" Desperately Johnny tried to fight down the desire that spiraled crazily inside him. "To hold you, touch you like this drives me crazy," he said in a strange, thickened voice, his mouth at her throat, then sliding up to close over her mouth hard and seeking. The searching movement parted her lips and he drank thirstily.

"Please, Johnny—"

"God help me for being such a weak son of a bitch," he snarled and stood with her in his arms. Long strides took him to the bedroom, where he placed her on the unmade bed and lay down on top of her, his mouth feasting on hers. The weight of him felt so good! She had missed, so much, the way he made her feel. This way, together, they relinquished control, and flew away into the sensuous world where there were only their hands, their lips, the hard strength of his male body and the softness of hers.

He wanted her, ached with the wanting.

"I shouldn't . . . I'll hate myself, but I have to—"

"I'm glad. I've never been anyone's but yours. Love me. Love me like you used to do. Make me forget everything but you."

"You're like a fire in my blood. I only have to think of you and I get like this." He brought her hand down to the hard and throbbing erection that was straining for release.

"I want to feel it. I want it in my hand—"

"I don't have a rubber—"

"It'll be all right—"

Between chopped breaths, he cursed with frustration. His desperation to be with her, inside her, made his hands clumsy. But finally, his jeans lay on the floor and he stretched out beside her, groaned, and rubbed his erection against her belly. She reached down and touched him, made a gentle fist with her hand, caressing, sliding, in the motion he taught her years ago.

He uttered a hoarse cry and burrowed, hard and urgent into the softness of her. He hesitated with momentary surprise at the tightness of the passage, then gave a swift thrust and embedded himself inside her with absolute possession. The pleasure was acute. The heat fierce. With his hands beneath her buttocks, he clutched her desperately, and made a moaning sound.

"I've missed you . . . missed you. Oh, Lord—"

She made a small helpless sound. "Open your eyes. Look at me. I love you—"

Dark eyes stared into blue ones. "Jesus! What am I doing to you?"

"Loving me. Don't stop." She raised her hips to meet his plunging strokes.

"I can't get enough of you," he groaned. "I can't get enough," he repeated.

Then, locked together they clung helplessly and surrendered to the sensuous void. The pleasure rose to intolerable heights, and she lost consciousness of everything but the powerful body that was driving her toward weightlessness. Her stomach clenched in fierce panic. She spun crazily, cried out wildly, and clung to the only solid thing in her tilting world.

Hands gently stroked her taut body. Soothing words calmed and reassured her. Her heart settled in to a quieter pace as the tension left her. Still joined to the man who had taken her heart, she began to cry.

"I'm sorry, honey. I'm sorry. I wanted you so damn bad—"

"Please . . . don't be sorry." She held his face in her hands and kissed him frantically. "I wanted you, too."

He withdrew from her, loosened his arms, and sat up on the side of the bed. "Go on. Go use the bathroom."

Kathleen slid out of the other side of the bed. She knew what he wanted her to do—sit on the toilet and let his sperm slide out of her in the hope that she wouldn't become pregnant. He needn't fear. She wouldn't be so lucky.

They had been married two years before she had conceived. At first Johnny had insisted that they use contraceptives because of their financial situation. But their appetite for each other had been so voracious that they had made love sometimes twice during the day and they didn't always take the necessary precautions.

Kathleen was elated. This was a new beginning. Johnny

hadn't said that he still loved her, but his tender loving of her said that he did. She washed, put a touch of toilet water behind her ears, and opened the door . . . to an empty bedroom. She hurried to the window to see Johnny's car going down the street.

She put her hand around her throat to ease the terrible ache there. She must not cry. If once she let herself weep, she would never stop.

"Johnny, Johnny." Her unsteady lips seemed unable to frame any other words. She felt sick and cold and terribly afraid.

Johnny cursed himself all the way to the clinic. When he got there, he sat in his car feeling nothing but contempt for himself. He had done the very thing that he had vowed not to do. He had exposed her to another heartbreak that could destroy her completely. And he let her think the door was open to the possibility of their having a future together.

She was lonely. She wanted a family. Hadn't she cried because she feared getting old and being alone? Christ on a horse! What had he been thinking of? She needed a clean break from him so that she could find someone who would give her the family she had always wanted. The thought of her with someone else was like a knife in his gut. He wasn't sure about what to do; but whatever it was, it'd have to wait until this thing with Isabel was over. In the meanwhile, he'd be careful not to be alone with her again.

Pete was in the reception room flirting with Millie when Johnny went into the clinic. Johnny was wearing what Pete called his Indian face.

"And good morning to you, too," he said cheerfully when Johnny didn't speak.

"How is Isabel?"

"I've not seen her yet. Reports aren't good."

"Henry Ann will be here tomorrow."

"You'd better prepare her for Isabel's nasty mouth. Even in her sleep last night, she spit out words I hadn't heard during sixteen years in the navy."

"Henry Ann's coming because it's what a decent person would do under the circumstances. If it upsets Isabel for her to be here, Henry Ann will know what to do." Johnny turned back to the door. "It upsets her to see me, too, so I'll go on back to the ranch and try to get some work done. I'll be back in tonight."

"I'll see how things are going here. If they put her under for a while, I'll come out and give you a hand."

Johnny nodded and left, leaving Pete puzzled as to the reason for his black mood.

"Mr. Perry," a nurse's assistant called from the doorway, "Nurse Frank said you can see Miss Henry now."

"Thanks, honey," Pete said, and winked. He then watched with pleasure the blush that covered the young girl's cheeks.

"Shame on you," Millie said after the girl disappeared down the hall. "She's young enough to be your daughter."

"But you're not . . . honey."

"No, and I'm old enough to know a rogue when I meet one." Millie stabbed at his chest with her pencil. "Flirt with someone your own age."

"And who might that be around here?"

"Theresa and Miss Pauley, the night nurse. Have you met her? I think the two of you would make a handsome pair." Millie pushed her glasses up on her nose, and poked the pencil into the thick gray hair over her ear.

"Flying catfish! That woman is sour as a lemon, cross as a bear, and is about as friendly as a case of the measles."

"Use that famous Perry charm on her. Who knows, with a kiss from the right man, Miss Pauley might turn into Betty Grable or Ginger Rogers."

"More than likely Marie Dressler or ZaSu Pitts," Pete grumbled, then walked away, grinning.

In the hallway he met Nurse Frank. Now, she was a pretty little thing, soft and sweet. Jude had told him that her husband had been killed during the war.

"Go on in, Mr. Perry. She's been sedated, but it hasn't taken effect yet or else it wasn't a big enough dose. Dr. Perry is afraid to give her too much because of her heart. Mrs. Cole is with her."

"My brother says she's going to die in a few days. Why can't you give her enough to let her sleep until the end?"

"Because it doesn't work that way. As long as there is life we must do what we can to prolong it."

"I guess I'm not quite as civilized as you and my brother."

The odor in the room was stronger this morning. He had smelled it at Johnny's and again in his car coming here. Jude said it was from the cancer that was eating away at Isabel's breast. Mrs. Cole looked over her shoulder when he opened the door, then adjusted a cloth over Isabel's upper body before she moved away.

"Get away from me, you . . . ugly bitch!" Isabel's voice was weak and slurred. "Where's Hardy? He'd take me . . . dancin'. Hardy is a son of a bitch. He screwed ever'thing on Mud Creek that moved. Even a rabbit, if he could catch one." Isabel turned her fevered eyes toward Pete. "You're a bastard, a cocksuckin' bastard. Know that?"

"Would you like a drink of ice water?" Pete asked.

"Hell no. I'll take a . . . cold beer. This broad-ass pussy here won't give me one. I want to . . . I want to go—" The words trailed away, but her mouth still worked as her eyes closed.

Mrs. Cole had turned her back and was putting the soiled bedclothes in a bag. Pete waited until she headed for the door, then stepped in front of her.

"I'm sorry you have to take this abuse." Pete put his hands on her upper arms. "Confound it. You shouldn't have to put up with this."

"Someone's got to. The poor thing doesn't realize what she's saying."

"I think she does." He tilted his head to look at her neck. "Dale! What happened to your neck. Did she grab you?"

"Heavens, no. She hasn't the strength." She attempted to go around him. "I've got to get this down to the laundry."

"If she didn't do this, who did? I've seen bruises like this before." He fitted his hand to the marks on her neck. She angrily knocked it away.

"Tend to your own business, Mr. Perry. What happened to my neck is no concern of yours."

Pete dropped his hand. "I'd like for it to be, Dale." He spoke so sincerely that her eyes caught his and held.

"I have a husband who looks after me, Mr. Perry."

"Did he do this to you?"

"No!"

"Is he out looking for the bastard who did? If you were

my wife, I'd hunt him down and take strips of hide off him. I'd make sure he never hurt another woman."

"But I'm not your wife—"

"No. I'd not be so lucky."

"I would appreciate it if you wouldn't make fun of me." Pete was shocked to see tears in her eyes.

"You . . . think that?"

"I know what I am, Mr. Perry. I am plain, overweight, and not a clever conversationalist. I know what you are, a man with a gift of gab. Also a flirt."

"What makes you think you're plain? It's what's on the inside of a woman that comes through and says whether she's plain or not. You may have a few extra pounds, but so what? I'd rather hold a soft woman in my arms than a bag of bones."

"Why are you telling me this?"

Pete ignored the question. "I had men come into the navy with an attitude like yours, and I sometimes found out that a father or a mother had constantly put the man down until he thought he wasn't worth anything. Is that happening to you?" he asked bluntly.

"I don't know what you're talking about. Please let me pass."

"Not until you promise me that you'll let me know if you ever need help. I'm going to stay here so I can be near my brother and my cousin, Johnny Henry."

"Why are you interested in my affairs?"

"Hell, I don't know. I just know I'm damn mad that some son of a bitch hurt you."

"I thank you for your concern." Dale lowered her eyes and then turned her head to look past him at the door as it opened. Jude stood there looking from one to the other.

"Excuse me, Doctor. I've got to get these down to the laundry."

Jude stepped aside, then came into the room and closed the door. He walked over to the bed and looked down at Isabel.

"I wish there was something I could do for her. There are so many things wrong with her that I don't know which to treat first." Jude picked up her limp wrist and felt her pulse.

"Johnny was here. He said that Henry Ann will be here tomorrow."

Jude nodded. He had seen death dozens of times, and it always affected him as if it were the first. He placed the thin hand back down at her side.

"She'll sleep now until early afternoon."

"She was talking about Hardy when I came in. Said that he would take her dancing. She talks mean to Mrs. Cole. I wish that she'd not do that."

"Mrs. Cole understands that sometimes a person in her condition is irrational."

"The woman's hurtin', Jude."

"Mrs. Cole?"

"Take a look at the bruises on her neck. Someone tried to squeeze the life out of her."

"I noticed as she passed me just now. Theresa told me about them."

"She denied that her husband hurt her. What do you know about him?"

"Nothing. He was here at the reception. Seems to be very personable. He works at the Gas and Electric Company. Office manager, I think."

"I might go down and have a little talk with him."

"You can't accuse him of anything." Jude looked at his

brother searchingly. Pete never could stand by and see a woman abused. He remembered Opal Hastings down on Mud Creek. If Pete had found out who raped her, he would have killed him. "What happens between a man and his wife is their business."

"Not if he's mistreating her."

"Even then, if she won't file charges. It's the law, Pete."

"Well, it's a shitty law."

"Theresa thinks Dale's husband mistreats her. She said Dale was crying this morning when she came to work."

"Did she say anything to Theresa?"

"No. She might sometime. They are good friends. Why are you taking such an interest in Dale? She's married and has a five-year-old boy."

"Hell, I don't know. She seems to be a damn nice woman who has a hell of a problem." Pete shoved his hands down into his pockets and walked out.

Jude watched his brother leave the room. In his youth Pete had been coarse, rude, and undisciplined. Mud Creek had never spawned another hell-raiser as wild as Pete Perry. Back then he would not have cared about Isabel. He would have voiced the view that she had made her bed and she'd have to lie in it. Nor would he have taken an interest in a woman who had a few bruises on her neck.

Pete had changed. War did that to a man.

# Chapter Thirteen

*T*heodore Nuding carefully stripped a length of paper from the wall of the room he was preparing for Kathleen. Looking at bright red-and-yellow roses climbing a white trellis day after day was bound to be annoying. Arranging a comfortable, safe room was taking much longer than he had at first believed. It had to be perfect for her to be happy here.

It was daylight now. He removed the pieces of carpet he used to cover the windows so that he could work at night without a light showing from the outside and stood back to admire the stout door he had put in place the night before. It would be necessary to keep Kathleen locked in until she became adjusted to being here. Then, like his mother, she wouldn't want to leave the room.

He washed, ate breakfast cereal, then set his alarm clock and lay down to sleep for a while. By noon he was parked on the rise outside of town with his weather-observing props in place should it be necessary for him to use them.

After scanning Kathleen's house with his binoculars

and seeing no movement there, he removed his notebook from the compartment beneath his seat and began to write.

*12:15 A.M. The timetable for bringing Kathleen to her new home will have to be moved to after Christmas. I am removing the old wallpaper and preparing the walls of her room for repapering. The room is next to the bathroom so I had only to close off one door and make another going out of her room. The fixtures are adequate. Later when I can have workmen here, I'll modernize the bath and maybe even put in one of those things French women sit on to wash their private parts. The furnishings in the house are of good quality, but for some things I'll have to make a trip to the city. I'll buy a lovely Persian rug, a few lamps, and other doodads that Kathleen will like. While I'm there I'll buy the best typewriter to be had and reams of paper so that when I have to leave her, she can amuse herself by writing her stories. I'll order toilet articles and a new wardrobe for her from Neiman Marcus. Only the best will do for my Kathleen.*

*Note: I was lucky last night. An opportunity fell in my lap to take care of a matter that could have consumed a lot more time than it did.*

"Adelaide! Come in."

"Brought you the latest *Gazette*."

"Thanks." Kathleen closed the door quickly behind her friend. "It's getting cold out there."

"It's that time of year. Thanksgiving will be here before we know it." Adelaide laid the paper on the table, headlines up, then took off her coat and draped it over the back of a chair.

*Johnny has been home for a month and I still don't know where I stand with him. What does he want from me?* Kathleen's next words were totally unrelated to her thoughts.

"When I was growing up in Iowa we always had snow before Thanksgiving."

"Over the river and through the woods to grandma's house?"

"My grandma always made a big deal out of Thanksgiving and Christmas. Grandpa would bring in a wild turkey for Thanksgiving and a goose for Christmas. They didn't have much cash money, but Grandma always set a good table."

"You're welcome to have Thanksgiving with me and Paul."

"Thanks. Barker and Marie mentioned my going to their place when they were here the other night. I'll let you know."

"Have you heard about Gabe Thomas getting killed?" Adelaide nodded to the headline.

"Johnny was here this morning and told me."

"This morning?" Adelaide raised her brows. "Early this morning? That's interesting—"

"—Don't let your imagination work overtime. Yesterday Gabe Thomas just walked into my house, as bold as brass, while I was washing my hair. I don't know where the man ever got the idea that I was interested in him. Anyway, he left when a fellow came to the door looking for someone. I told Johnny about it, and he was going to give him a talking-to this morning. He came by to tell me what had happened."

"I heard that you were out on the town last night with Johnny and Dr. Perry's brother."

"Oh, my goodness. You can't do anything in this town without it becoming gossip."

"Was it a secret?"

"No. Pete Perry is a nice man. Rough, but nice."

"Good-looking too, if you ask me. Why don't you use him to make Johnny jealous?"

"Adelaide, you'd be the first to flay me alive if I even suggested such a thing."

"I know, but at times I'd like to yank a knot in that guy."

"Johnny or Pete?" Kathleen plowed through her hair with all ten fingers, holding it off her face.

"Johnny. But I didn't come to talk about him. Well, maybe I did, but I want to talk about something else too."

"I'm all ears."

"I'm heading a committee to organize a fund-raiser to furnish a room at the clinic. They have only four rooms for overnight patients. Dr. Perry tells me that through a government program they will soon be getting an iron lung, and they need a room prepared to put it in. A boy from the southern part of the county died last summer before they could get him to a lung in Frederick."

"You don't have to sell me on the project. What do you want me to do?"

"We've come up with the idea of having a Christmas carnival at the school the week after Thanksgiving. We're asking all the church circles to have booths and sell crafts. The VFW will put on a barbecue. We will have a cake walk, a bingo room, a kissing booth."

"Count me out on that one."

"Chicken," Adelaide snorted.

"Paul wouldn't let *you* do it," Kathleen declared.

"Who'd want to kiss an old woman?"

"An old man."

"Want to bet? An old man wants to kiss something young. I wasn't going to ask you to be in the kissing booth. We're turning the gym into a ballroom and charging ten cents a dance."

"Good idea."

"A lot of men will come stag if they know they'll have someone to dance with. I want six of the prettiest girls in town to entice them to spend their money. If two or more men want to dance with the same girl, she'll go to the highest bidder."

"If you're asking me to be one of the *girls*. I'm not a *girl*, Adelaide. I'm old enough to have a *girl* in high school."

"You're one of the prettiest women in town. Say you'll do it. It's for a good cause."

"You're buttering me up . . ."

"Yeah, I am. I need you."

"What if no one wants to dance with me?"

"Are you dreaming? I'll have Paul keep an eye on you, and he'll see to it that you're not a wallflower. How's that?"

"Fine." Kathleen sighed. "I'll do it, even though I don't want to."

"Thank Jesus, Mary, and Joseph! Now there's just one more thing."

"I figured there would be."

"Don't be a sorehead. You'll be the most popular girl at the dance." Adelaide opened her notebook and scanned a list of names. "I'd appreciate it if you'd be on the committee to collect items for our auction to be held before the Christmas carnival."

"New or used?"

"Preferably new, but used if in good condition."

Kathleen glanced out the window. "Barker is here. You can hit him up for something."

Kathleen opened the door before he could knock. "Hello, Barker. Come in."

"Hello." He stepped inside. "Oh, hello, Adelaide."

"I was going to come out to see you today, Barker. You've saved me a trip."

"Better sit down, Barker. Adelaide is on one of her crusades."

"Marie took Lucas to the clinic this morning for a tetanus shot and heard that Johnny's sister, Isabel, is at the clinic."

"She's been there for a couple of days now. She's terminally ill, I'm afraid."

"I didn't know that she and Johnny had been in touch."

"As far as I know they haven't talked in years. I've never met her. She came to him because she was sick. He and a cousin took her to the clinic hoping Dr. Perry could do something for her. It's too late. She's dying."

"I'm sorry to hear it. What did you want to see me about, Adelaide?"

"Have you heard about our Christmas carnival?"

"Oh, yes. Janna has talked of nothing else."

"The teachers and the students are pitching in. Each room is going to do something to help us raise money. We want the families to have a good time. Will you donate an item from the tannery for our auction?"

"Of course."

"That's what I like to hear. I hate arguing with people to get them to cooperate." She glanced significantly at Kathleen.

"You didn't ask *him* to line up and wait for a lady to ask him to dance."

"I didn't ask you to wait for a lady to ask *you* to dance."

"I swear to goodness, Adelaide." Kathleen's tone was one of exasperation.

"I'm going. I've pushed as far as I can go today, but . . . I'll be back." Adelaide put on her coat. "As much as I'd like to stay and visit with you fine folks, I've got things to do."

"I'll be going, too," Barker said.

"Everyone is deserting me at once."

Adelaide paused at the door. "I just had a thought."

"Move back, Barker, this could be dangerous."

"Smarty. Why don't you write a Western story? Paul would set it on the linotype. We could sell autographed copies at the fair."

"No one would buy a story run off on newsprint."

"I think they would. When you're famous like Sinclair Lewis or John Steinbeck, an item like that would be worth a lot of money."

"Dream on, Adelaide."

"I think it's a good idea. I'd buy one," Barker said.

"You don't have to buy one of my stories, Barker. I get a dozen extra magazines from the publisher."

"Come down to the paper and go through the archives. Find something to write about that took place right here in Rawlings. Remember the story Doc Herman told us about the wife who met the woman on the street who had been sleeping with her husband, knocked her down and landed in jail for assault? That would be a good subject."

"I'll think about it. If I do it, will you let me off the list of dancing girls?"

"No, but I'll take you off the auction committee."

"You are taking advantage of our friendship."

"I sure am, sweetie!" Adelaide patted Kathleen's cheek. "Gotta go. 'Bye, Barker."

Barker lingered by the door after Adelaide left. "Has anything changed between you and Johnny?"

"I don't know. Sometimes I think he loves me and at other times I don't."

"Lucas keeps asking about him. It would be good for Lucas to get to know his brother. He thinks it's because we're Cherokee that Johnny doesn't want anything to do with him."

"That isn't it. It has nothing to do with Lucas. Right now he has Isabel to worry about, and he isn't sure how he's going to make a living on the ranch. He has applied for a GI loan. I'm not sure if he plans to use the money to buy cattle or more land. He won't use the money from the allotment check the government sent me while he was gone."

"I'd offer to help, but it would be like throwing gasoline on a fire." Barker's usually stoic features took on a look of sadness. "Come out anytime, Kathleen. We don't want to lose you, too."

Barker drove away from Kathleen's thinking about the day he told Johnny that he was his father. He hadn't known what reaction to expect, but certainly not the hostility he had received. Over the years his son had become less hostile, but the resentment was still there. Barker knew better than to jeopardize their fragile relationship by offering financial assistance. Johnny had grown up to be an angry man with strong feelings about most things.

When Barker walked into the reception room at the clinic, Millie looked up and smiled.

"Hello, Mr. Fleming."

"Hello, Mrs. Criswell."

"You're the third member of your family to be here today. Did Lucas suffer a reaction from his shot?"

"No. He's fine. I'd like to see Dr. Perry if he has a spare minute."

"I'll call the nurse—"

"—No, this is business."

"I see. I'll go back and see if the doctor can slip away for a few minutes."

Barker looked around as he waited. He remembered another time, seven years ago, when he had come to the clinic with Grant Gifford and two Federal Marshals to question Dr. Herman. The atmosphere was much friendlier now.

Millie returned. "It just so happens that the doctor is in his office." She went to the connecting door and rapped before she opened it. "Mr. Fleming to see you."

"Ask him to come in."

After shaking hands, the two men assessed each other. Grant Gifford had told Jude about Barker Fleming, rancher and owner of the tannery, and about his being Johnny's father. Jude remembered Johnny's being taunted by folks down on Mud Creek because of his Indian blood. This dignified, handsome man seemed to be a father any man should be proud to acknowledge.

"What can I do for you, Mr. Fleming?"

"You've known Johnny for many years." It was a statement. Jude nodded, and Barker continued. "I've known him for only seven," he said regretfully.

"We were fourteen when Johnny came to Red Rock, to stay with Ed and Henry Ann Henry. He had a chip on his shoulder a yard wide, but Ed Henry got around that by getting him interested in horses."

"I wish the man were here so that I could thank him."

"Johnny paid him back. After Ed died, Johnny worked like a son of a gun helping Henry Ann hold on to the farm."

"How is funding for the clinic going?" Barker asked, changing the subject abruptly.

"It's tight, but that's not unusual for a clinic in a town this size. We're getting a little government surplus, which is a great help, and the community is very supportive."

"My family has made a donation to the clinic each year for the past few. Absolutely anonymous, you understand."

Jude nodded. "It's appreciated."

"We are prepared to increase our donation this year, but with a string attached. I'll have our bank in Oklahoma City send a cashier's check so that the bank here will not know the donor."

"We would have no problem with that, if that's the condition."

"It is, and I'll explain."

Fifteen minutes later Jude walked to the door with Barker Fleming. "It was a pleasure to meet you, Mr. Fleming. You can be sure that your request will be carried out to the letter." He held out his hand.

"It was my pleasure," Barker said, shaking Jude's hand. "We would be honored to have you out to the ranch for dinner sometime soon." He smiled. "We're quite civilized. You'll not have to eat out of a communal bowl with your fingers as my ancestors did."

"I remember a time or two in Italy when I'd have been glad to eat out of a communal bowl." *And at home too, if my Pa had cared for me like you care for Johnny.* "I'll not forget the invitation."

"I'll have Marie or Mrs. Fisher give you a call. We appreciate your being here in Tillison County."

"And I'm glad to be here. Your donation will help us a great deal. All of us connected with the clinic thank you for it."

Jude sat at his desk for a few minutes after Barker left. A load had been lifted from his shoulders. Johnny Henry didn't know how lucky he was.

Johnny Henry worked the posthole digger as if he were trying to reach China before suppertime. Sweat dripped from the end of his nose even though the temperature was only 70 degrees. He dug the holes faster than Pete could set the posts.

"Slow down, dammit," Pete said gruffly. "Let's take a breather."

"What's the matter, sailor-boy? Have you gone soft in your old age?"

"You've been a hard dog to keep under the porch today and about as pleasant as a bobcat with a belly full of cockleburs." Pete sat down with his back to the post he had just set and pulled his cigarettes from his pocket. "What's eating you?"

"I'm anxious to get this done while I've got cheap help."

"I'll be around for a while. No need to work me to death today."

"It never occurred to me that you'd have a hard time keeping up with a youngster like me."

"She . . . it! We've set twenty posts. How many horses do you have anyway?"

"Keith tells me thirty head. But I owe him every other foal for taking care of them while I was gone. Hell, I might have to sell the damn horses anyway." Johnny sank on the ground and wiped his face with the sleeve of his shirt. "Keith will buy them."

"I thought you planned to build a herd from that stock."

"I did, but things have changed. I'll have quite a bill at the clinic, and then there's the burial. I'm thinking about giving up ranching for the time being and getting a job."

"What kind of jobs are to be had around here?"

"It doesn't have to be here."

"Yeah? I thought it did."

"The government is starting a rural electrification program up around Duncan. Eventually it'll work its way down here. I can operate heavy equipment. You name it, and I've driven it."

"What about Kathleen?"

"What about her?" Johnny looked up, his eyes boring into those of his friend.

"You don't plan to try and work things out with her? If you do, you can't do it while you're up around Duncan."

"Why do you ask?"

Pete shrugged. "Curious, I guess. She's special, and I like her."

A wave of sickness rose into Johnny's throat. He fought it down. Had Pete fallen in love with Kathleen? If so, Pete went after what he wanted and . . . he had a way of getting it. Henry Ann was the only woman Johnny knew that Pete hadn't charmed.

Johnny got to his feet. "I'll dig a couple more holes, then we'll stop for the day."

"Are you going back into town tonight?"

"Haven't decided."

"Before I go to the clinic, I'm going to stop by Kathleen's and pick up the magazines. I betcha I've read some of her stories. We had a load of Western magazines on board ship. They were read and reread until there was nothing left of them."

Watching Johnny, Pete noted that the posthole digger paused for a second or two on its way to the ground. He grinned with satisfaction.

"Okay, slave driver," Pete said, getting slowly to his feet. "You've worked the holy hell out of me today. I'll set three more posts, and then I'm on my way."

"Suit yourself," Johnny growled.

"Why don't you come along. I'm going to ask Kathleen to come over to Jude's for supper. I told him that I'd cook up a batch of corn bread to go along with the navy beans I cooked last night." Pete chuckled to himself when he saw that Johnny was now wearing his Indian face. Not a flicker of expression was on it.

Pete continued to ramble on while he worked.

"I never had a decent piece of corn bread all the time I was in the navy. I asked the chief cook about it one time when we were sitting out from the Marshalls. He said that if I didn't like what he baked, I could throw it overboard for all he cared." Pete snorted. "That bread would've sunk a Jap sub if I'd a been lucky enough to hit it. Hell, I can make better corn bread with my eyes shut than those belly robbers that call themselves cooks."

He watched Johnny attack the hole he was digging as if he were digging for gold.

*The darn fool is eating his heart out for her and is too damn stubborn to admit it.*

# *Chapter Fourteen*

"*Y*ou staying at Jude's or coming back out here?" Johnny asked as he finished pouring water into the wash dish and hung a towel over Pete's shoulder.

"Is that an invite?" Pete dipped his hands in the water and splashed his face.

"Yeah, I guess so."

"Are you going to the clinic in the morning?"

"I thought I'd go in about noon. Henry Ann's bus will be pulling in then."

"I'll help string the wire on those posts."

"It won't take more than a couple of hours." Johnny took off his shirt and headed to the bedroom to change his clothes.

"Henry Ann hasn't changed much," Pete remarked on the way to town.

"You still carrying a torch for her?" Johnny turned to look at him sharply.

"Yeah. I'll always have a soft spot in my heart for

Henry Ann. She was the driving force that made me want
to be more than Mud Creek trash."

"Don't be getting any ideas about Henry Ann."

Pete laughed. "Hell, if I did, she'd slap me down
quicker than a goose shittin' apple seeds. Don't worry. I'm
still more in awe of her than anything else. When I was
young, she was my idea of a queen. I'd act the fool to get
her attention. Couldn't stand it when she ignored me."

"She's more than a sister to me. She's—" Johnny
stumbled for words, then became quiet as he remembered
the hard times on the farm back in '32 when he and
Henry Ann were trying to save their cotton crop and Isabel was doing everything she could to make their lives
miserable.

They reached town and Pete turned down the street
where Kathleen lived. He slowed when he noticed a
woman hurrying along the sidewalk.

To Johnny he said, "It's Mrs. Cole. She's the nurse taking care of Isabel." He slowed the car, stuck his hand out,
and waved.

Dale managed a slight wave of the hand, kept her eyes
straight ahead, and hurried on.

"Know anything about her husband?" Pete asked.

"Only what Paul told me. The guy works for Oklahoma Gas and Electric, and he's a real horse's ass."

"Yeah? In what way?"

"According to Paul, he's not very well liked by the
men who work there."

"I think he's mean to his wife. If I find out it's true, I'll
catch him out some dark night and beat the shit out of
him."

"Christ on a horse, Pete. You've not changed much
after all."

"Nothing gets my dander up quicker than a man who beats up a woman or a kid. Far as I'm concerned, they're not fit for buzzard bait."

A pickup truck with a bedstead and a mattress was parked at Kathleen's house when they reached it. When Johnny snorted on seeing it, Pete glanced very quickly at him, frowned slightly, and looked away, then back again, as if puzzled.

"You don't approve of your wife's company?"

"It's none of my business who she keeps company with." Johnny opened the door and stepped out of the car.

"I'm glad to hear that. I was afraid you'd poke me in the nose if I asked her out on a date."

Johnny, rounding the car, paused. "Don't try to add Kathleen's name to your string of women, Pete."

"String of women? Hell, son, I ain't got no string. I ain't got even one woman."

Pete followed Johnny up onto the porch. The door was open. Johnny could hear Kathleen laughing. He opened the screen door and banged it shut to get her attention. She came through the living room from the kitchen, Barker behind her.

"Johnny, Pete, come in. Barker brought in a bed for me to use while Henry Ann is here. Pete, have you met Barker? Barker Fleming, Pete Perry. Pete is Dr. Perry's brother." Kathleen made the introductions, then stepped back. After the first glance at Johnny, she didn't look at him again.

The men shook hands, then Barker said, "How'er you coming with your corral, Johnny?"

"Good. Pete's given me a couple days' work."

"If you need help driving the horses up from Mc-Cabe's, let me know. Lucas and I will lend a hand."

"That's on hold for a while." Johnny looked directly at Kathleen. "Need help setting up that bed?"

"Sure. Barker hasn't brought it in yet. We were moving things around to make room for it."

The men went to the pickup. Pete and Johnny carried in the springs, Barker the foot- and headboards. Kathleen held open the door. Pete winked at her as he passed. It was more of a conspiratorial wink than a flirtatious one. She smiled.

Barker went back to the truck and brought in the bed rails and the slats while Johnny and Pete set up the bed. Kathleen watched. Pete was one of the most cheerful men she had ever met. His eyes flirted, his smile was continuous. He laughed at himself when Johnny told him that he was putting the side rails on upside down. There was a suggestion that, though he was probably slow to anger, he would make a very dangerous enemy when roused. Kathleen was sure that there was enough strength in his big, well-knit body to support that notion.

When the telephone rang, she hurried to answer it.

"Kathleen, this is Marie. Is Daddy there?"

"He's here. I'll get him. Barker, it's for you."

Kathleen stood in the doorway of the small bedroom while Barker spoke with his daughter.

"I didn't think about you having to get another bed when I asked if Henry Ann could stay with you." Johnny spoke as he tightened the nut on a bolt with the pliers Barker had left on the floor.

"I was talking to Marie on the phone and mentioned that your sister was coming. It was her idea to send over the bed."

Barker finished his conversation and hung up the

phone. "I have to go. One of the men has been hurt, and they need the truck to take him to the clinic."

"Not serious, I hope."

"Marie thinks it is, but then she's quite upset. We won't know until the doctor takes a look. The mattress is all that's left in the truck. I'll get it."

"I'll get it." Johnny was already out the door.

"Thanks, Barker," Kathleen called.

"Johnny's daddy, huh?" Pete said from behind her.

"Yes. Johnny has had a hard time accepting him."

"Why? Because he's an Indian?"

"Not that. He feels that he was just a seed sown in the wind, so to speak."

"That's nothing new. My pa had kids scattered all up and down Mud Creek as his pa had done before him."

"Did that make you think less of him?"

"I didn't think of it at the time. It seemed normal for Mud Creek."

"But did you . . . like him?"

"I respected his fists until I got to be as big as he was and learned to fight back. He treated me all right after that." He pinched her chin with his thumb and forefinger. "I'd better go help big, bad John with the mattress."

"He isn't bad," Kathleen protested, and got a grin from Pete.

After the bed was set up, Johnny went to take a look at the water heater.

"I'll come by with some tools and fix the pilot," he said when he returned.

"How about the Western magazines you were going to lend me?" Pete asked. He had noticed that Johnny and Kathleen avoided looking directly at each other. Something had changed since last night.

"I keep three copies of each," Kathleen said, as she placed a stack of magazines on the kitchen table. "Take what you want, but I would like them back."

"K.K. Doyle," Pete said admiringly and smiled his charming smile. "Did you really write these stories? If the boys had known that K.K. Doyle was a beautiful redhead, they would've been writin' for your picture."

"Not true, but it's nice of you to say so." Kathleen's face reddened. She glanced at Johnny.

"I've not read this one." He was gazing intently at the cover of *Western Story Magazine* that displayed her nom de plume in large print.

"That one takes place in the Texas panhandle and is one of the longest stories I've written. I just couldn't seem to end it. I try to move my stories around to different locations. The one I'm working on now is set in Montana."

Kathleen stood beside the table, terribly conscious that Johnny was standing beside her. She could feel the warmth from his body and smell the lotion he had put on his face after shaving.

*He's sorry that we made love. He must feel that it was my fault for clinging to him like a cheap floozy. And, I guess it was. I wanted him to love me.*

Suddenly she was aware that she was terribly afraid and didn't know why. It was something to do with Johnny. Everything was something to do with Johnny nowadays. When her eyes flicked to him, he was thumbing through the magazine, apparently oblivious to everything except what he was reading. *Look at him read! How did he learn to do that?*

"Get your bonnet and come have supper with us. I'm cookin' tonight." Pete's cheery voice sliced into her thoughts.

"You're cooking? Where?"

"At Jude's. I'll make you the best corn bread you've ever eaten to go along with the navy beans I cooked last night."

"Thank you, but I don't think so."

"Don't think, sugar. Just come. You'll not be sorry."

"I don't know your brother that well."

"You know me, and you sure as hell know Johnny. Come now, grab a coat."

"I can't go anywhere looking like this."

"You look damn good to me."

Kathleen glanced at Johnny and found him looking at her with indescribable sadness in his dark eyes. She took a hesitant step toward him before she could stop herself.

"Johnny?"

"You'll like Jude when you get to know him."

"I'm . . . sure I will."

"We'd better get going. We'll need to stop at the clinic and see about Isabel." Pete picked up several magazines. "I'll take good care of these."

"If someone is needed to sit with her at night, I'll take a turn."

"No," Johnny said quickly and emphatically. "I don't want you anywhere near Isabel."

"He's right," Pete said quickly when he saw the hurt look on Kathleen's face. "If you were my girl, I'd not want you near her either. I doubt that you've met anyone like Isabel."

"That's silly! I've heard bad language—"

"Are you coming to Jude's for supper?" Johnny asked, cutting off the argument.

"Will I be intruding on your time with your friends?" she asked boldly, looking directly at him.

"What gave you that idea?"

"Why do you always answer my questions with a question. It's terribly irritating."

Johnny shrugged, apparently unconcerned that he had angered her.

Kathleen ignored him. She headed for the bedroom, then turned, "I'd love to have dinner with you, Pete. Be back in a minute."

She sat between the two men in the front seat of the car. This time Pete was driving and it was Johnny's arm that was flung along the top of the seat behind her. His hand had rested on her shoulder briefly, then was quickly removed.

Down the street from Kathleen's a porch light was on and a small boy sat on the steps. Pete slowed the car.

"Is that where Mrs. Cole lives?"

"I think so."

"Do you know her?" Pete asked.

"I've met her a couple of times. She seems to be very nice."

"She's one of the nurses who takes care of Isabel."

Nothing more was said until Pete stopped the car behind Barker's truck parked at the clinic.

"Goin' in, sugar?" Pete asked Kathleen because Johnny had already opened the door.

"Might as well. I'll wait in the reception room."

Johnny waited on the sidewalk and, to Kathleen's surprise, took her elbow. She thought she heard him mumble something that could have been 'sugar'?

*My gosh! Is he jealous of Pete? Oh, Lord. I hope so. That would prove that he still loves me!*

Marie was the only person in the room when they opened the door. She jumped to her feet, went straight to

Johnny, and wrapped her arms around his waist before he could even get his hat off. Her face was streaked with tears.

"Oh, Johnny. It's all my fault."

"What's your fault?" he asked gently and, with his hands on her shoulders, held her away from him.

Of all the Flemings, this little half sister had been the one who crept past his resistance and wiggled her way into his heart. She had written to him faithfully all the time he was overseas, sent him cartoons, newspaper clippings, and funny stories.

"He was on that darned old stallion Daddy bought the other day and . . . and I went out as he was getting him into the pen, the wind blew my skirt, and . . . the horse went wild. He threw Bobby against the fence—"

"—Who?"

"Bobby Harper. His leg is broken, and his face—it's all cut up. He's not been home very long. Daddy gave him a job—"

"A broken leg is something that can be fixed. Dry up, now. Who's back there with him?"

"Daddy and Mr. Boone."

"The foreman?"

"No, his son. Mr. Boone isn't well, and Mack has been doing most of the work. Kathleen, I didn't even speak to you—"

Kathleen was pleased and surprised at how concerned and gentle Johnny was with Marie.

"Don't worry about that. Marie, this is Dr. Perry's brother, Pete. Marie is Johnny's sister," she explained to Pete, without looking at Johnny.

"Hello, I'm sorry for being such a crybaby. Johnny"— Marie was still holding on to him—"go back and see if he's all right. They told me to stay here."

"Stay with Kathleen. I'll see what I can find out." Johnny gently pushed Marie down into a chair and placed his hat on the seat beside her.

Pete followed Johnny down the hall. "Guess I didn't think of you having sisters on your daddy's side. That one is pretty as a picture."

"And way too young for you."

Pete took Johnny's arm and stopped him. "Let's get one thing straight, Bud. I can think a woman is pretty without wanting to hop in bed with her."

"I remember when she didn't even have to be pretty."

"You're not going to let go of that, are you? I admit that I was plenty mouthy when I was going over *fool's hill*, but I didn't do all that I bragged about doing. If I'd had a little sister like Marie, I'd have knocked every man on his ear that looked at her cross-eyed."

"I didn't notice you looking at her cross-eyed or I would've." Johnny grinned and hit Pete on the shoulder. "Let's see what we can find out for her."

Sitting on a couple of chairs at the end of the hall were Barker and Mack Boone. Johnny had never liked Mack. Before the war he had been a hard-drinking, reckless cowboy who had wanted to make it big in the rodeo circuit but had fallen short. Johnny had made it a habit to steer clear of him.

Barker got to his feet as they approached. Mack slouched in the chair, stretched out his legs, and crossed his booted feet.

"How's Harper? Marie's worried about him."

"We don't know yet. The doctor and nurse are with him."

Mack got to his feet. "I'll go stay with Marie."

Johnny moved slightly and stood in front of him. "No need. Kathleen is with her."

Mack's expression hardened into anger. It irked him that Johnny Henry stood so close he had to look up at him. He lifted his shoulders, stared at Johnny for a few seconds, and sat down. He was smart enough not to make a fuss in front of the boss.

Everyone in town knew that Johnny was Barker's bastard. The mystery was why Johnny didn't move into the big house and live high on the hog. That was what Mack was going to do as soon as he married Marie. It was too damn bad Bob Harper hadn't broken his neck instead of a leg. It was what Mack had wished for when he hit that stallion in the rear with his slingshot. It served Bob right for getting cozy with Marie.

Mack was not an ugly man, nor was he handsome. His eyes were too small and deep-set, his brows too heavy. He wore his hair long and combed back in a ducktail, a style he copied from the zoot-suiters he saw while he was stationed in California. He considered himself to be quite attractive to the ladies.

Miss Pauley, the night nurse, came out of Isabel's room. Pete and Johnny went to intercept her.

"How is Miss Henry?" Johnny asked.

"How do you think she is?" Miss Pauley said bluntly. "With all that's wrong with her, I'm surprised that she's still alive."

"Is she going to die tonight?" Johnny asked irritably.

"How do I know? Talk to Dr. Perry."

"Thank you," Johnny said with exaggerated patience and, to her back as she hurried down the hall, "You're a big help."

"She's a sour mouth, but Jude said she's a crackerjack nurse. I bet you a dollar to a doughnut that Isabel has been giving her a bad time." Pete went to the door of Isabel's room and listened, then came back to Johnny. "She's not yelling, so she must be sleeping."

Nurse Frank came out of the surgery and propped open the door.

"The leg has been set, but we'll need help getting him off the table and onto a gurney so we can move him to a room. The doctor wants to keep him overnight."

Mack got to his feet, but Pete moved smoothly ahead of him and into the room.

"I'll give you a hand. I've done this many times on board ship."

Nurse Frank motioned to Johnny. "It's hard for the doctor to lift because of his leg," she whispered when he came near to her. He followed Pete into the room.

In spite of the cuts on his face and a bandage on his forehead Johnny recognized the man on the table. He had been just a kid from a neighboring ranch when Johnny went to war.

"Hi, Bob."

"Johnny. Haven't seen ya since ya come back." He spoke out of the side of his mouth because of the stitches on his cheek.

"See you had a bout with a barbed-wire fence."

"He's lucky he didn't lose an eye," Jude said, washing his hands at a sink.

The nurse had pulled the gurney up alongside the bed. "If you two will get on the other side of the bed, slip both arms beneath and lift him while I pull on the sheet, we can slide him onto the gurney."

"The plaster isn't dry, so we'll have to be careful." Jude went to the end of the table to lift the foot of the plaster-encased leg. "After we get you into the room, we'll give you something so you can sleep."

"Before you do that would it be all right if Marie come in to see him?" Johnny asked. "She feels bad because she spooked the horse."

"It wasn't her fault," Bobby protested quickly. "I just wasn't anchored in the saddle. And . . . it's what I get for showin' off."

His face paled, but he didn't let out a sound as he was shifted from the table to the gurney and then to a bed. He lay in a white undershirt stamped US AIR FORCE. A sheet covered all but his broken leg which Jude had placed in a troughlike contraption so that he couldn't move it. The nurse returned with a hypodermic syringe and needle.

"It takes about fifteen minutes for this to take effect," she explained.

"I'll get Marie," Johnny said.

As he went out the door, he passed a scowling Mack Boone, who had stayed in the hall when Barker went into the room.

Marie had calmed when Johnny reached the reception room. Both she and Kathleen got to their feet when he entered.

"He's all right. He'll stay overnight so the plaster on the cast can harden. You can go see him."

"Oh, Johnny, thank you." Impulsively she hugged him, the top of her head a couple of inches beneath his chin. "Where do I go?"

"Go on down the hall. The door is open, and they know that you're coming."

# Chapter Fifteen

Kathleen thought that Johnny would go with Marie, but he lingered and finally sat down.

"Did you find out anything about Isabel?"

"Couldn't get anything out of the nurse. I'll have to ask Jude."

Silence settled down in the reception room so that the closing of a door in the back of the clinic sounded aggressively loud in the stillness.

"Marie was telling me about Bobby Harper," Kathleen said when she could stand the silence no longer. "She said that he was a gunner in the air force. He came home about the same time you did."

"He was just a kid when I left."

"Evidently he was old enough for the service. Marie said he enlisted when he got out of high school."

"Are they keeping company?"

"She didn't say. Why? Don't you approve of him?"

"I don't know him and, besides, it isn't any of my business who she keeps company with."

"Oh, Johnny," Kathleen said wearily. "You try so hard to distance yourself from anyone who cares about you."

Before he could reply, Barker and Mack Boone came in, followed by Pete and Marie.

"Daddy, I told Bobby we'd come back for him tomorrow, but I don't know how he can ride in a car with that leg in a cast."

"We'll think of something. Right now I've got to go tell his folks what happened."

"I completely forgot about that. Mrs. Harper should have been told right away."

"Take the truck back, Mack."

"I can take Marie with me, Mr. Fleming."

"Marie will go with me," Barker said, dismissing him. "And thanks for your help."

Mack left. Johnny knew that he was seething. His face was as easy to read as a road map.

"I've talked Theresa into coming and having supper with us," Pete announced. "How about it, Marie? Come have supper with us. We're all going over to Jude's. Johnny and I will take you home before we go back to the ranch."

Johnny looked at Pete and, for once, surprise showed in his expression. No one seemed to notice but Kathleen. Her heart beat high in her throat as she waited for Johnny's reaction.

"Oh, I don't know—" Marie fumbled for words, her dark expressive eyes traveling between her father and Johnny.

"You'll be well chaperoned by big brother here," Pete urged. "What'a ya say?"

Barker waited for his daughter's decision.

"All right. I'd like to go, if it's all right with you, Daddy."

"Johnny?" Barker looked at his tall son.

"I'll see her home," Johnny said, his mouth very grimly set. Again, none of the others seemed to notice.

Dr. Jude Perry's house was one of the finest houses in town. Built back in the prosperous 1920s, its rooms were large, its woodwork gleaming oak. Although the furnishings were the original and some of them needed to be replaced, the gas stove and refrigerator were new. Swinging doors, propped back, separated the kitchen from a formal dining room that would seat twelve.

The house, lacking personal possessions such as pictures, books, or other mementos, seemed cold to Kathleen. She wondered if the doctor noticed. Perhaps this was just a place to eat and sleep after he left the clinic.

Pete took over the cooking chore and made two large pans of corn bread. Kathleen found a head of cabbage in the refrigerator and chopped it with carrots and onions to make coleslaw. Theresa and Marie set the table.

Jude was tired, and his leg ached. That was evident in the lines in his face and in the way he absently rubbed his thigh. Theresa insisted that he sit and visit with Johnny. She had been disappointed to learn that Marie Fleming had been invited. Theresa felt heavy and awkward beside her. But to her surprise, the small dark-haired girl was not just a beauty; she was also nice.

As the evening progressed, Johnny loosened up a bit. He had asked Jude about Isabel and was told that her condition continually worsened and that the only thing they could do for her was to keep her as comfortable as possible.

"The Nuremberg military trials start tomorrow," Jude said after a moment of silence. "We'll probably hear only the verdicts."

"Paul, down at the *Gazette*, was telling me that before long transoceanic radios will be as common as a regular radio, and we'll hear everything that goes on all over the world."

"I'm probably like the ostrich with its head in the sand, but I don't want to hear the gory details of the trial. I've seen what the Nazis were capable of doing."

After that, Johnny and Jude talked about old times and both carefully avoided any mention of their experiences during the war.

"I'm eager to see Henry Ann," Jude said. "I'll never forget the two of you coming down to Mud Creek with blood in your eye because you suspected Hardy of rustling your cattle."

Johnny laughed. "We had more guts than sense. I don't know what I'd have done if your pa had grabbed me out of that car and wiped the ground with me."

"He wouldn't have done that. Hardy was scared of what Pete would do. Pete didn't want you to know it at the time, but the folks on Mud Creek knew that you and Henry Ann were off-limits and not to be bothered."

Johnny chuckled. "Not by anyone but him, huh?"

"All right you two," Kathleen said. "Get yourselves to the table."

Kathleen found the evening one of the most pleasant she had spent in a long time. They ate the corn bread and teased Pete that it wasn't fit for hogs and that the only thing good enough to eat was the coleslaw. He took the ribbing with his usual good humor. When the meal was over, the girls cleared the table and washed up the dishes.

"Now I know why they asked us to come for supper," Kathleen said as she hung up the dish towel she took from Theresa.

"I'll have to be going soon and get my little boy. I called Mrs. Ramsey, and she said that she'd give him his supper. He plays hard and is usually asleep by the time I get him undressed."

"How old is he?"

"He's four and big for his age."

"I'd like to see him sometime," Kathleen said wistfully. *Mary Rose would have been almost five if she had lived.*

"He's a handful at this age. I measured him when he was two years old. If it is true that he will be twice that height when he is grown, he's going to be six feet tall. Imagine me looking way up there at my little boy." Theresa's smile was beautiful.

"Aren't you through in here yet?" Pete demanded from the doorway. "You're holding up the rest of the program."

"And what is that?"

"Come on. You'll see."

The furniture had been pushed back, and from the radio came the signature tune of President Truman, "The Missouri Waltz."

"I should be going," Theresa protested.

"Not until I've danced with each of you beautiful ladies." Pete grabbed Kathleen's hand. "That's old Harry's favorite song." He swung her around the floor. Their laughter mingled with the music. "Jude, you and Johnny grab a girl. This one's mine for this dance and the next."

Theresa's heart jumped out of rhythm and her breath caught as Jude got to his feet and held his hand out to *her*.

She had been sure that he would prefer to dance with young and pretty Marie.

"Nurse Frank, would you honor me with this dance?"

"I'd be delighted, Doctor. But I must warn you, it has been years and years since I danced."

"Then it is time you did."

He pulled her to him and they moved slowly. It would have been all right with Theresa if they had not moved at all. When he lowered his head and pressed his cheek to hers, she closed her eyes, and her heart settled down into slow heavy thuds.

The music ended. She leaned back and whispered. "Your leg."

"What leg?" he said, and pulled her tighter against him as the music started up again and a female vocalist began to sing, *"I'll never smile again, until I smile at you—"*

"Do you want to try it, Marie?" Johnny asked when he saw her effort to fade into the background. "Come on. I'll try not to break your toes."

Marie was so small that her head barely reached Johnny's shoulder. He held her lightly and tried to keep his mind on the steps and not on Pete and Kathleen, who were talking and laughing as if they were having the time of their lives. He was sure that Pete was not interested in an affair with Marie, but he wasn't sure about Kathleen or Jude's Nurse Frank.

When the dance ended, Pete reached for Marie and Jude held out his hand out to Kathleen.

"It's the luck of the draw," Johnny said as he put his arm around Theresa and they began to move to the music. "I've never been much of a dancer."

"I've not done it a lot myself, so we'll be well

matched. I'll try not to step on your toes if you promise not to step on mine."

"Lady, I can't promise a thing." He smiled down at her. She was a soft, sweet woman and pretty even in that white uniform, white stockings, and heavy shoes.

The dance ended. Kathleen stepped back from Jude, not sure if Johnny would want to dance with her. On the radio the announcer was saying that this was the last number of the evening and to tune in next week for another hour of dance music. She felt a hand on her arm as Jude reached out for Marie.

Johnny pulled her into his arms. She went willingly and leaned against him. It was so good to be held by him. His arms encircling her pulled her so close that her breasts were crushed against his chest. They fit perfectly against each other. She could feel the warmth of his body through her dress, and the wild beating of her heart against his. Was his breath coming faster than usual or was it just wishful thinking on her part?

*"Good night, sweetheart, till we meet tomorrow. Good night, sweetheart, sleep will vanish sorrow—"*

Johnny pressed his cheek tightly to hers. Kathleen felt as if she was in another world. She closed her eyes and wished the song would never end.

But it did, and he pulled away from her.

"It's late. I don't like the idea of Theresa going to pick up Ryan by herself," Jude was saying.

"Doctor! I do it all the time." Theresa was putting on her coat.

"Not at eleven o'clock at night. I'd go with you, but I shouldn't leave the telephone."

"Don't worry, little brother." Pete picked up his coat

and handed Johnny his. "We'll follow Theresa and make sure she gets home."

"You don't need to do that," Theresa protested.

"Yes, he does," Jude insisted. "See you in the morning." Then he said to everyone in general, "This has been great. Come again, all of you."

"How about Thanksgiving?" Pete said. "I'll cook a turkey."

"I couldn't leave the family." Marie's dark eyes went from Johnny to Kathleen.

"Do you have plans, Theresa?" Jude asked.

"Why no. I'd love to come, but only if I can bring part of the dinner."

"That can be decided later. You and Johnny can come, can't you, Kathleen?" Jude stood at the door, waiting for his guests to put on their coats.

"I can, but I can't speak for Johnny." Kathleen was sure that her face was fiery red.

"He'll be here," Pete said confidently. "Wave a drumstick under that boy's nose, and he'll jump fences and wade across raging rivers to get to it."

Kathleen sat in the backseat of Pete's car with Marie as they followed Theresa's small car to Mrs. Ramsey's house. This was where she had boarded when she arrived in Rawlings seven years ago. Johnny had come to the newspaper office and had shown her the way. She wondered if he remembered.

Without a word, Johnny got out of the car and went to the house with Theresa. Soon they emerged, with Johnny carrying the sleeping child. Mrs. Ramsey waved from the doorway. Kathleen wanted to cry. He had never held their child in his arms.

If he married Theresa, he would have a son without

having to sire one and risk the deformity he feared. In the back of her aching mind she doubted that she was strong enough to endure the pain. If that should happen, she would never be able to go far enough from this place to forget him. Her heart would be broken.

He didn't come back to the car. He sat in Theresa's car, holding the child, and she drove to her house. Pete followed. Johnny carried the boy inside and came out immediately. He got into the car, turned to her, and said, "Mrs. Ramsey said to tell you hello and to thank you for lending Emily the books."

"It was nothing," Kathleen murmured.

"You'll have to show me the way to the Fleming ranch," Pete said.

Johnny got out again to walk Marie to the door. Johnny thought he smelled cigarette smoke as if someone nearby was smoking.

"This was so much fun. Thank you for telling Daddy you'd bring me home. Johnny . . . if you don't go to the doctor's house for Thanksgiving, will you come here? We were going to ask you and Kathleen."

"I'll have to go to Jude's. My sister, Henry Ann, may still be here, and that would be the logical place for us to go."

"I understand. You'll want to be with her as much as you can. Just don't forget that we want you, too."

"I won't forget."

Marie opened the door and slipped inside. Johnny stood for a second or two. He could feel that someone was near. It was the same sort of feeling he'd had while he was in the jungles of the Pacific. Usually the person had been a native, but a few times it had been a Jap who wanted to surrender but was afraid to show himself for fear of being shot, or a Jap spying on the camp. Johnny's eyes searched the darkness, seeing nothing. He went quickly back to the car.

Mack Boone stood flat against the wall of the house. He hadn't been able to hear what was said, but he knew that it was Johnny Henry with Marie. The old man's bastard was playing his cards close to his chest. The son of a bitch was planning to come out here and take over. Well, he, Mack Boone, was going to do his level best to see that it never happened. He had a few cards up his sleeve that he could play.

Kathleen went through the house one last time to make sure everything was in order before she left for town to pick up Henry Ann. She had seen Johnny's sister just a few times, the last before Mary Rose was born, but she felt that she had known her forever.

Kathleen had had a restless night and had risen early to sit at her kitchen table, drink tea, and think about the night before. Johnny had walked her to the door, held the screen while she put the key in the lock, then said good night and backed off the porch as if to get away from her as soon as possible.

He's afraid that he's made me pregnant, she thought now. He needn't worry. The chance of it happening that one time was one in a hundred, and she had never won anything in her life. One thing was sure. He was going to see to it that he didn't tempt fate again. He had made that clear by his actions.

She went to her car, thankful that the bad tire still had air in it. She would go to Eddie's and see if he could put on another tire or patch the one she had.

\* \* \*

From the rise above, Theodore Nuding watched Kathleen leave the house. Last night while she was at the doctor's house, he had taken his tire pump to her house and filled the tire as full of air as he dared because it would lose some before morning. Then, knowing that she was safe, he had gone back to work on her room.

He put down his binoculars, pulled his diary out from under the seat of the car, and began to write.

> *10:20 A.M. She is leaving the house. I believe that she is going to have company because the Indian brought a bed last night. It could be a relative coming to see that slutty woman who is in the clinic. I heard from the cleaning people that she was dying. Good riddance, I say. She was a whore who was taking up space and breathing good air that could be used by someone decent.*
>
> *The room is coming along, Mother. I wish I knew someone I could trust to help me. This small town isn't like the city. I have to be very careful and not draw attention to myself. The banker, John Wrenn, is the only weak link. He's ignorant, nosy, and likes to talk. If one word about me is leaked, it will be curtains for him.*
>
> *Mother, I miss you. But soon I'll have Kathleen, and my life will be full of joy again.*

Nuding read over what he had written, then quickly shoved the diary under the seat as a car approached, slowed, and stopped. It was Sheriff Carroll. Nuding grabbed his *props*, got out of the car, and stretched.

"Morning, Sheriff."

"Morning. How's it goin'?"

Nuding laughed. "Boring. Tornado season is about over. Another month will wind up my work here unless the bureau calls me in early." He shifted an instrument gauge and a chart clipped to a board to his other hand.

"We don't get much cold weather here until January. Out in the panhandle a northerner blows in once in a while."

"It's getting easier to predict them. Gives a fellow a little time to prepare."

"Where did you say you were from?"

"Louisiana."

"I was thinking you were from Texas. I don't know where I got that idea." Sheriff Carroll scratched his gray head.

"I may have said that. I guess I thought you meant where did I come from before I came here."

"Well, no matter. Hear that you're out at the old Clifton place."

"Yeah. A friend of my boss bought it. I'm staying there until a crew shows up to work on it."

"Kind of spooky, isn't it?"

Nuding laughed. "I haven't seen a ghost yet."

"I hope your luck holds. They say old lady Clifton is hovering around out there. I'd better get on down the road." The sheriff started his car.

"Thanks for stopping, Sheriff. It can get pretty boring sitting out here."

"See ya." The sheriff put his fingers to the brim of his hat in a gesture of farewell. A cloud of dust followed the car as he drove away.

"And I'll see *you*, if you get too nosy," Nuding muttered on his way back to his car.

\*     \*     \*

At the filling station, Eddie found a pinhole leak in Kathleen's tire, patched it, and put the tire back on the car. He also replaced the valve, which he thought could be another source of the leak.

"Johnny told me to let him know as soon as I got a shipment of new tires and to hold one for him."

"This old car isn't worth a lot. I don't want to put much money in it. By this time next year, new ones will be coming out, and I may be able to get a good used one."

"Used cars will be pretty well worn-out after being used all during the war."

"I'll just have to take a chance. I won't be able to afford a new one."

When she left the station, Kathleen stopped at the grocery store and bought a few things, then parked in front of the *Gazette*. She went into the office to wait for the bus that would be bringing Henry Ann.

# Chapter Sixteen

*H*enry Ann Dolan was a strikingly pretty woman with rich brown hair, heavy brows, and soft brown eyes. But it was her smile, revealing an inner beauty, that drew people to her. Not quite so slender as she had been thirteen years ago when she met and married Tom Dolan, Henry Ann had thickened slightly at the waist, and her breasts had rounded after three children. Still, she looked younger than her thirty-seven years.

Kathleen introduced her to Adelaide and Paul before bringing her home where they would wait for Johnny. She carried Henry Ann's suitcase to the small back room she had made as pleasant as possible on such short notice. Then she headed for the kitchen.

"The towels in the bathroom with the crocheted edges are yours. I'll fix us some tea while you get settled in," Kathleen called. "Would you rather have iced or hot?"

"Iced, if you don't mind."

Kathleen was a little nervous, aware that Henry Ann was curious as to why she was living here instead of out at the ranch with Johnny. Evidently Johnny hadn't told her about the separation.

"Oh, dear. I miss Tom and the kids already. This is the first time I've been away from them for any length of time." Henry Ann came in and sat down at the kitchen table.

"I bet they miss you, too." Kathleen dropped the chipped ice into the glasses and filled them from a pitcher of tea.

"I'm eager to see Johnny. He has called several times, but I've not seen him since he came home."

"He looks the same, just thinner and, of course, a little older. When he first got here, his hair was short, and he was brown as a berry. His hair has grown out now, and he looks more like his old self."

"I've not seen Isabel since she was fourteen. My, but she was a handful. I had no choice but to send her to the orphanage in the city. I'm sure she hates me for it."

"She had been out at the ranch for more than a week before I knew she was there. According to Johnny, Pete talked her into going to the clinic. She didn't want to be treated by Dr. Perry, but Pete promised to take her to a honky-tonk if the doctor gave his permission. Of course, he knew that wasn't going to happen."

"Have you seen Isabel?"

"I've never met her. Johnny didn't seem to want me to."

Henry Ann's expression showed her concern. "Kathleen, don't think I'm being nosy, but . . . there seems to be something wrong between you and Johnny."

Kathleen looked away for a moment, trying to blink the tears from her eyes before she answered.

"It depends on the viewpoint, I guess. Johnny thinks it right to be separated from me, and I think it's wrong."

"You love him?"

"I love him . . . and will always love him."

"He loved you when you first married. I've never seen him so happy. When he gave his heart, I was sure it was for keeps."

"We had two and a half wonderful years. Then he joined the Seabees, and I never heard one word from him while he was gone that four and a half years."

"I can't believe that . . . of him."

Kathleen said quickly, "Please don't mention to him that I said that."

"I won't if you don't want me to. Do you want to tell me what happened?"

"I don't know if I should. You're his sister. He loves you more than anyone in the world." Kathleen picked up the hem of her skirt and dried her eyes.

"Along with you—"

"No. No, I don't think he loves me. Sometimes I'm sure of that. I feel kind of disloyal talking about him to you."

"Then don't. I know he was hurt when you lost your little girl."

"Did he tell you that?"

"Of course. He called and cried like a baby."

"He . . . did?" The puzzled expression on Kathleen's face led Henry Ann to say, "Why are you surprised?"

"He never held Mary Rose. He never looked at her after . . . the first time."

"What . . . are you saying?" Henry sat back with a look of utter disbelief on her face. "Johnny has always loved kids. I looked after Tom's son Jay for a while before Tom and I married, and Johnny was so good with him. I thought at the time that he'd be a wonderful father."

"He was happy when I got pregnant, but after the baby came he changed overnight."

"I'm disappointed in him," Henry Ann said sadly.

"Oh, don't be!" Kathleen spoke in anguish. "He has his reasons, and they are real to him."

"They would have to be pretty darn good reasons."

"I'll have to tell you the rest so you'll understand. Mary Rose was not a pretty baby to look at, but she was my baby." Silent tears crept from her eyes and trickled unheeded down her cheeks. "She . . . had no skull on the top . . . of her little head and . . . her eyes protruded. She lived two days. She had no chance. No chance at all."

"Oh, Kathleen, I'm sorry." Henry Ann clasped both Kathleen's hands. "I'm so sorry."

"Johnny thinks it's his fault. He said the curse was passed down to him because of . . . incest in his family. He swore that he'd never have another child. He left me right after we buried Mary Rose and told me to get a man with better bloodlines if I wanted a family."

"That's not so. The curse of incest, I mean. Dorene was my mother, too. My children are perfect. It has always been rumored that Dorene's father seduced his daughter, and she gave birth to Dorene. I don't know how true it is. The people who lived on Mud Creek were a strange clan."

"Johnny said that his sister Isabel had always been a little . . . odd. He only remarked about it one time. After that he'd walk away when I brought up the subject."

"For goodness sake, look at what Jude has accomplished. He's a Perry. My children are as smart as whips.

What happened to your child was one of those unusual things that happen. I'll have to talk to him."

"Please don't, Henry Ann. He will be angry with me. He was so glad you were coming. I don't want anything to spoil it."

"Maybe he'll give me an opening—"

Kathleen jumped to her feet and disappeared into the back room. "They're here," she called. "I've got to wash my face. Go open the door, Henry Ann."

Henry Ann was waiting in the open doorway when Johnny came bounding up onto the porch, a smile lighting his face.

"Hen Ann," he exclaimed, using her pet name. He grabbed her the second he came through the doorway and hugged her tightly to him. "Lord, I'm glad to see you. Hell's bells, it's been a long time."

"Aunt Dozie would wash your mouth out with soap for swearing, young man." She leaned back to look at him with tear-filled eyes. "Oh, Johnny, I was so afraid for you when you were . . . over there. I prayed every night."

"It must have done some good, sis. I came back all in one piece."

She kissed his cheek again and again. "You rascal. Golly, how I love you."

"How about me, Hen Ann? Don't I get a welcome?" Pete asked from behind Johnny.

"I've seen you since you came home. And yes, you're a rascal too. Always have been." Henry Ann smiled at him. "As a matter of fact, you were a pain in the behind . . . for years!"

"Yeah, I was. But wait till you see Jude. That little pup is smart as all get out. He's a doctor. A real doctor. Can you believe it?"

"Why are you surprised that he's smart? He was smart enough to figure out who killed Emmajean Dolan and get you out of jail." Johnny was still holding on to Henry Ann as if he feared she would disappear.

"Yeah, I owed him for that, and what did I do? I went right out and joined the navy and left him to cope with our old man who was about as worthless as teats on a boar."

"It does us no good to look back. We all did the best that we could during those hard times. I thank God every day that both of you came back from the war."

"Even me, Henry Ann?" Pete asked.

"Of course, you. I was on to your game, Pete Perry. You wanted everyone to think that you were Red Rock's bad boy." Henry Ann reached up and kissed Pete on the cheek. "Don't tell my husband that I did that."

Johnny turned to see Kathleen standing in the doorway leading to the bedroom. She was wearing a green dress with a wide black belt cinched about her small waist. Her hair was its usual unruly mass of bright red curls, but she looked pale to him.

Kathleen had stayed in the background while Johnny met his sister. Now she came out into the room.

"I have sandwiches ready if you would like to eat before you go to the clinic."

"Sounds good to me." Pete sailed his hat into a chair and followed Kathleen to the kitchen. "Tell me how I can help."

"Wash your hands first, then chip ice for the tea."

"Bossy women," he grumbled. "Always tellin' a fellow to wash."

"That'll teach you to ask," Kathleen retorted.

"I'll remember that."

"This isn't much," Kathleen said as she set a plate of ham and egg salad sandwiches on the table, "but it will hold you for a while."

"Did Jude call?" Johnny asked as he sat down.

"Was he planning to?"

"Only if . . . we were needed."

"He didn't call."

"I told him that you'd be here before noon, Henry Ann, and that we'd come over there about one o'clock. They'll hold off putting her to sleep in case you want to talk to her."

"Oh, my. What can I say after all these years?"

"Henry Ann." Pete had genuine concern on his face. "If Isabel's awake, she's going to be . . . mean-mouthed. She's always been naturally mouthy, and now Jude thinks the syphilis or the cancer has gone to her brain. She has nothing good to say to anyone."

"Don't worry. I know she is sick, and I'll not take to heart anything she says. Even if she is . . . mean, she should have her family with her at a time like this. Johnny and I are all the family she has . . . that we know of."

The sandwiches disappeared from the plate so fast that Kathleen wished that she had made more than three each for the men and one each for herself and Henry Ann.

Henry Ann asked Kathleen to go with them to the clinic; but she refused, saying she would stay and work on her book although she knew that her mind was in such a turmoil that not a word would reach the page.

Johnny did not look directly at her during the meal. His eyes seemed to pass right over her. He did speak to her as he followed Henry Ann out the door when they left to go to the clinic.

"Thanks for the dinner and for picking up Henry Ann."

"You're welcome." Kathleen made sure that there were no tears in her voice. She wanted him to leave before she broke down and bawled. Talking to his sister about their child had stirred up all the misery again.

As soon as the car headed down the street, Kathleen went wearily to the bedroom, lay on the bed, and let the tears flow.

"Hey, beautiful doll, is Jude busy?" Pete asked in his cheery voice when they walked into the reception room.

Millie rolled her eyes to the ceiling. "The *doctor* is in his office, Mr. Perry."

"Mr. Perry? You were callin' me darlin' and sweetheart last night."

"You better be satisfied with Mr. Perry, *darlin'*. 'Cause I know a few other names I could call you."

Pete turned to Henry Ann. "She means it," he said with a mock frown.

Millie smiled at Henry Ann. "Go on in. Doctor knows you're out here." She tilted her head toward Pete and raised an eyebrow. "They probably know it down on Main Street."

Henry Ann moved to the doorway and gazed at the handsome man who rose from the desk and came to meet her. He was tall, slender, and confident. Her mind flashed back to recall the skinny kid from Mud Creek who had been so determined to get an education. He met her in the middle of the office, and Henry Ann wrapped her arms around him.

"Dr. Perry. I'm so proud."

"Hello, Henry Ann."

She hugged him for a long moment, then stepped back

to look at him, then at Pete and Johnny. Pete was beaming with pride. Johnny was smiling, too.

"Oh, you boys! I was sure none of you would amount to a hill of beans. Now look—you've turned out just fine."

"You turned out pretty good yourself," Jude said. "You were always the prettiest girl in Red Rock with a bunch of suitors, too."

"Ah, come on," Henry Ann scoffed. "It wasn't me they were after. It was the farm. Enough about me. How is Isabel?"

Jude's smile faded. "Not good, I'm afraid."

"Johnny said there's nothing you can do for her."

"We could have treated the syphilis. The cancer has spread beyond treatment. We're giving her morphine."

"How long?"

Jude shook his head. "I believe that her heart will fail before the cancer gets her. The end could come today, tomorrow, or a week from now. I've not had a lot of experience with cancer, but my nurse, Mrs. Frank, worked in the cancer ward at St. Anthony Hospital in Oklahoma City. She believes, and I concur, that if Isabel lives another week, it will be a miracle."

"Poor, poor thing. Maybe if I had kept her with me, she would have had a different kind of life."

"The world is full of *what if's*, sis. You can't blame yourself for how Isabel chose to live." Johnny's face was grim.

"Can we see her?"

"Sure. Anytime."

"Oh, before I go see her, I want to give you this." Henry Ann opened her purse and pulled out some bills. "Tom and I know that being in the hospital is expensive.

We want you to have this, and we will send more from time to time."

"Sis! No!" Johnny reached across and took hold of the hand holding the money. "I've already told Jude that I'll pay for Isabel's care—"

"Hold on, both of you," Jude said sternly. "Isabel Henry is an adult. Neither of you is responsible for her. This clinic has a built-in fund through anonymous donations to take care of patients who can't afford to pay. We either use that fund or we lose it. Isabel's care here will be paid for out of that fund. Put your money back in your purse, Henry Ann."

"No, Jude." Johnny shook his head. "That's charity. I'm not proud of it, but Isabel is my sister, and I'll pay, in time, for her care."

"Then you'll have to take her out of the clinic and find another place for her because I've already submitted her name as a patient qualified for the anonymous fund."

Johnny looked thunderstruck.

"You've got too much pride for your own good, Johnny," Jude said kindly. "Are you going to throw the generous donations back in the faces of the folks who gave them?"

Johnny didn't answer immediately, then insisted, "It goes against the grain to take charity."

"Then think about it the next time you offer to help someone or give someone a small part of something that you have plenty of."

"But, dammit, Jude—"

"Dammit, Johnny. I may be calling on you in the spring. I've plans to make some changes around here. I'll need all the donated help I can get."

"You'd have had it anyway," Johnny growled.

"I know that. Henry Ann, I'll take you down to see Isabel. Come on, Johnny. Pete won't be far behind. He never misses a chance to flirt with my nurses." Jude glanced over his shoulder at his brother and grinned.

At the door of Isabel's room, Jude said, "Wait just a minute." He opened the door a crack and looked in. Mrs. Cole was giving Isabel a drink of water. When she finished, he went in, motioning for the others to follow.

"Hello, Isabel," Jude said.

"Hello, Isabel," she mimicked. Her voice was raspy and weak, but still full of venom. "What'er you wanting? Cause I'm flat on my back . . . ya thinkin' to crawl on an' screw me? Cost ya two dollars for one time, three dollars for two . . . if you can go two times." She snickered.

Jude ignored what she said to him. "There's someone here to see you."

"A man?" She tried to look beyond him. "Has he come to take me dancin'?"

"Pete and Johnny are here, but someone else is, too." Jude stepped aside, and Henry Ann moved up beside the bed.

"Hello, Isabel."

Henry Ann would not have recognized the sunken-cheeked, bony, hard-faced woman who lay on the bed. Her hair was so thin you could see her scalp, and it stuck out from her head like straw. Her eyes seemed to be slightly out of focus. She said nothing at first, just stared.

"God's pecker and all that's holy!" she swore. "If it ain't Miss Tight-ass Henry Ann come all the way from that piss-poor farm to gloat over my bones."

"I just found out the other day that you were sick, Isabel."

"Hell, I ain't sick. Ain't sick," she tried to yell, but it

came out as a weak squawk. "Jesus, I hate your damn guts for sayin' I'm sick. I . . . ain't . . . no . . . way . . . sick! You ugly bitch."

"You're my sister, Isabel. I'd like to stay and visit with you."

"Shit a mile in broad daylight! I suppose that big-peckered, blanket-ass Johnny come, too. Damn turd-eater kept me locked up. Wouldn't let me go nowhere. Wanted to keep me there naked for him to use—"

"Isabel, that's enough!" Pete was beside the bed. "Dammit, shut up tellin' those nasty lies."

"Honey, wanta fuck me? Climb on. I ain't goin' to charge ya. And I don't care if prissy-tail watches." She chuckled. The sound was dry and scratchy.

Pete looked across the bed at Dale Cole. Her face had turned a rosy red. She glanced at him and then away.

"Henry Ann, don't stay and listen to this," he whispered. "She's not been this bad before."

"I understand that she's out of her head."

"I'm not so sure. She knew who you were."

"Son of a bitch," Isabel muttered in a dry whisper. "Goddamn son of a bitchin' whore. Bastard would screw a knothole if he had nothin' else. Pussy-grabbin' asshole—" Her eyes were completely unfocused.

"The poor miserable thing. I'll sit with her for a while. You and Johnny go on out."

Jude moved up to the bed, holding a hypodermic needle close to his side. Mrs. Cole held back the sheet and he sank the needle into Isabel's buttock. She didn't seem to be aware of it. When he removed it, Mrs. Cole quickly put a pad and a tape over the puncture and covered her with the sheet.

Johnny had already backed out the door of the room.

He felt sick to his stomach, to his soul. Jude came out and put a hand on his shoulder.

"How do you stand it, Jude?"

"This is a bad one. On the other side of the fence, when you make people well and they walk out of here, it makes it all worthwhile. A boy in Italy was like this in the end. The things he said were so foul they would turn your stomach. He had been a gentle, quiet boy planning to go to a theological school before he was drafted into the army."

"It's bad blood, is what it is."

"There's no such thing as bad blood that causes behavior problems. I could exchange your blood with a killer on death row, and if his blood was free of disease, you'd still be the same kind of man you were. Sometimes family traits are passed along, but it's all a matter of chance. Look at me and Pete. We're not alike yet we had the same father. You and Henry Ann are not like Isabel even though you had the same mother."

"Bad genes can skip a generation. I've read a bit about it. If I thought that I'd be like her, or had a child that would be like her, I'd shoot myself."

"Sometimes the books you read don't give a complete picture. If you're interested in the subject, I can give you a good medical book to read."

"Henry Ann is one of the best people I know and Isabel is one of the worst. It's strange, isn't it?"

"It is, but I've seen many strange things during the short time I've been a doctor."

"Doctor," Theresa called from down the hallway.

Jude started to go, then turned back to Johnny. "I hope you will come for Thanksgiving. Henry Ann, too, if she's still here. Kathleen has already said that she's coming."

"Henry Ann won't want to be away from Tom and the kids on Thanksgiving."

"Then I'll expect *you*." Jude smiled and walked to where Theresa waited for him.

Johnny went to the reception room to wait for Henry Ann. Jude had made him reconsider some of his ideas. He had some thinking to do.

# Chapter Seventeen

*H*enry Ann sat quietly beside the bed watching Isabel's ravaged face. The vile words that had come out of her mouth had shocked her. She had never heard such vulgarity. It was doubly embarrassing to listen to in the presence of the others. She kept telling herself that no woman would speak like that if she were fully in charge of her reasoning.

Yet Isabel had looked at her with pure hatred in her eyes. She had *reasoned* enough to know that she hated her. So sad. She had wasted her life hating. The poor creature would never know the love of a good man or the love of children. All that could be done was to pity and forgive her.

Henry Ann was conscious that Pete was still in the room. The nurse moved around picking up soiled linens and stuffing them in a pillowcase. She came to stand by Henry Ann and look down at Isabel. She smoothed the stiff dry hair back from her patient's forehead, a gesture Isabel would have sneered at had she been awake.

"The poor thing will have a few hours of peace now," Dale said softly.

"I'll sit beside her for a while."

"Stay as long as you like. Can I get you something? Water, tea, or coffee?"

"No, thank you."

"I've some other things to tend to. I'll be back in a little while."

When Dale Cole left the room, Pete was close behind her.

"Dale, wait a minute."

"Yes? Did you want something?"

"Just to talk to you for a minute. How are you doing?"

"Fine. Why are you interested in how I'm doing?"

"Because I can't get you out of my mind. I keep seeing those big sad eyes and the fingerprints on your throat."

She looked at him doubtfully and he saw a faint hint of color rise on her cheeks.

"Don't add to my problems. Please."

"That's the last thing I want to do. I passed by your house last night and saw a little boy sitting on your step. Yours?"

"Yes." Dale drew in a deep breath. "He . . . he saw you wave at me."

"Your little boy?"

"No. My husband. Please don't do it again." Large brown eyes pleaded with him.

Pete was stunned. Then his face hardened into a scowl.

"Did he hurt you?" The words came out in a husky whisper.

"No. But he . . . thought that . . . we—"

"Christ on a horse! Is the man insane? Can't a man

wave at you without him thinking you're having an affair?"

"He thinks that . . . a man wouldn't pay attention to me . . . unless he thought I wanted him to take me to bed. He says no man would pass up an invitation like that . . . even from me." The words were hard for Dale to say.

"Dale!" Pete's fingers closed on her arm. "That's not true. I'd be honored to have you for a friend, and that's all I intended . . . at first."

"At first?"

"Until I got to know you, saw the bruises on you. Oh, hell! Now I want to take that bastard out and stomp his guts out."

"Don't interfere in my life. I know what I am—"

"—Dammit, don't say it."

"For a short while I thought that I could work here at the clinic, use what I had learned in nursing school, maybe someday pass the exam and get my nursing license. It's not going to happen. He told me to give the doctor two weeks' notice."

"He's forcing you to quit?"

"He thinks I should be home with Danny."

"Why don't you stand up to him? Tell him that you'll not quit. You're needed here."

"You don't understand. Why don't you tend to your own business?" Tears of frustration filled Dale's eyes. "Now get away from me. I've got work to do."

"Wait," Pete said quickly when she started to dart into the laundry room. "If you ever need help, call me at Jude's house. I'll be there until I get a place of my own."

"You're staying around here?"

"I'm going to buy some land, start a horse ranch, and raise rodeo horses."

"Good luck," she whispered through trembling lips.

Pete stood in the quiet of the clinic hallway as the door swung gently after Dale passed through it. He didn't understand himself. He just knew that it hurt like hell to think of her being misused by the coward she was married to. The bastard was smart. He had kept her down by eroding her confidence. Pete dug his hands deeply into the pockets of his pants and went to find Johnny.

The reception room was empty when Pete reached it. He continued on out the door and saw Johnny leaning on the car, looking out over a broad expanse of prairie. Pete lit a cigarette and inhaled deeply.

"Come out to smoke?"

"Yeah. Henry Ann took it pretty good," Johnny said, when Pete leaned against the car beside him.

"Isabel was really out of her mind today. That's the worst she's been."

"While she was out at the ranch, she tried to tell me about men she'd been with, and I wouldn't listen. I'd just walk out. It appears to be all that's on her mind."

"She was a little slut at fourteen. I never touched her. I don't know whether Hardy did."

"It must be some bad strain that Dorene passed on to her."

"I never believed in this 'passing on' thing. If it was true, Jude and I would be down on Mud Creek with a dozen kids apiece."

"Some say that people are the products of their environment."

"That's not necessarily true either. I've known strong, brave men, whose folks were pure trash, and the other way around. I knew a preacher once . . . a real nice man, for a preacher." Pete grinned. "He had three sons: one was a preacher, one a teacher, and the other a killer who was executed over at McCalister. Figure that out."

"Did you ever know your mother?" Johnny asked after he lit another cigarette.

"No, she died when I was three or four. Hardy's ma took care of me until I was old enough to take care of myself."

"Was your mother a kin of Hardy's?"

"Hell, I don't know. Could have been a cousin. Dorene was the only sister he had. I think they had the same mother. Everybody on Mud Creek was related one way or the other."

"Blood can be so watered down by years of inbreeding that all that's produced are runts and freaks. I've seen it in cattle and horses."

"That's not the case with me. I'm certainly no runt. Hell, boy, you're not either. Jude may have got my share of brains, but seems like you got your share and so did Henry Ann."

"Years ago I was told that Dorene and Hardy are the kids of a father and daughter. Is that true?"

"I don't know that either. You probably heard that from Fat Perry's ma. That old woman could spin the wildest yarns you ever heard."

"It doesn't worry you that it might be true?"

"I've not given it any thought."

"What about your offspring?" Johnny persisted. "Do you plan on having children someday?"

"I'd like to think that I will. I've seen too many men grow old without anyone to care whether they lived or died."

"I'll never take a chance on bringing something in the world that people would call a freak."

A car drove up and stopped behind them. A man in a black suit and a brown-felt hat tilted forward got out. He passed Pete and Johnny without a glance and went up the walk and into the clinic.

"And good day to you, too," Pete said. "If he's a salesman, I hope Jude don't buy from him."

"He's Harry Cole. His wife was the nurse in the room with Isabel. I've seen him a couple of times."

"So that's him. Dale asked me not to wave at her anymore. He saw me do it and immediately thought we were having an affair."

Johnny grinned. "You work pretty fast."

"Yeah. It's one of my best qualities. I think I'll see what kinda car he drives."

Pete fingered the knife in his pocket as he sauntered around to the other side of Harry Cole's car. He came slowly around the back of it and up the sidewalk to where Johnny stood leaning against a front fender of his own car.

"Nice car," Pete remarked. "The only thing wrong with it is a flat tire on the back left side."

"Like I said, you work pretty fast."

"Mud Creek survival training," Pete explained without cracking a smile. "Shall we go in and sit for a while? Henry Ann will be wanting to go before long."

Harry Cole carefully took off his hat so as not to muss his hair when he went into the clinic. Millie looked up from her typewriter.

"I want to see Dr. Perry." He gave the woman a haughty stare. "Not as a patient, but on a personal matter."

"I'll see if he's free."

Millie did not like Harry Cole, had not liked him since the day he came to Rawlings. She liked him less since she had come to know Dale and to suspect that he abused her physically as well as mentally. The poor woman put on what Millie called her "happy-happy" act to cover her misery.

Millie knocked softly on the office door, then opened it and went inside, closing it behind her. The doctor was seated. Theresa stood beside him. Both heads were bent over a chart that lay on the desk. Millie waited until he looked up. Then she spoke softly.

"You've got a visitor. Harry Cole. He wants to talk to you about a personal matter."

"Uh-oh," Theresa said.

"Exactly." This came from Millie. "Want me to throw him out?"

"No. We'd better see what he has to say. What do you know about him? I've thrown out a few feelers and learned a few things."

"He's a snob. He likes to hobnob with the rich and powerful," Millie said with a sniff. "He loves to feel important and have people think he's a high muckety-muck. And, one more thing—he'd like nothing better than to be mayor or county supervisor."

"How about one of the trustees here at the clinic?" Jude asked.

"That, too." Millie nodded.

"I'm falling in love with you, Millie." Jude smiled.

Millie fluffed her hair. "You and your brother will just have to fight over me. I'll send Mr. Big Shot in."

"I'll leave," Theresa said. "Good luck."

"You're my luck, Theresa." His smile was so beautiful that she wanted to cry.

"And you are mine, Dr. Jude." The words were out before she realized it. She hurried out the side door. "Oh, my gosh! Why in the world did I say that?"

Jude stared at the door. He hadn't time to analyze Theresa's reply because the other door opened, and Harry Cole came in. Jude got to his feet and held out his hand.

"Mr. Cole, this is a coincidence. Mr. Wrenn from the bank was speaking about you yesterday. Please sit down."

Harry sat down and placed his hat on his knee. "Was John saying that I had overdrawn on my account?" he asked in a manner that said he knew that was not the case. His eyes glittered with interest.

Jude laughed. "Nothing like that. We were discussing men we considered highly qualified for county offices. Your name was at the top of the list. I hope you'll keep this conversation confidential. I don't want the others to think I'm spiking their guns, so to speak."

"You can count on it. Mum's the word." Harry leaned back in his chair and crossed his legs.

"Frankly, I kicked up a fuss because soon there will be an opening here at the clinic for a trustee. There are not too many men around who have had supervisory experience."

"I've had that all right. Supervising men is not the easiest job in the world."

"That's what I was telling John and the mayor. John thought you'd make a good mayor. It's something you could do and still keep your present job. Claude isn't sure he can handle the job for another term. Government surpluses will be pouring in next year. He said that we need someone with experience to direct them to the right place."

"It's gratifying to know that Claude has that much confidence in me."

"I'm sorry, Mr. Cole—"

"Harry. Please call me Harry."

"I'm sorry, Harry, I didn't mean to monopolize this meeting. What was it that you wanted to see me about?"

"Well, Doctor—"

"Call me Jude." Jude leaned forward as if he were eager to hear what the man had to say.

"I stopped by to tell you that my wife can help out here as long as you need her. We had discussed her quitting and staying home, giving her time for the fancy needlework and flower arranging she enjoys."

"I've noticed the bouquets she's brought to the clinic. She has a knack with flowers."

"We're not in need of the money she earns here. I spoke to her about volunteering her services—"

"—That's most generous of you, Harry," Jude exclaimed. "But I can't build a schedule around volunteers. I need to know when my helpers will be here and how long they will say."

"That's something I hadn't thought of, Jude." Harry nodded his head as he spoke. "I can see where that would be a problem for you."

"In the city we had volunteers who came in once in a while from the church groups. They have to be closely supervised. We thought we'd struck a gold mine when we came here and discovered Mrs. Cole. I was told that she was a great help to the doctor who came down two days a week after Dr. Simpson passed on."

Harry smiled. "Yes, she is very capable and very well organized. We've been married for six years and—"

"—I imagine that you had something to do with that."

Harry laughed. "I wasn't going to say so."

"You didn't have to, Harry."

When Dale glanced out the window and saw Harry's car parked in front of the clinic behind Pete Perry's car, fear kept her frozen for the length of a dozen heartbeats. Oh, Lord! What would she do if he raised a fuss? She went to the hall and stood for a moment, and the thought of fleeing came to mind. It was immediately discarded. Harry had come to tell Dr. Perry that she could not work here. He had warned her that that was what he would do if she didn't give notice.

*If it wasn't for Danny, I would walk out the back door of the clinic and keep walking across the prairie until I dropped. I can't leave my son to be raised by that man!*

Dale went to peer through the small window that allowed the nurses to view the reception area. She could see the back of Millie's gray head. Pete Perry and Johnny Henry were talking quietly in the corner. The rest of the chairs were empty.

Then she heard laughter coming from the doctor's office. *Harry was laughing!* What was he up to now?

"Ohhh . . ." She jumped when she felt a hand on her shoulder, and turned quickly to see Blanche, the clinic cook, standing behind her.

"Didn't mean to scare ya. I called but guess ya didn't hear. The lady back there with Miss Henry is calling ya. She sounds scared."

"Thank you, Blanche. I guess I was daydreaming."

Dale hurried down the hall. The door to Miss Henry's

room was open. Her sister was standing beside the raised bed.

"Something . . . is happening—"

Dale looked down at her patient and saw that the corner of Isabel's mouth had drawn down. She lifted a lid and observed that Isabel's eyes had rolled back in her head.

"She's having a stroke. I'll get the doctor."

Dale ran out of the room and down the hall. She threw open the door to the office.

"Come quick, Doctor. Miss Henry is having a stroke."

She hurried back down the hallway without even acknowledging Harry. Jude was behind her when she returned to Isabel's room. Henry Ann moved away from the bedside to make room for the doctor and nurse.

Dale pulled back the sheet and Jude listened to Isabel's heart through the stethoscope in his ears. He spoke to Henry Ann while still listening.

"Her heart is failing. It won't be long. If Johnny is here, he may want to come in."

"He's still here, Doctor. Shall I get him?"

Jude nodded, and Dale hurried from the room.

"She's dying," Henry Ann said sadly.

Jude nodded again and turned back to his patient.

Henry Ann was glad when Johnny and Pete entered behind the nurse. She moved over close to Johnny. He put his arm around her. The room was so terribly quiet. The rasping gasps for breath that had caused Henry Ann to call out had almost ceased.

Pete stood behind Henry Ann, his hand on her shoulder. He watched Dale, calm and efficient. Damn, but she was a fine woman.

Jude took the stethoscope from his ears. "There's nothing I can do. The stroke brought on a heart attack." He moved to the end of the bed to give Henry Ann and Johnny an unobstructed view of their dying sister.

Henry Ann stood with her head bowed, trying not to remember how uncaring Isabel had been the night her father died.

"Ain't my daddy," Isabel had said when asked to turn down the radio.

Now Isabel was dying. Henry Ann cared, not because she was her half sister, but because she was a human being.

Five long minutes passed. Then Jude moved back to the bed and placed the end of the stethoscope on Isabel's chest. When he lifted it, he pulled the sheet up over her face.

"She's gone."

"Do you think that it was my being here that got her so worked up that she had the stroke?" Henry Ann asked.

"No, I don't think that. Her blood pressure was terribly high, and I couldn't get it down to a safe level. Her kidneys were failing, and water was forming in pockets all over her body. That and the cancer that had spread led to the stroke that caused heart failure."

"I'm glad that I came today. Something told me that I should."

"I'm glad you're here. Isabel had her family with her in the end, even if she had rejected them."

Johnny had not uttered a word since he came into the room. He stood with his back to the wall and ran his fingers through his dark straight hair. He had seen enough death to last a lifetime but was never prepared to see life leave a human body.

"Will you call the funeral home, Jude?" Johnny's voice

was low with respect for his dead sister. "We'll take Henry Ann back to Kathleen's. Then I'll go make arrangements."

"Sure. If there's anything I can do, let me know."

"Oh, look. That poor man has a flat tire," Henry Ann said on the way to the car.

"Yeah," Pete said. "Seems so."

Harry Cole had driven his car past Pete's before he realized the back tire was flat. Driving on the rim had ruined the tire. Harry had removed his coat, jacked up the car, and was struggling to put on the spare.

"Hey, mister," he called as Pete rounded the front of the car to get in on the driver's side. "Do you have a tire pump?"

"Nope." Pete kept walking, got in the car, and started the motor.

Henry Ann looked questioningly at Pete. "I can't believe you don't have a pump."

He grinned at her, tromped on the gas, and darted around the man squatted beside the car, his wheels stirring up a dust cloud.

"This car's got a lot of pickup," he said as if pleasantly surprised. "It's hard for me to hold it down at times."

As soon as Dale was free, she hurried to the window to see if Harry's car was still there. He had moved it and was fixing a flat tire. How did that happen? He hated getting dirty. He would never do physical work if there was any way to get out of it.

She went to the reception area. "Millie? What's going on?" she asked fearfully.

"I don't know what happened in the office, honey, but

I've got reason to think that Doc fixed things. Mr. Big . . . ah . . . well, he came out all smiles and even spoke to me. He said to tell you that he had some business to attend to and that he might be a few minutes late getting home for supper. He didn't want you to worry."

"He said *that*? Millie, are you sure?"

"Honey, I'm sure. Butter would not have melted in his mouth. He and Doc were laughing like old friends."

"I wonder what happened."

"If I find out, I'll tell you. I've got a feeling that things are going to work out. Doc knows how to get around folks."

"I hope you're right."

# *Chapter Eighteen*

"Where is your pride?" Kathleen muttered against the cold,wet cloth she held over her face. "He does not want you. Can't you get that through your stupid head?"

She removed the cloth and looked at herself closely in the mirror above the lavatory. Her eyes were swollen from crying and her face was blotchy. She stared into the sky-blue eyes looking back at her. Other women had survived disappointments in the men they loved, and so would she. There really wasn't such a thing as a broken heart—badly bruised maybe, but not broken. Kathleen felt stubbornness rising in her, a will to do what she pleased, to get out from under the depression that had held her down since Mary Rose was born.

She was luckier than most women; she had a career in writing that she could pursue. *I am master of my own fate. I will stop moping around and get on with my life. I may even find a man who really loves me.*

With those thoughts in mind, she changed into a dress with a soft full skirt, put on her hose and high-heeled shoes, and fixed her face, using a little more makeup than usual. She put on her good black coat and picked up her car keys.

"Where am I going?" she asked herself.

Kathleen stood on the porch and looked around. The back of her neck began to tickle. She had an eerie feeling that someone was near, but she didn't see anyone. She shrugged. She'd had the feeling before, and it had gone away.

She drove slowly down the street. *Double Indemnity* with Barbara Stanwyck and Fred MacMurray was showing at the Rialto Theatre. After Henry Ann's visit was over, she decided, she would go see every movie that was shown. She loved movies and had no one to please but herself.

Kathleen came to a decision suddenly. She drove around the block and angle-parked in front of the red-brick building that housed the law firm of Alan Fairbanks and Son. She had to take the first step. It was what Johnny wanted her to do.

The time had come to break the tie, but Father in Heaven, it was hard to do. She forced herself to put one foot in front of the other until she reached the office and was standing in front of the woman at the desk.

"Is Mr. Fairbanks in?"

"Yes, he is. Your name is—"

"Kathleen Henry."

"Just a moment."

"Send her in, Janet," a male voice boomed from the back office.

The woman lifted her brows and shrugged, then sat back down. Kathleen walked around the partition and into the office behind it. The portly man behind the desk stood and held out his hand.

"Well, well, well. I haven't seen you since you came back."

"Nice to see you, Mr. Fairbanks," Kathleen said, shaking his hand. Seven years ago, he had been supportive of the effort she, Adelaide, and Paul had made to rid the town of Dr. Herman and his influence.

"Sit down, Kathleen. You're lookin' pretty. Doesn't seem like the years have changed you much."

"Oh, but they have. The war years have changed all of us."

"I was glad that Johnny came home all right. So many of our boys here in Tillison County didn't come home, and some of them who did are crippled for life." He shook his head. "War is a sorry business."

"It is that, Mr. Fairbanks. But we were forced into it."

"You're right, my dear. Now what brings you to my office."

*Now was the time. Could she do it?*

"Mr. Fairbanks, I . . . don't know if you are aware of it, but Johnny and I have been separated for quite a while."

"Of course, you have. How long was he over there?"

"Four and a half years. I . . . ah . . . don't mean that kind of separation." She rushed on before she lost her nerve. "Before he left, Johnny told me to get a divorce."

The lawyer leaned back in his chair and twisted the pencil he held between his fingers. He pursed his lips before he spoke.

"Did you?" he asked.

"No. I thought he might change his mind when he came back."

"He is the one wanting the divorce? Not you?"

"I guess I want it, too. I don't want to be married to

someone who doesn't . . . want me." Kathleen swallowed the lump in her throat and lifted her chin.

"Does he have another woman?"

"No. I don't think he's been seeing anyone else."

"How about you?"

"No, of course not. I worked at an aircraft plant in Oklahoma City while he was gone. When the plant closed, I came back here. I still have an interest in the *Gazette*."

"Humm . . . What grounds do you plan to use to get the divorce? You can't claim that he deserted you when he went to war."

"I'd never claim that. Why do there have to be grounds?"

"That's the way it works. The judge would ask you why you want a divorce. You have to give a reason. Has he refused to support you? Has he threatened you with bodily harm? Has he refused to live with you as husband and wife?"

"No to the first two and yes to the last one."

"That could be the one we could use. In that case, we can go for alimony—"

"No. I don't want anything from him." Kathleen stood. "I've got to think about this."

"Good idea. Do you want me to talk to Johnny?"

"It wouldn't do any good. He's made up his mind."

"But you haven't made up yours."

"Yes, I have, Mr. Fairbanks. I don't have a choice."

"Think about it for a day or two. We'll come up with grounds of some kind."

"Thank you."

She was at the door when he said, "You don't have any children, do you, Kathleen?"

"No," she said, over her shoulder because she was afraid that she was going to cry. "No children."

She got into the car and drove away as if she really had someplace to go. She stopped in front of the library, turned off the motor, and stared at the steering wheel. Minutes passed while her thoughts tumbled one on top of the other. What should she do? She didn't want people to know that Johnny refused to sleep with her— that's what living as *man and wife* meant, didn't it?

She had no idea how long she sat there when a tapping on the window drew her attention. A man with a stupid looking billed cap and big glasses was looking at her. He wore a gray, foreign-looking mustache. She rolled down the window.

"Do ye be all right, miss," he asked.

"Oh, yes, I'm fine. I was just thinking."

"'Tis sure ye be deep in thought. Is it trouble ye be havin'?"

"No. I'm a writer and I was thinking about the plot of my story. Thank you for your concern. I'm going now." Kathleen quickly rolled up the window and started the car.

The prickly feeling was at the back of her neck again. She wanted to turn and see if someone was hiding in the backseat of the car. She watched the man walk leisurely down the street and around the corner. His accent was Irish or Scottish. She was sure that she'd never seen him before. She wouldn't do this again. It was obvious even to a stranger that she was troubled.

Kathleen reached her house and was surprised to see Pete's car parked in front. When she entered, Pete and Henry Ann were sitting on the couch in the living room.

"Hey, sugar, you're all dressed up." Pete stood and helped her off with her coat.

"Not really. How is Isabel?"

"She's gone," Henry Ann said. "I was with her for only a couple of hours when she passed away."

"Oh, I'm sorry."

"Johnny and Pete are going to make the arrangements."

Johnny came from the kitchen with a glass of ice water and handed it to Henry Ann. *He was making himself at home in her kitchen.* If he looked at her she never knew it because she kept her eyes turned away from him.

"You sure do look pretty, sugar," Pete was saying. "How come you're all dressed up?"

"I had some business to take care of."

"When we get back, let's all go down to the Golden Pheasant for supper."

"Thank you, but count me out. I'll have a sandwich and work for a while. Now if you'll excuse me, I'll get out of these high heels."

Kathleen closed the bedroom door, leaned against it, and closed her eyes. *I will not mope around like a puppy with its tail between its legs any longer!* Her eyes popped open and she jerked open a bureau drawer and pulled out a pair of faded, baggy slacks. They were blue with white dots. Ugly. The top was equally ugly—white with blue dots, some of which had bled onto the white. After washing her face, she examined herself closely in the mirror, then pulled the hair on the top of her head back and secured it with one of her precious, prewar, rubber bands.

She stared at the stranger looking back at her from the mirror over the lavatory. She stood there trembling, accepting that sooner or later she would tell Johnny that she had been to see Mr. Fairbanks.

"Lord, help me," she muttered, and looked away from the pale face and vacant eyes.

Just as she was getting ready to leave the bedroom, she heard the front door open, then close. She looked out the window to see Johnny and Pete going out to Pete's car. She sighed with relief and went into the living room, where Henry Ann was reading the latest *Rawlings Gazette*. She looked up.

"This is a much better paper than the one we have in Red Rock."

"Paul Leahy, Adelaide's husband, is responsible. He worked for a big paper in Texas before he came here. The *Gazette* is one of the best small-town papers in the state."

Henry Ann folded the newspaper and placed it on the table beside the chair.

"I feel kind of guilty leaving the funeral arrangements to Pete and Johnny."

"I'm sure they don't mind."

"We decided to have a graveside service tomorrow afternoon. Isabel didn't know anyone here except Jude and Pete, Johnny and me."

"A few of Johnny's friends will be there out of respect for him."

"He doesn't expect anyone."

Kathleen shrugged. "People in small towns are very good about things like going to funerals."

"I was so shocked when I saw her. Oh, my. She looked so old and was so . . . hard."

"Barker Fleming, Johnny's father, tracked her down in Oklahoma City seven years ago. She was working in the toughest part of the city. She told him that Johnny had a ranch near Rawlings. That's how he found him. Barker told me, back then, that Isabel was quite ah . . . shameless."

"Jude said the sickness had damaged her brain. I hope that was the reason for the filth that spewed from her mouth." Henry Ann was quiet for a while, then said, "I'll go home the day after tomorrow. I miss Tom."

"I was hoping you would stay longer."

"I have to go back before Thanksgiving. I couldn't be away from home at that time."

"That's understandable. When I was going to school in Des Moines, I traveled through a snowstorm to get home for Thanksgiving. I couldn't stand the thought of not being with my grandparents."

"Our daughter will be in the school play next Tuesday. I made Tom promise to help her with her lines."

"I envy you. Husband and children. It's what I always wanted." Kathleen immediately regretted saying the words, but once said words cannot be taken back.

"They are my life. I hoped for the same for Johnny. He is as dear to me as my children."

"We all want different things from life. Can I get you some more tea?"

"No, thanks." Henry Ann sighed and leaned back on the couch. "I feel like I've been through a wringer."

The phone rang, and Kathleen excused herself to answer it. It was Marie.

"Kathleen, we heard that Johnny's sister died."

"Yes, he's making funeral arrangements now. The plans are for it to be tomorrow afternoon at the gravesite."

"Daddy wants to know if there is anything we can do."

"I wouldn't know, Marie, but I'll pass the message along to Johnny when he gets back."

"Tell Johnny that we'll be there."

"I will, Marie. 'Bye." Kathleen hung up the phone. "That was Marie Fleming, Johnny's half sister. You'll meet her and Johnny's father tomorrow. They will be at the funeral."

"It's nice of them to come."

"They are nice people."

When Pete returned, he was alone. "After we finished up at the funeral parlor, I took Johnny out to the ranch to do chores. He'll be back in to take you to supper, Henry Ann."

"I forgot to mention to him that Isabel would need a burial dress."

"It's taken care of. Mr. Klein asked about it. We went to the dry goods store, bought a gown and a lacy bed-jacket thing to go over it." Then to Kathleen, "How about going out tonight and cuttin' a rug, sugar?"

"I don't think so." Kathleen laughed in spite of her dark mood. "But thanks for the invitation."

"Come with Johnny and me, Kathleen." Henry Ann's face showed concern.

"No, but thanks. You and Johnny should have some time alone together. Tonight is the night I like to listen to the Andrews Sisters and the Riders of the Purple Sage. They're on that *Eight-to-the-Bar* show."

"Jay is a Bob Wills fan," Henry Ann said with a smile. "He likes Eldon Shamblin, the guitar player." Jay was Tom's son from a former marriage. He was four years old when his father married Henry Ann and would graduate from high school this year. Henry Ann was intensely proud of him.

"I'm losing my charm. I struck out all around," Pete said. "I wonder what Millie is doing tonight."

Pete left after a while, and Henry Ann went to freshen up before going out with Johnny. Kathleen sat on the couch and allowed her face to relax. Was this to be her life? Always on the edge? Always hoping? She really should move away from here. She didn't have to stay in Tillison County while getting the divorce.

When Johnny stopped in front of the house, Kathleen went to the small kitchen and busied herself at the counter putting away the dishes she had allowed to dry in the drainer, leaving Henry Ann to open the door. She heard their voices, then Henry Ann came to the kitchen door.

"Are you sure you won't go with us, Kathleen?"

"Oh, yes, I'm sure. I have things to do."

She turned to see Johnny staring at her over Henry Ann's shoulder. He was freshly shaved, his dark hair brushed back from his forehead. He had on a string tie and a new suede jacket. He'd dressed up for the occasion. She looked back at him without visibly flinching. She was glad that she looked tacky. That would show him that she didn't care a whit what he thought about her.

"See you later," Henry Ann was saying. "I'm early to bed tonight. This has been a trying day."

The days were short this time of year. The lights were on in Dale's house and the car was parked out front when Pete drove slowly past. He had not had a chance to find out from Jude why Harry Cole had come to the clinic. Whatever it was, it apparently was handled cordially. When he came from Jude's office, the bastard was all smiles. Thinking about the flat tire that had awaited Cole, Pete chuckled. It was Mud Creek justice, pure and simple.

Since meeting Dale Cole, Pete had found himself thinking about her at the oddest times. At first it had been her perky personality and sharp comebacks that had caught his attention. He had observed her obvious dedication to nursing and her calm in the face of Isabel's insults. He had seen women who had been knocked around. But the cruel evidence Dale bore had made him want to hurt whoever had done that to her.

He didn't remember ever being so interested in a woman that he wasn't trying to get in bed, and he was puzzled by it. He had known prettier women, more shapely women, but when he looked into the big sad eyes of this woman, he wanted to take care of her. What the hell was wrong with him?

Inside the house, Dale was equally puzzled, but about something altogether different. Harry hadn't mentioned his visit to the clinic or where he had gone when he left there. He had been in a good mood during supper, talking to Danny about school, and even telling her that the chrysanthemums in the backyard were especially nice this year.

"We've not had a hard frost."

"Maybe you should pick a bouquet and take it to the clinic before the frost gets them."

It was fortunate for Dale that he didn't expect an answer because she was so dumbfounded that she couldn't have given one that made any sense at all. She discovered the reason for his good humor after Danny had gone to bed.

"I had a long talk with Jude today."

"Dr. Perry?" Dale was wiping dishes, and Harry lingered in the doorway of the kitchen.

"I told him that you could help out at the clinic for as long as he needed you. I want your best effort, hear? What you do reflects on me."

"I always do the best I can."

"Jude is thinking about proposing me as a trustee at the clinic. When that happens, I'll make some changes out there. They need organization. I didn't tell him that I'd even consider it because I've also been approached about running for mayor, maybe even county supervisor." He took in Dale's surprised reaction, then said, "Jude is behind me a hundred percent."

"Why, Harry, that's wonderful."

"It's about time someone in this hick town recognized my abilities. I could have gone anyplace. Oklahoma Gas asked where I wanted to go. I chose this place or they'd have got that half-ass supervisor from over at Ardmore. I put this place in order in no time. It's the best run Gas and Electric in the state."

"You're a good organizer, Harry."

"Damn right. Don't you do anything out there to embarrass me."

"I won't."

"Don't be swishing your fat ass at anyone around there either. I heard that big-muscled goof-off that hangs around is the doctor's brother. Stay away from him. He's a womanizer. I can tell one a mile away."

"I don't know him, Harry. I've only seen him a time or two at the clinic."

"He waved at you that day. I saw it with my own eyes. Jesus, Dale, you ought to know that he's making up to you for a reason. He's probably goin' to hit me up for a job. It'll be a cold day in hell when I give him one."

Harry had been seething since the brush off he'd been

given when he asked for a tire pump. He'd had to go to the station on a tire that badly needed air. He was surprised the tube hadn't been cut to ribbons by the time he got there.

Eddie had looked at his ruined tire and said that he must have run over a really sharp object to put such a hole in the tire and tube. He'd told him that he could put a boot in the tire, and with a new tube he could use the tire for a spare.

"By the way, Dale, clean the knees of the pants I wore today and press them. My coat needs a good brushing, too." Harry yawned without covering his mouth. "I'm going to bed."

# Chapter Nineteen

*C*urious eyes followed Henry Ann and Johnny to a table at the restaurant. In a town were everyone knew or had heard of everyone else, Henry Ann was someone new to wonder about. All that was known about her was that she had come in on the bus and had been met by Kathleen Henry. It was hot gossip in town that Kathleen had left Johnny and was living in town. Hell of a note, some said. A man goes to war, comes home, and his wife won't live with him.

If Johnny was aware of the curious glances following him and Henry Ann, he didn't show it. After they were seated, Henry Ann looked around, then plucked the printed menu from between the salt and pepper shakers and the sugar bowl. She glanced at it and handed it to Johnny.

"See anything you want?" he asked.

"The special. Roast beef, mashed potatoes, and gravy."

"Sounds good to me, too."

"If Rawlings is anything like Red Rock, people are wondering who I am."

"Shall I get up and make an announcement?"

"What would you say?"

"I'd say, 'Folks, I would like to present Mrs. Tom Dolan from Red Rock. This lady, who is only five years older than I, took in a mean fourteen-year-old city kid and changed my life. If not for her, I would probably be serving time in McCalister Penitentiary. She's my sister and my best friend. I think the world of her.' That's what I would say."

"Oh, Johnny. I may disgrace myself and cry."

"You will never disgrace yourself in my eyes, Hen Ann."

"I wish Aunt Dozie had lived to know that you came home from the war and that you turned out to be such a fine man."

"She probably knows I came home from the war." His dark eyes, usually so somber, laughed at her.

After the waitress took their order, Henry Ann said, "It's strange, and I feel guilty, but it doesn't seem like a member of the family died today."

"She was sicker than I thought when I took her out to the ranch. She complained about everything. I don't know what I would have done with her if Pete hadn't come when he did."

"You stood by her when she had no place else to go. You couldn't have done more for her. She lived the kind of life she wanted to live," Henry Ann said sadly.

"After I bought the ranch, I saw her in Oklahoma City. I told her that if she wanted to, she could come stay with me. She laughed and said it would be a cold day in hell when she moved to the sticks. I never heard from her again until Sheriff Carroll called and said she had asked him to get in touch with me and tell me to meet the bus."

"Tom and I will help with the burial expense."

"No need for you to do that. Pete gave the undertaker fifty dollars. I put in another fifty. That takes care of the burial, the plot, and a small stone."

"It wasn't Pete's obligation."

"Tell that to Pete. He's stubborn as a mule at times."

Henry Ann glanced at the diners in the booths that lined the sidewall. One man sat hunched over his meal. He looked up. His eyes slid over her and Johnny and then back to his plate. He had a chart of some kind lying on the table and he looked at it from time to time.

"Tom and the children are wondering when you're coming to see us."

"I'd better wait until I can get some decent tires."

"You could take the bus. Come and bring Kathleen. Tom would like to see her, too."

"I don't know about that, sis."

"Oh, dear. I told myself I'd not bring this up, but I've got to say it. I just hate it that you and Kathleen are not together." Henry Ann's expression was troubled.

"It isn't something you need to worry about."

"Why not? I love you both. Do you want to talk about it?"

"I'd rather not. Kathleen and I want different things out of life."

"What things?"

"She wants children. I do not."

"Johnny Henry! You'd make a wonderful father. I remember how you were with Jay—"

"Here's our food." Johnny smiled with relief.

The waitress, thinking that the smile was for her, giggled happily. Johnny didn't remember her, but she remembered him. All the high school girls back before the war had a crush on the Best All-Around Cowboy of Tillison County. Then he had to up and marry the redhead from the newspaper. It was rumored that they had separated.

"If you need anything else, Johnny, just give me a whistle," she said brightly.

"I'll do that, thank you."

"You're welcome, I'm sure."

"She was flirting with you," Henry Ann said. "Doesn't she know that you're married?"

"She's just being friendly."

The food was delicious, and Henry Ann was hungrier than she thought. Hot beef sliced, heaped on bread, and covered with gravy was one of her favorites.

"Pete has suggested, and I'm giving it some thought," Johnny said halfway through the meal, "that he and I form a company and put on rodeos. I'm not sure how much money it would take to start. It's just in the talking stage now."

"That's a great idea." She smiled into his eyes. "Pete is a talker. He could promote and you could manage behind the scenes."

Johnny looked at her with surprise. "It's just what I thought. We're both interested in raising rodeo horses."

"Do it, if you feel it's right. Henry & Perry Rodeos. I like the sound of it. Rodeos are just bound to get more popular now that the war is over."

"Folks like to see someone thrown on his rear. I always got the biggest hand when I hit the dirt." He grinned, remembering. "I doubt that I can get the money through the GI Bill to finance something like that."

"You could mortgage your ranch."

"I can't do that. Part of it belongs to Kathleen." He

looked away, veiling his expression. "I wouldn't ask her to take the risk."

It was completely dark when they left the restaurant and walked down the street to Johnny's car.

"Days are getting shorter," Henry Ann remarked.

"And cooler. On Guadalcanal I wished for a cool night like this."

When they reached the house, Johnny walked with Henry Ann to the porch. The lights were on in the front room and in Kathleen's bedroom.

"Are you coming in?"

"No. I'd better get back. You'll have a trying day tomorrow. I'll be here to take you to the burial. Pete and Jude will be there. Good night, sis. I'm glad you're here."

"I'm glad I'm here, too."

Theodore Nuding rubbed his face with his hands and pressed his fingers to his temples. He had eaten his supper at the restaurant, a treat he allowed himself occasionally. Now he sat at the table in the room he was preparing for Kathleen. His notebook was spread out in front of him. His had been a busy day. He picked up his pen and began to write.

*9:30 P.M. Mother, I am tired tonight. I don't like to admit it, but I've not felt the best lately. I've been working hard. So much to do and so little time. A lot happened today. My darling Kathleen went to see a lawyer. She looked so desolate, so lonely afterward, that I risked talking to her when she parked in front of the library and sat in her car. She is so beautiful. I wanted to stay and look at her, but I didn't dare. She will be happy here in her room, where she will have everything she needs. I'm making out a list and over Thanksgiving, I'll go to Dallas and place an order.*

*Johnny Henry's slutty sister died today. I knew that someone had died when the undertaker went to the clinic. Johnny Henry and the doctor's brother went to the funeral parlor, then to the cemetery to pick out a plot. He was at the cafe tonight with a woman. She is the one who came in on the bus today from Red Rock. It must be his other sister.*

*I've been having splitting headaches lately, Mother. At times they are so bad I can hardly see. I wish Kathleen was here. I would lay my head in her lap and she would rub the hurt away.*

Henry Ann, Johnny, Pete, and Jude were four of the eleven people who stood at Isabel's gravesite that knew her. The others were Barker Fleming, his two daughters and son, Adelaide and Paul Leahy, and Kathleen.

Lucas Fleming, in a dark suit, with his hat in his hand, fidgeted beside his father until Barker gave him a quelling glance. Marie and Janna, who towered over her older sister, both wore dark coats and hats.

Early this morning Marie had come to the house with a baked ham, potato salad, and a couple of loaves of Mrs. Fisher's freshly made bread. Kathleen had introduced her to Henry Ann.

"I'm glad to know you, Mrs. Dolan," Marie said.

"And I'm glad to know you. It was nice of you to bring food."

"Daddy insisted we start preparing right away as soon as we heard that Johnny's sister had died."

"I hope I get the chance to thank him."

"You will. All of us will be at the funeral."

Kathleen had avoided Johnny when he came to the house. She left it to Henry Ann to tell him about the food Barker had sent over. When she came out of the bedroom, wearing her dark coat and hat, Pete and Jude were there. And when they left the house, she had ridden in Pete's car to the cemetery.

Now it was over. The minister, whom the undertaker had engaged to read a simple service, had finished. The casket sat lonely beside the heap of red Oklahoma soil that would cover it. As the group began to move away, Kathleen invited Adelaide and Paul as well as Barker and his family to come to the house.

"You furnished the food, Barker, and besides, you should get to know Henry Ann, Johnny's sister."

"I would like that if it wouldn't be an imposition." Barker nudged his youngest daughter, who groaned at the thought of spending more time with the adults.

"I'll have Pete drop me off at the clinic." Jude took Henry Ann's hand in both of his. "Will I see you again before you go?"

"I'm going back in the morning. This is the first time I've been away from Tom and the kids. I'm homesick for them."

"Lucky Tom and the kids. Take care of yourself. Tell Tom hello."

"Take care of yourself, too. Seeing you has renewed my faith in human nature. Find a nice girl and start a family. That's where true happiness lies."

Jude kissed her on the cheek, lifted his hand to the others, and went to where Pete waited beside the car.

"I'll ride with Adelaide and Paul, Pete," Kathleen

called. "Come to the house after you deliver Jude." Ignoring Johnny, she took Adelaide's arm.

At the house, Kathleen insisted that Henry Ann visit with Johnny, Barker, and the Leahys while she and Marie prepared the food. She sliced the ham, and Marie set out plates and silverware.

"There's a cake in the lower cupboard, Marie. I baked it last night."

"What can I do?" Janna asked.

"Cut the cake," Kathleen said.

"Are you sure you want her to?" This came from a smiling Marie.

"I can do it," Janna insisted, and stuck her tongue out at her sister.

"She'll do just fine."

"Now here's a roomful of pretty women." Pete crowded into the small kitchen. "Better let me do that," he said, taking the slicing knife from Kathleen's hand.

"Gladly. I'll slice the bread."

"This knife is dull as dishwater, sugar. Don't you have a whetstone?"

"Sorry. You'll just have to make do. Janna, let's move the kitchen chairs to the other room. There isn't room in here for everyone to sit down."

After the meal, the men went to the porch to smoke.

"If you're looking for land," Barker said to Pete, "You may want to look at the Clifton ranch. I understand that it sold recently, but the owner isn't going to run cattle. It's good pastureland."

"Any of it tillable?"

"Might get a hay crop. It wasn't tilled during the dust storms. It's got good topsoil."

"The man who bought it is a famous writer, so John

Wrenn said. It didn't sound like he'd do much ranching himself. He will lease out grazing rights." Paul and Pete had hit it off. Paul liked a gutsy man who had had a few hard knocks and survived them.

"Is anyone living out there?" Pete asked.

"The writer hasn't moved in yet. A fellow from the weather bureau is staying out there looking after the place. Sheriff Carroll says he sits out west of town watching the clouds and making notes on a chart."

"Now that's a job that would grow mold on the brain." Pete's laughter was sudden and spontaneous. Lucas joined in, causing Pete to look down at him sitting on the edge of the porch. "You a cowboy?"

"Yeah." Lucas glanced at his father, then said, "Yes, sir."

"You like rodeos?"

"Yes . . . *sir*!"

"I'm trying to get Johnny to go in with me and put on a rodeo in the spring."

Lucas's eyes went to Johnny. "You goin' to?"

"I'm thinking about it."

"Could I have a job?"

"If you can cut the mustard."

"Ya . . . hoo!" Lucas jumped to his feet, and threw his hat in the air. The Stetson came down in the yard, and he ran to get it.

"We'll need someone to pick up horse turds, won't we, Pete?" Johnny teased, his dark eyes dancing with amusement.

"I'll do that, Johnny," Lucas said quickly. "You'll let me ride sometimes, won't you? Wait till I tell Janna. She's been practicing barrel racing. She's not very good," he scoffed.

"She'll get better." With his booted foot on the edge of the porch, the other on the ground, Johnny spoke to Barker.

"Sherm, the man living out at my place, found two of your steers in my back lot not fifty feet from the barn."

"How did they get there? Two steers don't usually wander off by themselves. A dozen maybe, but not two."

"Hell, I don't know. Sherm drove them down that dry gulley and back onto your land. One of them had an ear tag."

"I'll look into it."

"How is Bobby Harper doin'?" Paul Leahy asked.

"Dr. Perry said that he'd be off his leg for a while even after the cast is off."

"I'd keep my eye on Mack Boone if I were you."

"He's not the man his father is. I keep him on because of Victor."

"Watch him around Marie and Janna."

"Have you heard something?" Barker was instantly alert.

"A few brags is all."

"I don't like him," Lucas said.

"Any special reason?" Barker's dark gaze honed in on his son.

"Just don't." Lucas wondered if he should tell about seeing Mack with a slingshot the day Bobby Harper was bucked off and broke his leg. He decided that he'd wait and tell Johnny. "You'll not let Mack work at the rodeo, will you, Johnny?"

"The rodeo is just in the talk stage. Don't count on it just yet. We may not be able to swing the deal at all."

"I hope you do it, Johnny."

"We'd better get back home, son. You've got chores before dark. Go in and see if your sisters are ready to go."

"Yes, sir." Lucas bounded up on the porch, and Paul watched him.

"That's a dandy boy, Barker. He's full of beans and vinegar, just like he's supposed to be at that age."

"Not too bad yet. The time will come when he'll want to sow his wild oats. The hard part for me will be turning him loose."

Kathleen said good-bye to Paul and Adelaide and to the Flemings. She stood on the front porch and waved, dreading to go back into the house where only Johnny, Henry Ann, and Pete remained. She had managed to avoid Johnny all day, but now with just the four of them, it would be more difficult.

He spoke to her as soon as she entered.

"I'm taking Henry Ann out to my place. Do you want to come along?"

She swallowed once, hard, and avoided looking at him when she answered.

"No, thank you. I've got some cleaning up to do."

"Come, go with us," Henry Ann urged.

"No. This is your time together. You don't need me butting in."

"Come on, Henry Ann." Johnny took his sister's arm. "She doesn't want to come. Coming, Pete?"

"I'll stay here and give Kathleen a hand," Pete said.

Johnny slapped his hat down on his head as he went out the door and never looked back.

Pete followed Kathleen to the kitchen. "What do you have to do?"

"Well . . ." She looked around. "Nothing, really."

"I didn't think so. Let's go down to the drugstore, get a Coke, then go to the picture show."

"Do you know what's on?"

"*The Outlaw*, with Jane Russell."

"It must have changed today. Yesterday it was *Double Indemnity* with Barbara Stanwyck."

"I could go for that Jane Russell," he said with an exaggerated leer.

Kathleen laughed at his antics. "The show doesn't start until seven."

Pete looked at his watch. "We'll get a Coke, sit on Main Street, and watch the people go by, then go to the show."

"Sounds good. I haven't had a cherry Coke in ages."

Pete ordered the Cokes to be put in paper cups and brought them out to the car.

"I remember when cokes were a nickel," he grumbled as he got into the car and handed her the cup.

"Thanks. Cokes went up to ten cents during the war."

"I was land-based in the Pacific for one stretch. We looked forward to when the Salvation Army people came. They never charged us for cigarettes or candy bars."

"I've heard other servicemen say that." Kathleen sucked on the straw. "This is good, but not as fizzy as in the bottle."

"You and Johnny have a set-to?" Pete changed the topic of the conversation so smoothly that she wasn't prepared for the question.

"Ah . . . no. Why do you ask?" Her eyes were unwilling to meet his.

"You didn't look at him all day."

"Was it that obvious?"

"Probably not to anyone but me."

"Thank goodness for that." She sucked up the remainder of her Coke, then said, "Were you surprised when you met Johnny's father?"

"Yeah, I guess I was. Jude likes him."

"And you?"

"I like what I've seen so far. He doesn't seem to throw his weight around like you'd expect a man of his means to do."

"I like him very much. I like all the family. Johnny keeps them at arm's length."

"Johnny still has a chip on his shoulder."

"He has a right to have one. Look at what he's had to overcome." Kathleen jumped quickly to Johnny's defense. "He'll get over it one of these days—in his own time."

"Are you two ever going to get back together?"

"I don't think so. I saw a lawyer yesterday. I waited for Johnny to come home from the war and hoped that he'd want me back. He's made it clear that he does not want to live with me as man and wife." She couldn't keep the tears from her voice and swallowed repeatedly. "I need to make a clean break and . . . and start over."

"He wants you. It's eating him up."

"You're wrong. But stand by him. He needs friends like you and Jude." She looked at her watch. "If we're going to the show, we'd better get on down there."

# Chapter Twenty

"*I* had a really good time," Kathleen said, as Pete stopped his car behind Johnny's. "I love movies. I guess that's the storyteller in me. I'd see a movie every night of the week if I had the chance. Movies were all the entertainment I had during the war." Kathleen knew that she was rambling. Realizing that Johnny was in the house unnerved her.

"I like movies, too. *Casablanca* will be on next week. How about going with me?"

"Can I decide later?"

"Sure."

"Come in and say good-bye to Henry Ann. She's leaving on the eight-thirty bus in the morning."

On the way to the porch Kathleen stumbled on the rough ground. Pete caught hold of her arm and they were laughing as they stepped up onto the porch, still laughing as Kathleen opened the door. Johnny was sitting in her armchair, and Henry Ann was on the couch. He had a bland look on his face, but Kathleen knew him well enough to know that for some reason he was furious. *Too bad, Bud. I'm not waiting around for you any longer.*

"We've been to the show," she said cheerfully, and slipped out of her coat. "Now Pete's got a crush on Jane Russell."

"Who wouldn't? She's built like a brick outhouse," Pete declared. "That Hughes fellow knows how to pick 'em. I read that he gave her part of the profit to get her to take the role."

"Then she's set for life."

"I also read that he designed the . . . you know . . . the bra she wore to make her look more . . . buxom."

"Well, for goodness sake." Henry Ann laughed. "You must read a lot."

"I do when I find good stuff like that. Where shall I put the coat, sugar?"

"In on my bed. There's still ham left if anyone wants a sandwich."

"You don't have to ask me twice." Pete came out of the bedroom. "How about it, Johnny?"

"None for me."

"Have a seat, Pete, and visit with Henry Ann. I'll make some sandwiches and a pot of coffee."

"Thanks, sugar." He sat down on the couch. "It isn't often I have a pretty woman waiting on me. I'm going to take full advantage of it. You're leaving in the morning, Henry Ann?"

"I'm anxious to get back to the family. I'm glad I came. It was a sad occasion, but I got to see Johnny, Kathleen, and Jude."

"And me, Hen Ann?" Pete teased.

"I saw you a couple of weeks ago when you came to Red Rock looking for Jude. I've wondered about Isabel over the years. When Johnny called, he said that she was sick. I never thought she would go so quickly."

"She and Jude got along like a cat and dog when she was young, and in the end it was Jude that eased her passing. Ironic, isn't it?"

"Thank you for helping with the burial expense." Henry Ann reached over and placed her hand on Pete's. "It wasn't your responsibility."

"I wanted to do it. I may have helped contribute to her wayward ways. I wasn't too smart myself back then."

"We were all doing the best we could to get along."

"I'm glad you've got a good man, Henry Ann."

"He is a good man. You need to find someone and settle down, raise a family. Tom says that reformed rogues make good husbands." Her eyes smiled at him.

"If that's the case, I ought to be a jim-dandy."

"I always suspected that you were not quite as bad as you wanted folks to think you were."

Johnny got up suddenly and went to the kitchen. Pete's eyes followed him.

"Kathleen is going to get tired of waiting for him to decide what he wants to do. I'd hate like hell for him to lose her."

"I would, too. But they'll have to work it out. He won't talk to me about it."

Kathleen moved the coffeepot to the stove and turned to see Johnny's tall body blocking the doorway. He stood with one shoulder hunched against the doorjamb. With her movements going on automatic, she lowered the flame under the pot, then reached under the counter to bring out a cloth-covered platter that held what was left of the ham. She looked at him then, full in the face, and was proud that she could do it.

"Have you changed your mind about wanting a sandwich?"

"No."

"Cake?"

"No."

"Coffee then?"

"Maybe."

"It will be ready in ten minutes or so." Kathleen squatted in front of the small icebox and came up with a covered dish of butter.

"I'll be here in the morning to take Henry Ann to the bus."

"I figured you would." Kathleen spoke with her back to him.

"I appreciate your letting her stay here."

"It was my pleasure to have her."

"What's got your butt over the line?" Johnny snarled suddenly. "You've hardly looked at me for the past few days, much less spoken to me. Did I impose on your private life by asking if Henry Ann could stay here?"

Kathleen didn't answer. She began to butter the slices of bread she had laid out on a plate.

"That's it, isn't it? You didn't want my sister to stay here."

"I just told you that it was my pleasure to have her. Don't be a bigger ass than you already are!" Kathleen swung around, her eyes bright with anger. "Henry Ann is one of the nicest people I know. Far nicer than you are."

"I'll not dispute that. I never claimed to be an angel, but I'm not a devil either."

"No. You're a stubborn jackass with a one-track mind. You think that you are always right about everything."

"Not quite everything. I don't know you anymore."

"And you don't want to. I'm tired of waiting around for you to make up your mind about whether or not you want to be married to me. I went to see Mr. Fairbanks yesterday."

"And—?" His voice lowered to a mere whisper.

"—And as soon as we can decide on the *grounds* for the divorce, he'll file it."

"What do you mean . . . grounds?"

"We have to give the judge a reason why we want a divorce."

"A *reason*?"

"Yes, a reason. He'll want to know if you beat me? No. Did you refuse to support me? No, even though I don't need your support. Have you been unfaithful? I don't know. Did you refuse to live with me. *Yes!*"

"Why do there have to be grounds?"

"How the hell do I know." Kathleen was snarling now. "I've never been divorced before. Do you think that I'm proud that everyone in town knows that my husband refuses to live with me? I have endured that embarrassment as long as I'm going to."

"Still can't hold your temper."

"Why should I? You've treated me like a doormat ever since you came back. Damn, damn, dammit to hell! I'll lose my temper. I'll swear and even throw things if I want to. This is my house, and if you don't like it, you can get your sorry butt out of it."

"You've really worked up a full head of steam, haven't you?"

"I've got my pride, too."

"Have you got something going with Pete? Is that the reason you went to see a lawyer?"

"Maybe," she said just to irritate him. "I've got my eye on several eligible men."

"Including Barker."

"Barker is your father, for Christ sake!" She was almost yelling.

"He could give you everything you want!"

"How do you know what I want? Have you ever asked me? No, it's only about what you want, or don't want."

"I don't want to go through what we went through before. You know that."

"You're too thickheaded to go find out for sure why Mary Rose was born the way she was. You think that you have all the answers. Well, maybe you've got it into that pea-size brain of yours that it was something I did that caused it."

"You know damn good and well I don't think that!" Johnny turned his head quickly to look in the living room when he heard the front door close.

"Henry Ann has gone out onto the porch so she doesn't have to listen to your ranting."

"If you didn't want your sister to hear me calling you a horse's ass, you shouldn't have come in here and started it."

The coffeepot began to boil over. One step took Johnny to the stove, where he shut off the gas cutting off the flame beneath it. He went back to the doorway.

"Let me know when you want me to sign the papers."

"Oh, you'll know. I'll make damn sure you know," she snarled, and slapped a slice of bread down onto the plate.

"I'll be here in the morning."

"I can hardly wait. As you leave, tell Pete his sandwich is ready."

During the rest of the evening, Kathleen managed to hide to some degree her feelings of smoldering anger. She sat with her guests at the kitchen table. Pete squeezed her shoulder reassuringly when he came in, then proceeded to be amusing. He told stories about things that had happened while he was in the navy, funny things usually at his expense. After that, he and Henry Ann reminisced about their younger days in Red Rock until it was time for him to leave.

When they were alone, the two women silently prepared for bed. Kathleen was grateful when Henry Ann didn't mention Johnny or the overheard words that had passed between them. Heartsick and frightened, she turned out the lights and got into bed.

The years ahead would be long and lonely.

Kathleen told Henry Ann good-bye on the front porch while Johnny waited in the car. He had nodded good morning when he came to the porch for her suitcase, and she had nodded coolly in return.

"Regardless of what happens between you and Johnny, I want us to stay in touch. Besides being Tom's niece, his only connection to Duncan, his brother, you are very dear to us. Write and let me know how you are doing. I pray that things will work out between you and Johnny."

"A lot of time has gone by. Every day that passes we get farther apart. Tell Uncle Tom that as soon as I get a better car, I'll be over to see you-all. Just listen to me, I've been down South so long, I'm even saying *you-all*," Kathleen said lightly. She had to keep things light or she'd cry.

"I'll tell him. Take care of yourself."

"You too."

Kathleen waved, then went back into the house as soon as the car began to move.

What would she do with the rest of the day? She wasn't in the mood to write for her book or to read, which was her favorite pastime. She sat down in the big chair where Johnny had sat the night before, reached over and turned on the radio.

*"Jack Roosevelt Robinson, a Georgia-born son of a sharecropper and grandson of a slave will join the Montreal club, a Brooklyn Dodgers affiliate of the International League. A spokesman said that the signing was not to be interpreted merely as a gesture toward solving the racial unrest. Robinson, who has been playing in the Negro League—"*

Kathleen turned the dial and discovered that news was on almost every station this time of morning.

*"Today the first refrigerator plane crossed the country with a full load. It is the beginning of a new era. The president of the airline has predicted that within a few months fish will reach the consumer within hours after it leaves the sea.*

*On another note: Shoe rationing will end November 23. Meat and butter rationing ends December 20 just in time for Christmas."*

Kathleen switched off the radio when the phone rang. It was Marie.

"Has your company left?"

"She left this morning."

"Would you mind riding with me over to Frederick this morning? I need to see the dentist, and Daddy says I can't go alone. He would go with me, but he can't leave the plant until late afternoon. I had counted on Thelma, but she isn't well today."

"I'm at loose ends today. I'll be glad for something to do."

"Oh, good. I'll be by in about thirty minutes. Is that too soon?"

"Not at all. I'll be ready."

Johnny and Henry Ann sat in his car as they waited for the bus that would take her back to Red Rock.

"When will I see you again, Johnny?"

"I don't know, sis. I'm trying to get some things sorted out."

"Have you applied for your GI benefits? You're entitled to twenty dollars a week for a year."

"I haven't applied. That's for men who can't find a job. I could get one operating heavy machinery, but it would mean leaving here. I don't want to give up on my ranch."

"The ranch or Kathleen?" Henry Ann reached for his hand and clasped it tightly. "I'm sorry. I promised myself I'd stay out of your private affairs."

"I have no private affairs where you are concerned, sis." He watched the big Greyhound bus come lumbering down Main Street and stop in front of the *Gazette* Building.

"She loves you."

"She did at one time. That may be coming to an end."

"Women don't fall out of love easily."

"You saw how happy she was with Pete."

"Being happy and having a good time with someone doesn't necessarily mean falling in love with them."

"You know how he is. If she should fall for him, it

would be like jumping out of the frying pan and into the fire. He'll never be faithful to any woman."

"You could be wrong, Johnny. Pete puts on a good show because he's not sure of himself or where he stands with people. I believe now that was why he was so obnoxious when he was young. If he ever meets a woman who believes in him and loves him, he'll be faithful."

"Time will tell, won't it? We'd better go. They're loading up."

Johnny set her suitcase down beside the bus. The driver opened a side door and shoved it into the compartment.

"Get aboard, folks."

"I want to see Tom and the kids, but I hate to leave you when you're so troubled." Henry Ann clung to Johnny's hand. "Talk to Kathleen."

"I will. Tell Tom and the kids hello."

"'Bye, Johnny." Henry Ann had tears in her eyes when she kissed him on the cheek.

"'Bye, sis. I'll be over sometime soon."

Johnny stood on the sidewalk and waited for the bus to leave. Henry Ann waved and he waved back. When the bus turned the corner and was out of sight, he went back to his car. He didn't think that he had ever felt more lonely in his life.

Talk to Kathleen, she'd said. What could he say to her? *I know what you want? I can't give it to you, but I don't want to lose you? How can I live with you as my wife and not make love to you? We would have to be so careful that you didn't get pregnant. The constant worry could, in time, drive us apart. I'm sure there isn't a protection that is a hundred percent safe.*

Last night he had intended to talk to her calmly, to tell

her that he and Pete had talked about promoting rodeos and to ask her if she would be willing for them to refinance the ranch. But she had gone out with Pete when she had refused to go with him and Henry Ann. He had said things that he wished he could take back. It was stupid of him to throw Barker up at her. He knew deep down that she would never marry his father.

Johnny started the car. He had told Henry Ann that he would talk to her, and he would. He would explain to her once again that it had taken the heart right out of him when he saw the pitifully deformed body of their baby. He had seriously considered blowing his brains out. At the time he had thought, what the hell good was he to humanity?

The answer had come when he saw the poster of Uncle Sam pointing a finger. *We want you.*

He had enlisted. But not a day had gone by that he hadn't thought of her. Not a night that he didn't ache for her.

Johnny pulled his car into the driveway behind Kathleen's Nash. She should have another car, he thought as he got out and walked up onto the porch. That thing wasn't going to last much longer.

He rapped on the door, waited, then rapped again. Her car was here. He had not seen her walking to town. Had she seen him and was refusing to come to the door? He opened the screen and tried the doorknob. Locked. Then it occurred to him that she had gone somewhere with Pete. He stomped off the porch, got back in his car, and headed out of town.

# Chapter Twenty-one

*T*he weather turned bad two days before Thanksgiving. A cold rain kept Kathleen indoors. It proved to be a good time to work on her book. She forced herself to concentrate on it . . . then she became interested again, and it became easier to immerse herself in the story.

She had not seen Johnny since the morning Henry Ann left. Pete had come by from time to time. He told her that he, Barker, and Lucas had helped Johnny drive his horses up from Keith McCabe's ranch.

Theresa called to let Kathleen know what she was taking to Jude's for the Thanksgiving dinner.

"I wanted to make sure that both of us didn't make pumpkin pie."

"Any pie that I made would be tough enough to dance on. I'll bring the cranberry sauce, sweet potatoes, and apple salad."

"Pete is cooking the turkey. I'll bring the corn bread dressing and the pie. I'm looking forward to it. I hope we don't have an emergency at the clinic."

"I'm wondering how many turkeys Pete has cooked in the past. Maybe I should make a meat loaf."

Theresa laughed. "He says that he can do it. I hope he remembers to take the insides out."

Thanksgiving morning Kathleen was up early. After preparing the food she was going to take to the dinner, she took a bath. Looking at herself in the mirror after she got out of the tub, she was surprised that her face was so pale. She examined herself closely.

Her hair was shoulder length now. She picked up the scissors and snipped until she had short curls across her forehead and from the corners of her eyes to her jawbone. Satisfied that her face didn't look so *bald*, she applied light makeup.

The dress she had chosen to wear was forest green jersey with a gathered skirt and full sleeves caught at the wrist with a wide cuff. It was a soft dress, the color was good, and it made her feel feminine.

The day was bright and sunny, not at all like the Thanksgivings she remembered in Iowa, where, if snow hadn't already fallen, there was the promise of it in the air. Telling herself that she hadn't mashed the sweet potatoes and added butter and cinnamon because that was the way Johnny liked them, but because it was the only way she knew how, she packed the food in a box and set it in the backseat of the Nash.

Only Pete's car was parked in front of Jude's house. He saw her drive up and came out to help her with the box.

"Am I the first one here?"

"Theresa is here. Jude had me go get her while he went to the clinic. Someone over there had a pain or something." Before they stepped up onto the porch Pete stopped. "Kathleen . . . Johnny isn't coming. He went down to Vernon to the McCabes."

For some reason Kathleen was not surprised and swallowed her disappointment.

"That means all the more turkey for us," she said brightly.

"I hope it's fit to eat. I never cooked one before."

"You . . . never cooked one?" She held the door open for him.

"No, but if anyone else can do it, I can. I went right by the instructions Dale gave me. I had her write them down."

"Dale Cole?"

"Yeah."

"I hope she told you to take off the feathers."

"She did. Hey, you've got to meet Theresa's boy. He's a ringed-tail tooter." He set her box down on the kitchen table. "Let me take your coat."

Theresa came from the pantry. "Hello, Kathleen. Do you have anything that should go in the refrigerator?"

"The salad and the cranberry sauce. Oh, my, isn't it a beauty." Kathleen ran her hand over the door of Jude's new refrigerator. "I'm going to have one of these one day."

"The sweet potatoes will stay warm on the back of the stove."

Pete came back to the kitchen with a small, pixie-faced boy riding on his shoulders.

"Know where I found this little peanut? Hiding in the closet. When he grabbed my leg, I was sure that a Jap was about to cut my toes off."

The child giggled happily and held on to Pete's head.

"Kathleen, this is my son, Ryan. Say hello to Mrs. Henry, Ryan."

"How-dee-do, pretty lady," he said in a deep voice, then giggled uncontrollably.

"Ryan," his mother said. "Where did you learn to talk like that?"

Still giggling, Ryan patted the top of Pete's head. Pete swung him down off his shoulders and set him on the floor.

"All right," he said gruffly. "You gonna rat on me ya got to pay." He grabbed him around the middle and, with him dangling from under one arm, left the kitchen.

"What ya gonna do, Pete? What ya gonna do?"

"I'm going to make me some peanut butter."

Sounds of laughter and thumps came from the living room. Theresa rolled her eyes.

"I hope they don't break anything. I don't know which one is the biggest kid. Honestly. Ryan adores Pete, and Jude, too."

"Obviously Pete likes him."

"It's been wonderful for Ryan. He's not had men in his life except his grandfather on his father's side. Believe me, he was nothing like Pete and Jude."

"I don't think there's anyone like Pete."

Jude returned after stitching a man's split lips and a bad cut over his eye.

"Too much whiskey and not enough brains. He'll not be eating turkey for a while."

It became obvious to Kathleen that Theresa and her son had been frequent visitors to Jude's house. She wondered if it was at Jude's invitation or Pete's. Theresa seemed to know what Jude had in the way of china and silver, bowls and pots.

After he proudly brought a golden brown turkey to the table, Pete handed the carving knife to Jude.

"Have at it, brother. You need the practice," Pete said, and sat down beside Ryan. "He might need to take off a leg or two in the next few days or do a little slicing here and there," he explained in a loud whisper.

"Pete, that's awful!" Kathleen's hand went to her mouth.

"Mom, what's awful?" Ryan asked.

"I'll tell you after dinner."

Kathleen enjoyed herself even though she didn't have much of an appetite. Johnny had not been mentioned since Pete's announcement that he wasn't coming. It was Kathleen's fifth Thanksgiving without him, so it wasn't anything new.

During the meal Kathleen noticed Jude's eyes straying often to Theresa. She wore a blue dress with tiny darker blue flowers. Her cheeks were flushed, her eyes shining. Before sitting down, she had whipped off a frilly apron.

After the meal Theresa carefully wrapped the leftover food and put it in the refrigerator.

"Now if Pete's gone tomorrow, the doctor will have a meal."

"Is Pete going somewhere?"

"I heard him tell the doctor that he was going to the city to see about buying some land."

"In the city?"

"Here, but whoever it is he has to see is in the city."

While Ryan napped, the two couples played cards. Pete called the game Pitch; Kathleen called it High, Low, Jack, and the Game. Despite the argument over the name of the game, Kathleen and Pete played well together and skunked Jude and Theresa. After two hours, Jude threw up his hands and protested that they had cheated.

As Kathleen prepared to leave, she told Pete to tell Dale that the turkey was cooked perfectly.

"The dinner was wonderful, the company outstanding. I enjoyed myself immensely," she told Jude.

"Come again, Kathleen."

"Hey, sugar," Pete called as she went toward her car. She paused and he caught up with her. "Shall we see the movie tonight?"

"Ah, Pete, why don't you take Theresa?"

"And have Jude serve my head up on a platter? No, sir, my head's too important to me."

"Is . . . he? They?"

"I think he likes her a lot. I'm not sure if she has gotten to that stage. I'm working on it."

"Why . . . you matchmaker, you!"

"Pretty smart of me, don't you think?"

"You want to get out of the house tonight and give them some time to be alone, is that it?"

"You've hit the nail on the head, sugar."

"Come over and we'll listen to the radio and play two-handed solitaire."

"You got a date."

During the week that followed, Kathleen worked with Adelaide on the Christmas carnival to be held on Saturday. They were raising funds to pay for the remodeling of the room at the clinic to accommodate the iron lung that had already arrived and was set up in a storage room in case of need.

Posters were up all over town, and flyers had been sent to surrounding towns. Because it was an affair that would benefit not only Tillison County, but surrounding counties, announcements had been made on the Frederick radio broadcasts.

Adelaide confided to Kathleen that Paul was working on getting a license to operate a radio station in Rawlings.

"It's something he has always wanted to do. I hope he is able to swing it. He already has a backer."

"Backer? Oh, and I bet I can guess who that is."

"You'd be guessing right, of course. Sometimes I think that Johnny Henry is dumb as a doorknob. He has no idea what a remarkable man his father is."

"Only a few people know what Barker does for this town. The rest of them see him as an Indian and resent what he has. His father made a lot of money, but he taught his children how to use it. Most people, if they had Barker's money, would be sitting around doing nothing. He works."

"Well." Adelaide sniffed. "I didn't mean for you to get on a soapbox. And, by the way, Barker approached Paul with the idea. Not the other way around as you would expect."

"It hadn't occurred to me to expect anything. Paul has a wonderful speaking voice for the radio."

"Everything about Paul is wonderful."

"Oh, Lord. I've started the ball rolling. She'll go on for hours."

"No, I won't," Adelaide said pertly. "I've got to get down to the schoolhouse."

On the day of the carnival, Kathleen worked on decorations all day. She tied up balloons the high-school boys had inflated with an air hose at Eddie's station. She hung strips of crepe paper and made signs on big sheets of butcher paper donated by Miller's grocery.

She was so busy that she hadn't had time for a passing thought of Johnny until, on a trip to the *Gazette* office, she saw his car parked in front of the drugstore. Then, fearing that she would run into him, she grabbed up the newsprint Paul had rolled off. It was to serve as a backdrop on the small stage that had been set up in the gymnasium where the dance would be held. She flung it into the car and hurried back to the school.

The five-member band was not of Bob Wills's class, but they were up-and-coming local musicians and were donating their services. For the carnival they were calling themselves Willie and the Chicken Pluckers. They showed up in hillbilly costumes: straw hats, ragged overalls, oversized shoes with the toes cut out. Just looking at them put Kathleen in the mood for a good time.

People were beginning to arrive when Kathleen dashed home to change clothes. As she dressed, it occurred to her that she had not had her monthly period. The date had come and gone and she had not noticed because occasionally she would go for as long as five or six days beyond her due date.

With one stocking on and one off she went to find a calendar. It had been over five weeks. Now that she was thinking about it, she had only flowed a part of a day during her last period, which in itself was not unusual; three days was her limit. It would just be her luck to start tonight. For safety's sake she put a couple of tampons in her purse.

She was amazed at the number of cars parked around the school when she reached it and had to park half a block away. It was a warm evening for the first week in December, and she didn't mind the walk.

The booths had opened in the classrooms. People, some in costume, were wandering up and down the hallway. Criers were standing in the doorways enticing them to enter. Kathleen made her way to the gymnasium and through the crowd that milled behind the area roped off for dancing.

Pete had been pressed into service to act as announcer at the dance. The band, playing to liven up the crowd, was putting on a show. The fiddler jigged as he played his violin; one of the guitar players plucked wildly while trying to stomp on the toes of the band members who were not wearing shoes. The drummer, wearing a helmet, kept hitting himself on the head, and the piano player, his overalls on backward, wore an oversize tattered straw hat that covered his ears. The crowd was enjoying their antics.

Kathleen made her way to the stage to join the dime-a-dance girls. Four of the five chairs were filled. She recognized one girl who worked in the Golden Pheasant and another who worked part time at the library. The other two were high-school girls. All four women were pretty. Kathleen was sure they would all have paying partners before she did. As soon as she took her seat, Pete picked up the microphone and began to talk.

"Folks, we are about to get this little shindig under way. It's only going to cost you ten pennies to dance with your lady love. Willie here tells me they will be long dances, so you'll get your money's worth. The band members have donated their time and talent so that every dime that you spend here tonight will go toward that polio room in the clinic.

"For you gents who chained your wives to the washtub so you could come here tonight"——Pete paused for the laughter——"there are five pretty girls sitting up here on the stage who will dance with you, if . . . a big if . . . you've got a ticket. Kathleen, that pretty redhead on the end, is a knockout, don't you agree? The little blonde next to her is just as cute as a button. The brunette will dance your legs off as will that one with the pretty brown hair next to her. The little 'un on the other end was made for a slow, cuddlin' waltz. Sugar, I'm goin' to dance with you before this night is over.

"Willie's going to start the evening off with our own Bob Wills's 'San Antonio Rose.' If you haven't got a ticket, gents, go get one, get two or three dozen. You'll use them before the night's over. Remember just ten cents. That's two packs of chewing gum. Wouldn't you rather dance with your sweetheart or one of these pretty girls than chew gum or smoke a ten-cent cigar?

"One more thing, folks. If you don't dance, that's all right. You can drop a donation in the jar right over there on the ticket table. It could be your kids or your neighbor's kids who come down with polio. They'll have a better chance if we have that iron lung set up and running." Pete drew a string of tickets out of his pocket. "I'll start it off with the beautiful redhead."

He came to the stage and held his hand out to Kathleen. By the time they got to the middle of the dance floor, men were coming through the gate with a partner or hurrying to choose one of the four girls on the stage.

"You've missed your calling." Kathleen matched her steps to Pete's. "You should have been a ringmaster at a circus."

"Think so?" Pete laughed and whirled her around. "Honey, I'm just now gettin' warmed up."

Willie had a surprisingly good voice. Following "San Antonio Rose", the band played "Tumbling Tumbleweeds", a slow waltz.

"Looks like a good crowd."

"Each dance will last a little over ten minutes. Think your feet will hold out?"

"I'll not dance every dance."

"Wanna bet? We'll have to limit the number of consecutive dances or one of these gents will hog you all evening."

Kathleen laughed. "Wanna bet?"

She would have lost the bet. The five girls never had a chance to sit down. Men stood in line to dance with them. Kathleen danced with men she had never seen before. Some of them danced really well, while others merely swayed back and forth, which was fine with her.

The band was playing "When I Grow Too Old to Dream" when Kathleen stepped into the arms of a well-dressed man with dark hair, graying at the temples. His coat was an expensive tweed.

"Good evening, Kathleen." The words were said softly in her ear as they moved across the floor.

"Good evening."

He held her firmly to him, making it easy to follow his steps. She wondered vaguely at the familiarity of his using her first name, then dismissed the thought.

Theodore Nuding was sure that she could feel the pounding of his heart. After seeing her name listed as one of the ladies who would be available for dancing, he had taken great pains with his disguise. He had darkened his hair, put in the false gray, colored his eyebrows, and even darkened the skin on his face. He was better at making himself look old, but tonight he had wanted to look attractive.

He turned his head until his nose touched her hair and breathed in the scent of her. She was so lovely, so graceful. He spread the fingers of the hand on her back in order to feel more of her. They danced slowly. He knew that he danced well. His mother had taught him.

The dance was over all too quickly for Nuding, but he

was a patient man. He released her and stepped back. She had not said a word after the initial greeting, but it had not been necessary to hear her voice. He knew it as well as he knew his own.

"Thank you, my dear," he said, and quickly walked away before she could examine his face too closely. By the time Nuding reached the back of the crowd where he could watch her unobserved, she had another partner and was dancing.

Kathleen was a little puzzled. Something about the man she had just danced with was familiar. Her mind, accustomed to ferreting out details for her stories, searched her memory and came up with nothing.

To her utter surprise, when it came time to change partners again, she found herself in Johnny's arms.

"Where did you come from? I didn't see you here."

"You've been too busy to look."

When Willie began to sing, "Thanks for the Memory," Johnny's arms tightened around her just a fraction. They didn't talk. Kathleen couldn't have carried on a coherent conversation because she was flooded with conflicting feelings: resentment that he had stayed away for so long and gratitude that he was here and holding her. She closed her eyes and enjoyed the wonderful feel of him, his breath in her hair, the warmth of his hand on her back and his heart beating against hers.

The dance was over before Kathleen realized it. They stood together in the crowd waiting for the next song.

"How are your feet holding out?" Johnny asked. "You've danced every dance. We can sit this one out."

"They're still all right."

"If you don't want to polka, we'd better move over to the side." The song was the "Beer Barrel Polka," and some of the dancers were showing off. He took her hand, and she followed him to the side of the dance floor.

"I'll use a couple of my tickets and you can sit out if you're tired."

"I'm not that tired."

Words dried up between them, and they watched the dancers. Dale Cole was dancing with her husband. Theresa was dancing with Doug Klein from the funeral home. Millie was there and didn't lack for partners. Kathleen saw Judy taking pictures of the band for the *Gazette*. Later she was dancing with a cowboy with sandy hair and sideburns. After one dance with Theresa, Jude mingled with the crowd, explaining about the iron lung.

"We're going to have a tag dance, folks. This is the way it works." Pete's voice came over the microphone. "All you men without a partner give your ticket to the gate keeper and come on in. For the next twenty minutes you can tap a gent on the shoulder and take his partner. After you've been tagged, you can tag another gent. Now this is going to be fun. Turn the lights down, boys. Everyone enjoy the dance."

Pete watched, thinking that Harry Cole might lead Dale off the floor and was relieved when they started dancing. Cole was playing the big dog. He had swallowed hook, line, and sinker Jude's line about his run for public office the day he had come to the clinic to give notice that Dale was going to quit. Pretty clever of Jude. If it had been left up to Pete, he'd have just rearranged the bastard's face. Pete waited until a dozen couples had exchanged partners before he tapped Harry on the shoulder.

"You're tagged. My turn with this pretty woman," Pete said cheerfully.

Harry looked at him first with surprise, then as if he'd

like to run him through with a rapier. Pete paid him not the slightest attention, just elbowed him aside and took Dale in his arms. They moved away from the stunned man.

"Why? Why, did you . . . do that?" Dale gasped.

"Because I wanted to dance with you." Deep in the crowd, he tightened his arm around her. Pete was a strong dancer and she followed him easily. "Is it so wrong to want to dance with you?"

"He'll be furious." The distress was notable in her voice.

"I gave him the chance to get off the floor if he didn't want to be tagged." Pete moved his cheek against her hair.

"He . . . never thought anyone would want to dance with me."

"He was wrong! I've been waiting for the chance."

"You'll be stuck with me."

"I hope so. Are things going all right?"

"I guess so."

Johnny tapped him on the shoulder. "Go away."

"Not on your life. Give up, man, or I'll deck you."

"I'll be back, Dale."

Pete looked for Kathleen, knowing that they would dance for only a minute or two before someone cut in. He tapped her partner on the shoulder and took her in his arms.

"How ya doin', sugar?"

"Good. Johnny saw you dancing with Mrs. Cole. Her husband is giving you dirty looks. He looks mad enough to chew nails."

"Is that why Johnny cut in?"

"I don't know. Someone cut in on him."

"That bastard beats her. Did you know that?"

"I'd . . . heard—"

Pete was tapped on the shoulder by the man in the tweed coat. When he took Kathleen's hand she noticed he had a deep white scar across the back of his hand. A man she knew at the plant in the city had one like it. She turned to look up into his face, but they were too close.

"Hello, again." His voice was a mere whisper in her ear.

"Do I know you?"

"Name's Robert Brooks."

"Kathleen Henry, but you knew my name."

"The announcer said, 'Kathleen, the pretty redhead.' He was right about you being pretty."

"Thank you."

Johnny tapped the man on the shoulder. His arms dropped reluctantly from around Kathleen, and he moved away.

"Who is that guy?"

"He said he was Robert Brooks."

"He's been watching you like a hawk."

"Maybe I remind him of someone."

Johnny had to give Kathleen over to another partner. He looked for Pete and found him dancing again with the nurse from the clinic.

"I wish you . . . hadn't—" Dale was saying.

"Why hasn't he cut back in?"

"He's too . . . angry."

"Godamighty, Dale. As bad as I wanted to dance with you, I'd not do anything to get you hurt. What's the matter with that son of a bitch?"

"He's always been like that." Her voice quivered.

It was the last few minutes of the dance before intermission. The lights were turned down even more. Pete pressed his cheek tightly against hers.

"You don't love him, do you?"

"I've forgotten what love is."

"Leave him. Dale, honey. I'll take care of you and the boy." They were barely moving now.

She stirred in his arms and looked up at him. "You don't know what you're saying."

"Yes, I do. I'm in love with you. Don't ask me why. I just am. I've given this a lot of thought. I've been looking for a woman like you all my life."

"You can't be!"

"I am! He's made you feel that a man wouldn't find you desirable. Godamighty! I should beat the hockey out of him just for that. I damn sure will if he hurts you again."

"Please. I'm married to him. He'll take Danny."

The music ended, and seconds later the lights came on.

"Thank you, Mrs. Cole," Pete said loudly enough for those nearby to hear.

"Intermission," Willie was saying. "We need time to smoke and wet our whistles. We'll be back in fifteen minutes."

Pete turned away when he saw Harry walking across the floor toward his wife.

# Chapter Twenty-two

"*T*here's a fellow out there slappin' the shit out of his woman."

The piano player, a veteran, leaning heavily on his cane, came in from outside where he had gone to smoke.

"What did you say?" Pete jumped to his feet.

"Some no-good fart-knocker is out there beatin' up on a woman. Somebody's got to do somethin'. Hell, I can't do nothin' with this bum leg," he added, as Pete shot out the door.

In a shadowed corner away from the door Harry was holding Dale against the wall with his forearm against her throat. His other hand was fastened in her hair.

"You're a worthless slut. You're a goddamned trashy whore. You've been carryin' on with that mouthy son of a bitch. You've disgraced me—" He slapped her, his hand against her cheek making a loud clapping sound.

"Get away from her!" Fury tore through Pete, shutting off his breath. He started to speak again, choked, and gulped down spittle and air. He grabbed Harry by the back of the neck.

"Bast . . . ard! I . . . ought to kill you!"

Harry was snatched back so suddenly that he stumbled and never had a chance to regain his balance. Pete's fist slammed into his mouth, knocking him off his feet. Blood splattered over his white shirt.

"Get up, you shithead. You're goin' to know what it's like to get some of what you've been givin' her."

"No! Please . . ." Dale caught Pete's arm.

Pete was too angry to hear her pleading. He shrugged her arm away, reached down, and grabbed Harry by his coat and hauled him to his feet. He backed him against the building and slapped him first on one side of the face and then the other, rocking his head back and forth. Blood from Harry's nose ran freely down over his mouth and onto his shirt. Pete continued to slap him, cursing him with every blow. Harry hung almost limp against the building.

"You sorry, rotten piece of horseshit. You're not fit to lick her shoes. Try picking on someone who'll fight back, you low-down, stinkin' coward!"

"Hey, fellow, that's enough." Willie put a hand on Pete's arm. "Leave enough of him for the sheriff."

Pete stepped back, and Harry slumped to the ground.

"What's going on here?" Sheriff Carroll, his flashlight illuminating the area, came out the door of the school. Johnny was behind him.

Pete went to where Dale leaned against the building, her face hidden in the crook of her arm. He put his hands on her shoulders and turned her toward him.

"I'm sorry. I'm so damn sorry. I caused this by dancing with you, didn't I?"

Dale stood with her head bowed. "He would have found another excuse."

It was some time before the men watching Dale realized that she was crying. There was no contortion of her features, no quivering lips, only a soundless outpouring of grief as tears crept down her cheeks.

"He'll kill me now, and Danny will be alone with him," she said hoarsely.

"What happened here, Mrs. Cole?" Sheriff Carroll asked.

"He was . . . angry with me."

"Did he hurt you?"

"He slapped me."

"This isn't the first time," Pete said. "I've seen bruises on her, around her neck, where he's choked her. He's a yellow coward. A man who beats a woman is as low a son of a bitch as there is."

"Looks like you taught him a lesson. Mr. Cole, can you get on your feet?"

Pete didn't wait for Harry to move. He reached down, hauled him up, and leaned him against the wall.

"Put the yellow-backed, belly-crawling shithead in jail. He's not man enough to fight anybody but a woman."

"I can't arrest him because he slapped his wife. There's no law against it."

"Now that's a hell of a note!"

"Can't help it, son, that's the way it is."

Harry came out of his daze and away from the wall. He pulled a handkerchief from his pocket, held it to his nose, and pointed a shaky finger at Pete.

"He attacked me."

"You're lucky he got to you first," Willie said. "I'd of broke your damn neck. Wife beaters are at the bottom on my list of human beings."

"Who are you to judge?" Harry sneered.

"Take over for me in there, Willie." Pete put his arm around Dale.

"Yeah. It stinks out here."

"If you even think about doing this again, I'll strip the hide off you and feed it to the buzzards." Pete shoved Harry back up against the wall.

Harry stiffened his legs and with a show of defiance moved from the wall. "Let's go home, Dale."

"She's not going."

"She's my wife."

"Dale?" Pete held her arms and looked into her face. "I'll find a place for you. You don't have to go with him."

"I've got to. Danny." The look of hopelessness in her eyes tore at Pete's heart.

"You and Danny. Make the break, Dale," Pete pleaded. "I promise you that he'll not hurt you or Danny ever again."

"Come on, Dale. You're only making things worse for yourself." Harry turned to the sheriff. "I have a standing in this town. You arrest this ruffian, or I'll have your job."

"You can have it anytime you want, Harry," Sheriff Carroll said calmly.

"Mr. Cole to you. I'll be down Monday morning to file charges."

"I'll be out of town all next week, *Harry*."

"Come on, Dale." Harry moved away, fully expecting Dale to follow. When she didn't, he turned. "Come with me now or you'll be on your fat ass out in the street tomorrow morning . . . without Danny. Don't expect to see him again. I'll not have him corrupted by trash like you're hanging around with."

Pete looked at Dale, waiting for her answer. She was staring at Harry as if she had never seen him before. Slowly she shook her head.

"I'm through with you, Harry. You've hit me, shamed me and Danny for the last time. I wish I never had to see your mean face again." There was a fearful tremor in her voice.

"That does it! You been screwin' this—"

"Say it, and you'll be swallowing teeth," Pete threatened. The men standing around, even Johnny and the sheriff, grinned.

"Well, it seems you've made your choice," Harry sneered. "I'll get my son and take him home."

"The boy belongs with his mother," Pete said, with his fist drawn back. "Stay away from him."

"I'm taking my son. The law will back me. Isn't that right, Sheriff?"

Sheriff Carroll looked steadily back at Harry. "The boy stays with his mother."

Harry exploded in a rage. "You'll be sorry for this." He pointed his finger at the sheriff. "I'll ruin you! I've got influence in this town."

"We'll see how much influence you have after folks find out how you treat your wife."

Harry was too angry to comprehend the sheriff's words. He pointed a finger at Pete.

"As for you, you'll wish you'd never come to this town, this county or this state."

"Go home, Harry," Sheriff Carroll said firmly. "You've caused enough trouble here tonight."

Almost choking on his fury, Harry stumbled off into the darkness.

"Sheriff, will you go with me and Mrs. Cole to get

some things for her and the boy?" Pete asked when Harry had left.

"Why sure. Be glad to."

"Where is the boy, Dale?" Pete asked gently.

"In the playroom."

"Do you know him, Johnny?"

"No, but I'll find him."

Pete came close, and whispered. "Take him to Jude's. We'll be along."


Kathleen was dancing with the man in the tweed coat again. Johnny waited for the dance to end, then beckoned for her to come to the side of the dance floor.

"What's going on? Where's Pete?" Kathleen asked him. "Someone came in and said he was in a fight."

"It wasn't much of a fight. Dale Cole's husband was slapping her around, and Pete lit into him like a tornado." Johnny chuckled. "Pete's a caution when he's riled up."

"Good for Pete."

"Mrs. Cole is leaving her husband. Pete asked me to find her boy and take him to Jude's. Do you know him?"

"I've seen him, but from a distance. He goes to Emily's grandmother's house after school. Emily is right over here." Kathleen tilted her head toward a pretty blonde girl. "She'll help you find him."

"That fellow in the fancy coat is still watching you." Johnny had started to walk away, but turned back. "How many times has he danced with you?"

"I haven't counted them." Kathleen felt a little thrill that Johnny might be jealous. "He's kind of good-looking and real nice. He hardly says a word."

"He's a stranger around here. I wouldn't get too friendly with him. I'll get Emily and find the boy."

After Johnny left, Kathleen sat down and slipped off her shoes, a hint that her feet were tired. Paul came and sat down beside her.

"Tired, huh?"

"My feet feel like they weigh a hundred pounds each."

"Addie said you've danced every dance."

"She got me into this. I'm thinking seriously about putting a wicked spell on her."

Paul chuckled. "I just bet she'd handle it."

"People turned out, didn't they? They know how important the clinic is to the town."

"We've made a tidy sum for the clinic tonight. The donation jar over there is stuffed. Someone put a couple of hundred-dollar bills in it."

"No kiddin'? That's great. Usually when someone donates that much they want credit for it."

"The booths did well, but the dance took in the most money."

"It's a good band. Is Willie and the Chicken Pluckers really their name?"

"It was Will Hartman and the Boys. They've got a good gimmick going with the hillbilly outfits. If I were them, I'd capitalize on it and keep the theme and the name permanently."

"Even with a gimmick, the music was good."

"Someone said Pete got into a fight outside. I'd hate to tangle with that bruiser. Being in the navy for sixteen years, he's probably fought his way out of a hundred bars."

"Johnny said it was because Mr. Cole was slapping his

wife. I hope the sheriff files a report, then we could put it in the paper. Maybe the Gas and Electric Company will transfer him out of here or, better yet, fire him."

Paul's homely face lit up in a smile. "I'll talk to Sheriff Carroll."

Emily and Johnny came by. Emily held the hand of a small blond boy.

"Emily is going with me," Johnny said as they passed. "Danny is more comfortable with her. He doesn't know me."

"Anything changed between you and Johnny?" Paul asked after Johnny left.

"Nothing has changed. I intended to see Mr. Fairbanks again this week, but he's away for a few days working in the city. I don't want to talk to Junior."

"Going to make it final?"

"It's what Johnny wants." She slipped her feet back into her shoes. "Do you think I'll be deserting the ship if I leave now? The crowd has thinned down, and I am tired. Your wife worked my tail off today."

Paul chuckled. "She's good at that. She can get more work out of people with her sweet ways than an overseer can with a whip. Go on home. You've done your duty."

There was more traffic than usual because of the carnival. Kathleen didn't notice the car that followed her at a distance, stopped with lights off and sat there until she was in her house and the lights were on.

Theodore Nuding lingered for several long minutes in his dark car and stared at the lighted bedroom window. After a while he drove slowly out to the Clifton place, parked his car in the shed, and went into the house.

The front hall was jammed with boxes and crates that had been delivered the night before. He had given strict orders that the truck arrive at twelve o'clock midnight, not a minute earlier or later. A bonus of fifty dollars to each of the two men would be the reward. The cargo was unloaded quickly and silently. After the men were paid, they had left quickly and silently.

Nuding went to the small room where he kept his personal belongings. After removing his good clothes, he dressed again for work and went up the stairs to Kathleen's room. This was where he spent most of the time while he was in the house. He loved to be here, where she would be. He settled in the comfortable chair at the table and opened his observation diary.

*11 P.M. Mother, dear Mother. This has been the most wonderful evening of my life since I lost you. I danced with Kathleen five times. I wanted to dance every dance with her, but I had to be careful and not be too conspicuous. I held her in my arms, Mother. I actually held her. She is slender as a reed and moves like an angel. I pressed her against me—her breasts and her belly. She is perfect. Her skin is like smooth silk, and on her nose are tiny little freckles. I wanted to fall at her feet and worship. I had so wanted her here for Christmas, but I fear I will not be ready. It is taking me a little longer because I tire so quickly. I've already decided how I will take her. A man in Dallas advised me and arranged for me to have what I need. It is wonderful what money can do. For a while I thought I might have to eliminate Johnny Henry. Now*

*I don't think it will be necessary. They are drifting
away from each other. Doing away with him would
not be difficult, but the death of a war hero would
bring attention to Rawlings. Any number of officers
would be poking about, and I don't want that. I am
still not feeling well, Mother. I tire easily. I was so excited tonight that I forgot to be tired until I was on the
way home. Tonight I will go to bed early so that I can
work in her room all day tomorrow. The sheriff
wouldn't expect the "weatherman" to be out on Sunday.*

Nuding closed the journal on his rambling entry,
leaned back, closed his eyes, and relived the time he had
spent with Kathleen.

By Monday noon the town was buzzing, not only about
the success of the carnival, but about the supervisor at the
Gas and Electric beating his wife. At Paul's urging, Sheriff Carroll had filed a disturbance report which could be
legally used as a news item in the paper. Paul wrote the
story, which would appear in the Tuesday edition of the
*Gazette*.

The success of Saturday night's carnival to
raise funds for the polio ward at the clinic
was slightly marred by an altercation that required Sheriff Carroll's attention.

Harry Cole, manager of the branch of Oklahoma Gas and Electric, became enraged at
his wife for dancing with another man during
the tag dance. The sheriff was called by a
concerned citizen who discovered Mr. Cole

abusing his wife outside the school. The lady suffered bruises on her face, a cut lip, and a black eye which were attended to by Dr. Jude Perry. Charges are pending.

Pete hired Junior Fairbanks to appear with Dale in front of a judge to get a restraining order against Harry Cole, which was granted after the judge saw Dale's face. She and Danny had spent the night at Jude's, with Millie Criswell acting as chaperone. The humiliation of the town's knowing Harry had been beating her was making Dale physically ill. She had walked the floor most of the night. Concerned, Pete asked Theresa and Jude to talk with her.

"He is the one who should feel humiliated," Jude counseled Dale. "You've done nothing to be ashamed of. The higher you hold your head, the less people will think of him. You are an excellent nurse. We value you here at the clinic. If you choose to, you can work toward getting your RN."

"I love nursing, but can I make a living for myself and my son?"

"You can work full-time here," Jude said gently.

"Thank you, Doctor. Now I'm wondering why I put up with him for so long. The final straw was when I realized the influence he would have on Danny."

"You put up with it because he was 'the devil you knew'. You were afraid of going into the unknown. We all are."

Jude was amazed at the depth of Pete's feelings for Dale Cole. Although a very nice person, she was far different from any woman he had thought Pete would be interested in. She was mature, had a child, and was rather plump. None of this seemed to matter to Pete. He had fallen in love.

Later that day Pete moved Dale's and Danny's things into the room at Mrs. Ramsey's, where Kathleen had stayed when she first came to Rawlings. It had been Theresa's idea for them to rent the room; she felt that Dale should not be alone at night because that was when Harry would most likely try to harm her.

"I'm glad to have you here." Mrs. Ramsey put her arms around Dale. "I suspected what was going on at your house from the things Danny would say. You poor dear. You have put up with a lot."

Harry, of course, put out his version of what happened on Saturday night. The four employees at the Gas and Electric listened politely and didn't believe a word of it.

"I tried to get her to come home with me. She may have had a drink of something. She never acts the way she did unless she's been drinking. She fought me like a wild woman. Look at the marks on my face. What was I to do?"

To Harry's way of thinking, the stink in the town would die down. He was worried about word getting back to his bosses in the city. Tuesday, when the *Gazette* came out, he became so angry he put his fist through the partition in his office.

The "weatherman" read the *Gazette* at the Frontier Cafe while he was eating his lunch. The article in the box on the front page caught his interest, and he read it through twice.

On the one occasion that he had been to the utility office to have electricity turned on at the Clifton place, he had witnessed Harry Cole's treatment of an employee. The man had not understood his instructions. Harry Cole had berated him, calling him a stupid lout. Nuding had wanted to put his fist in Cole's face. The employee, needing the job, had stood quietly and taken the insults. At that moment Nuding had formed an instant dislike for Harry Cole.

An idea was beginning to form in his mind. Most men were animals, in Nuding's opinion, and a man who abused a woman, God's most perfect creature, was the lowest form of animal life. Nuding folded the paper and sipped his coffee.

With his weatherman props in his hand, Nuding rose, paid his bill, and left the restaurant. He drove to his place on the hill. The sky was cloudless, giving him no excuse for being there. He took a roundabout route back to the Clifton place, left his car in the shed, and went to his secret room.

From a locked box he took out a sheaf of handwritten notes, a carefully labeled vial of clear liquid, and a syringe with a needle attached. For the next half hour he studied the notes. One part stood out from the rest. *An injection of more than one cc is fatal. (destroy syringe and needle after use.)* Nuding had purchased it for his own use should something go wrong with his plans to keep Kathleen with him. He could never endure the consequences of an arrest and had made plans to join his mother should that happen.

At the restaurant it had occurred to him that he should test the potency of the liquid to be sure it would work if he needed to use it on himself. A man who would beat a woman was the ideal guinea pig for him to try it on. He filled the syringe with one and one half cc's of the liquid, placed it in a small metal case, and slipped it in his pocket.

He knew what he was going to do. He just had to plan carefully when he was going to do it.

# Chapter Twenty-three

*I*n the days that followed, Kathleen found herself thinking about the man in the tweed coat. Something about him made her uneasy. She couldn't put her finger on what it was. He had been a perfect gentleman and a very good dancer. During a rather fast fox trot, his breathing had become labored as if he was tiring; but he didn't hesitate and murmured a rather breathless "thank-you" when the dance was ended.

Kathleen described him to Adelaide, but her friend didn't know him. They explored the possibility that he was a salesman passing through town who had come to the carnival because there wasn't much else to do.

The only news she had of Johnny came from Pete.

"We were having a beer last night at the Silver Spur and Mack Boone came in. His daddy is Barker's foreman, but he's been laid up for a while and Boone has been taking over."

"I know who he is." Kathleen poured herself more tea and refilled Pete's coffee cup. "He used to compete at the rodeo and seemed to be a sore loser. It was always some-

one else's fault if he didn't place. The animal didn't perform or he wasn't given the mount he drew. Johnny
called him a whiner even then."

"Sounds like him. He's got his claws out for Johnny.
Threw out a few remarks about Fleming cattle wandering
over to the Circle H. Johnny ignored him for a while.
Then Mack said something to one of the cowboys about
Marie Fleming having the hots for him and following him
around until it was hard for him to get his work done.
Faster than you could spit, Johnny had him by the throat
and shoved up against the wall."

"Marie can't stand Mack Boone. She's in love with
Bobby Harper; she told me so the day we went to Frederick."

"Johnny's got a short fuse these days. He would've
strangled Boone, if I hadn't interfered. He thinks more of
the Flemings than he lets on, especially the kids."

"Lucas has always looked up to Johnny as a kind of
hero. I wish Johnny would pay more attention to him."

"He did a pretty good job of it when we drove the
horses up from McCabes's. They were thicker than
thieves. Barker kept his distance, probably so the boy
could be with Johnny. Lord, I wish I'd had a daddy like
Barker when I was growing up."

"Barker should be told that Mack is making remarks
about Marie."

"Johnny warned Mack that if he ever heard of him
even mentioning either of the Fleming girls, he'd be
walking spraddle-legged for the rest of his life. Then he
added that he had a witness who saw him driving Fleming cattle onto Henry land, hoping Johnny would be ac-
cused of stealing them. Johnny told him that if it
happened again, he would go to the sheriff and swear he

had tried to sell them; that is, after he had strung him up by the thumbs and left him hanging all night.

"The way he said it would have put the fear of God in me. Johnny can be a mean son of a gun when something doesn't set right with him. Must be his Cherokee blood."

"The last time I saw him was at the carnival."

Pete reached over and squeezed her hand. "If you'd ask me, I'd say he's missing the boat. Once in a man's life he has a chance to catch the brass ring. If he misses it, he's out of luck."

"Have you caught your brass ring, Pete?" she asked softly.

"Yes, and I'm going to hold on to it. Dale is filing for divorce. She hasn't said that she would marry me. It's too much to ask her to make a decision like that right now. I don't want her to come to me because she thinks she can't make it on her own. I want her to want me as much as I want her."

"You're a good man, Pete Perry. Dale is lucky you fell in love with her."

"Lordy, sugar." Pete laughed, and his blue eyes gleamed. "No one's ever called me a *good* man! I've been a horse's patoot most of my life."

"I don't believe it."

"Johnny could tell you things about me that would curl your hair."

"Pete Perry, have you looked at me lately? If there's anything I don't need, it's more curls in my hair."

The end of the week marked the seventh week since Kathleen's last menstrual period. She didn't dare to hope that Johnny had made her pregnant six weeks ago when they made love. She had been heartbroken when she came out of the bathroom and found him gone. She had curled up in the bed and sobbed. Maybe it was then that one of his sperm had made its way into one of the eggs her body had released. *God, please let it be true.*

The doctor who delivered Mary Rose had said that he had no idea what had been responsible for her deformity. All these years Kathleen had wondered if something she had done during pregnancy had caused it.

Johnny, however, had been certain that his heredity was to blame and had left her. When she had needed him the most, he had let her down. Why was she still madly, crazily in love with him?

On the spur of the moment, Kathleen decided that she would go to the clinic and talk to Jude, not as her friend, but as Dr. Perry, MD. She called Millie and made an appointment, fearing that if she thought longer about it, she would change her mind.

The morning of the appointment she was so nervous she couldn't drink her tea. She considered canceling. Then strengthening her resolve, she bathed, dressed, and walked to the clinic so that on the way she could plan what she was going to say.

"Good morning." Millie's was a cheerful greeting when she entered the reception room at the clinic. "Have a seat. Doctor will be with you in a minute."

Before she could sit down, Jude opened the door of his inner office. "Morning, Kathleen. Come in."

"Oops. Short minute," Millie exclaimed with a good-natured smile.

Kathleen's legs felt like stiff sticks as she walked into Jude's office. He went behind his desk and motioned for her to sit down.

"I never got to thank you for your part in making the

carnival such a success. Enough money was raised to out-fit the polio ward. Now let's hope we don't have any pa-tients. The medical journals indicate that researchers are close to a polio vaccine, but it could still be years away."

"Working toward a good cause usually brings a com-munity together. A lot of people had a hand in making the carnival a success."

Kathleen chose to get right to the point of her visit be-fore she lost her nerve. She swallowed hard before she began.

"I realize that you're busy. But there are a few things of a personal nature that I'd like to discuss with you . . . confidentially, of course."

"Of course, and take as much time as you want." He leaned forward and studied her pale face.

"You may have heard that Johnny and I had a baby in 1942 before he went to war." She paused to take a deep breath. "Mary Rose lived only forty-eight hours. She was . . . she was—"

"I have the medical records," he said kindly, and reached for a folder on his desk. "Theresa and I have gone over them carefully. Do you want to know what we think about the birth?" Kathleen nodded and he contin-ued. "Your baby was born without a cap on her skull. It's a condition called anencephaly and is not compatible with life. It was a miracle she lived as long as she did out of the womb."

"What caused it? Johnny thinks he . . . that his mother—"

"Let me help you," Jude said, seeing her struggle for words. "Johnny thinks that his mother is the product of an incestuous coupling. He had convinced himself that her resultant defects were passed along to him and to Isabel, each in a different way. It made Isabel wild and uncaring for anything except her sexual pleasure, and it made him unable to sire normal children. He has no explanation as to why the *blight*, as he referred to it, skipped over his other sister, Henry Ann."

Jude went to the bookcase, pulled out a large volume, brought it back to the desk, and opened it to a place he had marked with a scrap of paper.

"I don't know if Dorene was the product of incest. If she was, so was my father, Hardy. They were brother and sister. No one disputed that or the fact that the folks on Mud Creek were a lusty clan that took their pleasure whenever and wherever it was convenient." He sighed in disgust.

"It's a medical fact that continuous incest within a family for generations will produce people of an inferior intellect, stunted stature, and deformity. Not one thing points to this being the case with your baby."

Kathleen sat in frozen silence, her eyes riveted to his face.

"I believe that a natural but rare failure to develop properly in the womb is what happened to your baby." His palm was covering a picture on the page of the book. "This may be difficult for you to view, but I think you should at least glance at this, if only to convince yourself that such birth defects have been recorded in other pregnancies and were no fault of yours or Johnny's."

Jude removed his hand. Kathleen looked down at the sketch of a baby, then quickly away. Her eyes filled rapidly with tears.

"Is that comparable to the way Mary Rose looked?" Jude asked gently.

Kathleen nodded, her face crumbling. While she com-

posed herself, he returned the book to the bookcase, then
waited for her to wipe her eyes.

"I must tell you that I've not had much experience in
pediatrics. Theresa worked for a year in that department
at St. Anthony in the city. We discussed this case after Isabel died and Johnny mentioned 'watered-down blood.'
Of the hundreds of babies born during the time she was
there, Theresa can recall only one case similar to your
baby's condition. It was definitely not the fault of the parents. They had already had four perfectly normal beautiful children."

"Thank you," Kathleen whispered. She allowed the
tears to roll down her cheeks unchecked. "I wish I had
known this . . . back then."

"Is this what's keeping you and Johnny apart?"

Kathleen gulped and looked away from the kindest
eyes she had ever seen.

"He may have fallen out of love with me and used the
baby's birth as an excuse to leave me."

"That doesn't sound like the Johnny I used to know.
That Johnny would have said plainly why he was going."

"He did. Later."

"Had he been looking forward to the baby?"

"He could hardly wait. We had names picked out for a
boy, and a girl, but we just knew it would be a boy. The
last few weeks he wouldn't go any farther away than the
barn for fear that I would need him. We talked about a little girl with red curls, or a boy with dark hair like his.

"On the morning my water broke, he was so excited.
Then when it was over, they brought Mary Rose to me
and let Johnny come into the room. They had given me
the bad news and told me how she would look, but they
hadn't told Johnny. I'll never forget the look on his face.

Nothing has been the same between us since. He became more and more distant. Then he enlisted—not to beat the draft; his number was not that high on the list. He just wanted to get away from me."

"Did he talk about the baby at all?"

"No. All he said was that he couldn't give me the family I wanted. He told me to get a divorce while he was gone and find someone that would." Kathleen twisted the handkerchief in her hands and blurted, "I may be pregnant."

Jude sat back in his chair, showing not a trace of the surprise he was feeling.

"I still had on my nightgown the morning he came to tell me that Gabe Thomas had been killed. It just happened. I know he was sorry because he got right up and left the house."

"You've missed your period?"

"Yes, but sometimes I'm late."

"How do you feel about the possibility of being pregnant?"

"I don't dare hope—"

He pushed a calendar toward her. "Show me when you had your last period and when you made love with Johnny."

Kathleen's finger traced along the dates then stopped. "Here. I seldom go more than three days." Her finger moved to another date. "And this is when we . . . were together."

Jude turned the calendar toward him. "At that time you were in your most fertile period, Kathleen."

"But . . . one time? After so long?"

"Oh, yes. Many women conceive after long periods of abstinence."

Kathleen began to smile. "Jude . . . ah, Doctor, I'll thank God every day for the rest of my life if he lets me have this baby."

Jude frowned. "Don't get your hopes up . . . yet."

Kathleen didn't listen. "I can't help but hope. If there is the slightest chance . . . I'll hope. I don't want Johnny to know. Please. You won't tell him?"

"If you're pregnant, it isn't my place to tell him; but I think he should know." His voice was grave, his eyes somber.

"No. He'll be angry and think that I tricked him into my bed. I don't want him to know. He doesn't want to chance having another child. I don't want him putting a damper on my happiness." Kathleen's voice was almost shrill. Her blood was pounding.

"We may be getting the cart before the horse here."

"When will we know? I'll not be able to stand the suspense."

"If your dates are right, you are six weeks into your pregnancy. Have you experienced any morning sickness?"

"Not really. I haven't been drinking my tea or eating my toast for the past few mornings, but I chalked that up to a case of the nerves."

"If you want an examination, I'll call Theresa to prepare you. She'll stay with you. She's very good at this."

"Will you be able to tell with any degree of certainty?"

"I believe so. While you're being prepared, I want to refer to some of my medical books. I've not gotten to the place yet where I think I know everything." His smile was beautiful. *The woman who gets you, Doctor Jude Perry, will be a lucky girl.*

\* \* \*

Kathleen walked home from the clinic with a smile on her face.

Her heart was celebrating.

At first she had been horribly embarrassed about Jude looking at her private parts. A sheet had been hung so that she couldn't see the doctor or the nurse during the examination. With Theresa being there and acting very professional, as if this was something they did every hour of every day, it had been easier than she expected.

When the examination was over, Jude came around the curtain and smiled down at her.

"I can say, and Theresa agrees, that seven and a half months from now, you may expect a permanent addition to your family."

Kathleen had burst into tears. No way on earth could she have stopped them.

Before she left she asked again that the visit be confidential, and was assured word would not leave the examination room.

At home, she sat down in the big chair, leaned her head against the back, and allowed her mind to absorb the wonderful news. Next August she would have Johnny's baby. It would be all right. God wouldn't be so cruel as to give her this happiness, then take it away.

She placed her hand on her stomach.

"Oh, baby, I'm so glad you're here. There may only be you and me; your daddy may not want you, but I want you so much, and I'll love you so much—"

Theodore Nuding watched Kathleen when she left the house and walked to the clinic. She would be doing some volunteer work, he presumed. If she had been sick, she would have driven the car. When she returned a couple of hours later, she was waltzing along, swinging her purse as if she didn't have a care in the world.

When she was safely in the house, Nuding checked his watch, started his car, and drove to the Gas and Electric office. He had been carefully studying the schedule of the employees. This was the time that he could catch Harry Cole alone in his office.

Harry Cole was looking through the mail left on his desk, searching for a letter from the head office in Oklahoma City. Two days after Dale left him, he had written asking for a transfer to another office. He was having difficulty here, he explained, because of his wife's indiscretions. He had put up with it as long as he could; now he wanted out of the marriage and out of Rawlings.

He rocked back and forth in his swivel chair thinking that he wouldn't have to put up with the stupid cow. She had served her purpose; getting her pregnant right away as he had planned, hoping to stay out of the war.

Harry was sure now that he would not be asked to run for public office nor be offered the position of trustee at the clinic. The *bitch* had seen to that. He had been humiliated when he was served the order restraining him from going near her and Danny. But anger, resentment, and knowing that he was right overrode the humiliation.

This was best for him after all, he decided. He was tired of living with a wife who acted like a whipped puppy. He wouldn't have any trouble getting another woman. This time he would be more choosy. He leaned back in his chair and visualized a young blonde with a slim waist and high, pointed breasts urging him to come to bed.

He'd not marry again. He was certain that he could get what he wanted without tying himself down. There were other advantages as well. The money he earned could be spent entirely on himself. His daydreams were interrupted when he heard someone come into the outer office.

"Office is closed until one o'clock," he called. "Didn't you see the sign on the door?"

He listened for the door to close; when it did not, he got up from his chair and went to the counter where customers paid their bills. A shabby-looking man in an old brown hat stood there.

"Didn't you hear what I said? The office is closed until one o'clock."

"I heard you and I saw the sign. I want to report that one of your electric poles is down and wires are on the ground."

"Where? Did you run into it?"

"I'll show you on the map."

"All right, but make it snappy." Harry went back into his office. A large map of the area was under a glass on his desk. He sank down in his chair.

"I thought it important that I report the wires down."

"The road crew will be in soon, and they'll know about it; but show me if it'll make you happy, then leave. I'm busy," he said harshly.

Nuding moved around behind him to look at the map over his shoulder.

"Humm . . . It was along here somewhere near where the two main roads meet." He made a few humming sounds, and a grunt or two as if studying the map while he took the syringe from the metal box.

"This is the place. Right here," he said, and jabbed the needle just above the hairline in the back of Harry's neck.

"What the hell?" Harry jumped.

"I'm sorry about that. I must have had a pin in my tie."

Nuding returned the syringe to the metal box and moved around to the front of the desk. "I lied about a pole being down."

"Get . . . out—"

Nuding looked at his watch. "In about fifteen seconds."

Harry's face began to sag. His hand fell from the edge of the desk onto his lap.

"What . . . Why—" Then the slack mouth opened and closed without making another sound, reminding Nuding of a fish.

"Why did I do it? Because you deserved it. I did you a kindness and injected you above the heart, so that it wouldn't take long. Good-bye, Mr. Cole."

Harry's eyes glazed over and his head fell to the side.

Nuding nodded with satisfaction, walked calmly out of the office and back to his car. *It was good to know that the poison developed by the Nazis during the war was as deadly as the seller said it was.*

Harry Cole's sudden death of a heart attack was a shock to all who knew him. An employee had found him sitting at his desk when he returned after his noon meal. Dr. Perry, acting as coroner, could not find a mark on him and had to assume, without an autopsy, the cause of death to be heart failure. Sheriff Carroll agreed, and an autopsy was not ordered.

Dale learned the news when Doctor Perry returned from the Gas and Electric office. She was stunned. Harry was not a good man, but she hadn't wanted him dead.

"Could my leaving him and the humiliation he suffered have brought on the heart attack?"

"He appeared to me," Jude explained, "to be a man

who was constantly under stress. I can't say that a little more pushed him over the edge. From what I learned while talking to the people who worked with him, he seemed during the past few days to have accepted your leaving and was looking forward to a transfer and a new life somewhere else."

"He was always angry at something or someone. If it wasn't me, it was Danny, the men at the Gas and Electric, or someone that he imagined had slighted him in some way. It's strange, but Harry was only happy when he was angry."

"The stress finally caught up with him."

"I've got to tell Danny."

"Pete has gone to the school to get him."

"Thank goodness for that. I should leave now, Doctor. I'll have to make funeral arrangements."

"You'll have all the help you need. I'll take you to Mrs. Ramsey's. That's where Pete is taking Danny."

Later that day Dale was given a letter marked *personal* that had arrived at the office. The message inside came from the main office in Oklahoma City and was a dismissal.

> *Numerous complaints about conduct unseemly in a manager of one of our substations have been made over the past year. We have no choice but to dismiss you immediately.*

Dale ripped the letter to shreds and flushed it down the toilet. Harry was dead. Danny need never know that his father was fired from his job on the day he died.

After the funeral, Dale and Danny moved back into the house. Life had suddenly opened up for Dale. The fear she had lived with for so long was no longer there. She tried to feel sorry about Harry's death, but she felt only relief.

Pete had been very discreet about the help he had given Dale, knowing that it would be easy for tongues to start wagging. Now that he knew what he wanted, he was satisfied to wait.

Instead of leasing or buying land for his horse ranch, Pete decided to put all his assets into the rodeo promotion plan. He spent time talking to Keith McCabe in Vernon, whom he had met when he helped Johnny with his horses. Keith was crusty, a fount of information about the rodeo business and willing to share his knowledge. He had contacts who could supply the information he didn't have.

Johnny had become as irritable as a cow with its teat caught in the fence, and Pete told him so . . . often. Finally one morning, Johnny told him to find another partner for his rodeo scheme because he would be unable to raise the money for his part without mortgaging the ranch, and he would not do that because Kathleen owned part of it.

"Why the hell don't you go see her?"

"I don't want to intrude," Johnny retorted sarcastically. "She seems to have plenty of company."

"What do you mean by that?"

"Every time you come out here you've got something to say about her. She's had her hair cut. She's making progress on her book or Barker came and fixed her sink. She baked a peach pie or some other bit of news."

"I like going there. She's good company."

"It's a free country."

"Dammit, Johnny. You're going to mess around and lose that woman. She'll pack up someday and hightail it out of here and you'll never see her again."

Johnny turned and leaned over the motor he was working on. Not with a flicker of an eyelash did it show that his heart had jumped up into this throat.

"Is she leaving?"

"No, but for some reason she seems to smile and laugh a lot more than she did. She's happy about something."

"Maybe she filed for the divorce."

"Have you been notified?"

"No, but—"

"Then she hasn't filed."

"I suppose you've been divorced and know all about it."

"I've not been divorced, and I will never be if I can help it. When I marry, it'll be for as long as I live."

"Good luck," Johnny said, and walked away.

It no longer worried him that Pete would make a play for Kathleen now that he was so enamored with Dale Cole. It was a relief in a way that Pete was keeping an eye on Kathleen. It shook him when Pete said something about her moving away. He hadn't thought of that prospect.

He hadn't seen Kathleen since the night of the carnival two weeks before. If he went to see her now, just six days until Christmas, he'd have to have a reason. He couldn't just walk in and tell her that he was so hungry for the sight of her that he couldn't eat or sleep, or that wanting to make love to her was causing his guts to boil just thinking about it.

The only rational thing he could say was that he wanted her to have the gifts he had made for her that first year he was away. The year when he really didn't care if he lived or died.

He would wait, he decided, until a couple days before Christmas, then go see her and take the chance that she wouldn't slam the door in his face.

# Chapter Twenty-four

$K$athleen was both happy and fearful. She was happy because of her pregnancy and fearful each time she went to the bathroom that she would see color, which would mean that she was aborting. She didn't even mind the morning sickness that usually lasted not more than an hour. It was unpleasant, but she endured it gladly because it meant that she was really pregnant.

She longed to tell someone about this wonderful thing that had happened. If she told Adelaide, she would argue that Johnny should be told. So would Marie and Pete. They all loved Johnny. She loved him too; but when he found out, he would hate her. She couldn't bear having him think that she tricked him into making love with her so she could have this baby when she knew he had sworn never to father another child.

The days passed one after the other without as much as a call from Johnny, not that she expected one. The book was half-finished. She wrote to her editor and promised the complete manuscript by April. At night she would read one of the books she brought home from the library.

Her favorite authors were Zane Grey and Bess Streeter Aldrich. She read *A Lantern in Her Hand* twice, something she almost never did.

Mrs. Frisbee, the librarian, told her about a new book by another Kathleen, Kathleen Winsor. *Forever Amber*, a rather racy historical novel, was one of the year's best-sellers. It was enjoyable reading, but Kathleen was not particularly interested in English history.

Her other pleasure was the movies. She went on Sunday nights when fewer people were there. The big nights were Friday and Saturday. Some of the Rialto movies were old. She didn't mind. She went to see an old W.C. Fields picture even though she didn't like slapstick comedy.

As Christmas approached, she got into the spirit and decorated her living room with red paper bells, and silver 'icicles' hung on the green ropes she looped across the window. She mailed Christmas cards to Tom and Henry Ann in Red Rock, Hod and Molly in Kansas, and to the McCabes's.

Pete had been by to tell her that she was invited to spend Christmas at Jude's. In addition to Theresa and her boy, Dale and Danny would be there.

"I don't think I can come, Pete, but thank Jude for inviting me. Barker asked me several days ago. Invite Johnny. If he knows that I won't be there, he'll probably come. I hate to think of his spending Christmas alone."

"I'll ask him. Hey, you look awfully chipper. Did someone die and leave you a million dollars?"

Kathleen laughed. "I'd look a lot more chipper than this if that happened."

"I'll have to bring you some mistletoe. There are big

clumps of it in the trees along the road. I'll hang it in the doorway so I can kiss you every time I come over."

"You don't have to go to all that trouble." She reached up and kissed him on the cheek. "You are a dear, dear friend, Pete. I want you to know that."

Pete was to remember those words in the days ahead.

Nuding was exhausted. He sat in the chair in *her* room and looked around at what he had accomplished during the past two weeks: the plump high bed, satin coverlet and fancy pillows, the Persian carpet on the floor, the armoire filled with clothes from Neiman Marcus, lamps, the desk and typewriter, the dressing table with drawers filled with creams and perfumes. He even had a selection of books for her to read.

He had gone to her house Sunday night while she was at the movies. It had been easy to come across the back field and let himself into the back door with a special key he had. For half an hour he had moved through her rooms, touching her things and wondering why he had not given himself this pleasure before.

She was neat. He knew she would be. Her clothes were aligned in the closet: dresses, skirts, blouses. He buried his face in them, breathing in the scent of her. Before he left, he treated himself to a handkerchief from the drawer of her dresser.

Nuding's main purpose in going there had been to type a note on her typewriter saying that she was leaving. He didn't want anyone looking for her right away and hoped to convince her friends that she was leaving Rawlings to start a new life. He seriously considered burning down the house, but he didn't want to leave Kathleen, once he had her, to come back and do it.

The next day he had gone to Frederick to buy Christmas bells for her room and paper to wrap the gifts he had for her. Now all he had to do was wait until Sunday.

*10:20 P.M. Mother, I worked day and night to get the room ready for Christmas. It's in shades of green, her favorite color. What isn't green is ivory. It is somewhat like your room, Mother, except your room was in two shades of blue. After she has been here a while and has become content, she will let me know if she wants a different color. I wish I wasn't so tired. By Sunday I will feel better because then Kathleen and I will be together forever.*

Nuding closed the journal, took the handkerchief from his pocket, and held it to his face. This time next week he would be sitting here with his darling Kathleen, his princess, his angel. She would be his, all his.

Christmas had come to Rawlings and with it cold weather. The temperature went down to freezing. Kathleen put a sweater on under her coat, a scarf on her head, and walked to town. She remembered that her landlady's daughter had been told to walk some every day while she was pregnant.

The downtown was decorated with ribbons, lights, and artificial swags of greens. Kathleen prowled the stores, bought a scarf for Mrs. Ramsey and perfume for Emily, aftershave lotion for Pete and Jude and Paul. A week ago she had bought gifts for the Flemings. They were wrapped and ready to take when she went there on Christmas Day.

At the ten-cent store she bought a small toy for Theresa's son, Ryan, and one for Danny Cole. Then, remembering that she had nothing for Theresa and Dale, she went to the drugstore and chose a fancy box of bath powder for each of them. She walked along the street looking in the stores' gaily decorated windows. When she reached the men's store, she stopped. She had gifts now for everyone except Johnny.

Leroy Grandon had owned the store when she first came to Rawlings. He had wanted to date her, but she'd had eyes only for Johnny Henry. During the war Leroy had sold the store, married a war widow, and moved to Ardmore. The store was more up-to-date now.

An attractive display in the window caught her eye. A light blue cowboy shirt with dark blue piping and buttons was draped over a brown-leather saddle. A wide leather belt lay coiled beside it. The enterprising merchant was playing Christmas music. The song grabbed at her emotions and made her want to cry. *I'll be home for Christmas, if only in my dreams*—

On an impulse, Kathleen went in, bought the shirt and the belt and asked for them to be gift-wrapped.

Leaving the store, she continued on down the street. At the corner a gust of wind hit her. It was so cold that it almost took her breath away. She turned her back to it and didn't see Johnny coming toward her. Holding her scarf under her chin to keep it from blowing off, her shopping bag in her other hand, she started across the street. When she stepped up onto the curb, he was there in his old sheepskin coat, his hat pulled low on his forehead and the leather straps of a horse halter looped over his shoulder.

"Don't you look before you cross the street?"

"Hello, Johnny. I looked." Her cheeks were rosy from the cold. Her breath came out in small white puffs.

"Where's your car?" *Dear Lord! He had dreamed about Christmas at home with her.*

"At home. I walked."

"Won't it run?" *He was home now, and it was Christmas, but they were miles apart.*

"It did yesterday. I walked because I wanted to. How have you been?"

"Fine. Working."

"Pete said you got your horses up from Keith's. How's Ruth?"

"All right. They miss Granny. She died a year ago."

"I'm sorry to hear it."

"Ruth asked about you and said to tell you to come down."

"There's not much of a chance of that. I'm pretty busy."

"I'm pretty busy myself. I came in to the leather shop to get this halter sewed. If you've finished your shopping, I'll give you a ride home."

"I'm not through, but thank you anyway."

"I can wait. I'll get a haircut."

"Thanks, but I'll walk." *I need the exercise because I'm carrying MY child, you uncaring dolt!*

"Suit yourself."

Feeling as if he had been slapped in the face with a wet towel, Johnny walked on down the street. She had changed. She had looked him steadily in the eye and declined his offer of a ride. She had passed the time of day with him as if he were a neighbor she met on a street corner instead of a man with whom she had lived, loved, and had a baby. At one time they had been so close that each had known what the other was thinking.

*Was she seeing someone else? The lawyer's son, Ju-*

*nior Fairbanks? Had she fallen in love with Jude? The idea of the job in Central America was becoming more tempting all the time.*

Johnny was so absorbed in his thoughts that he forgot to stop in at the barbershop and went on down to where he had left his car. Just as he was getting in, Barker stopped across the street and called out to him.

"Hold on a minute, Johnny." After he parked, his father came across the street. Johnny threw the halter in the back of his car and waited. "It's cold. We might get a norther out of this. You got plenty of hay?"

"Yeah. I got a load from McCabe. What's on your mind?"

"Quite a bit. Let's get in the car out of the wind. I'm getting so damned old my bones creak."

Johnny almost smiled. "Guess I've got eighteen years before I get old and my bones creak." He went around and got under the wheel. Barker slid into the seat beside him.

"I heard what happened between you and Mack Boone. Not from Mack, but from another one of my men who was there."

"Yeah. What about it?"

"Thanks. What he said about Marie wasn't true. She and Bobby Harper have something going. I don't know how serious it is yet."

"Bobby's a good man. I've not heard anything about him that would change my mind."

"I've no objections to Bobby. Mack turned his attention to Janna. It was a mistake. Janna is not Marie."

"She's half his age for chrissake!"

"He put his hand on her, and she hit him across the face

with a rope." Barker's face, usually stoic as the head on the nickel, creased in a smile.

"Good for Janna."

"He won't force himself on her. He knows that if I didn't kill him, you would."

Johnny sat quietly and watched Kathleen going into the *Gazette* building.

"I warned him."

"I had a talk with Victor and told him I had to let Mack go. He understood. Mack had a few words to say about you before he left. He's out for trouble. Be on the lookout for him."

"He's a two-bit crook. He drove your cattle onto my land, planning to call the sheriff and say that I'd stolen them. If he'd been smart, he'd have put them in the barn."

"He can't take credit for having many brains, that's sure." Barker opened the car door and stepped out. "By the way, we'd like for you to come out for Christmas. Kathleen will be there."

Johnny chewed the side of his jaw, then said, "Okay."

"See you then." Barker shut the door and backed away, not wanting to press his luck by saying more. By the time he reached his car and started the motor, Johnny was headed out of town.

From the window of the *Gazette* office, Kathleen saw him drive past. She placed her shopping bag on the floor beside the coat rack and pulled the scarf from her head.

"You've had your hair cut," Adelaide said, coming in from the back room. "I like it."

"And hello to you too."

"Your cheeks are rosy and your nose is red, Santa Claus."

"Ho, ho, ho. Have you been a good little girl?"

"Have you?" Paul leaned in the doorway. "We've not seen much of you lately."

"I'm working on my book. I promised to have it finished by April."

"Do you need any help researching the kissing scenes?"

"With you? Your wife would cut my throat."

"It might be worth it." Paul leered and twisted the end of an imaginary mustache.

"All right, Tyrone, just simmer down." Adelaide gazed with mock anger at her husband.

"Tyrone Power?" Dramatically, Kathleen placed the back of her hand to her forehead. "Tyrone Power, right here in Rawlings."

"Well for crying out loud," Adelaide exclaimed. "You're sure in a feisty mood."

"It's Christmas, Addie." Kathleen sat down in the swivel chair. "Anything earthshaking to write about?"

"Paul's working on a couple of stories that came in on the radio. General George Patton died from the injuries he received in that car accident in Germany a few weeks ago. And Cordell Hull won the Nobel Peace Prize."

"It's a shame that a man like General Patton, who goes all through the war, is killed in an accident when it's over."

"What are you doing Christmas? Judy and Sheriff Carroll are coming over. Want to come?"

"I would, but Barker asked me to come for dinner."

"Will Johnny be there?"

"I doubt it. More than likely he'll go to the McCabes'."

"Have you seen much of him?"

"Not since his sister's funeral." She didn't think it necessary to mention that she had seen him just now on the street corner.

"Have you given up on him?"

"Yes." The answer was quick and blunt.

"Well, I guess that takes care of that."

Kathleen slipped into her coat. "I better get along. I want to stop at the library, and I fear that it's getting colder by the minute."

"Paul and I will come by Christmas night if you're going to be home."

"I'll be there."

The wind was so cold that Kathleen decided against walking the extra blocks to the library. By the time she reached home she was out of breath. Leaving her packages and her coat on the couch, she went to the kitchen and lit a fire under the kettle to heat water for tea.

She felt good about her encounter with Johnny. She was pleased that seeing him didn't hurt quite so much. *It's because of you, baby. I know now that I'll always have a part of him with me.*

The following day was Saturday. Pete stopped by.

"Hello, sugar. Is the coffeepot on?"

"I can put it on in a hurry. Leave your coat there on the couch and come to the kitchen. What's in the sack?"

"Donuts. Fresh. With sugar on 'em."

"Well, now, you're the kind of company I like to have."

"I need your expert advice."

"Bribing me with the donuts?"

"Yeah. Pretty smart, huh?"

"I'm glad you came by. I have a sack of presents for you to deliver."

Pete took a package from the pocket of his coat and

carefully unwrapped it. He lifted the lid on a pink box. Inside was a gold-colored oval vanity that held face powder and a bottle of Coty perfume.

"It's beautiful," Kathleen exclaimed.

"Do you think Dale will like it?"

"Of course, she'll like it. Any woman would."

"I want to give her something that a woman would like, but wouldn't buy for herself. I don't think she's had many things like this."

"That's sweet, Pete."

"I wondered if I could get you to wrap it kinda fancy."

"Of course. I have some pretty Christmas paper and green ribbon."

"I bought some toys for Danny. Dale says he still believes in Santa Claus, so we'll have Santa leave them."

"You're happy, aren't you, Pete?"

"Does it show that much?" He grinned nervously. "I've not had anyone to do things for for so long that I forgot what Christmas was about. It makes all the difference when you have someone you care about."

"Yes, it does."

"You're a great gal, Kath. I hate seeing that sad look in your eyes."

"I'm not sad! I'm happier than I've been in years. I've become reconciled to the fact that Johnny doesn't want me. I've decided to go on and make the best life that I can for me and . . . for me."

"Are you staying here in Rawlings?"

"No. I can't stay here. After the first of the year, I'll decide where I'm going. My book is due in April. I'd like to get settled somewhere by the end of January."

"That's just a month away. Is there anything I can do to help?"

"I would hate leaving my furniture. I may call on you to help me with that. Barker is such a good friend. He'll help me find a place." Using both hands she gestured widely. "One thing about my kind of work. I can do it anywhere."

Pete watched the expressions flicker across her face. He could have fallen in love with her if he hadn't met Dale. Dammit. Johnny could have the world right here in his hand and he was letting it slip away.

# Chapter Twenty-five

$B$y Sunday, the wind had gone down, but it was still cold. Kathleen had planned to go to church services, but her morning sickness had lasted a little longer than usual. She sat in her big chair, nibbled on toast, and listened to the radio.

In the middle of the afternoon, while she was making Christmas cookies to take to the Fleming's, Marie called.

"Are you going to the Christmas Eve service at the church tomorrow night? If you are, I'll stop by and pick you up."

"I'm not sure, but if I decide to go, I'll meet you there."

"We're looking forward to having you here Christmas."

"I'm looking forward to it, too. I'm making cookies to bring. See you then if not before."

Kathleen was not sure that her cookies would compare with Mrs. Fisher's, but she enjoyed cutting out the bells and the stars and sprinkling them with colored sugar. After they baked she placed them on a cloth on the counter. By the time she returned from the movie, they would be cool enough to pack in a tight tin.

She arrived at the theater only minutes before the movie, *Going My Way* with Bing Crosby, started. She liked Bing Crosby in anything and had been looking forward to this movie. She settled down happily in the middle of the theater to watch.

When the show was over Kathleen stopped in the lobby to wish Mrs. Lansing, who had been selling tickets at the theater for years, a merry Christmas. Then humming "White Christmas," she drove home and parked the Nash in the driveway.

Kathleen unlocked the door, pushed it open, reached and flipped the light switch. Nothing. The room remained in total darkness. *The bulb had burned out.* She closed the door and groped her way toward the bedroom and the switch just inside the doorway.

When a hand was pressed to the back of her head and a cloth to her nose, she hardly had time to struggle before she went limp, and a blanket of darkness settled over her mind.

"Good morning."

Kathleen's eyes were open, but her mind was fuzzy. She squinted against the bright sunlight that blazed through a high window.

"Are you hungry?"

Hungry? The thought of food was revolting. Her stomach lurched. She gagged. Her hand found something soft and held it to her mouth. She tried to lift her head and focus her eyes. Her vision cleared enough to make out a man sitting beside the bed.

"I'm . . . going to . . . puke—" she gasped.

"Oh, my goodness."

He moved quickly and placed a bowl on the bed beside her face. She bent over it, gagged and gagged, but very little came up.

"I'm sorry you're sick. I gave you a very small amount of chloroform. Just enough to get you here."

"You gave me . . . chlor—" She gagged again.

"What do you need?"

"Cracker. Piece of . . . bread."

The man left her sight. Kathleen's head fell back against the pillow. Her mind was clearing enough for her to know that she had to get food into her stomach. She felt something pressed into her hand and lifted her lids enough to see that it was a soda cracker. She chewed it and swallowed, then waited a minute before she attempted to open her eyes again.

When her stomach had settled enough so that she could think, she realized that she was in a strange, very comfortable bed and a man had held a basin for her to throw up. He had also brought her a couple of crackers and placed a wet cloth on her forehead. Carefully she opened her eyes. He was sitting there looking at her. His shirt was white, his tie dark. His face was a blur.

Alarmed, she lifted her head, made an effort to focus, and looked around. *What place is this? What am I doing here?*

"Where am I?" she demanded. "Did you say something about chloroform?" She tried to sit up. He gently pushed her down.

"You're not strong enough to get up."

She looked wildly about, then beneath the covers. She was wearing something made of heavy cream satin.

"Where are my clothes?" Panic made her voice shrill. "Who took off my clothes?"

"You'll not need those old things anymore. You've a wardrobe of new things. The very best."

"Who are you? Where am I?" She tried to get up again.

"No, don't get up yet." He was strong and held her down. "I don't want to use the constraints."

"Am I in a hospital?"

"Goodness, no. You're at home."

"No. I'm not at home."

"You are. This is your home now. You will learn to love it here and never want to leave."

"This isn't my home!" she insisted and peered intently at him. "Oh, my Lord, you're Ted Newman!"

"You remembered," he chuckled delightedly as he moved off the bed and onto the chair. "Yes, I'm Ted Newman, who worked a few feet away from you in the personnel department at Douglas Aircraft. I thought you were the most beautiful thing I'd ever seen. I took care of you then, too. I followed you home every night to see that you got there safely."

"Why, Ted, why?"

He smiled at the puzzled look on her face. "When I first saw you standing beside the water cooler, I knew that someday you would be mine, and I wanted to protect you until I could make a safe and beautiful place for you."

"What in the world are you talking about?" she gasped.

"I know it's hard for you to understand now, but you will. You see I took care of my mother for thirty years. The last twenty of them in a room much like this. She depended on me for everything. When she died I had to give her up."

"I'm sorry she died, but what has that to do with me?

Did you follow me to Rawlings? I haven't seen you around town."

He smiled again. "I have many faces. Remember the man who came to your door the day that garage man confronted you in your house? I was guarding you. I would have killed him then if he had touched you."

"It was an . . . old man who came to the door."

"Yes." He looked pleased. "I can be old, young, a Scottish immigrant, or a businessman who likes to dance with a pretty woman with red curly hair at the school carnival."

Kathleen's mouth opened and closed without saying a word. She was stunned and terrified and weak all in one. She feared that if her eyes left him, he would pounce on her.

"You . . . You were nice . . . then." The words came in a hoarse whisper.

He leaned forward. "You needn't worry that I'll hurt you, Kathleen. I would die before I harmed a hair on that beautiful head."

"You . . . undressed me!"

"I had to get you out of those awful clothes. I never touched you in a lewd way. I never will."

"Yeah? You perverted son of a bitch! You try to rape me, and I'll scratch your eyes out."

"I swear on my mother's grave that will never happen. That aspect of life doesn't interest me."

"Then why in the hell am I here?"

"Hush! I won't put up with swear words coming from your mouth. It is coarse and unladylike. There are a few rules that I insist must be obeyed. No swearing is one of them."

"That's just too bad." She threw back the covers. "I'm leaving."

She swung her legs off the bed and felt something drag. She looked down in shocked horror. A cuff circled her ankle, and attached to it was a small chain. When realization struck, she stood and lashed out at him with her fist. He took the blow without flinching and grabbed her wrist.

"I had to do that, Kathleen. When you get used to being here, I will take it off." He released her wrist and stepped back out of her reach.

"I'll never get used to being here!" Sobs rose in her throat.

"You will, my darling girl. I promise you will. It will take a little time. I'll take care of you, be so good to you that you won't want to leave me. I've arranged all this just for you." He waved his hand around the room. "We will sit together in this lovely room in the evenings. During the day while I'm away, you can read or write a book. You can't know how I've dreamed of seeing you here."

"Why?" she managed to say over the sobs in her throat.

"Why you? I understand your wanting to know that," he said kindly. "You are everything that is lovely, virginal—"

"I'm not a virgin. I'm married!"

"I know, but that doesn't matter. You have not been with a man other than your husband. I admire you for that. To me you are virginal—"

"I'm pregnant! You stupid fool. You could've killed my baby with that chloroform!"

When he heard her words, his face seemed to freeze;

then his nostrils flared. Ice-blue eyes bored into hers, and she felt cold chills run down her spine.

"Whose?" he asked, the calm voice belied by the cold look on his face.

"My husband's," she retorted sharply, her anger over-riding her fear. "I'm not a slut!"

The cold mask dropped from his face in an instant. He smiled, his eyes shining with pure pleasure.

"This is wonderful, Kathleen! Oh, my dear, beautiful, darling girl. We will have our own little princess."

Kathleen looked at him in astonishment then said softly, "You are out of your mind."

"Not at all, my angel." He laughed; and when he did, she had to admit that he was quite handsome. "We will make plans. You can have anything you want for little Kathleen."

"Little Kathleen?"

"Of course. My mother was Kathleen, my angel is Kathleen, and our little princess will be Kathleen."

She sank down onto the bed, her mind groping for an explanation. He was crazy, but in a way that she hadn't ever heard of before.

"It could be a boy," she said dully.

"No! It will be a princess. I will not tolerate a male. Is that understood?"

She leaned forward and put her face in her hands. She had to think. He had said that he wasn't going to rape her, but she couldn't be sure. He had undressed her. At the thought of having lain naked in this strange bed with his eyes on her, her face grew hot beneath her hands. If he raped her, she would lose the baby. She had to think . . . to plan, and she needed time.

"Don't be afraid of me, my angel. I'll not hurt you." His voice was as soft as that of a lover.

"I will hurt *you*, if I can." She spoke forcefully with her face still in her hands.

"I know, and I can't blame you for that. You don't know me yet or understand the depth of my feelings for you."

"I don't want to know you. I want to go home."

"Are you hungry yet? I'm going to have to leave and fix you something. This is Christmas Eve. You can open your gifts tonight. That will cheer you up."

"I've got to use the bathroom."

"Of course." He opened a door opposite the bed. "I'm embarrassed that this closet is so crude. I didn't have time to prepare it as I wanted. Everything you need is here: toothbrush and paste, soaps, shampoo, and a supply of sanitary napkins, which you will not be needing." He picked up the box and set it beside the door to take out when he left.

"How do I get in there? I'm chained like an animal."

"The chain reaches to any corner of the room, my Kathleen. I'm sorry I had to go to such extremes. I'll take it off in a month or two—"

"Month or two?" Despair gave way to tears, and she began to cry. "I want to go home! Please take the chain off and let me go home. It's . . . Christmas—"

"Don't cry, darling girl. I'd take the chain off if I dared. Look. You have a new typewriter, the very best, and reams and reams of paper. You can write all the stories you want. I have a collection of your stories.

"Wouldn't you like to see the clothes I bought for you at Neiman Marcus? I went down to Dallas and asked for a model with red hair to try on the clothes. She wasn't nearly as pretty as you, my angel, but she was about your size. I showed the salespeople your pictures. Oh, yes, I have many pictures of you. Someday I'll show them to you, if you like."

If Kathleen had not been so confused, she would have noticed the beads of perspiration on the man's forehead and how his hands shook as he brushed back a strand of his brown hair.

"Do you like this?" He opened the wardrobe and brought out a lovely green dress of pure silk. "Look at the lounging robes at this end. All the shades of green. You are especially lovely in green."

"What shall I call you?" Kathleen scarcely looked at the clothes he was showing her.

"Ted or Teddy. Mother called me Teddy. She hated it when someone called me Theo."

"Teddy, I need to use the . . . closet."

"Oh, I'm sorry." He went to the other side of the bed, knelt, and removed a padlock he had fastened through several links to shorten the chain. "Now you can go to the closet, or to any part of the room. Is the ankle bracelet comfortable?"

"I hardly know it's there," she replied sarcastically.

The ankle-length garment she had on was made of heavy satin, high at the neck and with long sleeves. It was modest for a nightgown.

"Excuse me," she said pointedly.

He tucked the box of sanitary napkins under his arm. "Push the button here at the side of the door if you want me. I'll be back with your breakfast."

Teddy unlocked the door, went out, and closed it. Kathleen heard a heavy bolt slam in place. He had wanted her to hear the clang, to know that she was locked in.

The chain on her ankle was amazingly light. She lifted the nightgown and sat down on the toilet. Her bladder was full. She couldn't believe that she was here, locked in a luxurious room, at the mercy of some kind of psychopath. He must be totally mad if he thought that she would ever be content to stay here and let him "take care" of her, as he put it.

She went back to the bedroom and looked around. She knew instinctively that he would hurt her before he would let her leave despite his denials. He had gone to too much trouble to get her here. With the baby to consider, her options were limited, and she must plan carefully. First she had to find out where she was. Was she still in Rawlings, or had he taken her to some other place?

Logic told her that she was near Rawlings. He had been watching her . . . guarding her, he claimed. He had been spying on her. How else would he have acted so quickly when Gabe Thomas came into her house?

Look at this! She read the titles of books on the shelves inside the glass door of a tall, ornate secretary. A shelf of Zane Grey, works by Hemingway and Daphne du Maurier, including *Rebecca, Frenchman's Creek*, and *Jamaica Inn*. How did he find out that these were some of her favorite books? A stack of Western magazines lay on the bottom shelf. They were from the company that published her stories.

The slanting lid on the secretary opened to provide a writing desk. Inside the pigeonholes were fancy notepaper and envelopes. Several good fountain pens rested in a holder alongside a bottle of ink.

Kathleen moved past the small gas heater that made

the room toasty warm to the dressing table. Hardly noticing the expensive creams and perfumes, she sat down and
gawked at herself in the mirror for a full minute. She felt
as if she were living a nightmare. Nothing seemed to
make sense.

A rap sounded on the door. "Kathleen, may I come in?"

"How can I keep you out? You've got the key."

He unlocked the door, swung it open, and picked up a
tray from the table beside the door. Kathleen could see
out into a hall to what looked like the railing of a stairway. Teddy stood hesitantly in the doorway.

"I brought toast, jam, and a pot of tea. But there is
something I forgot to tell you. The other end of the chain
around your ankle goes through the floor to the room
below. You can't leave this room even if you should
knock me senseless. If anything should happen to me, my
precious girl, you would stay in this room and starve to
death. I wanted you to know that so that you'll not be
tempted to do something foolish."

"I would yell and scream and make enough noise to
raise the dead."

"There is no one to hear you. No one." He smiled.
"You're a spunky woman, my angel. Your mind is working right now on ways to get away from me. Save yourself the effort."

"My husband will be looking for me. He'll tear you
apart."

"He won't find you. If I had thought he'd be a threat, I
would have eliminated him. Here, I found some green tea
in Dallas. It's your favorite, isn't it?"

"What . . . do you mean . . . eliminate him? Would you
have killed him?"

"Let's not be crude, my darling. Killing is not a subject

ladies should be concerned with. Would you like to have your tray there on the dressing table?"

"I want to know. Would you have killed Johnny if he had gotten in the way?"

"Maybe we should clear the air on this subject and be done with it. I would have killed him if it had become necessary. Johnny Henry or any other man means no more to me than a fly on the wall. Now may we drop the subject?"

Kathleen stood slowly. "He wouldn't have been easy to kill."

Teddy laughed. "There are a hundred ways to kill a man without his knowing he is about to die. I know them all."

"You tell me this and expect me to be content to stay here?"

"I told you because you insisted on knowing. Drink your tea and eat the toast. The jam is strawberry and comes from Canada. It is very good."

"Ted Newman couldn't have afforded all this. Who are you . . . really?"

"Theodore Nuding, my precious heart. I had reasons for using the Newman name in the city. Now be a good girl, eat your breakfast, and change into something pretty. This is Christmas Eve, and you are my Christmas gift."

# Chapter Twenty-six

Johnny sat at the kitchen table hunched over a plate of pork and beans and a helping of cottage cheese. He was tired. Today he had pulled the old tractor into the barn to work on it out of the wind. In the process he had smashed his finger and cut the back of his hand. To top it off, he found he had only a sliver of the Lava soap he needed to wash the grease off his hands. He was not in a very good mood.

His thoughts returned to Christmas Eves he had enjoyed on the farm in Red Rock. Aunt Dozie had bustled about, cooking pies, baking bread, and scolding him for being underfoot. Henry Ann had sneaked around wrapping presents and hiding her gifts. She always insisted that he hang a stocking and on Christmas morning, childish though it all was, he'd find a gift as well as an orange, an apple, and stick candy tucked inside.

After he and Kathleen married, she always cooked a special dinner on Christmas Eve just for the two of them. She decorated the table with candles and wore a sprig of mistletoe in her hair. On Christmas Day they would go to the McCabes' or to Paul and Adelaide's. One time she had persuaded him to go to Barker's with her.

Johnny finished his meal. Sherm had gone to spend Christmas at his sister's. Pete, no doubt, was with Dale Cole and her boy, and Jude would be with Theresa and Ryan. Johnny had thought about Kathleen all day, especially after he had dug down in his duffel bag to find the bracelet and necklace he had made for her the first Christmas he was in the Pacific.

While washing the dishes, he began to think about going into town, stopping by her house, and giving her the presents. What the hell could he say?

*I made these on Guadalcanal the first Christmas I was there and forgot to send them to you.*

*I just discovered these in my duffel bag.*

*All the guys made this stuff when they didn't have anything else to do.*

Hell, he'd not say any of those things. If he intended to give the presents to her, he should go in tonight and knock on her door, give her the package, and get the hell off her porch. While he was in town, he'd give Barker a call and tell him that something had come up, and he couldn't make it to dinner tomorrow, and that would be that. Christmas Day would be like any other day. He'd spend it working on the tractor.

Now that he had a plan of action, Johnny put on his sheepskin coat, picked up the tissue-wrapped package, and went out to his car.

The stars always seemed brighter on Christmas Eve. Tonight the sky was studded with millions of them. He thought back to the night in '38 when he and Kathleen had driven back from visiting the McCabes. It was a night like this, but not so cold. She had snuggled close to his side with her hand resting on his thigh. They stopped at the ranch and made love for the first time. She was everything he had ever dreamed about. He had never been so close to heaven in his life.

Deep in thought, he reached town before he realized he had arrived. Twilight Gardens was closed when he passed, as were most of the businesses along Main Street. Lights were on in houses all over town. Families had gathered for Christmas Eve behind closed doors. Pete's car was parked a block from Dale Cole's house. He was being careful to avoid gossip, which told Johnny that Pete must really care for the woman.

Johnny's car was the only one moving on the streets. He drove to the edge of town where Kathleen lived. Along the way lights shone from every house. When he reached hers, it was dark. He stopped in front of the house, disappointment weighing heavily on him. The Nash was there. Had she gone to Adelaide's or to Jude's? He doubted that she would go to Jude's. She'd not wanted to intrude on him and Theresa.

Maybe he should just drop by Paul and Adelaide's place and be surprised that she was there. He moved the car on down the street, turned around, and went back up Main Street. There were no lights in the back room at the *Gazette* office and none in the apartment upstairs.

Johnny looked at his watch. It was only a little after seven. It seemed later because the days were short at this time of year. Would Kathleen have gone to bed? Maybe she was sick. He turned the car around again, went back, and parked behind the Nash. He knocked on the door and shook the doorknob. She had taken his advice and locked it. After knocking several times, he went back to his car, sat for a minute, then headed back to the ranch.

* * *

After a sleepless night, Johnny was up at daylight. He drank warmed-up coffee and went out to do chores in the crisp cold air. He couldn't decide if he wanted to go to Barker's for Christmas dinner. He might feel like a fish out of water. He debated the pros and cons in his mind.

What if Kathleen completely ignored him? What if she gave him a present and he didn't have one for her? He had already decided he wasn't going to give her the gifts he had made during the war in front of the Flemings.

By damn, he'd forgotten to get anything for Lucas and the girls. The drugstore was usually open for a few hours. If not, he could get Stan to open for him. He could get something for the girls there . . . but Lucas was another matter.

An idea hit. He went through his navy duffel bag and found a knife he'd taken off a dead Jap on Ondonga, a small island in the Pacific, where unexploded Japanese shells and buried mines were more of a danger than the nightly air raids. Even now he could smell the mud and rotting vegetation on that hellhole. That was all behind him, thank God.

He worked on the blade, polishing it with steel wool, then sharpened it. It was a wicked weapon. The grip had a notched bow called iron knuckles. Barker would make sure that Lucas understood that the knife was a memento from the war and not a plaything.

Dressed in his good tan twill pants and a blue shirt, Johnny left the ranch. He reached town just as Stan was locking the door of the drugstore. Fifteen minutes later he was back in the car with Blue Waltz perfume and Tangee lipstick for the girls, fancy soap for Mrs. Fisher, and a cigarette lighter for Barker.

At Kathleen's he parked behind the Nash. With her gift in hand, he knocked on her door. After a minute or two he decided she wasn't there, that one of the Flemings must have come for her. Disappointed again, he went back to the car and drove slowly out to Barker's ranch.

Marie, followed by Janna and Lucas, answered the door.

"I'm so glad you came. Merry Christmas, Johnny."

"Merry Christmas to you."

"Hang your coat there on the hall tree, Johnny, and come on over by the fire," Barker called from his easy chair beside the fireplace.

A Christmas tree stood in one corner of the room with presents on the floor beneath its branches.

"Here are a few things to add to the tree. I didn't put names on the packages, but I know what goes to who." Johnny handed the sack of gifts to Marie.

"We thought you might go by and bring Kathleen. We were waiting for the two of you before we opened the presents."

"I stopped by, but she wasn't home." Johnny hung his hat above his coat. "Her car was there, so I thought you'd picked her up."

"I offered, but she said she'd drive out." Marie set Johnny's gifts beside the tree. "We saw Adelaide at church last night, and she was surprised that Kathleen wasn't there. Janna and I and Mrs. Fisher went by the house after the service, and she wasn't at home then, either. She doesn't usually go out at night except to the movies, and then she drives the car."

"She'll be along." Barker was pleased that Johnny was there. It was the first time since he came home from the war. "How are things going out at your place, Johnny?"

"Pretty good, I guess." Johnny backed up to the fireplace. The heat felt good on the hands clasped behind him, but he continued to worry. "When did you last speak to Kathleen, Marie?"

"It was Sunday, I think. She was baking cookies, then she was going to the movie. She usually goes to the show on Sunday night. I asked her to go with us to church Christmas Eve. She said she'd meet us there. That's why we went by her house last night."

"She said that she'd be here at a certain time; it's not polite to be this late and especially at Christmas." Mrs. Fisher, concerned about the meal she had prepared, spoke bluntly.

"Kathleen is never inconsiderate." Marie jumped to Kathleen's defense.

"No, she isn't," Barker said. "And she is one of the most punctual people I know."

"Maybe she's sick and can't get out of bed to answer the door." Janna voiced what had suddenly occurred to the others.

Johnny immediately started putting on his coat. "Do you have a key to the house?"

Barker reached for the sheepskin hanging on a hook beside the door. "Yes. I have a master key."

"Why don't you wait a little longer?" Mrs. Fisher said. "You may pass each other, then we'd have to wait for you."

"She's almost an hour late. I think they should go." Marie had a worried look on her face. "Will you call, Daddy, if . . . she's sick or something?"

Barker nodded. "Why don't you go ahead and open a few presents."

Janna and Marie shook their heads. "We'll wait." Lucas scowled.

Barker followed Johnny to his car. Johnny didn't speak until he had parked behind the Nash and they had walked up onto the porch.

"The window shades are still down."

He rapped on the door several times, then stepped back to let Barker insert the key. The door opened easily and Johnny went inside.

"Kathleen," he called.

Hearing no answer, Johnny walked quickly to the bedroom. The bed was still made. With his heart in his throat, he passed through the bathroom to the other small room and then into the kitchen. Barker was behind him.

"Sunday she told Marie she was baking cookies. They're still here on the counter." Barker opened the back door and looked out, then closed it.

"It's cold in here." Johnny touched the small gas heater in the corner of the living room. It was cold.

In the bedroom once again, he opened the wardrobe. Her clothes were there. The pages of her manuscript were neatly stacked beside her typewriter. A sheet of paper was in the machine. He glanced at it and back when a word or two caught his eye. His heart was thudding in his ears when he jerked the paper from the roller.

*After thinking about it for a long while I have de-*
*cided to leave Rawlings. I don't want anyone looking*
*for me, and I don't want anything in this house that*
*would remind me of the past.*
*I AM STARTING A NEW LIFE*

Johnny read the note twice and handed it to Barker. Sick with fear, he watched as Barker read the note.

"She didn't write it," Johnny declared when Barker handed him back the note.

"How do you know?"

"Because if she had made a decision to go, she wouldn't have baked cookies and she wouldn't have left her purse."

Johnny reached down beside the bed, picked up a brown-leather handbag and opened it. Kathleen's driver's license was inside, as well as six one-dollar bills. In another compartment, he found her wedding ring.

"She wouldn't have left without this. She was taken by force and during the night because the shades are still down."

"Who would do such a thing?"

"Call the sheriff. I'm going outside to look around."

After Barker made the call, he phoned Adelaide to see if Kathleen was there.

"The last time I saw her was on Friday. Paul and I were planning to go over to her place tonight. You can't find her? Oh, my Lord. Is there anything we can do?"

"The sheriff is on his way. We'll let you know."

Johnny didn't wait for the sheriff. He went directly to Dale Cole's house, where he knew he would find Pete.

"Is Kathleen here?" he asked as soon as Dale opened the door.

"What's up?" Pete appeared in the door behind her.

"We can't find Kathleen. When did you see her last?"

"Saturday. She said she was going to the Flemings' today for dinner."

Johnny told them about finding the note and Kath-

354 / Dorothy Garlock

leen's purse. "She wouldn't walk away and leave her purse, even if she didn't want the rest of her things."

"She's not at Jude's. I was by there before I came here to get Dale and Danny. We were getting ready to leave. I'll take them to Jude's and help you look for her."

Four hours later Johnny had to face the fact that Kathleen had vanished without a trace. He went back to her house for the fourth or fifth time to see if there was any news. Marie was there by the telephone. Bobby Harper, on his crutches, was with her. Adelaide and Paul were there, too. Barker met Johnny on the porch.

"Anything?"

Johnny shook his head. "We need men on horseback to look into every building or vacant shack. Some sick bastard may have taken her to an out-of-the-way place like that and left her there." Johnny's eyes were bleak with worry. "Barker, I've not asked you for anything, but—"

"You don't have to ask, son. Kathleen is family. I'll call out the men at the ranch, the tannery, and some people I know on the reservation. We'll organize a search in the country. You handle the one in town."

"Thanks."

"Johnny, Dr. Perry wants you to come by there when you can," Marie said from the doorway.

"Does he have news?"

"No. He asked if we had any."

"I'll go over there."

Johnny had to keep moving. The thought that he might never see Kathleen again was tearing him to shreds. He drove automatically and stopped automatically in front of Jude's house and got out. Jude came to meet him. Johnny shook his head when he saw the question in the doctor's eyes. Jude turned to Theresa, who stood in the doorway, and relayed the "no news" message.

"Let's sit in the car," Jude suggested. "You look worn out," he said after they were seated. "Have you had any dinner?"

"No, but Marie brought some food to Kathleen's." There was a world of misery in Johnny's eyes. "She wouldn't have just walked away leaving her purse, her money, her clothes. Her picture album is there and her grandmother's crocheted dresser scarf. She wouldn't have left the manuscript she's been working on. Someone else wrote that note or made her write it."

"I've not known her long, but I can't see her just up and leaving on Christmas and not telling anyone. She sent over a sack of presents with Pete. He asked her to join us for dinner, but she said she was going to the Flemings' today."

"What did you want to see me about, Jude? I need to go check out a few things."

"I've been struggling with my conscience. Yes, before you ask, I do have one."

"I've not given it a thought one way or the other," Johnny said tiredly.

"That was a little play on words because I'm nervous about breaking a promise in telling you this. But under the circumstances, I think you have a right to know that Kathleen came to see me right after the school carnival."

Johnny's head jerked around. "Was she sick?"

"No. She was pregnant."

"What?" Johnny leaned forward as if he had been struck in the back of the head. His hand reached out, then fell back. "What?" he said again more softly as breath returned to him.

"She came to talk to me about the baby you had that died. She wondered if something she had done could have caused its congenital defect. I explained to her that the baby had failed to develop in her womb which occurs without any apparent reason to one fetus out of several thousand."

"Whose is it?" Johnny turned his head and looked blindly out the window when he asked.

Jude was quiet for so long that Johnny turned to face him. "Whose, dammit?"

"She's your wife. Do you need to ask?" Jude answered quietly, but his words were laced with anger. "I guess I understand now why she didn't want you to know."

"I've been with her only one time in five years."

"Once is enough."

"But . . . it took a long time before."

"Kathleen is pregnant. She's about two months along now. If you have any doubt that it's your child, take it up with her."

"I have no doubt." Johnny rubbed his hand over his face.

"She made me promise not to tell you. She said you swore you'd not have another child, and she didn't want you putting a damper on her happiness." Jude regretted that his words were so cutting.

"She knows why I didn't want another child," Johnny said harshly. "I let her go because her top priority was having a family. She wanted a dozen kids if she could get them because she was an only child and never had any family except her grandparents."

"She was smiling from ear to ear when she left the clinic that day. She kept asking me if I was sure."

"Would being pregnant make her ... do something like run away?"

"Not Kathleen. She'd not do anything that could cause her to miscarry."

"God, Jude! What am I going to do if I can't find her?"

"I don't know, Johnny. I'm here to do anything I can."

"Thanks. Tell Dale that Pete has gone out with one of the deputies. He said that he'd come by for her later."

"I'll tell her." Jude got out of the car. "Would you take a sandwich or something with you?"

"No, thanks. I've got to get on back."

Johnny drove down the street and stopped. He needed to think. He had sensed something different about Kathleen when they met on the street. Now he knew what it was. She was leaving! She was going to go off some place, have his baby, and never let him know. Godalmighty! What a mess he had made of his life and hers.

Unaware of the tears in his eyes until his vision blurred, Johnny started the car moving again, then braked. Something Jude had said suddenly came to his mind. *Undeveloped in the womb ... one in several thousand births.* Dear God! Had he been wrong all this time thinking that their deformed child was his fault? He had been so sure! He had deprived himself of being with the woman he loved because he was so sure. And Kathleen. What had he done to her?

She had come into his arms willingly, eagerly that morning. She had been as loving as a woman could be. He had touched a little bit of Heaven again; but feeling undeserving of her and angry at himself for having been carried away by the moment, he had rushed off. He hadn't considered how she felt then. Now that his child was growing within her, what was her attitude toward him? Would he ever know?

Kathleen might have come to the end of her patience with him. Even if that were true and she was going to leave, she would not have done it in this manner. She wouldn't have wanted to cause pain to Adelaide and the Flemings . . . especially not on Christmas.

God, let her be all right! He had to tell her that he had never stopped loving her; that was why he never stopped wearing his wedding ring. He wanted to be with her when she had his baby. He wanted them both, even if this baby was like Mary Rose.

Why would she even consider taking him back? He put his head on the arm folded across the steering wheel and cried the harsh, dry sobs of a man who was a stranger to tears.

# Chapter Twenty-seven

*FIRST DAY OF CAPTIVITY.*

*W*hen evening came, Teddy, as he wanted to be called, rolled in a serving cart with a tray of food and a pot of tea. On the lower shelf were several fancily wrapped packages. Kathleen was served noodles in a sauce, green peas, bread, and a sliced orange. The food was good, and she was surprised that she could eat.

Wearing a white shirt and tie and the tweed coat, he silently watched her while she ate. When she finished, he removed the tray to the hallway and placed the packages in her lap.

"Are you giving these to me?" When he nodded, she asked, "Why?"

"Because it makes me happy to give you pretty things."

"I have nothing for you."

"I told you, my Christmas gift is you." He handed her an oblong package. "Open this one first."

Kathleen removed the paper and lifted the lid from the box. She gasped. Lying on dark velvet padding was a large emerald suspended on a silver chain. Her eyes flew to his face. He looked like a child on Christmas morning.

"I can't accept this."

"Don't you like it?"

"That isn't the point. I can't accept something like this from someone I hardly know. It cost too much money."

"I have plenty. Open the other packages."

In the other boxes were a set of earrings and a ring. All were set with large perfectly matched green emeralds.

"I don't know what to say."

"'Thank you, Teddy', would be nice."

"I can't accept them, but thank you for the kind thought."

"Put them away. We won't talk about it now." He didn't seem to be offended by her refusal. "This is your first day here. You may want to go to bed now. Play the radio if you like. Sometimes music is soothing. I'll see you in the morning."

"Is there a lock on the door?"

"Yes, but I won't lock it. You have the chain."

"I mean on the inside."

"Why would you want one?"

"So that I can undress in privacy," she shouted.

"No need to yell, my precious. I will never come into this room without knocking first."

"I would rather you didn't call me endearing names. I am your prisoner, not your precious."

He laughed. "My darling, beautiful Kathleen. You are far more wonderful, more precious, to me than I dreamed. Everything about you is perfect from the top of that glorious red hair to the tip of your lovely toes. I would worship at your feet, but"—he paused—"you might kick me," he said, chuckling.

"And you would be right, Mr. Know-it-all!"

He went out the door laughing.

## SECOND DAY—CHRISTMAS DAY.

By the end of this day, Kathleen was acutely aware that she was at the mercy of a man who was highly intelligent, terribly kind to her, but mentally deranged. All her wit and courage would be needed to escape from him.

She began to form a plan, make some rules for herself to follow. She could not afford to irritate him, yet she would not be docile. She would eat the food he brought her, not only because she would be needing her strength, but because of her baby. If she could make him think that she had accepted her captivity, he might grow more lax and maybe even remove the chain.

He had measured carefully. The chain allowed her to go anyplace in the room, but not out the door and into the hallway. Slipping the chain from her ankle was out of the question. She had tried it. It was a snug fit within the cushioned pad.

*How did the idiot think she could put on the underwear he had supplied with the chain on her ankle?*

She decided not to mention it to him. In a dress without panties, she felt naked. So she wore two of the nightgowns and a robe and, because she didn't want to anger him, the emerald necklace, the earrings, and the ring.

## THIRD DAY.

Kathleen cried most of the day. The dam that had held back the tears for the last couple of days had burst. The sobs surged out of the depths of her misery. She wanted to go home. She longed for the safety of Johnny's arms.

Did Marie or Adelaide wonder why she wasn't at church service on Christmas Eve? Had Barker come to see why she hadn't come to dinner Christmas day? Adelaide and Paul had planned to stop by in the evening. Surely they were wondering what had happened to her.

Kathleen continued to cry. She wanted Johnny! Would she ever see him again? *Johnny, I love you. Please don't forget me. Remember that I love you.*

"Why are you crying, my darling?" Teddy asked when he came in and found her sobbing on the bed.

"I guess . . . I'm just lonesome." It was the first thing that came to mind.

"Why don't you put on one of the pretty dresses I bought for you? That should cheer you up."

"I can't put on stockings."

"I'm sorry about that, my angel. You understand, don't you, that I can't take the chain off. I can't lose you, my precious girl, now that I finally have you."

Kathleen wanted to hit him. She wanted to scream for him to get out of her sight and stop groveling at her feet as if she were a goddess. His constant, cloyingly syrupy endearments grated on her nerves and made her want to scratch his eyes out.

## FOURTH DAY.

Kathleen no longer feared that Teddy intended to rape her. Her plans, should he try, were to grab his testicles with one hand, squeeze and twist, and shove stiff fingers in his eyes with the other. A girl at the aircraft plant had told her that was how she had warded off a rapist.

Teddy knocked each time before he came into the room. Usually he sat in one of the chairs and watched her. Once he brought a notebook and wrote several pages. He was very open about it when she asked him what he was writing.

"A journal. A man never knows where he's going if he can't recall where he's been."

"You're terribly smart, Teddy. Where did you go to college?"

"My dear, you flatter me. I didn't go to college. Mother taught me at home. She was brilliant."

"You must have loved her very much."

"Yes. She was the most magnificent creature I had ever known until I met you."

"Teddy, I could in no way be like your mother."

"Precious girl, you outmatch Mother in sweetness and in beauty. She knows that and understands it."

Kathleen searched for another topic of conversation, not knowing how to respond when he spoke of communicating with his dead mother.

"Read me what you are writing."

"Would you like to hear it? Really?" His eyes smiled into hers when she nodded.

"*Three-thirty-five*. I put down the time because feelings are sometimes different at different times of the day."

"I hadn't thought of that."

"*Three-thirty-five P.M.*" He read from the journal. "*Mother, this is my fourth day with my darling Kathleen. I am so happy. She is everything I told you that she would be: beautiful, intelligent, kind, and understanding. It is amazing that God could make such a vile creature as a man and such a perfect creation as my Kathleen. She has been so—"*

"—Teddy, please don't read any more. I'm not any of the things you say I am, and it's embarrassing to hear you say so. I can be mean, quarrelsome, and I have a terrible temper. My grandma said it went with red hair."

"You couldn't be mean, my heart. You're modest. It's part of your charm, your goodness."

"Do you mind if I lie down and rest for a while?"

"No, my sweet. I'll just sit quietly and watch over you."

"You don't need to do that. I'm sure you have things you want to do. I'll be all right." *Please go! Pl . . . ease go!*

Kathleen lay down on the bed and turned her back to him.

"I do have a few things to do. Rest, my wonderful one. I'll be back soon."

When she heard the door close, she turned her head to be sure that she was alone, then heaved a sigh of relief and let the tears roll down her cheeks. How much longer would she be able to endure this without having a screaming fit?

## *FIFTH DAY.*

Kathleen suspected that Teddy wasn't well. He hadn't touched her since the morning she awakened in this room. He had been strong then, holding her down on the bed. And it had taken strength to carry her out of her house and up the stairs.

Long ago she had dismissed the notion of trying to overpower him, not only because of the chain on her ankle. She couldn't let herself be hurt in any way that would harm the baby.

Kathleen began to notice that at times Teddy winced at some apparent pain, and his face became wet with perspiration. Something was wrong with him. Dear Lord, don't let him have a fatal heart attack. The thought of being chained in this room until she died of starvation was so horrible it made her stomach heave.

## SIXTH DAY.

Teddy's face was pale and his hands trembled when he brought her breakfast.

"Are you sick, Teddy?" Kathleen asked with concern.

"Only a headache, sweet girl. It will go away. I'll lie down for a while and be good as new."

"Teddy, don't leave me chained. Please. If you got sick, I'd die up here." She had promised herself she wouldn't beg, but suddenly she was terribly frightened.

"My precious girl." He cupped her cheek with his palm, the first time he had touched her since the first day. "I'll not leave you. When I depart from this world, you and the little princess will be with me."

His words were not comforting. They implied a deadly intent that frightened her more than ever.

He didn't come back until evening. He brought bread and cheese, an apple, and a pot of tea. He sat in the corner of the room and watched her. When she finished eating, he took the tray and left with only a few of the sugary words she had come to detest.

*SEVENTH DAY.*

Theodore Nuding, also known as Robert Brooks, sat beside the oven in the kitchen of the large Clifton house hugging a blanket around his shoulders.

This was supposed to be the happiest time in his life, the fulfillment of his dreams. It was not fair, Teddy thought, that the curse had chosen this time to rear its ugly head.

"It runs in the family, my dear Teddy," his mother had said. "It has dogged my Greek ancestors down through the ages. I can't avoid it and neither can you. You must constantly keep your affairs in order."

He had heeded his mother's advice, even to the filing of his will. The means of his escape from a painful, lingering death had been tested. Unlike his mother he had prepared for the inevitable. She had left it up to him, and even if he did say so, he had performed his duty admirably.

When he went to meet her in Heaven, he would take his darling Kathleen and the little princess with him. He couldn't bear to think of going without them.

A random thought struck him and brought a smile to his face. What was the date? The thirtieth of December. Tomorrow would be the last day of the year 1945—the perfect time for him to take his darling little family to meet his mother.

Johnny and Tom Dolan waited in front of the *Gazette* office for the Greyhound bus that was bringing Hod Dolan down from Kansas. Tom had arrived on the fourth day of Kathleen's disappearance and this was the seventh. The whole town had turned out to look for her, yet not a single clue had turned up.

Johnny was near exhaustion. He couldn't sleep, had hardly eaten anything. His whiskered cheeks were sunken. The eyes he turned to Tom were flat and bleak.

"I hope Hod will have some new suggestions for us. Unless Kathleen has shelter, she can't last much longer."

"I hate to say this, but she could be out of the state, out of the country by now."

"She's near. I just feel that she's around here somewhere. Someone took her who wanted to get back at me, or at Barker. Maybe something was printed in the paper that hit someone the wrong way. She's part-owner of the *Gazette*."

"You've not been home long enough to make many enemies," Tom said.

"I made one. He worked at the Fleming ranch until Barker fired him. Pete got to him before I did. He said he didn't know anything about Kathleen. Guess he smarted off at first, and Pete mopped the floor with him. Here's the bus." Johnny and Tom moved out away from the building and waited for the door of the bus to open.

United States Marshal Hod Dolan stepped down. He was a tall, impressive man in a black suit and a dark hat. Except for the streaks of gray in his black hair, he looked enough like Tom Dolan to be his twin.

"Hod! God, it's good to see you." The two men clasped hands and shoulders.

"How'er ya doin', Tom. It's been a hell of a long time."

"Too bad it takes something like this to get us together."

"Johnny. Lord, man. You're no longer that skinny kid

who helped me track the Barrow gang." Hod grasped Johnny's hand.

"A lot of water has gone under the bridge since then, Hod."

"Dammit, Johnny, I don't know what to say. Kathleen is not only our brother's daughter, she's special."

"Thanks for coming, Hod. We're about at the end of the rope. We need someone to show us a new direction."

"Molly said to say hello. She would have come down, but she's got her hands full with the kids."

"The car's over here. We'll go on out to the house, and Tom and I will fill you in. Barker has a crew out on horseback and so does Pete Perry. They may be back by now."

"What's this? Kathleen's old Nash? This old heap still runnin'?"

"Yeah. My old car doesn't have but one seat. I kind of rearranged the inside so I could haul stuff."

It was almost dark by the time Johnny parked the Nash alongside Kathleen's house. Three other cars were parked along the street: Pete's, Barker's, and Bobby Harper's.

"Nice little house," Hod said when they stopped.

"Kathleen has been living here since she came back from the city. Come on in. There should be some food in there if you're hungry. Folks have been good about bringing it in."

Bobby Harper met them at the door. He flung it open, then stepped back on his crutches to let them in.

"Bobby, this is Hod Dolan. Kathleen's other uncle."

"Howdy." Bobby stuck out his hand.

"Johnny?" Marie came from the kitchen and put her arm around Johnny's waist. "Any word?"

Johnny shook his head. "My sister, Marie Fleming, Hod. She's been coming every day. We didn't think it a good idea for her to be here alone, so Bobby took on the job of staying with her."

"Hello, little lady. I bet Bobby didn't mind takin' on the job a'tall."

"No, sir. I sure didn't." Bobby grinned broadly.

"Put your things in the bedroom. I'll have supper on the table soon if Bobby will help me. Have you seen Daddy, Johnny?"

"Not since morning. Has anyone called?"

"A lot of people have called wanting to know if there was any news." She reached up and put her hand on his rough cheek. "You've got to eat something. You'll be sick and not able to help Kathleen if she needs you."

"All right, little sister. I need to go wash off some of this road dirt."

Johnny and Tom had filled Hod in on everything from day one to the present by the time Pete and Barker came back to the house. Johnny introduced them to Hod, and the four continued the discussion at the supper table.

"Paul, down at the *Gazette*, made posters with Kathleen's picture and the offer of a five-hundred-dollar reward for information. Every town within fifty miles has been saturated with them. Paul saw to it that every paper in the state of Oklahoma and some in Texas received a news release."

"No bites?"

"Nothing."

"News coverage and a reward of that size will usually get you something if there's anything to be got." Hod was sorry he had been so blunt when he saw the look of despair cross Johnny's face.

"We've gone over the whole county by car and by horseback. We've looked into every nook and cranny."

This came from Pete, who had put in almost as many hours as Johnny looking for Kathleen.

"Maybe we should go back over the area, slowly, starting at the edge of town and fanning out to search every foot of ground. You're reasonably sure she's not in town?"

"Folks in town have known about the reward for five days. I believe that if anyone had noticed anything slightly suspicious, we would have heard about it by now."

"Fifty men from the reservation will be here at daylight. Some will be on horseback and some afoot," Barker said quietly. "Some speak very little English; but they are good trackers, and I'll be with them."

Hod studied Barker. If he had not been told that the man was Johnny's father, he would have guessed it. Johnny had his father's classic Indian features.

"The volunteers will meet in front of the *Gazette* in the morning at seven." Pete helped himself to a piece of corn bread. "Mayor White is in charge of them. We'll have to decide what we want them to do."

"Hod, Keith McCabe will be back here the day after tomorrow. He'd been here since the first of the week and had to go home today to tend to some business." Johnny had eaten to satisfy Marie, but the food was sticking in his throat.

"It'll be good to see that son of a gun. By the way, what was Kathleen wearing when she was last seen?"

Johnny answered. "She went to the show on Sunday night. The ticket seller said that she was wearing a green dress and a black coat."

"Her coat had a round collar and big gold buttons

down the front," Marie said while filling Johnny's coffee cup.

Pete got up to leave. "See you in the morning, old hoss," he said, and clasped Johnny's shoulder.

"I'll be going, too. Are you bringing Marie, Bobby?" Barker asked.

"Yes, sir. I'm learning to drive pretty good with one foot."

Marie put on her coat. "I'll be here tomorrow, Johnny."

"Tomorrow is New Year's Eve," Tom said. "Maybe it will bring us some good news."

# Chapter Twenty-eight

*EIGHTH DAY.*

*K*athleen knew immediately that there was something different about Teddy, aside from the fact that he was pale and not quite steady on his feet when he came to her room with her breakfast.

His eyes shone as if he were terribly excited, and his face was damp with perspiration. He was freshly shaved, which was not unusual, but he had also trimmed his hair.

"Eat your breakfast, my precious pet. I have things to do downstairs, then I'll be back." He placed the tray with a pot of tea and a piece of toast on the dressing table.

"Teddy, unchain me and let me come down and help you."

"No, no. There's no need for that. You'll be free of the chain soon enough, sweet one. Would you like for me to wash your hair this morning?"

"No, thank you. I washed it last night."

"It's lovely, my darling. You're lovely. Eat your breakfast like a good girl."

"Teddy, do you feel all right? It scares me for you to be sick."

"Because you love me, sweet one?"

"I . . . could learn to care for you," she told the lie easily because it was what he wanted to hear. "What if you get sick? If I'm chained in this room, I can't help you."

"It will not come to that, I promise. Eat your breakfast before your tea gets cold. And, my beautiful Kathleen, put on the emeralds: the necklace, the earrings, and the ring. I want to see you decked out like the goddess you are. Humm?"

He went to the wardrobe and pulled out a foam green peignoir with a gown to match.

"You haven't worn this. Wear it for me, angel girl. It will make me happy. I'll be back soon."

Kathleen was trembling with fear by the time he left the room, his feet spread apart in an effort to keep his balance. As soon as the door closed, she went to the place where the chain disappeared in the hole in the floor and tugged on it for the hundredth time.

*Eat your breakfast.* How many times had he said that today? Enough times so that it seemed to be more important than usual.

She lifted the top from the teapot and sniffed. It smelled the same but had he put something in the tea? She held the strainer over the cup, poured the tea through and carried it to the toilet. She emptied the second cup, then crumbled the toast in the toilet before she flushed it.

Fear ran rampant through her.

*You'll be free of the chain soon.* What had he meant by that? If he wasn't going to turn her loose, the only way she would be free of the chain was if she were . . . dead?

*He is going to . . . kill me!*

Since that first day, she hadn't considered that he would do that. He had said that she would come to love it here. She took that to mean he planned to keep her here for a long time. Did he think that he was going to die and wanted to take her with him?

The thought sank into her mind like a chunk of lead.

She told herself that she wouldn't panic. She had to plan what to do if she was going to live to have her baby. If he put something in the tea, it was to put her to sleep or to make her drowsy and easy to handle.

She had to suppress the anger that made her want to scream and throw things. She couldn't afford to allow rage to cloud her mind when she was going to need every bit of courage she possessed in order to be ready when he came back to the room.

Kathleen hurriedly dressed in the green gown and peignoir, fastened the necklace around her neck, and attached the earrings to her earlobes. With the ring on her finger, she lay down on the side of the bed nearest the door. Hugging a pillow close to her, should she need it to protect her baby, she tilted her head so that she could see the door through the slightest lifting of her eyelids.

With her heart beating like a tom-tom in her breast, she waited.

*Johnny, will you ever learn that I've never stopped loving you? Will Jude tell you that I was going to have your baby?*

Time went slowly, and her mind raced. She wondered how she would be remembered if she didn't make it through the day. Would Johnny grieve for her? He had loved her fiercely at one time, and she had been sure he loved her the morning she conceived the baby. She wondered if her body would ever be found, or if Teddy would bury her in some dark hole somewhere.

During the hour that followed, she moved from time to

time so that her arms and legs would respond when she needed them. She began to think that he wasn't coming back, that his plan was for her to stay here in this room until she died. Then she heard his footsteps on the stairs and repositioned herself so that she could see him when he came in.

He rapped softly on the door.

She didn't answer.

He rapped again louder. After a few seconds of silence he opened the door. It took all the control that Kathleen possessed to lie still when he entered the room. He paused just inside to look at her.

"Are you asleep, my angel?" His words were slurred.

He was in formal attire. His black suit had satin lapels. His shirt was startling white, his bow tie black. On his feet were black patent-leather shoes.

"Did you drink your tea, darling girl?" He glanced at the tray, where the tea strainer was filled with leaves. "I see that you did, my heart. You are my good sweet girl."

He brought his hand out from behind him. In it was a hypodermic syringe with a needle attached.

Kathleen felt a gigantic surge of fear and with it a fierce determination to fight him to the last breath! Not sure what she was going to do, she watched him as he watched her.

"Queen of my heart," he murmured. "My darling Kathleen. You and I and our little princess will soon be together forever. I have adored you since I first set eyes on you. I have guarded you and killed your enemies while I waited for this day. It's all written in the journal, dear one.

"Remember the supervisor at Douglas who wanted to take you out and called you a bitch when you refused? He is no more. Nor is the garage man who went into your house uninvited." He held up the surgical syringe. "I tested this lovely product on that detestable creature who beat his wife. It worked beautifully."

Teddy rocked back on his heels, almost lost his balance, and grabbed onto the doorjamb with his free hand.

"You are so beautiful in the green gown. The emeralds are lovely only because it is you who wear them, my precious girl. You drank your tea, humm? I didn't want you to be frightened. I had not planned to do this now, but the curse is on me as it was on Mother."

He stopped his rambling and began to cry.

"There is no one to help me, so I must do it myself. I had hoped for more time so that I could see our little princess. But this is the way it must be. You will feel no pain, my lovely one. Within fifteen seconds, I will be with you."

Kathleen hugged the pillow. It was hard to wait for him to approach the bed. Adrenaline was pumping through her veins. She thought of nothing but keeping him from injecting her with the needle.

"It's time to go, darling," he crooned, and came to the side of the bed.

When he bent over her with the needle poised, Kathleen's eyes flew open. She reared up with the pillow in front of her and, with the strength of desperation, she rammed it against him. Her feet hit the floor, found purchase, and she shoved again. He toppled back, staggered, and fell, his head hitting the floor. He tried to rise but fell back.

Dragging the chain, Kathleen went around him to the dressing table and grabbed the heavy crockery teapot. She was ready to bring it down on his head when he opened his eyes, looked up, and smiled.

"I'm dying, my precious. I pierced my hand with the . . . needle. It will take a minute. Let me look at you. You will join me, for no one knows that you are here. If you wish to do it without suffering, use . . . the needle—" His mouth remained open when breath left him. Ice-blue eyes continued to stare up at her.

When Kathleen's numbed mind came to realize that he was dead, she dropped the teapot, backed away as far as the chain would allow, and screamed and screamed.

The air was so cold that their breaths were visible when more than a hundred men and boys spread out over the countryside in search of a clue to Kathleen's whereabouts. In ten groups of ten or more, they moved across the prairie searching every wooded area, every shack and shed.

Barker and his Cherokee worked the land south of Rawlings on horseback and on foot. Johnny covered the western area with a dozen volunteers. His horse zigzagged through a small forest, with Johnny leaning from the saddle searching the ground for anything that would be foreign to the area. It was warmer in the woods out of the wind. He dreaded finding evidence that would tell him that she was dead. *God, please don't let it happen.*

He met up with his crew on the other side of the woods. The plan was for all the crews to meet at the crossroads directly south of town at noon to exchange information. Volunteers, organized by Adelaide, would join them, bringing a noon meal.

A dozen cars were lined up at the crossroads. The women had built fires in the ditch along the road, and coffeepots were sending plumes of steam into the air. Blankets, on the ground, were spread with sandwiches, pies, and cakes.

Johnny dismounted and removed the saddle from his horse. After slipping a halter on the animal, he attached a long lead rope to the bumper of the end car. The tired horse began cropping the short dry grass.

Pete came in with his crew, then Barker and a group of Cherokee. The Indians put hobbles on their horses and turned them loose. Another group galloped toward them from across the prairie. The quiet, subdued circle of men took sandwiches, then squatted down on their haunches to eat and to drink the hot coffee.

Johnny made the rounds to talk to the leaders of the crews. Barker stood with a man Johnny didn't know. He was a Cherokee, wearing a leather tunic. His hair hung past his shoulders in two braids.

"Anything, Barker?"

"Nothing. Johnny, meet Jacob Rides Fast. Jacob, this is my son, Johnny Henry."

"Howdy." Johnny stuck out his hand.

"I'm glad to meet you and sorry to be doing it under these circumstances." To Johnny's surprise Jacob Rides Fast spoke with an accent similar to that of the men he had met during the war who were from the eastern states.

"Jacob brought the men down from the reservation, Johnny. He's a member of the Cherokee Nation Council."

"I appreciate the help," Johnny said.

"We will come back if you need us."

One of the Indians spoke to Jacob in Cherokee.

Understanding the language, Barker said. "I'll go with them."

"They are hesitant about going to the fire for coffee and food," Jacob explained to Johnny after Barker left.

Barker returned with two cups of coffee. He handed one to Jacob.

"Tom and Hod rode in," Barker said.

"Maybe they've found something."

As Johnny moved away to find Kathleen's uncles, his eyes moved over a group of young Indian boys scuffling and tossing a ball. He looked away and then back. One of the boys was wearing a black coat, and he had seen a flash of a gold button. His heart thudded, then sank with disappointment when he realized the coat was mid-thigh on the boy. Kathleen's coat had been long.

When the boy, running to catch a ball that had been thrown, ran toward Johnny, he noticed that the coat was ragged along the bottom and that the lining hung down. It had been cut off. Johnny ran across the field toward the boy.

The boy peered up at Johnny with fright when he grabbed him and swung him around. Johnny had eyes only for the coat. It had a round collar and gold buttons down the front to where it had been cut off.

"Where did you get this coat?" Holding the frightened boy by the shoulders, Johnny yelled again, "Where did you get this coat?"

The boy said something in Cherokee, then repeated the words over and over.

"Johnny, Johnny." Barker repeated his name, and shook his arm to get his attention.

"It's her coat!"

"He doesn't speak English. Let me talk to him."

"What's he saying?"

"He's saying that he didn't steal it."

"It's Kathleen's coat. Where's Pete? He'll know it's her coat."

Barker pulled the frightened boy aside. He was not much older than Lucas. He and Jacob talked to him for several minutes. The boy pointed as he spoke to them. Johnny waited, his heart filled with hope, his head telling him that this could be the dreaded end of the search.

"He found the coat yesterday while we were looking around the old Clifton place. He was out with me and the men from the ranch. His father works for me. He said he found it in a place filled with boxes. He thought the coat had been thrown away. He cut it off with his knife. He wanted to wear it because he was cold."

"Hasn't anyone searched the Clifton place?"

"We went there the first day and back again yesterday. The house is boarded-up and locked. Two sheds on the place are padlocked. Wind said that he climbed in a little window and found the coat in a box. He didn't tell me because he thought I'd make him put it back."

Hod and Tom arrived to hear what Barker had to say. The boy stood trembling and looking up at the tall, angry-faced men.

"Where is this place?" Hod asked.

"Four, maybe five miles." Johnny headed for the cars. "You and Jacob coming, Barker?"

Barker spoke to Jacob, then said, "Jacob will wait here and look after the horses."

Two cars left the crossroads, Johnny driving the Nash, Tom, Hod, and Barker with him. Pete had flagged down Sheriff Carroll and hopped in the car with him, telling him the news as they followed the Nash.

"Tell me what you know about this place, Johnny," Hod said.

"Not much. Do you know anything about it, Barker?"

Barker leaned forward to rest his arms on the back of the front seat so he could be heard.

"It's been for sale for a couple of years. It sold recently to a man who hasn't moved in yet according to Wrenn at the bank. I looked up the deed because I was interested in buying some of the land. The deed was made out to Hidendall, Incorporated. All the stock in the corporation is owned by a man named Theodore Nuding."

"Hell and damnation, Johnny. Slow down," Tom cautioned, as the back wheels on the Nash skidded at a corner.

"The Clifton ranch is a big one," Barker continued. "I leased some of the land before Mrs. Clifton died. No cattle were run on it during the war."

"How many acres?"

"I'd say maybe a couple thousand or more. It goes into the county east of here."

"That's it ahead," Johnny said.

"Don't go into the driveway just yet."

Johnny slowed, then pulled up onto the grass off the drive. The sheriff parked behind, and he and Pete got out. Pete reached into the car for a crowbar.

The big old house with a porch on two sides was boarded-up. Not a sound was to be heard except for the wind sweeping the dry leaves on the front lawn.

"Let's go in."

"Wait a minute." Hod stood on the edge of the driveway. "A car has been going in and out of here. It's the same car, according to the width of the tires. A heavy truck has been here since the last rain."

Sheriff Carroll seemed content to let the U.S. Marshal take the lead. The men followed Hod up onto the porch. The door was locked. The drive led around the side of the house to a shed with doors wide enough to let a car drive through.

It was padlocked, but that did not deter Pete. He slipped the crowbar under the hasp and with one yank pulled it free of the wood. The rest was easy. The doors were pulled back.

"Laws!" Sheriff Carroll exclaimed. "That looks like the car that belonged to the weatherman. He was here for a couple of months checking clouds, but he's been gone now for several weeks."

Pete and Tom searched the shed, Hod and Johnny the car. Across the front seat of the car lay charts, several small instruments, and a pair of powerful binoculars. Nothing pointed to Kathleen's having been in the car.

"Goddammit!" Johnny backed away from the car and wiped his face with his hands.

Pete popped the lock from the shed close to the house. It had one small window that only a skinny kid like Wind could have squeezed through. And as he had said, it was full of boxes. The men went through them, throwing them out the door after they were checked. Some of the boxes contained scraps of wallpaper; empty food cans or were filled with wrapping paper and smaller boxes.

"Johnny," Tom said in a hushed voice, and pulled a green dress from a small box.

"It's hers." Johnny had to steel himself before he asked, "Anything else?"

"Underwear, shoes."

"Oh, God!"

Pete stood in the yard and cursed silently, then headed for the house with the crowbar.

Hod looked at Tom and shook his head. The signs were not good. If Kathleen's body was not in the house, he was almost certain that it would never be found. Not much is worse for a family than not knowing what happened to a loved one.

The wood splintered when Pete yanked the screws from the lock. Then without the slightest hesitation, he rammed his foot against the door. It flew open with a force that banged it against the wall.

In the attic room at the top of the house, Kathleen heard the sound, but was afraid to hope. She stood as close to the open door of the room as the chain would allow and listened. No other sound reached her. Disappointment brought tears.

"Damn you, you old son of a bitch," she said to the body on the floor. "I hate you, despise you, I'm glad you're dead!"

She was still crying when she heard male voices. She grabbed the teapot and threw it out the door of the room. It bounced against the wall and broke. She threw the hand mirror, the brush, and finally a jar of face cream. Anything to make noise.

"Help me!" she yelled. "Help me . . . please. I'm up here. Somebody help me!" She thought she heard sounds but didn't know what they were or where they came from. "Help me! Please . . . I'm up here, and I can't get out! Please come up here!"

From down below came a shout that rolled up the stairway.

"Kath . . . leen."

A door opened. "Kath . . . leen!" Johnny's voice.

"Johnny! Johnny! I'm up here!"

"Kathleen!"

There was more shouting downstairs, then the sound of boots on the stairs. Kathleen was crying uncontrollably when Johnny reached the top and rounded the corner so that she could see him. Her arms reached out to him. He grabbed her to him, lifting her off her feet, kissing her wet face.

"I love you, love you," he murmured over and over. "Are you all right? Honey, are you all right?"

"I'm all right. I'm all right, now. Don't leave me, Johnny." She clung to him as if she would never let him go.

"I'll not leave you . . . ever. Sweetheart . . . are you sure you're all right? It's been so long—" He looked down into her face. "I've been out of my mind."

Men crowded the hallway outside the room. Johnny's smile spread all over his face as he turned to tell them she was all right. From the shelter of her husband's arms, Kathleen saw first her uncle Hod, then her uncle Tom. Tears flowed as she kissed each of them. Barker, Pete, and then the sheriff filed in. They looked around the luxurious room at the top of the old house with amazement.

"I've a lot to tell you," Kathleen said, seeing the astonished looks on their faces. "The man on the floor is Theodore Nuding. Be careful when you lift the pillow and don't prick yourself with the needle. I shoved it back at him before he could stick me with it. Whatever's in it killed him."

"He doesn't look like anyone I've seen before," the sheriff said.

"He was the man in the tweed coat, Johnny." Kathleen snuggled closer after Johnny opened his coat and folded it and his arms around her. "He said he killed Gabe Thomas and Mr. Cole. I'll tell you everything, but . . . please take off the chain so we can go home."

# *Chapter Twenty-nine*

*P*ete drove away from the Clifton house with Tom and Barker crowded in beside him. Johnny and Kathleen, with their arms around each other, sat in the backseat of the Nash. Hod and the sheriff stayed at the Clifton house to wait for the undertaker.

"There are some valuable things here," Hod said, picking up the emerald necklace Kathleen had thrown down on the dressing table. "All this stuff should be loaded up in some of the boxes we found in the shed and taken away for safekeeping until it's decided what to do with it. Folks will be coming to look the place over."

"I told your brother to send out my deputy. No use telling Johnny to do anything. His head was in the clouds." Sheriff Carroll shook his gray head. "Can't blame him a doggone bit. That boy was half out of his mind."

"This is one of the strangest cases I've ever come across. Kathleen said he never hurt her and that he didn't as much as hint of anything sexual with her. He bought all this in her size and in colors to suit her."

"He did all this work here. If he'd hired anyone from town, word would have got out. How in the hell did he do it?" Sheriff Carroll looked down into the still face on the floor.

"It's odd that he seemed to worship her as an idol. Maybe after we read his journal we'll understand it."

"He sure had me fooled. I never thought that he was anything but what he said he was, a weather observer."


Pete began to honk the horn as he approached the cross-roads. The men who waited there and the women who had not yet left after serving the noon meal lined up alongside the road to cheer. Pete slowed the car to a crawl as they passed. Kathleen waved with tears streaming down her face. The car stopped only long enough to let Barker come out to thank the men who had donated their time to search for Kathleen.

The excitement was just as great in town. Pete honked the horn, and soon a dozen cars fell in behind with horns blasting. The procession went slowly up Main Street. Smiling people came out onto the sidewalks and waved.

At her house, Kathleen left Johnny long enough to go into her room and put on old familiar slacks and a flannel shirt. She tossed the green gown and peignoir and the other robe she had worn over it in the corner.

*Teddy had not purchased a coat. He had not intended for her ever to leave the room.*

It was dark by the time people stopped coming by. Marie, preparing to leave, hugged Kathleen.

"Daddy and I decided we'll have Christmas next Sunday. Will you come?"

Kathleen looked at Johnny. He smiled and nodded.

"We'll be there."

Marie, blinking back tears, and with Bobby Harper beside her, escaped out the door Barker held open for her. Kathleen went to him and put her arms around him. He patted her on the shoulder.

"I'm so glad I'm a member of the Barker Fleming family. Tell that little boy who found my coat that I'm going to buy him the best sheepskin coat I can find."

"I'm glad you're home, daughter."

Johnny stepped forward and held out his hand. "Thanks, Barker. I never knew what having a family was like . . . till now."

"You are part of us, Johnny."

His face showed no emotion, but Kathleen was aware of the turmoil churning inside this wonderful, kind man who was Johnny's father.

When all who remained were Pete, Tom, and Hod, Pete rose and put on his coat.

"I'm taking Tom and Hod over to Jude's to spend the night. We were thinking it might be a little crowded here."

"That's the best thought you've had in a month of Sundays." Johnny handed him his hat, and they all laughed.

"You'll be back in the morning?" Kathleen asked her uncles.

"I'm going back to Red Rock on the noon bus. Hod is staying on a while, then coming over to my house before he goes back to Kansas. I want him to see my boys and my pretty little girl."

"I have to see them before they sprout wings and fly away," Hod said. "He's done nothin' but brag about them for the past hour."

"You're staying awhile, Uncle Hod?"

"For a while. Kidnapping is a Federal offense. I'll stay

until the case is assigned. The sheriff feels that he may be in over his head here."

"Come on, Mr. U.S. Marshal," Tom said. "Let's get out of here and leave these two alone. Are you so darned old you can't remember when you wanted to be alone with Molly?"

"Remember? I still want to be alone with her." Hod hit Tom with his hat. "What about you and Henry Ann?"

"She was gone four days when Isabel died. That's the last of that monkey business. My wife sleeps in my bed every night from now on."

"Then you understand how I feel." Johnny opened the door and waved them out. "Good night, gentlemen. I'll thank you tomorrow."

Pete had a parting shot as he went out the door. "We'll be back about midnight with a shivaree."

"You do and you'll get a load of buckshot in the rear." Johnny closed the door and opened his arms. "Come here to me, Mrs. Henry. I don't know how I'm going to do it, but I'm going to make up for five years of lost time."

When he kissed her, she returned his kisses fervently. She was afraid that after she told him about the baby, this wonderful loving man would feel that she had betrayed him.

"I've something to tell you." She closed her eyes and buried her face against his collarbone.

"I have a lot of things to tell you. Let's go to bed so I can hold you while I tell you how much I love you." He brushed her hair back from her face and looked into it earnestly. "Honey, this has been the worst week of my life. Worse than the week in the New Georgia Islands when eight thousand Japs were less than a mile away, bombing us at all hours of the day and night."

"I've always loved you. I want you to know that."

"I do. And I was a fool to put distance between us." He reached behind him and turned off the light.

In the bedroom, Johnny turned back the covers, took off his clothes, and got into bed. Kathleen came from the bathroom, leaving the light on and the door ajar.

"Do you mind if I leave the light on?"

"Leave it on, sweetheart. Just come here." He folded back the covers and held out his arms.

She slipped in beside him, closed her eyes when his arms went around her, and pressed her full length against him. *God*, she prayed. *Please don't let him turn from me when I tell him.*

"Oh, Lord! You feel so good." He sighed. "I've missed you so much."

"I've got to tell you—"

"Let me tell you." Johnny kissed her, then whispered, "I went to see Jude, and he told me that about next August we were going to have a baby."

Kathleen went still and waited.

"Is that what you were going to tell me?"

"Yes, but I was afraid—"

"He explained what had happened to Mary Rose. One baby out of several thousand is born like that. It wasn't my fault or yours. I was an ignorant, prideful fool who was too stiff-necked to go to someone who could explain it to me. Jude thinks that I'm a damn fool and don't deserve you. I knew that even before I thought I'd lost you."

"You want the baby?"

"I want the baby, sweetheart. I want all the babies you want to give me. Don't cry, honey. I love you so much. I didn't know how I was going to get through the rest of my life without you."

She kissed his neck, his chin, his rough cheeks until he desperately sought her lips with his. The kiss lasted a long time and was full of sweetness.

She whispered that she loved him and she had been afraid he would think she had tricked him that morning.

"I was so hungry for you that a team of mules couldn't have stopped me from making love to you."

"I bought you a Christmas present."

"Yeah. What?"

"I'll give it to you Sunday when we go to Barker's."

"I was there Christmas. When you didn't show up for dinner, Barker and I went looking for you. He pulled every string he could trying to find you. Somehow I've got to make things up to him, too."

"He's been a good friend to me, Johnny. I think a lot of him and all the Flemings."

"I guess I've been jealous of all he could give you that I couldn't."

"I just wanted you, Johnny. From the first, it was you, only you."

"The first Christmas I was overseas, I made some things for you, but I was afraid to send them."

"I wish you had. I was so lonesome for you."

"You won't be lonesome anymore. Kiss me again and tell me you love me."

He pressed her hand to his chest. She could feel the powerful beating of his heart. Her fingers stroked the short hair curling from his brown skin. Leaning over him, her lips drifted down his chest, the taste of his warm, moist skin on her tongue. His body quivered, and she became aware of the movement against her thigh.

"You'd better stop, or I'll not be able to," he whispered.

"I don't want to stop."

"You've been through a lot today."

"But I'm here now . . . with you. You'll never get away from me again. I'll nag you, chase you, hang on to you." She nipped his chin.

"I want you. I'm about to burst wanting you."

"I know," she said happily. "I can feel it."

"Maybe you should rest for this little cowboy's sake." His big hand covered her belly.

"He won't care. He's in there snug as a bug." She slipped her arms around his neck. "I want you to love me."

His lips crushed hers hungrily. "Then I'll love you— that is, if you think he won't mind." He punctuated his words with soft, but firm kisses.

# *Epilogue*

AUGUST 23, 1946

## MOTHER AND CHILD FINE

### FATHER A NERVOUS WRECK

Mr. and Mrs. Johnny Henry are the proud parents of a dark-haired seven-pound boy who was promptly named John Barker Henry. Dr. Jude Perry, assisted by his wife, Nurse Theresa Perry, was forced to eject the father from the delivery room for causing a commotion.

The story ran in a black box on the front page of the *Rawlings Gazette*. Paul and Adelaide jokingly considered putting an extra out on the street.

The morning after the birth, a spotted pony was tied up in front of the clinic with a gift tag that read: To little Johnny from Uncle Pete and Aunt Dale. Johnny swore to get even when at noon, he had to leave Kathleen and the baby, carry a bucket of water to the pony, and clean up a pile of manure.

\* \* \*

It had been a year like no other.

For months Kathleen's kidnapping and what occurred afterward had been the talk of the town, county, and state. Much had been learned about Theodore Nuding. To sum it up, he was wealthy, very intelligent, cunning, and insane.

When the autopsy was performed on his body investigators found no evidence that he was ill. The doctors theorized that he believed so strongly that a curse had been passed down to him from his mother that when he started having severe migraine headaches, he was convinced that he was about to die. It was the poison that had killed him, as it had Harry Cole.

His attorney came forward to claim the body, and Nuding was buried in a corner of the Rawlings cemetery with only the attorney present.

The only explanation of Theodore Nuding's obsession with Kathleen seemed to stem from the fact that her name was Kathleen and her hair was red. Pictures of his mother, whose name was also Kathleen, had shown that she, too, had red hair. According to his journals, for more than twenty years he had kept his mother in a room similar to the one he had prepared for Kathleen.

The story of Theodore Nuding was so amazing that the University of Oklahoma Medical School asked permission from his estate to study his journals.

A few days after the burial, Kathleen and Johnny received the startling news that Kathleen was the sole heir to the Nuding estate, which included the stock in Hidendall corporation, property in Oklahoma City, the Clifton ranch, thousands in savings bonds, and almost a hundred thousand dollars in cash in a lockbox at the bank in Oklahoma City.

The will had been signed and dated a month before the war ended and while Kathleen was working at the aircraft plant. It was unclear why Theodore was working there. He was financially secure and was not in danger of being drafted into service. He was registered as 4-F, because he had a major heart murmur.

The first words out of Kathleen's mouth when told of the inheritance were, "I don't want it."

"There is a provision made for that," the lawyer said. "If you should refuse to accept the inheritance, the entire estate will go to Iva Togori."

"Let her have it."

"Iva Togori is the woman known as Tokyo Rose. Mr. Nuding believed you to be a patriot who would not want a traitor who had broadcast propaganda to our men in the Pacific Theater to take money back to the Japanese who had killed so many of our men."

"What shall I do, Johnny?"

"The decision is yours, honey."

"I don't want her to have it."

"Mr. Nuding was counting on that," the lawyer said. "Do you have a lawyer in the city?"

"Johnny, would Mr. Gifford be our lawyer? You've known him for a long time."

"Grant Gifford?" the lawyer asked. "I know him well. He's out of public office now. If you wish, I'll work with him on this."

Grant Gifford took over as financial advisor and manager of the estate. At first, Kathleen feared Johnny would be stiff-necked about the inheritance. She immediately had it transferred to both names, meaning that his signature was required on all documents.

As soon as the money was available, a large portion of it was given to the clinic so that a wing could be built and a surgeon added to the staff.

The Rawlings library was enlarged to include a children's section, and funds to support a reading program and extended evening hours were provided.

A sum was set aside for Emily Ramsey's college education. She was the little girl whose mother was killed by Marty Conroy.

The Henry/Fleming scholarship fund for children of the Cherokee Nation who wanted to continue their education after high school was established, with Barker Fleming and Jacob Runs Fast as the trustees.

Johnny and Kathleen decided together that they would keep the Clifton ranch, but they would never live in the ranch house.

In the spring a full page ad was placed in the *Gazette* announcing that the Clifton house was being demolished. Anyone who in any way had helped search for Kathleen Henry when she was kidnapped and taken there was welcome to come and take whatever they wanted: windows, doors, stair railings, flooring, plumbing and electric fixtures, or lumber.

After two days, there was hardly enough left to make a good-sized bonfire.

Kathleen gave the wardrobe full of clothes to the church for their bazaar. Johnny suggested that she keep the emeralds and put them in a lockbox at the bank.

"They will be your security, honey, if we should have another Great Depression. The man owes you that for what he put you through."

In July the first Henry/Perry rodeo was held at the Rawlings fairgrounds. Willie and the Chicken Pluckers put on a warm-up show and were such a success that Pete booked them for rodeos in Ardmore, Duncan, and Elk City.

In August the remodeling was completed on the Circle H ranch house in time for Johnny to bring his wife and son home.

CHRISTMAS, 1946

The old Nash, sporting new tires and a fresh paint job, stopped in front of the Fleming ranch house. The Henrys were reluctant to give up the old car even though a new Dodge sat in the garage at home.

Johnny, carrying his son, followed Kathleen with a basket of gifts, to the door. Barker opened it immediately.

"Merry Christmas," sang the chorus behind him.

"Merry Christmas to you," came the cheerful reply.

"John Barker, go to grandpa while I take off my coat," Johnny said after he had stepped inside the door.

Barker took the child to the rocking chair beside the fireplace.

"You'll never guess what Daddy got John Barker for Christmas," Janna said from behind her hand.

"Don't tell me it's a tomahawk." Johnny, now totally at ease at the Flemings', liked to tease his youngest sister.

"How did you know?" Janna retorted, and flounced away.

"Surely not!" Kathleen grabbed Johnny's hand and held on to it tightly.

"If his grandpa gave him a tomahawk, we'll hang it on the wall until he's old enough to use it."

"Johnny!"

He pulled her to him. "Lord, honey. No one could have made me believe last Christmas that I could be so happy this Christmas."

"You always have been too stubborn for your own good, Johnny Henry, but I love you . . . mightily!"

"But not as much as I love you, Kathleen Henry."

"All right, you two, stop necking." Marie was sitting with Bobby on the couch. "This year we're going to open the presents on Christmas Day. Last year we didn't open them until New Year's Day."

"That's not a bad idea. Let's do it this year." Johnny held Kathleen close to him.

"It's a rotten idea," Lucas snorted.

"What do you know about it? You're just a skinny, ugly kid." Johnny roughed Lucas's hair.

"Soon I'll be big enough to whop your . . . ass—er . . . hind." Lucas darted a quick glance at his father.

"All right, boys." Barker held John Barker firmly against his shoulder and gently patted his back. "Settle down or I'll have to get up and whop both your hinds."

"We'd better watch it, Lucas," Johnny said in a loud whisper. "The chief is about to go on the warpath."

The girls giggled.

Lucas snickered.

Johnny laughed.

Kathleen stood back and watched the horseplay between her husband and his young brother and could almost thank Theodore Nuding for the despicable act that had brought them all together as a family.

# PETE PERRY'S CORN BREAD

½ cup flour
2 cups yellow cornmeal
1 egg, slightly beaten
1 teaspoon salt
3 teaspoons baking powder
2 tablespoons sugar
1 small can cream-style corn
½ cup milk
Mix and Beat Vigorously

Add:
½ cup finely chopped green onions
¼ cup chopped bell pepper or green chilies

In a 9 x 13-inch cake pan, or 12-inch heavy iron skillet (preferred) melt a large tablespoon of lard, Crisco, or meat drippings in a 375° oven. Pour melted grease into the cornmeal batter, mix well. Bake in the skillet or pan until golden brown 35 to 45 minutes.

Dear Reader Friends,

This is the last book of the Dolan and Henry family stories. I hope that my characters have given you a glimpse of life as it was in the 1930s and at the end of World War II when the brave men and women who fought for our country came home to their loved ones.

I am sorry to be leaving the Dolans, the Henrys, and their friends. I have grown close to all of them, as I hope you have. When the time is right, and if they wish to do so, they may appear in future books.

Now I am starting a new venture into life with the Jones family, citizens of Fertile, Missouri, in the year 1922. World War I has ended and, thankfully, the flu epidemic. Though they cannot know it, they are about to be caught up in a decade of amazing changes as, even in towns as small as theirs, people are waking up to a daring new day.

As always, I appreciate your letters, calls, and e-mails and take note of your suggestions. For those of you who have asked for them, all of my Warner Books are kept in print and may be ordered through your local bookstore.

Until next time,

*Dorothy Garlock*

Julie Jones was convinced that life was passing her by. Living on the edge of the town of Fertile, Missouri (Population 1802) in the year 1922, on a hilly, rocky, hard-scrabble farm, she felt immobilized by her responsibilities. Since her mother's death, four years earlier, Julie had been charged with running the household and raising her brothers, Joe, Jack, and Jason, and her sisters, Jill and Joy. All those "J" names, hers included, had been her mother's idea, prompted by her own name, June, and her husband's, Jethro. Wasn't it bad enough, Julie wondered, to be poor, burdened, and isolated without names that were a town joke?

Julie dreamed that someday when the children were grown, she would leave Fertile with a handsome man who, when he learned her dark secret, would not care a whit and would love her devotedly. She was sure her dream man had come to town when Corbin Appleby arrived in Fertile. Until then, only Evan Johnson, silent and hardworking, had paid attention to her. She thought about Appleby a lot. He was the only exciting thing to hit town—until the big flood came . . .

Look for *The Edge of Town* by Dorothy Garlock